Abe and Molly:
The Lincoln Courtship

by
Frederic Hunter

Nebbadoon Press
Santa Barbara

Abe and Molly:
The Lincoln Courtship

© 2010 Frederic Hunter

Nebbadoon Press
800 500-9086
www.NebbadoonPress.com

ISBN 978-1-891331-16-9

Printed in the U.S.A.

Cover photos from the Library of Congress
Cover design by Gary S. Albright

1840 and 1841 Mary Todd letters to
Mercy Ann Levering are quoted by permission
of the Abraham Lincoln Presidential
Library and Museum.

For my wife
Donanne
and
our son
Paul

CONTENTS

INTRODUCTION

Some years ago while researching a film project for PBS, aired as *Lincoln and the War Within*, I stumbled on the story of the courtship between Abraham Lincoln and Mary Todd. What a classically romantic tale! She called him Mr. Lincoln. He called her Molly. Two young people attracted across barriers of class and background who manage to break down those barriers to grab a bit of happiness. Great stuff!

In the England of Jane Austen it is the women who are poor—and destined to lives of genteel poverty—unless the men wake up, realize how exceptional they are and rescue them. In the middle America of the nineteenth and early twentieth centuries it is the young men who are poor. They seek fulfillment with women of higher social standing. (Check out F. Scott Fitzgerald and Theodore Dreiser.)

In *Abe and Molly* the story is anchored in the actual lives of two people familiar, almost legendary, to most of us. Lincoln, impoverished and socially awkward, is trying to conceal a backwoods heritage. He has undeniable talents, including a tremendous capacity for growth, but he's also full of self-doubt. Molly, of extraordinary education and aristocratic background, hardly more than twenty, is vivacious, witty and sharp-tongued. Despite the opposition of her family, she and Lincoln fall in love; they decide to marry. But

1

the family interferes. The engagement is broken. After the breakup, they live separate lives for eighteen months. And a lot more happens.

Why are such stories a staple of people's imaginative lives? Because they reassure readers that perseverance in the face of opposition leads to happiness and enlarged capacities.

Readers may say of Austen's Elizabeth Bennet and Mr. Darcy that it's only a story. The particular pleasure of the Lincoln courtship story is that it's mainly true—and would be entirely true if only we knew the threads that have been lost across time.

Our story takes these young people no farther than their wedding. Most readers will know what happened to them later on. But our story knows them only as a young man and woman moving forward into life with hopes and ambitions—and with no knowledge of whether or not they will be fulfilled.

Our story adheres to the historical facts, at least as far as we know them. Educated speculation fills in what is not known. This speculation involves the interpretation of facts, character and probabilities. Many people have mulled these facts, characters and probabilities, and interpretations of them differ.

There's an unusual aspect to this volume. It includes extensive notes about how the interpretations offered here came to be. It also notes how other interpreters have arrived at different conclusions.

This is mainly a true story. But it's not history. The dialogue makes no pretense of being factual. Did Molly Todd's first look at Abraham Lincoln occur just after she arrived in Springfield? Just as he threw a drunken shoemaker into a trough to discipline him for beating his wife? That's what we have here. It probably did not happen that way. But Lincoln and some friends did toss the shoemaker into the trough and saw to it that his wife beat him.

If you'd prefer to encounter the story after first learning what's fact and what speculation, you may want to start at the back of the book and read the notes first. Wherever you start, may you enjoy the story!

CHAPTER

1

Molly had been riding all day in a glow of expectation. The expectation involved the new life she was about to begin, a life of more freedom than she had known under the supervision of a stepmother who was both neglectful and meddling, a life that promised introductions to young men of ambition and a talent for hard work, with one of whom she would cast her fortune. The expectation was real, but the glow was a trifle hard to maintain crammed, as she was, into a stagecoach that jounced and jolted, tipped and almost toppled as the team of horses pulled it across the Illinois prairie.

With the exception of Cousin John Hardin, a prince of the family who acted as her chaperone, the men stuffed beside her were not the kind with whom she expected to share this new life. They were calloused-hand frontier types smelling of sweat and tobacco. During the day it had amused her to observe them as they burped and farted in their open-mouthed sleep with dust settling like tiny castles on their teeth. One of them was made so queasy by the coach's motion that he flung himself through the open coach door window to spread groans and his breakfast across the prairie.

When these men were not sleeping, they told stories, scratching themselves, and scrutinized her, looking away when Cousin John warned them off with narrowed eyes. They noticed the fineness of her clothes. They examined her clear complexion and the lustrous, well-brushed brown hair. They told themselves that this was not a woman who spent long periods of time outdoors. They noticed the smallness of her hands, the absence of a wedding ring, and guessed correctly that she was not a woman who worked with those hands. Her feet did not reach the floor of the stage; she rested them on one of the many pieces of her luggage that had been unloaded the previous evening from the Illinois River paddleboat. They saw—or imagined—that her ankles were tiny and well-turned, the kind of ankles that made a man swallow. They did not realize how much dust she was tasting in her throat.

Most of all, they noticed how pretty and animated she was, especially when she whispered to her escort and her blue eyes flashed. When she giggled, glints of pleasure lighted the men's eyes. The melody of her laughter made them want to share the joke. Despite the pounding of the hooves outside and the shouts of the driver, the music of Molly's laughter made them thrill.

Early in the evening, the long day and the two-week trip finally nearing its end, Molly opened her eyes, no longer pretending to nap, and recognized the landscape from her visit two years before. "Cousin John," she asked, "am I dreaming?"

"Springfield's just ahead," he assured her. "Capital of the state now."

"My heavens! There it is!" She had glimpsed the new State House cupola rising above the prairie. "I'll wager you can see Kentucky from the top!"

All day it had seemed to Molly that the stage was moving too slowly. Now suddenly it seemed to fly along the packed expanse of earth called Jefferson Street, past stores, taverns and workshops.

Idlers emerged from the taverns; they stepped out along the street to see whom the stage was bringing to town.

The driver blew a horn. The stage pulled to a stop outside Spottswood's Rural Hotel. Cousin John Hardin leaned close to Molly. "Just so you know," he whispered, "the proprietor of this establishment calls himself Colonel George Washington Spottswood. A blood descendant of the father of the country. So he claims."

"Indeed!" said Molly. "A true colonel?"

"A bloodline colonel. Without weapons experience. He will undoubtedly want to greet you. The fine Southern families must stick together."

Molly raised an eyebrow.

"He may want to marry you," Hardin teased. Molly struck him a blow on the arm. "Fortunately for you, our laws prohibit bigamy."

By the time the stagecoach came to a halt, a clerk was ringing a large bell mounted on top of the hotel. Spottswood's was a two-story structure, both hotel and tavern, recently built of wood planking, not logs, and it also served as an office for stage lines operating through Springfield. Stable hands hurried from behind the hotel to take charge of the horses. The driver jumped to the ground and flung open the coach door.

Cousin John helped Molly out of the coach. She scrambled through the door on legs that seemed numb beyond moving and emerged into the twilight of the spring evening. Beside Hardin stood a man with more girth than height. He grinned up at her and offered his hand. She took it and let the man and her cousin guide her onto the wood plank porch of the hotel.

"Welcome to the capital of the State of Illinois," the round man said, bowing. His tavernkeeper's clothes smelled lightly of corn whiskey.

"Colonel," Hardin said, "I would like to present Miss Mary Todd, my cousin, Molly." He turned to her with an ironic sparkle in his eye that Spottswood could not see. "Molly," he said, "this is Colonel George Washington Spottswood."

"I'm honored, Colonel," Molly said, curtseying ever so slightly.

"Todd is one of the great family names of Kentucky," said the Colonel, standing as tall as he could. "Your cousins Dr. John Todd, the noted surgeon, and Mr. John Todd Stuart, the esteemed attorney and Congressman, are making it one of the fine names of this fair state as well."

Molly nodded demurely as a carriage pulled up before the hotel. Out of it stepped a tall man of aristocratic bearing who turned back immediately to help two women to the ground. Molly grinned and ran toward her sisters. "Look who's here at last!" she said, throwing her arms about Elizabeth and Fanny. "At last! At last!" Molly laughed and gave each sister a squeeze.

Elizabeth stepped out of the embrace to appraise her younger sister. Six years older than Molly, Elizabeth would now be supervising her entry into society. Ninian Edwards, Elizabeth's husband, would assume the role of her guardian. Elizabeth scrutinized Molly, seizing the mantle of Determined Protector while retaining the aura of what she unquestionably was: young Springfield Matron of Consequence. "I'm sure you feel you've been traveling forever," Elizabeth said. "You look tired."

"Well, I'm not!" Molly assured her. "I feel like my life's beginning!"

"And so it is!" agreed Fanny. "You'll be so glad you're here!" Two years older than Molly, Fanny, a bride-to-be, fairly purred with contentment. Within a few short weeks she would embark on the adventure for which her whole life had prepared her: marriage and motherhood. "My real life began here. So will yours."

Now Elizabeth's husband joined them. Son of a man who had served as an appointed governor of the Illinois Territory and had been elected to the United States Senate, Ninian Edwards, although only thirty, exhibited a commanding presence. He bent to kiss Molly's cheek, said, "Welcome," and offered his hand to Hardin. "Shall we get up the hill where the air's more fragrant?"

As they moved toward the carriage, they heard wailings and cursing. Turning, they saw four young men running hard along the packed earth of Jefferson Street. They dragged a fifth man by his arms and the rope belt that held up his pantaloons. As his boots stirred up puffs of dust visible in the fading light, the man roared drunken obscenities at his tormentors. The Edwards party stopped to see the commotion, the men alarmed lest profanity in the presence of gentlewomen should require them to take action.

The four men hurried past. They circled the horses tied at Spottswood's hitching post, approached the horse trough, and with a splash, tossed the drunk into it. After a moment he rose to the surface, blubbered and floundered. Ninian and Hardin chuckled. The women stepped back, hands pressed to their throats, Elizabeth and Fanny averting their eyes. Molly watched the drunk thrash at the water, then sit erect in the trough, roaring vulgarities. The horses at the hitching post neighed and grew skittish; they began to dance at the ends of their reins. To halt the obscenities one of the men put beefy hands on the drunkard's shoulders and pushed downward. He resisted, shouting vigorously, then slipped below the water. His arms flailed in the air. Now an unusually tall, steeple-thin, black-haired fellow straddled the trough; he pulled the drunk out of the water. Coughing as if he might bring up his intestines, the drunk went on cursing. The tall man put a hand over the blaring mouth and gave Molly and her sisters an embarrassed look.

"Shall we go into the hotel?" Elizabeth suggested.

"Let's do," said Ninian. "This isn't the best part of town."

Ninian, Elizabeth and Fanny started into the hotel. Molly stood her ground, Hardin beside her. "I want to catch the flavor of the frontier," she explained. She watched the tall man and his partners lift the drunk out of the trough. They stripped him of his shirt and laid him across the hitching post. The drunk roared louder than a pig being slaughtered in a barnyard. Molly felt his roars like a breeze of whiskey. "Cousin John," she asked mischievously, "will you tell me what he's yelling?"

"Not a chance. We're not quite civilized here yet."

"Well, we're civilized on the hill," said Ninian. He had returned with Molly's sisters. "Let's go to the carriage and get home."

The setting sun had turned the clouds orange, red and finally purple. Now the twilight was giving way to night. As Molly went to the carriage, she saw the four men rope the drunk to the hitching post, his back bent across it. The tall, black-haired fellow led a woman toward the drunk. She looked terrified. The tall man bent beside her, speaking quietly, encouraging her. Another of the men handed her a switch. She hesitated. Then suddenly, nodding her head, in the grip of a strange ecstasy, she stepped toward the drunk and raised the switch over her head. Molly heard it whistle through the air and snap against the drunk's back. He screamed. "Light in! Light in!" the four men urged the woman. "He does it to you! Let him know how it feels!" She struck him again. The drunk wailed.

Ninian stepped forward, placing his back to the hitching post. He gestured the women to hurry into the carriage. "Evening, Lincoln. Gentlemen," he greeted the four men. Hardin spoke to them as well.

"Hardin. Edwards. Ladies," said the tall man in a high-pitched voice that seemed strange for one so tall. He bowed slightly to salute the ladies. "Fine evening, isn't it?" He added, "We're doing civic education."

A moan escaped the lips of the woman, a sound that was half wretched, half exalted. Once again she laid the switch onto the back of the drunk. "Stop!" he cried, sobered by the blows. "Stop her! Stop her!" The woman laid into him. Again and again she switched him.

"Heavens!" exclaimed Elizabeth. "Don't look, Molly. Fanny!"

Molly could not help looking. The very tall man with the black hair was no less a frontier type than the passengers in the stagecoach. But Molly noticed his gentleness with the woman and had a strange sense that her expectation about her new life in Springfield would be fulfilled.

Molly felt Elizabeth's hand on her arm. "Molly! Come along!" She pulled her toward the carriage.

The Edwards party settled itself inside the vehicle. "Hurry on!" Ninian told the driver and off they went down Jefferson toward First Street.

"What kind of prairie education was that?" Molly asked, looking behind at the figures still clustered beside the pump. "Do you know those people?"

"Wasn't that the shoemaker?" Fanny asked.

"And his wife," acknowledged Ninian.

"What was going on?" asked Molly.

"When the shoemaker gets drunk," Ninian explained through tightened lips, "he beats his wife. I take it those gentlemen decided to offer the wife a chance to teach him a lesson."

"Hooray for them!" cried Molly. "I hope she scars his back." Beside her Elizabeth shuddered. Molly craned her neck, looking back for a glimpse of the woman and the tall, rail-thin fellow with black hair. But she could make out only the lamps glowing in the darkness outside Spottswood's.

"Mary, please," cautioned Elizabeth, using her given name now. "Don't crane your neck. We are Edwardses. That means something here."

They started down Jefferson Street in the silence the gentry required to separate themselves from commoners. Ninian raised a disapproving eyebrow to Elizabeth, as if he should have come to fetch Molly alone. Molly asked, "Who were those men?"

"Those vigilantes?" asked Elizabeth.

"The civic educators," replied Molly.

Cousin John Hardin remarked, "All four of those fellers were Whigs," because he knew their political affiliation would interest Molly. "Our people."

"Their behavior," commented Elizabeth, "gives the lie to the notion that all Whigs are propertied and gentlemen and educated."

"There were attorneys among them," added Hardin, teasing Ninian and himself, who were also attorneys, and grinning at Molly. "Though, needless to say, not graduates of Transylvania University. Like present company."

Ninian was Illinois's foremost graduate of Transylvania University in Lexington, Kentucky. After a moment and as if it were a confession he felt obliged to make, he acknowledged, "The tallest of that bunch is one of my brother legislators."

"One of the 'Long Nine,' as they call the Sangamon County boys," Hardin reminded Molly. "That's 'cause they made such tall promises to get the capital moved to Springfield." He winked at her.

"Lincoln's a bumpkin," said Ninian.

"That's harsh," Hardin replied.

"A farm boy with native wit and political cunning," Ninian continued, ignoring Hardin. "He has that peculiarly American kind of frontier-bred ambition to be something he'll never be." After a moment he reflected, "I confess that sometimes I have grave doubts about democracy."

"It's refreshing to see that kind of civic education," Molly said. "A man who beats his wife ought to get beaten once in a while himself." She noticed Ninian once again raise an eyebrow at his wife. It delighted Molly to see that she had administered a slight shock to Ninian's stateliness. She exclaimed, "Oh, I can't tell you how delighted I am to be here! I truly am." Then, because it was now her town, too, she craned her neck and peered behind her. But the gathering darkness closed off any view of vigilantes.

The carriage drove a mile south of Jefferson Street, up a gentle hill to an area where the orange glow of candles shone in the windows of large homes. It turned in at the circular drive before the Edwards residence, crunching over gravel, and deposited its passengers. The five people moved into an entryway filled with candlelight. Ninian led Hardin off to the parlor. Elizabeth took her sisters upstairs to the nursery where the Irish girl was sitting with Julia, now over two years old.

"My darling Julia!" Molly enthused, lifting the child out of her crib to hold her close and kiss her. "How you've grown!"

"Thank you so much," Elizabeth said to the Irish girl as she left the room. Turning to the child, she grinned and announced, "This is your aunt Molly from Kentucky."

"Moddy! Moddy!" the little one exulted.

"What a fine daughter!" Molly marveled. She held the child, enjoying the warmth of her against her body, breathing in her child's smell, and told her sisters about the trip. "The Ohio River was teeming with people moving west," she said. "You'd see flatboats and huge rafts with whole families on them, including their livestock and wagons. I was so grateful to have passage on a steamboat."

She told them the news from home: As usual, their father was away as much as he was at home, off on business for the state-owned Bank of Kentucky, of which he was president, or in Frankfort for meetings of the state assembly or down in New Orleans buying cotton yarn and other merchandise for the Todd & Oldham store. As always, Molly said, quoting him, he was "not so poor as to beg my bread, nor so rich as to forget my Maker."

Miss Betsey, the sisters' stepmother, sent her love. She was still producing a child every fifteen months, "a little like a prize sow," Molly observed, making her sisters giggle. "The farther we limbs of Satan are from Lexington," Molly observed, "the more she loves us." The sisters' maternal grandmother was healthy; so were their three full-blooded siblings, Ann, Levi and George, the youngest, whose birth had brought on the death of their mother. The house was practically a tavern so many visitors came. The slaves were well. Nelson had driven Molly to and from Ward's School every weekend for the past year. Mammy Sally, by whom she was charged to send a report of her sisters' health, was still helping runaway slaves on their way north; the fence outside the Todd home was still marked so that runaways knew they could find rest and a meal there before hurrying onward. "If Father knows about it, he's never said a word," Molly noted.

"Father's opposed to slavery," said Fanny. "But he needs help running a household full of children and entertaining all those guests."

"Help is certainly nice," remarked Elizabeth. "And Chaney and Betty and Mammy Sally all know their jobs." She sighed, smiled with exasperation and lowered her voice to a whisper. "My Irish girls need so much training. They always want to move on as soon as they can."

"Help is nice," agreed Molly. "But I'll be happy living in a state where men do not go sneaking down to slave cabins at night for recreation."

Elizabeth and Fanny nodded their heads to that.

Molly gazed at the child she held in her arms and rocked her gently, smiling at the eyelids slowly closing. "In fact," she went on, "I'm glad to be out of Kentucky all together. I'm tired of living in a place where men educate their daughters only to marry them off to men who prefer their wives not to think, and treat them like infants." Her sisters watched her tenderness with the child, reassured that motherhood and domesticity were where she was headed despite all the education she'd acquired, much more than any woman would need in Springfield. "As if all women want is sweet candy and fancy dresses," Molly said. "If I'd've stayed in Lexington, I'd've opened a school." The sisters seemed surprised at this remark. "Of course, Father opposed the idea. Miss Betsey absolutely forbad me to mention it. 'Todd women do not work,' Miss Betsey said. As if I was acting like an impoverished German or Irish girl washed up on the shores of America."

"Starting schools is what young men do in Illinois," said Elizabeth. She rose and took the sleeping child. "They teach school and read the law and then become lawyers." Molly wondered if Elizabeth meant that she was not to think of opening a school in Springfield. "And young women enjoy the best times of their lives."

"Is that what you've been doing, Fanny?" Molly asked.

Fanny smiled her bride-to-be smile.

"For a brief springtime season," said Elizabeth, "a young woman gets to be a full moon shining brightly in a dark night. She casts a lovely light on everything. The whole town watches her."

"Thank you," said Molly. "But I have left the place of the slave auctions. I do not intend to be put on the block, however much you talk of moonlight."

"Enjoy this time, Molly," Elizabeth advised. She put Julia into her crib.

"She's right," agreed Fanny. "This is your moment." While Elizabeth leaned over the crib, tucking a blanket about her child, Molly studied Fanny. She had blossomed in the two years since Molly had seen her. She smiled more readily, walked more self-assuredly, held herself with more confidence. She was no longer a waif in her sister's house, a refugee from Kentucky, hoping some man would offer her a role in life. If there was to be a waif now, she would be Molly. Fanny's man had come and by offering her marriage had raised her to a position of respectability in town. Molly would be expected to follow this path.

"Ambitious and adventurous young men will pay you court," Elizabeth assured her, moving away from the crib. "Some of them are talented and destined for great things."

"And as soon as one of them wins me," Molly observed, "he will turn me into a brood cow. And if the high hopes he has for himself are not realized, he will blame me." While her sisters smiled at how little she knew of what she really wanted, Molly pulled herself to her full height. "I do wish sometimes I could be a lawyer or a lawmaker or a politician," she declared. Her sisters glanced at one another in surprise. "I'm surely better educated than most members of the Illinois legislature. Not that education is everything."

"We must accept what we cannot change," Elizabeth said.

"We may have to accept it," agreed Molly, "but we don't have to like it."

"But generally speaking," Elizabeth replied, "we're happier if we do." Molly might not agree, but allowed Elizabeth the last word. After all, it was her house.

As the three sisters left the nursery, Molly thought to herself, "Think of being that shoemaker's wife! Married to that kind of man and unable to get away."

After they had gotten ready for bed, Fanny sat in the wing chair in the room they would share and watched Molly unpack the large trunk that had accompanied her. She placed its contents into bureau drawers.

"I was hoping we'd go into Spottswood's," Fanny confided. "The most famous room in all of Illinois is in that hotel."

Molly looked up from arranging stockings to find Fanny smiling as if she had a secret. "Why didn't you tell me? I could have fainted and been carried inside."

"Ninian and Elizabeth say it's a low tavern."

"What in heaven's name happened there?"

"A cold-blooded murder." Molly stopped arranging the bureau. "With witnesses." Fanny's eyes brightened as she spoke the words. The victim, she recounted, was Jacob Early, a man well known in central Illinois as a physician, Methodist preacher and Democratic politico. He had been sitting in Spottswood's parlor after dinner just left of the fire, reading a *Sangamo Journal*, when a man he knew, Henry Truett, the son-in-law of Congressman William May, entered the room. He was carrying a gun.

"Wait," Molly interrupted. She sat on the bed near where Fanny lolled in the chair watching her, ready to bite at this gossip. "Didn't May and Early have a bitter political feud? May was a Whig and Early a Democrat."

"How do you keep all that straight in your head?" Fanny exclaimed. "It's two years since you

matic and ironic tone. "This is my moment! I'm a full moon shining brightly in a dark night, casting a lovely luminous light o'er the landscape." She giggled, then asked, "Did Truett get off?"

"Can you believe it?" exclaimed Fanny. "The bumpkin convinced the jury that he feared for his life. Said he had personally fought with Jacob Early in the Black Hawk War and knew that a chair in his hands was a deadly weapon. The jury acquitted."

"Sometimes bumpkins surprise you." Molly rose from the bed and returned to arranging her bureau.

"There's more," Fanny said. Molly turned to find a curious grin on Fanny's face. Molly frowned, wondering what had gotten in to her sister. "You saw him, that man," Fanny said.

"I did?"

"Outside Spottswood's. The tall fellow with black hair."

Molly remembered Ninian and Cousin John greeting the man by name. What had they called him? "Didn't Ninian call him—was it Lincoln?"

Fanny nodded. "They serve together in the Legislature."

"'Native wit,'" Molly remembered. "Ninian said he had 'native wit.' I guess he must."

"And political cunning," Fanny added. "Lincoln's as responsible as any other legislator for getting the state capital moved to Springfield."

Molly cocked a mischievous eyebrow at her sister. "And has a peculiarly American ambition to be something he'll never be," she recalled her brother-in-law's words. "Which, if Ninian says it, must mean someone like him."

"Oh, he'll never be like Ninian," Fanny assured her. "Socially he's hopeless. Ill at ease. Has no idea how to talk to a woman."

"Do we know him socially?" Molly asked.

"Not socially," Fanny said. "He comes to the house sometimes. With the Coterie." Fanny shrugged as if that gesture might cover social irregularities on the frontier. "After all, he's in the Legislature with Ninian." Dispensing with murders and men, Fanny went to her side of the bed. "You must be exhausted. Finish unpacking tomorrow." She began to blow out the candles. "I tell you that story, dear sister, to assure you that there are interesting men in Springfield. Joshua Speed is still unattached."

Molly brought up a memory of Speed, part owner of a store. He had the good looks that reminded ladies interested in poetry, which Molly was, of the famous Lord Byron. "The handsome Mr. Speed paid no attention to me two years ago," she said.

"He was probably in love. He falls in love quite regularly. Never mind. There are other interesting men in this town."

"Let me assure you, dear Fanny, that I did not come here to find a husband."

"Neither did I." She smiled, leaning over the final candle. "But find one I did." Matter-of-factly she added, "It'll take at least a year." She blew out the last candle.

Tall, lanky Lincoln strolled down the middle of Main Street, gazing at the stars and enjoying the breeze. He kicked the dust off his boots, let himself in at the James C. Bell & Co. mercantile store, walked without needing a light to the winding stairway and climbed it to the second story. "We took the shoemaker swimming, Speed," he remarked to the young man reading by lantern-light.

"He take the temperance pledge?"

"Judging by him, I think I'll take it."

The man sat down on a chair and pulled off his boots. "Looks like another of Ninian Edwards's wife's sisters has come to town."

"Edwards'll be holding a ball one of these days so we can get looked over."

"She's a tiny thing. Men over five feet eight need not apply."

"You get the shoemaker's wife to beat him?" Speed asked.

"We did."

"Will that make it a better marriage?"

"I wouldn't be surprised if the two of 'em are snuggling in bed together this very moment, pledging to each other that it'll never happen again."

"You know nothing about marriage, Lincoln," Speed offered.

Lincoln laughed softly and replied, "And maybe I never will."

CHAPTER

2

Molly appraised herself before the mirror in her bedroom in Elizabeth's house. This evening she was being introduced to the best young people in Springfield, the young people of her class, to the Coterie. This was Molly's moment, her sisters contended. She was at the height of her beauty and vivacity. There was only laughter now in her blue eyes, only the curve of a smile on her lips, only music in her voice. No gray yet in the soft brown of her hair, no wrinkles in the clear freshness of her complexion, in her lovely neck and shoulders. Men of the Coterie would notice these features. They would line up to dance with her. And she would charm them all, fill them with rapture and delight. She would flirt and bat her eyelids and show not a care in the world.

All the while she would be sizing up which of these swains had prospects and which were as leaves blowing past in a windstorm. Only two paths lay before her: marriage and spinsterhood. She had too much pride to go hunting for a husband and charm enough not to need to. Let beaux discover her and embark on their campaigns. She had no intention of staying in Elizabeth's home as the spinster sister; Ninian, she knew, had no intention of allowing her to do so. So as she danced and flirted this evening, she must stay alert for a man who could set the bells ringing within the belle.

Beside her, also appraising herself in the mirror, primping out of habit, stood Fanny, a few weeks from her wedding. "My last ball as an unmarried woman," she said. "I must remember not to smile too much. I am almost a wife."

"What is it about getting married," Molly asked, "that makes a girl who's done nothing but giggle all her life suddenly grow so serious?"

"I haven't giggled all my life," objected Fanny. "I'm about to have a position in society, Molly. Position carries responsibilities. It requires dignity."

"Gracious," said Molly. "You've been listening to Elizabeth."

"I have done a lot of flirting," Fanny admitted. "We were trained to do that. Now I must remember not to. Except discreetly with Dr. Wallace." Fanny smiled, hummed a self-satisfied little tune and said, "It may happen to you tonight."

"It. It. It." said Molly. "I don't care whether 'It' does or not."

"You'll look across the ballroom and there'll be a glow about him. It will distinguish him from all the other men in the room."

"That's how you picked out Dr. Wallace?"

"He picked me out. It took a little time. But once I knew, I tingled whenever I saw him. It's going to be that way for you."

"How do I look?" Molly asked. She appraised the organdy frock, pink with lace, the pink slippers and the stockings inside them.

"You're beautiful!" Fanny enthused. "Lovely! That pink does wonders for your eyes." After a moment she cautioned, "Don't let them guess how educated you are. Men don't want women to be smarter than they are."

"I'll dance and sway like a nimble-footed flirt." Molly looked again in the glass. "I am so short," she said. "Only a dwarf would take me for a swan."

In the lilac-scented evening air two men climbed the gentle rise of the hill. A breeze stirred softly. The sun had slipped below the horizon and the last light was fading from the sky.

"Lincoln," said Speed, "you have not spoken a word since we left the store."

"You've been whistling the entire time," Lincoln observed. "You're acting—well, not quite like a dog in heat, though it puts me in mind of that."

"A dancing party," replied Speed. "The best young ladies of the town dressed up to please us. I thank them for that."

"They've dressed up to please us," Lincoln said, "and we've dressed up to please them." He touched the stiff black silk cravat at his throat and let his hand slide across the satin of his waistcoat. "Whenever I'm with the 'best ladies,' I never know what to say." He felt much more comfortable with less pretentious prairie girls that he could tease and joke with.

"Tell them how pretty they are."

"I can't make a conversation out of that."

"I can," said Speed. Lincoln laughed. "Talk about the law. Talk about politics."

"Never knew a woman interested in politics," said Lincoln.

"Maybe you'll meet one tonight. They want us to find them beautiful, you know. And interesting. That's what's so pleasant about a ball."

Lincoln said nothing. Speed danced well. He didn't even know the steps.

"They've thought of nothing for days except us holding their waists and whirling them around the dance floor. They've been dreaming of falling in love."

"And so have you."

Speed whistled merrily, not denying the charge.

"You expecting to fall in love with Miss Molly Todd?" asked Lincoln.

"I'm just hankering to find a girl who doesn't think a kiss is a contract to marry. I'll steal one off her."

"Only one?"

"One's a start."

As they reached the crest of the hill, they saw other young men approaching the Edwards house, some on horseback, most of them walking. Carriages were waiting on the drive to disgorge their passengers. Before entering, guests lingered in the evening quiet. They stood chatting on the arcaded verandah, greeting one another, the men shaking hands, the women exchanging kisses on the cheek. Above them, visible through the large open windows of the second story, young women positioned themselves so as to be seen—although they would never have acknowledged this intention. Having finished their toilette, they paraded slowly past the windows. The more demure ones walked with their backs to the young men who cast glances at them from below; the more forward searched the crowd, bestowing a smile or a wave when they caught sight of a favored young man. From a distance the sound of music floated from the parlor, muted by the merry voices and the silver laughter of young women that floated from the second story windows.

As the two men approached the mansion, a voice called out, "Lincoln, is that you?" Lincoln and Speed glanced in the direction of two men standing at the side of the road. The man who

28

spoke laughed with good-natured mockery. "When I see a moving ladder, I know it's Abe Lincoln."

"Douglas?" Lincoln called. "That Shields with you? You two leprechauns are so tiny I thought you must be a pair of prairie dogs watching the swells."

"It's us who're the swells, my lad," replied Jim Shields in his Irish brogue.

"We may not be Whigs," said Steve Douglas, "but we're swells."

"In the Democratic party every man's a swell," called Shields. "It's our platform."

"Can't you fellers talk anything but politics?" asked Speed. "I'm for ladies."

Molly and Fanny moved down the staircase to join the swirl of guests below. Molly hesitated for a moment on the landing, beholding the energy, push and vitality of the citizens of Springfield, so different from the stately and self-consciously genteel, the formal and effete citizens of Lexington. Here folks, as they called themselves, were scrambling to build a society. It could not yet be called a way of life, which is what the leading citizens of Lexington thought they had created, a civilization. The rawness and dynamism of Illinois both amused Molly and energized her.

She glanced at Elizabeth and Ninian, greeting guests at the entryway. They stood, exemplars of Lexington culture, Elizabeth in wine-dark satin with brocaded flowers on a skirt that flared out from the tiniest waist a tightly cinched corset could afford her. Ninian stood beside her, smiling proudly behind his well-trimmed beard and brushed eyebrows, his coat tight at the waist and wrists. Molly was amused that although the ball was designed to introduce her—in her virgin's pink-colored frock—Elizabeth's embodiment of fashion guaranteed that her guests would not overlook their hostess. Her voluminous sleeves puffing gigantically from shoulder to wrist emphasized by contrast the slightness of her waist. The wide neckline displayed the graceful slope of her shoulders and hinted at the beauty of her breasts. *"Bonsoir, les garçons,"* Molly heard her sister say as four young men entered. *"Enchanté de vous voir."* The men, to whom she was proselytizing the finer way of life—woodsmen in waistcoats, Molly thought—took the strange sounds in stride.

"There's the gallant Mr. Speed," whispered Molly. She studied the town's most eligible bachelor, a kindhearted charmer of twenty-four or twenty-five, from a fine Louisville family and a man no woman ever tired of beholding. In addition to dark good looks, long curly hair, blue eyes and a Byronic face, Speed shared with Lord Byron a propensity for falling in love. His passions were as deeply felt as the poet's and just as fleeting. But a merchant, not a poet, he took no actions to compromise a woman's good name. "I do declare!" Molly said. "A beau with the magnetism of a highwayman—and at my sister's house in Illinois." Speed glanced up at the landing and gave Molly a smile, an Illinois welcome. To her surprise Molly returned the smile.

Fanny lifted her fan delicately to her mouth and spoke behind it. "A sweet, sweet man, afflicted with a very fickle heart."

Speed smiled again at Molly and turned back to Elizabeth. She lightly touched his arm, speaking to him, though presumably not in French. "Who's that beanpole with him?" asked Molly. The man glanced up at her, rural in appearance, almost homely, certainly in contrast to his friend.

He had a dark, heavy brow, a solid nose, a no-nonsense mouth.

"That's Lincoln," said Fanny. "The man disciplining the drunk at the horse trough the night you arrived."

Molly hid her mouth with her fan. "So we do know him socially."

"Well, yes, for a party like this. He's Cousin John Todd Stuart's law partner."

"He's a scarecrow in a waistcoat."

Fanny laughed behind her fan. "I shouldn't indulge your wicked tongue, Molly Todd. I dare you to converse with him. That'll test your talents!"

Molly gazed at Lincoln, remembering the man's tall presence the evening she arrived, the way he had lifted the drunk from the trough as if he were a corncob doll. Then he'd seemed in his element. Now he did not. She noticed a melancholy sadness in his eyes. "Does he ever laugh?" she asked. "Who're the others? The shorties?"

"The one speaking French to Elizabeth is Jim Shields," whispered Fanny. "From Ireland—and not nearly as handsome as he thinks."

"And the other? I doubt he's as tall as I am."

"Stephen Douglas from Vermont. The 'little giant,' the politicians call him. A comer, racing as fast as a comet."

Molly appraised him. "Look at the size of his head!" she whispered. "I bet he tore the insides out of his mama coming out of her."

Fanny began to giggle. Then remembering her place as an almost married woman she fought to control herself. "You do have a nasty tongue," she scolded, taking her sister's arm and leading her down the staircase. "And I suggest you curb it now because you're going to meet men who may change your life."

"Welcome," Molly said to Speed, affected by his highwayman's magnetism.

"You remember my sister Molly, Mr. Speed," said Fanny, recovered now from her giggles.

"Indeed, I do. Welcome back, Miss Molly." Speed stepped closer and inquired conspiratorially, "What was the joke up there?"

"So many handsome men," said Molly, mocking and teasing and flirting all at once. "That does make girls giggle."

"And so it should," said Speed.

"Mr. Abraham Lincoln. My sister Molly."

The scarecrow exuded a strong, firm masculinity that sought to be civilized, but had not yet achieved that state. Molly looked into his eyes for only a moment—"Miss Molly," he said—and then Fanny was introducing her to Douglas and Shields. In fact, Douglas stood an inch or two taller than she did; he held himself very erect. James Shields bowed slightly, grinning an ain't-I-handsome grin that put Molly off.

"Show my little sister a good time tonight, gentlemen," said Fanny. "I want every one of you to dance with her. She can dance till dawn."

The men grinned, for to Springfield bachelors every bright, pretty young woman was a prized ornament. As they moved off among the guests, Molly glanced at her sister, her eyes flashing with annoyance. "Why'd you say that?" she asked. "They'll think I came here to catch a husband."

""If you dance with Mr. Shields," Fanny whispered, "he will squeeze your hand. He does it to every girl. If you dance with Mr. Lincoln, he will step on your toes."

Molly did not quite dance till dawn, but many men lined up to squire her around the floor. She waltzed with Speed and Cousin John Todd Stuart, a member of Congress with talented feet, and never had Springfield seen such graceful gliding. She polkaed with Reverend Charles Dresser, the minister at Elizabeth and Ninian's church, and with the handsome Irishman James Shields. Old Parson Dresser moved with a confidence that belied his years. When the dance ended, he was winded and laughing, but pleased to remember what polkaing was meant to be with a partner so accomplished. He would be leaving the party shortly, he explained with regret, because he was preaching the next morning. He wanted to be in good form then so as not to be criticized by parishioners who did not hold with dancing. "There are some of those in every congregation," he confided. "I hope to see you in church tomorrow, Miss Todd. Promise me you'll come."

Molly gave him a flirtatious look. "I will surely try, Reverend," she assured him and saw that he was not immune to her charm. "But when a girl is being introduced to society, she has an obligation to dance with every man who asks her. Don't you agree? That may tucker me out. You wouldn't want me nodding in church, would you?" She batted her eyelids. "Though I'm sure no one's attention flags during your sermons." The parson chuckled at this flattery, happy to hope it was true, and returned Molly to the edge of the floor. There James Shields awaited his turn with her.

Shields grinned at her, for he was confident of his good looks. His footwork, refined on Irish jigs, incorporated a bantam cock's swagger both as they walked onto the dance floor and as they whirled around the room. "Born in County Tyrone,

I was," he soon told Molly. "And a reckless fellow I was at a very early age." She inquired as to what sort of recklessness that might be. "When I was still a stripling, I challenged a man to a duel."

Molly gasped, for that seemed the expected reaction. "You are brave," she said. And reckless indeed, she thought, though she did not say it. She wondered if he might dance her out onto the verandah and kiss her, a prospect that both thrilled and unnerved her.

"He was a veteran of the Napoleonic wars." Shields continued. "Being Irish, I took exception to his praising British soldiers and slapped him across the face." Molly gasped again as he spun her around. Shields grinned and explained, "I had ancestors at the Battle of the Boyne where the Brits took over Northern Ireland. So I was not about to be having someone praise the Brits."

Mr. Shields did not appear to need drawing out, but even so Molly offered, "I take it you prevailed."

"Good fortune prevailed. I was not smart enough to run off. So I met my adversary on the field of honor early the next morning. I took one of the pistols he'd borrowed from a friend. We stood back to back, counted off the steps, turned, aimed and—the longest moment of my life. It's terrified I was. Neither pistol fired. We tried again. Same result. So instead of killing each other, we became fast friends. He taught me French and I taught it to scholars in the wee village of Kaskaskia down south of St. Louis when I first arrived in Illinois. But like Ireland Kaskaskia was too small for me."

Laying out all his masculine credentials, Shields told Molly he had fled Ireland lest he be hanged as a rebel. He had been marching local boys in close order drill and the Brits took offense at that. He'd been shipwrecked while fleeing. He, another seaman and the ship's captain alone survived. Later, he'd plied some, though not all, of the seven seas. A mast had fallen on him during a severe storm off New York. He had been nursed for three months before he was back on his feet.

"You dance marvelously for a man who's suffered two broken legs," Molly praised him.

"I came to this country for opportunity," Shields said, "and plenty of that, there is, for the man who knows how to recognize and seize it."

The dance ended. There was more to tell, Shields assured her, squeezing her hand as he held it. He would relate the rest the next time they were together.

Next she danced the galop, first with Edwin Webb and then Ned Baker, both of them legislators. It seemed that the entire legislature had come to the ball. Mr. Baker, originally from England, made interesting conversation, but unfortunately was married. Mr. Webb was a widower. "Call me Bat," he said. "From Batterson, my middle name. Everybody calls me Bat." But that was too frontier for Molly; she called him Mr. Webb. Another small man, he looked close to forty. The galop winded him a bit. He smiled at Molly like a wolf ready to make a meal of her and confessed that he had two young children. She expressed her condolences about the loss of his wife and thought of her father who was out scratching around for another woman to give him children hardly before his wife, Molly's mother, was cold in her grave. So hasty was his pursuit and his acceptance by Miss Betsey Humphreys that their behavior caused talk in two counties of Kentucky, facts she might never have known had her maternal Grandmother Parker not made sure she heard them.

She danced Virginia reels with Anson Henry and Elias Merryman, both doctors. And schottisches with Stephen Douglas and James Conkling. Douglas was even smaller than Shields and Webb, but with a head so massive, a self-confidence so out-sized, a dynamism so overpowering and a personality so aggressive that he gave an impression of size. "The Little Giant," Molly said when he asked her to dance.

"That's what some call me, Miss Molly," he acknowledged, "And others call me names too indelicate for a lady's ears.

"Your fame precedes you, sir."

"What use is fame to a man," he asked her in his deep baritone, a twinkle in his eye, "unless it precedes him. Does it do me credit?"

"You succeeded my cousin John Hardin, who escorted me to Illinois, as state attorney for Morgan County." After a pause she added, "That was due, I believe, to a set of shenanigans much too complicated for me to remember."

"I hardly remember the circumstances myself. But I'm sure there were no shenanigans." He grinned at her as if to confirm that shenanigans there certainly were and that he remembered them. "Hardin and I are good friends these days."

"And you opposed my cousin John Todd Stuart for Congress last year."

"The Todds are certainly numerous in Illinois," observed Douglas.

"And there was scuffling, I believe I heard, during the campaign."

Douglas grinned. "Well, what's a campaign without a scuffle? There's sure to be scuffling if only thirty-six votes out of thirty-six thousand separate the candidates."

They began to move around the floor, Douglas leading her with a firm hand. "But let's talk about you. Your sparkling eyes and lilting voice are certainly welcome here. Are you likely to stay this time?"

"I believe so. What led you to settle here?" Molly asked. Douglas had been gracious in throwing the conversation back to her, but she sensed that a man so full of self-confidence and good feeling about himself would prefer to do the talking.

"I felt the West beckoning me. Growing communities need lawyers."

"And politicians."

"Yes, indeed. Politics, politics, politics. I love it."

"And you're very good at it, I understand," said Molly.

As they spun gaily around the floor, she noticed tall Mr. Lincoln. He stood at the edge of the dancers, his arms held stiffly behind his back as if he were manacled. It was not the first time she had spotted him, obviously ill at ease, but now Douglas whirled her away from any view of him.

Molly smiled again at her partner. "You've rocketed to success in Illinois."

"You flatter me, Miss Molly. But I eat politics, drink politics, sleep and dream politics." He examined her and grinned. "What are yours, may I ask?" Molly shrugged. "Whiggish, I suppose. But if you've got an open mind, I'd like to invite you to a great party, the Democratic Party."

"Whigs give very good parties," Molly teased, "if this is any example."

"But this party ends tonight. My party goes on and on."

"The leader of the Whig party, Mr. Henry Clay, is a neighbor of ours down home. I'd die if he ever learned that I'd been seen at the wrong party. A lady must be careful of her reputation."

"I'll keep after you about this, Miss Molly. Be warned."

After thanking Stephen Douglas for the polka, she left to "refresh" herself. She went upstairs and stood at a window for a breath of air. By herself while a waltz played in the ballroom, she quite unexpectedly found herself thinking of the scarecrow Lincoln. Fanny had dared her. Should she talk with him?

Downstairs, she found Elizabeth and said, "Present me to Abraham Lincoln, will you, please? He must be miserable. He's been standing all evening like a stork at the edge of a pond, afraid to get his feet wet."

"He's awkward around women. And does not dance," said Elizabeth.

"For religious reasons? Is he one of those?"

"Mr. Lincoln is not religious," said Elizabeth. Then she whispered, "I am quite sure Mr. Lincoln does not dance because he does not know how to dance."

"Does he smile?" Molly asked. "I want to get him to smile. Surely he smiles."

"Tells stories not fit for a lady's ears, so Ninian says. And cackles while he tells them."

"Perhaps I can get him to tell one to me," said Molly.

"I declare, Molly," said Elizabeth, smiling and shaking her head. "You are that limb of Satan Miss Betsey always contends you are."

"Present me to him. He's just across the room."

The two sisters circled the dance floor and approached Lincoln. He glanced at them, gave them a half-smile and moved back beneath a candle sconce to let them pass. They stopped before him. "Mr. Lincoln," said Elizabeth, "I don't know that you've had a chance to talk with my sister Molly. She's a new arrival from Lexington. She thinks our prairie countryside suits her taste."

Having provided these bits of information, Elizabeth smiled at Lincoln expecting him to take the cue, ask a question or make a comment. He only nodded, a look of mild apprehension on his face, and held his hands more tightly behind his back. Elizabeth turned to Molly, a smile frozen on her lips, and waited for her sister's Lexington social graces, well learned at the knee of Madame Mentelle from Paris, to come to the rescue.

"Are you a preacher, Mr. Lincoln?" Molly chirped brightly.

Lincoln looked surprised at this suggestion and shook his head.

"Excuse me," Elizabeth said. "A hostess must never be still." She moved off, leaving Molly to cope with this fellow famous for his gawkiness, odd clothes and black hair that seemed always to escape the discipline of a comb.

"I ask," said Molly, "because the evening I arrived here I saw you baptizing."

"Baptizing, ma'am?"

"In a horse trough." Lincoln smiled sheepishly. "You must be a very fine Christian yourself."

Lincoln watched her, leaning back, smiling quizzically as if uncertain what was happening. Molly supposed no woman had ever talked to him this way.

She continued, "I believe you're one of the famous young men of this community."

Lincoln looked surprised at these words coming from this vivacious young woman with soft brown hair and flashing eyes. He, a famous man of the town?

"Are you not famous, Mr. Lincoln?" Molly teased. "Did you not get a murderer acquitted because he was threatened by a deadly chair?"

Lincoln gave a guilty half-smile and said nothing.

Molly appraised him. "You are so tall, Mr. Lincoln!" she burbled. "Longest of the 'Long Nine,' I've heard. Is that so?"

Lincoln shrugged as if his tongue were tied in knots.

The "Long Nine" were a group of legislators from Sangamon County, all standing over six feet tall. The group's signal achievement had been to lead the wheeling, dealing and conniving needed to get the state capital moved from Vandalia to Sangamon County's own Springfield, an effort consuming several years.

Molly leaned back exaggeratedly, mocking Lincoln, setting her small hand across her brow. "Well, you must be the tallest of them. You're seven or eight feet, I daresay. I can hardly see your brow. How's the weather up there?"

Lincoln smiled, but was still too uncertain of himself to speak.

"You mustn't be discombobulated that I called you famous. Fame comes and goes."

"Does it? I haven't made its acquaintance."

"You will, Mr. Lincoln. I assure you. I have a sense about these things and I'm never wrong."

Lincoln shrugged, pleased with this flattery, and stole a look at Molly.

"You're the partner of my cousin, Congressman Stuart, are you not?"

"Yes, ma'am."

"You served together in the Black Hawk War, I believe I heard. And chased those Injuns right across the Mississippi River. And became a hero. Am I right?"

Lincoln grinned sheepishly and stared at his feet. Molly leaned backwards exaggeratedly, her fingertips at the middle of her back as if to keep her erect.

"I hardly know what to say, Miss Molly." His voice was strangely high-pitched for a man with such a long throat in which his sound could resonate.

"You're not a war hero?" Molly asked.

"We did have a fine time soldiering. Maybe 'cause we hardly saw an Injun."

"Really?" Molly grinned at him flirtatiously. It was always amusing to see how men reacted to flirting. Douglas reveled in it; this one seemed hardly to know what to do. She chirped on, "All these Kentucky cousins of mine who served with you tell me the fighting got as hot as the Revolutionary War."

Lincoln looked uncertain of what to say. She was so bright, so full of wit, that if he were not careful he would say the wrong thing. Certainly he must not contradict the boasts of those Kentucky cousins.

"Maybe it was the sun that was hot," Molly suggested, "and not the fighting." She appraised him. "You serve on the Town Board, do you not?"

"Yes, ma'am, I do."

"And in the Legislature?"

"I do."

"Why, Mr. Lincoln! We've only met and you're already saying 'I do' to me!"

Lincoln laughed and blushed.

"Is that all you have to say for yourself?"

"I could say this, Miss Molly. I want to dance with you in the worst way."

Molly led Lincoln to the dance floor and raised her arms to dance with him. Her hands barely reached his shoulders. His length seemed to require him to stoop to put his hand at her waist. Even so, he held her firmly. But their difference in height was sure to make waltzing awkward. It did not help that the dancing school Mr. Lincoln had attended, wherever that might have been, had taught a different version of the waltz than Molly had learned from her dancing masters in Lexington. They moved in opposite directions. They heard contrary rhythms. He stepped on her toes; she gritted her teeth but did not cry out. But she did wonder if she would ever again be able to wear the pink dancing slippers.

Once around the ballroom was all she could manage. She led him off the floor, saying that she had done too much dancing. He seemed relieved to stop, but reluctant to withdraw his hands from her. They got punch and walked out onto the verandah where other guests were lounging, a few of the men smoking. Molly led Lincoln to a quiet corner, for she was certain he would disappear into himself if she joined a group of others. As it was he felt so awkward that he quickly emptied the punch cup, then stared into it, uncertain what to do with it.

Molly took the punch cup and put it on a small table. "Do you ride circuit, Mr. Lincoln?" she asked for he seemed to have no conversational ploys to offer.

"I do."

Although it crossed her mind, she did not tease him again about saying "I do" to her. "And do you ride or go by a one-horse shay?" She appraised him. "I'll wager you ride, Mr. Lincoln. You give me the impression of a man who sits a horse well."

"I do ride, ma'am." The faintest flicker crossed his eyes. "And if the horse is swayback, my feet touch the ground."

She laughed, pleased with him. "And if it rains?" she asked. "I declare, it must rain a good deal. What do you do? Shelter under a tree?

"I carry an umbrella."

"As you ride, you carry an umbrella? My, my." She giggled at the thought of him, riding a sway-back horse in the rain, his feet dragging on the ground, as he held an umbrella above the two of them.

Lincoln smiled at her. "I carry it only when it rains, Miss Molly. The horse carries it the rest of the time."

"And how do you carry it?" she asked.

"I tie it to the saddle with a strand of twine. It's too big to be carried inside my hat. Specially when my head's in the hat."

Molly giggled. "You generally carry things in your hat?"

"Legal papers. They keep dry in there."

She laughed, picturing him in her mind, his swayback horse plodding through a thunder-storm, his boots splashing along under it, with the umbrella held high above the stovepipe hat in which he carried his legal papers, safe and dry. He smiled down at her, pleased to amuse her.

"Do you take political soundings when you travel about?" she asked. "It must be a fascinating way for a politician to gauge the likes and dislikes of voters."

"The voters I talk to most are ones with legal problems."

"Are they interested in issues of the day?"

"Mostly they're interested in solving their legal problems."

"I'm sure of that. But what about internal improvements, for example? Are they interested in them?"

Lincoln looked at her strangely. "Are you interested in them, Miss Molly? I don't know I've ever talked politics—"

"With a woman, Mr. Lincoln?" He saw that there was fire in her as well as flirtation and teasing. "Do you suppose politics are too complicated for us delicate creatures to understand?"

"Why no. In fact, I'm all for women's suffrage."

"I saw you teaching a woman how to beat her husband on Jefferson Street."

"I can teach you if ever there's a need to know." He paused and there was a twinkle in his eyes. "I'm always for women's suffrage when I talk to women.'

But she was not amused. "Just like you're for emancipation when you talk to Negroes?"

Was this just party talk? Or did she want to know? He could not tell. She was from Kentucky, and he knew that her father owned slaves. The former Kentuckians around Springfield were strongly opposed to abolitionist, moralist meddlers who presumed to tell them how to run their lives, something that Ninian Edwards, for one, detested.

"I always try to see the other feller's point of view," Lincoln said carefully.

"Even when he's not a feller?" Miss Molly shot back at him.

"Specially then, I reckon," he said. "What are your views on the issues of the day?"

She cocked her head and gazed at him saucily. "You taking a sounding right here?"

"Right here on Coterie Hill, ma'am."

"Is that what they call it in town?"

"Sometimes 'Quality Hill.' I want to be able to represent 'Quality Hill' well in the legislature."

"I'm sure you are making fun of me, Mr. Lincoln."

"I suspect you've been making a little fun of me, Miss Todd." With an amused smile on his face he looked down at her from under his heavy brows. She wondered what kind of stories he told men when they were alone. Probably she would not even understand them.

Molly saw her friend Mercy Ann Levering and James Conkling moving toward them across the verandah. Mercy Ann had just arrived from Baltimore for an extended stay with her brother Lawrason and his wife Bri, the Edwardses' closest neighbors. Conkling, a recent graduate of Princeton College in New Jersey who possessed the polish that Lincoln so obviously lacked, had been practicing law in town less than a year. He seemed pleased to be with Mercy Ann. They smiled as they approached and Molly realized the musicians had stopped playing. She thought, Merce thinks I'm stuck and is coming to my rescue.

"What a lovely party!" Merce exclaimed. "We just had some refreshments. They are so good."

"Do you all know each other?" Molly asked.

"Of course," said Conkling. "Lincoln and I often practice in the same courtrooms."

"I think half the men in town are lawyers," said Merce. "There must be an awful lot of troubles in Illinois to keep you all busy."

"We aren't all busy," said Conkling. "Some of us are loafers."

"I was going upstairs for a few minutes," Merce told Molly in a half whisper. "Want to come with me?"

"I'm fine for the moment," Molly said. "Unless there's—"

"No, no. I'm fine, too," Merce assured her. "This is such a beautiful evening for a party. What a wonderful springtime we're all going to have in Illinois."

They made Coterie chitchat for a time, speaking about who had come to the ball, who was indisposed and who was out of town. They praised the musicians, especially the show-off at the piano, and wished that balls like this one could last until sunup. Molly noticed that Lincoln had put his long arms behind him once again as if to hide them. He said not a word and seemed to be fading into the darkness.

Finally the music struck up once more. "That's our cue," Conkling said. "I guess we'll go in again."

Molly watched Merce and Conkling move off. When she turned back to Lincoln, he was trying to be invisible again. The melancholy expression was on his face. She wondered where he'd gone off to in his head. "We were talking politics, Mr. Lincoln," she said cheerily, not simply because it was his subject, but because it was also hers. "Is Mr. Conkling planning to put his toe into politics?"

"I can't speak for Conkling's toe, ma'am," Lincoln said, fully back now.

His hands were still clutched behind his back. Molly wondered why. "I hope it does not shock you to talk politics with a woman."

Finally he allowed, "It intrigues me, Miss Molly. I mean that."

46

"The fact is," she said, "I have strong views on the issues of the day. And I daresay I'm more informed about them than most of your constituents."

Lincoln just grinned at her, warmed by her vivacity and spirit.

Molly stated her views on the issues: internal development (good policy); protective tariffs for infant industries (an excellent idea); conservative banking and a stable currency (essential; her father was president of the Bank of Kentucky, she mentioned); the irascibility of President Andrew Jackson (unfortunate although, of course, she applauded his victory at New Orleans); his tendency to make policy choices based on personal favoritism or animosities (abhorrent).

Lincoln listened, a slight smile riding on his lips. Molly could not tell whether it was a smile of enchantment or amusement, but her training and instincts warned her that she must redirect the conversation toward him. "What do you do when you are not strategizing legal maneuvers? Do you hunt?"

"Not much for hunting," Lincoln said.

"Do you ride?"

He shook his head.

"Take rambles in the country?"

"I get my fill of rambling when I'm on circuit. I guess I read."

"What do you read?"

"Poetry mostly. Right now I'm studying a book of Euclidean geometry."

"Really?"

"It's pretty much Greek to me. Which isn't surprising, Euclid being—"

"Greek." Molly and Lincoln laughed. She took a closer look at him for it was well nigh unheard of in her experience for a man to admit that he did not know something. "I studied Euclidean geometry," she said. "I remember it well."

"Could you help me figure it out?"

Molly studied him. Had he really said this? Had he truly asked for her help in understanding mathematics? "I don't mean to pose as a know-it-all slyboots."

"Could I call on you with my book in hand?"

"Come tomorrow evening if you like."

"All right."

Molly had thought of opening a school. But she hadn't expected teaching to come at her in this way. She laughed, a little embarrassed by her boastfulness. "Oh, goodness," she said. "Now I'll have to try to remember what I've crowed about knowing."

As the two Democrats walked back down the hill, Shields observed, "Molly Todd's a good match for you. Bright, lively, intelligent. Rather pretty."

"I thought she might be a good match for you," Douglas told his friend.

"Sure, it's hard to tell whether she's flattering or mocking you."

"Probably both. It was both with me. She is pretty."

They walked along without speaking. "Ninian Edwards is an odd duck," Shields said at last. He was thinking of an ancestor, a good Irish lad, who'd seen a boat carrying two young ladies capsize on Lough Neagh. The ancestor swam out to rescue the ladies and ended up marrying one of them, the daughter of the local English lord. Shields wondered if that ancestor had felt the same way about entering his father-in-law's castle as he himself felt about entering Ninian Edwards' home. "And his wife telling us, *'Enchanté de vous voir,'* speaking French with a Kentucky drawl." Shields chuckled with amazement. "And didn't I hear he gave his graduation speech at Transylvania University in Latin?" He laughed aloud. "Latin!"

"Illinois is a strange place to be an aristocrat," said Douglas.

"And them just land speculators who got here first."

"If you'd gotten here first," Douglas teased him, "you'd be putting on airs, too. You'd be a Whig inviting us peasants to your castle."

"Not I," said Shields. "Down with aristocrats!" After a moment he wondered, "You think Molly Todd's come here looking for a husband?"

"Could be," said Douglas. "Her sister Fanny found one easy enough."

"A lot of good men there are out here."

"A first class bunch. But if she's looking for an aristocrat, this is not the place."

As the two Whigs walked down the hill, Lincoln asked, "Did you find some girl to steal kisses from?"

"My friend," said Speed, "a gentleman never answers such questions."

"I'm not asking a gentleman."

"Then I'll have to say 'Alas! No!' and let you wonder. Did you dance?"

"If you see Miss Todd limping you'll know she danced with Abraham Lincoln."

"Did she get you talking?"

"She talked politics. She's a good little Whig."

"I saw her dancing with Douglas. They're well paired."

"Indeed. Neither one's taller than a bug."

Lincoln glanced over at his friend. He had been whistling on the way up to the party, but was not whistling now. Apparently Speed had failed to fall in love this evening.

Well, he had not fallen either. Not that he had the money to afford a wife. All in good time, he told himself. It was something he had been telling himself over the years about so many things: the law, politics, money, women. All in good time, he thought, trying to believe it.

Molly sat at her vanity brushing her hair. Ordinarily before going to bed she brushed one hundred strokes on each side. But she was comfortably tired tonight, music still playing in her head, Fanny already asleep in their bed. She had lost track of the count. Well, the world would survive if she did not get to her one hundreds.

Fanny stirred in her sleep, a smile on her mouth. Glancing at her, Molly wondered if she truly loved her "sweet doctor." Would she even know? Men and women inhabited such separate universes, Molly thought. Maybe members of the two sexes never really knew one another.

As she yawned, it occurred to Molly that Elizabeth and Fanny were Lexington women at heart. They seemed content to bear and raise children, dress well, give parties to advance their husbands' status and play well the roles society expected of them. Not for me, Molly thought. She had received a better education than any woman of her acquaintance. She vowed to herself that she would never marry without love.

But would she recognize love when it came? That sudden rush of feeling that came over her sometimes in the presence of certain men. Was that love? She had felt that fleetingly for Cousin

John Hardin when they were traveling together. But he was married and out-of-bounds. A lot of men might be out-of-bounds on the frontier, men who came from nothing. "Never forget that you are a Todd," Elizabeth always said. Would being a Todd keep her from finding a man she could love?

A knock came at the door. Elizabeth entered, looking tired from the work and strain of giving a party and trying to let none of it show.

"What a beautiful ball, Elizabeth," Molly whispered with a smile. "Little wonder you're known far and wide as the leading light of Springfield society."

Elizabeth sighed and sat on Molly's bed. "You are launched," she said.

"And who was ever better launched than I've been?"

Elizabeth looked over at Fanny and smiled. "A lot of beaux at the ball. Any one of them specially take your fancy?"

"I can't even remember who they all were. I'll write down the names of the ones I remember tomorrow."

"You and Stephen Douglas make a handsome pair."

"He's a Democrat, Elizabeth. How could that work?"

"Leave politics to the men. We do the important business of this country: raising strong families to people the land. Forget the man's politics. Worry about the man."

Molly went back to brushing her hair. "I lost count of the strokes," she said. "Do you suppose I've done enough for tonight?" Casually she added, "Abraham Lincoln asked me to teach him Euclidean geometry. And I just may."

Elizabeth smiled at Molly being Molly and let a tired hand slip through her hair. "You and Lincoln are completely mismatched. He's everything you're not."

"I never met a man at a ball who admitted he didn't know something." Molly turned to watch Elizabeth's reaction. "You have to agree: that's amazing!"

"Lincoln is amazing," Elizabeth acknowledged. Agreement sometimes outmaneuvered Molly. "He entered the Legislature wearing a suit Ninian says he borrowed the money to buy. Got elected from a village that's now abandoned by telling the best stories of all the backwoods rowdies. He could outrun them and throw any of them when they wrestled." Molly went back to brushing her hair. "He looks like a farmboy," said Elizabeth. "But he's a political operator."

"I must get to know this man." Molly turned back to Elizabeth and grinned cheekily. "He said he wanted to dance with me in the worst way. Which is exactly what he did." The sisters laughed.

"Molly Todd, you have a wicked tongue," Elizabeth admonished with a smile. Her expression grew serious. "Don't break his heart," she said. "Mr. Lincoln is not one of us. And never can be."

Molly set the hairbrush down. "I'm sure I've done enough." She took the hands of her tired sister. "Thank you so much for the party."

She rose when Elizabeth did and embraced her. As Elizabeth tiptoed from the room, Molly got in bed beside Fanny. Listening to her sister's breathing, she thought about what Elizabeth had said. Of course, raising families was important, obviously the most important thing of all. But politics was important, too. Too important to be left to mere men. Elizabeth was right about Lincoln: canny or not, he was impossible. As for Stephen Douglas, there was no way she could marry a Democrat!

CHAPTER

3

The cackle of roosters woke Molly. The first light of dawn dimly lit the room. The rhythm of remembered waltzes tippy-tapped lightly through her head and she smiled, dancing with someone in her head. She yawned, turned over, nudging Fanny who snored lightly beside her, and went back to sleep. Later the sound of the stable boy harnessing the horse to the carriage woke her again. Because Ninian was mindful of the fact that Reverend Dresser counted on them to set an example of faithfulness for all Springfield, Ninian and Elizabeth would be attending church. Fanny would accompany them—she had already left the room—in order to see Dr. Wallace.

Brilliant sunlight spilled from the window. Molly smelled the aroma of fresh-baked bread rising from the kitchen; the Irish girls would have already returned from mass. Molly stretched, wondering whom she'd been dancing with when she woke earlier, and was grateful to Elizabeth for not badgering her to attend church. She lay with her eyes closed, feeling a breeze stirring through the open window. When she heard the carriage leave the yard, she sat up in bed, took pencil and paper from the bedside table and, resting against the pillows, began to list the potential beaux she had danced with. She wrote the first name . . .

Stephen Douglas. Never had she seen such an enormous personality crammed inside so diminutive a package. Still, there was something magnetic about him: the sparkle in his eyes, his easy laughter, the resonance of his deep voice. He exuded self-confidence in a way that drew people to him. She had felt drawn to him herself—like a willing subject to a mesmerist. Hmm. She stared across the room at the spring sunlight flooding through the window. She would be careful about Douglas. She laughed: he was so tiny! Why, any one of the Long Nine could toss him half way to Lexington! She smiled at the idea of his flying through the air, trying to regain his self-possession. Then she realized, of course, that he would not have lost his self-possession. He would turn that flight to his political advantage.

She wrote: James Shields. The blarneying, hand-squeezing Irishman. Hard to tell if there was any heft of personal qualities. Shields claimed to have taught French to farmers' sons in Kaskaskia. She giggled, shuddering to think of *quelle sorte de français* it was, *effroyable,* probably. At least she'd been smart enough not to start chattering away to him in the society French Mme. Mentelle had taught her.

She wrote: _____ Webb. She couldn't remember the first name. A widower. Also small. Much too old. With children. That tempted her to cross him off. Around the Long Nine it was hard to be impressed by small, wispy men.

James Shields was good-looking. Too bad he was so aware of the fact.

She wrote: Joshua Speed. The truly good-looking man was Speed. Also very personable. Think of having him across the breakfast table for thirty years! There'd never been a spark between them. Too bad. But then he was a store keeper. Without the intellectual weight or mental cunning of the lawyers.

She wrote: Elias Merryman. Anson Henry. Both doctors. She barely remembered them.

She wrote: Abraham Lincoln. The so very tall Mr. Lincoln. She stared at the ceiling. Surely it was a mistake: boasting to him about all the geometry she knew. Certainly Fanny was right. Not a good idea to remind men on the edge of a frontier that was still being settled that she was smarter and better educated than they were.

She wrote: James Conkling. The Princeton College graduate. She could parade her education to him and they would only laugh about it. So many of these frontier men were self-taught. Lincoln, Shields and Douglas must have all come to the law by reading law books in the corners of lawyers' offices. Young ladies with a lot less schooling than she, girls who only had instinct to guide them, knew better than to brag about how smart they were.

She crossed out Conkling's name. Taken. The previous evening she had known just as surely as she had ever known anything that one day he and her dear friend Mercy Ann would marry. Merce did not know it yet. Conkling probably had hopes but dared not mention them yet for fear of killing the bud before it could blossom. Molly would do nothing to make Merce regard her as a rival. Merce and Conkling were both Easterners, venturesome in their native environments but rather colorless for the frontier. Jim Conkling, she imagined, would practice law until he retired, serving the community in ways appropriate to a lawyer. Merce would have and raise his children, tend his home and entertain their friends. In their dotage both would think correctly that they had lived good, useful and even interesting lives. That life journey would be enough for them, Molly assumed. But for her? Probably not.

She looked over the list. Might she actually marry one of these men? Speed? Douglas? One of the doctors? Gawky Mr. Lincoln with those sad eyes testifying to the struggle he had faced in becoming Coterie-worthy? Mr. Lincoln, who had not only taught himself, but was still doing it. How different he was from Douglas, humbly acknowledging that he was studying something that befuddled him.

She wondered if he would actually appear that evening with his book of Euclidean geometry carried in his large hand. If he did, she was not going to parade her brains.

At midafternoon a knock came at the front door. It was Stephen Douglas, wondering if Miss Molly would care to take a walk. Molly was tending two-year-old Julia while Elizabeth rested. She sent word that she'd be down presently and considered bringing Julia along. She decided, however, that this might suggest an impatient proclivity toward motherhood that would scare off Mr. Douglas. She alerted Elizabeth, who was not sleeping, that a beau had come calling. Elizabeth insisted she go, but not far.

"I'm sure you're too busy to take me for a walk," Molly said as she greeted Douglas.

"I had an afternoon when I could get away," he told her. "I thought I better take advantage of it."

They strolled around Elizabeth's garden, chatting about the party, the shrubs and flowers, the weather, where they hailed from. "Tell me about the East," Molly implored Douglas. "Are people very different there?"

Douglas recounted tales of the green mountains and valleys of Vermont where he was born, of rugged winters in upstate New York, being snowbound and cold and underoccupied all winter when the temperature made a boy want to be active, doing chores all summer when sun and heat made him lazy. "I realized early I wasn't cut out to be a farmer," he said. "I got my first taste of political work in Middlebury. I was working for a cabinetmaker, turning table legs on a lathe, making bedsteads and washstands. My employer was an Adams man. That may have made me rally to General Jackson." He grinned, his deep baritone voice bursting into laughter. "But I liked what Jackson stood for, too. Friends and I ran around town tearing down John Quincy Adams handbills." He relished the story, pretending to snatch handbills off lilac bushes. "Old Hickory had executed five militiamen for desertion during the War of 1812 and those handbills all had coffins on them. We found a coffin for those bills!"

To credential himself as an educated man, he told her about attending Canandaigua Academy in upstate New York, the region's finest school. "I tried my hand—and my voice—at debating there." He laughed at himself once more. "I knew I needed a stage even before I knew what a stage was. I needed to be lifted above the crowd and it was a nuisance that my physical dimensions were not as large as my aspirations. As soon as I saw what lawyers did—got up and orated, righted wrongs, sent malefactors to jail, saved the innocent from the gallows—I knew that was for me. And I was fitted for it. My tongue could talk the stripes off a tiger."

Molly laughed at the way Douglas made a stage of wherever he was and became a commanding figure upon it. He allowed her to seem specially chosen to strut across it with him. She enjoyed the fact that he could laugh at himself as he pranced. He was not a man who wanted a woman to do a lot of talking. With him a woman's role was to listen, nod appreciatively when that was expected and laugh when that was. Molly was happy with these duties, at least on a walk around a garden.

"I was drawn to politics," he told her, "because it was a better stage than lawyering. You could draw crowds. There was applause." He grinned at her and she laughed. "I believed in things, too, of course. I trusted the voice of the many and believed in the doctrine of equal rights. Once I got my bearings in Illinois—I taught school the first winter I was here, had forty young scholars—it wasn't hard to see what was calling out to be done. Turn the prairie into farmland. Make the internal improvements that would help farmers get their produce to market. Find the financing to do it. I found myself putting dreams into voters' heads that common sense should have put there. Not every man can do that," he said.

"Only very special men, I should think," replied Molly.

He gave her a sidelong glance. "You're flattering me," he accused.

Of course, I am, you silly, she thought. Wasn't that what he expected? What he wanted?

She said, "You're the Little Giant. How could you not be special?"

"I believe in the people," he told her. "The government is for them. And by them, through the ɔr entatives they choose. Their government s n obligation to make them secure. To give en freedom and an opportunity to better ther -

come to a bed of roses, pink, scarlet and yellow, Molly tiptoed among the blossoms. "Come smell them," she urged. "They're wonderfully fragrant." Douglas stepped beside her and breathed in their perfume. "I think there's lemonade in the house," said Molly. "Would you like some?"

While they drank lemonade, Elizabeth appeared with Julia to show Mr. Douglas that Molly was properly chaperoned by her family. She had a sip of lemonade, then left the child with Molly and disappeared. Douglas mentioned that while campaigning the next year he would give dozens of speeches to Irishmen.

"To Irishmen?" Molly asked.

"Indeed," boasted Douglas. "There are hundreds of them right now digging the Illinois and Michigan canal. The Democrats are going to deliver the vote to them. And they're going to deliver their votes to us." Douglas grinned like the cat that swallowed the canary.

"How can Irishmen vote?" Molly asked. "They're not citizens."

"What a Whiggish attitude!" Douglas made a face at her. "Nothing in the Illinois constitution says a man must be a citizen to vote. A white man living six months in the state qualifies." This assertion surprised Molly. She would have to consult with Ninian. Douglas grinned. "You think those Hibernians will vote Whig? Not after we've sent Jamie O'Shiel to talk to them."

"And who's Jamie O'Shiel?" she asked, provoked by his confidence.

"Jim Shields. He'll thicken that brogue." Douglas assumed a brogue that Molly barely understood. "You're not after telling me you'll vote Whig now, are ya? It's us who's taking care of you, lads.

It's us who're needing your votes." Douglas laughed heartily. "Watch us!" he said.

Preparing to take his leave, he clasped Molly's hand in both of his. She felt a flush of excitement flood through her body. He looked at her deeply and smiled. She feared that she might blush and commanded her pigments to behave.

"May I call again?" he asked.

"I hope you will," she told him, turning to pick up Julia so that their gaze would not linger, so that she would not blush. She watched him skip down the walk, whistling, and turn at the gate to wave. She waved back. She kissed the child's forehead and whispered, "Auntie Molly has met someone she likes."

At supper Molly asked Ninian about Douglas. "Brilliant," he said. Elizabeth made a face. Watching Elizabeth's reaction, Molly understood why Douglas thought the Whigs were a party of wealth and privilege. "Also combative," said Ninian. "The politician as pugilist. He'll stoop to any trick to get ahead."

Molly said that Douglas was confident that the Democracy would carry Illinois in the upcoming 1840 campaign. "He's relying on the Irish canal diggers' vote."

"We've got him blocked on that," Ninian assured her.

"He speaks with great passion about our democratic system. It being designed to benefit humble people, the citizens, not the propertied."

"The 'humble members of society,' as Old Hickory, the old hick, calls them," said Ninian. He wore an amused smile. "Holding the fort against a moneyed aristocracy systematically exploiting the humble toilers."

"He has idealism and fervor." Molly defended him because Ninian's expression was patronizing. "If I were an Irishman, I'd probably vote with him."

"But you're not," Elizabeth reminded her. "You're a Todd."

"We all agree," said Ninian, "that American government takes its authority from the people. But it must also protect property. People of property hold the country together. They have a stake in its success. People who have nothing can riot and break things. And often do."

"I'm sure Douglas is exciting to be around," Elizabeth said. "But don't forget. He's a parvenu." Molly felt confused. Only last night Elizabeth had spoken highly of Douglas; now he was a parvenu. Hearing his political ideas must have changed her mind. Elizabeth nodded to her husband. "Tell her about Cousin John Hardin."

Ninian told how Douglas, hardly a year in Illinois, had teamed with a crony in the Legislature to maneuver Cousin John Hardin out of the state's attorney's job in Jacksonville. Douglas had drafted a bill making the position elective by both houses of the Legislature; the crony had introduced it. After it passed the Legislature that had a Democratic majority, Douglas got the state's attorney's job in Jacksonville for himself. "Smart operator," said Ninian. "Only twenty-one then and he hardly knew any law."

"Just enough to draft a bill," observed Molly.

"He so provoked Cousin John Todd Stuart during a campaign speech he was giving," Elizabeth said, "that John got that massive head in a neck lock and danced him around the market place. Douglas bit his thumb and he still carries the scar."

Molly laughed. "I'd like to have seen the two of them doing that galop!"

"When politicos were jockeying to relocate the state capital, Douglas sold his vote," said Ninian. "That's the rumor. Sold it to become the Registrar of the Land Office. He found enough money in that job to resign a few months ago to devote himself entirely to political organizing."

This accusation shocked Molly. Douglas was rumored to have done something a Todd would never do. "Who'd he sell his vote to?" she asked.

With a sly smile Elizabeth said, "The Long Nine."

Molly turned to Ninian. "You're one of the Long Nine. Is it true?"

Ninian gave his sister-in-law a condescending look. "I never dignify rumors by commenting on them," he said. He grinned. Elizabeth and Molly laughed and Molly was left wondering if the rumor was true.

As the sun was leaving the sky, Abraham Lincoln came to call. In his enormous, long-fingered hand he carried two books. Molly invited him into the parlor. They sat together on the horsehair settee, Lincoln perched uncomfortably. If her feet hardly reached the floor, his seemed to stretch almost to Peoria. His trousers inched well up his legs, revealing his ankles and the nether regions of his long calves. His hands hung between his legs as if, thought Molly, his fingers might scrape the floor. He said nothing, glanced quickly at her, then stared downwards.

"Why, Mr. Lincoln," Molly started with false gaiety, "you've brought your Euclid."

Lincoln nodded, but made no reply.

This evening would test her wiles, Molly thought. Still, she had been schooled to handle this kind of situation. The only way she knew to rescue herself was to flirt. Men liked that. "I'm sure I've misled you into thinking I'm some kind of mathematical genius," she said coquettishly. "But I'm not. If you've come to learn Euclid, that arcane Greek, I'm afraid you'll be disappointed."

He glanced at her again. "I'm not disappointed, Miss Molly."

"Why, thank you!" she said. She assumed he meant to compliment her. It was true that men did not always know how to make polite conversation. Even so, Lincoln's awkwardness was more of a challenge than she was accustomed to facing. Especially after a session with Stephen Douglas, that nonstop talker. "I do apologize," she went on. "I did rather exaggerate my skills." She batted her eyes.

"But you did study Euclid?"

"My dear sir," Molly objected as if offended, "I did not prevaricate." She felt herself beginning to hit her stride. "To exaggerate is not to prevaricate." Her pleasure in rhyming allowed her to risk an admission. "I studied because my home life was not very happy." Lincoln said nothing. He glanced at her and sensed that this was neither exaggeration nor prevarication. "I suppose I studied to get away from home."

"That's why I studied," Lincoln said. She smiled to encourage his talking. He looked back at his hands. He had accustomed himself in Springfield, especially at the Edwards place up on Coterie Hill, never to speak about his background. He would not elaborate on his remark to say that he would have done almost anything to escape a life of toiling on the land. He would not tell her, who had been to fancy schools, that he had mainly taught himself by firelight, lying on a cabin floor. "Why did you want to get away from home?" he asked.

The question surprised Molly. She did not want to answer it. She did not believe that a man who had come from where Lincoln had—wherever that was—would be interested in why she had chosen to flee a life of ease.

She looked toward the books in his hands. "Is that Euclid?" she asked. He handed her the book of mathematics. She thumbed through the pages and laughed. "Let's see . . . What do I remember of geometry?" She assumed a pose of thinking. Lincoln watched her; she knew she entranced him.

"Axioms," she said. "I must remember something. Give me a hint."

"The shortest distance—"

"Between two points is a straight line." She laughed triumphantly.

"Unless there's a river between them," observed Lincoln, "and a footbridge just down the way."

"All right angles are equal," offered Molly. "You can draw a circle if you know its center and any given point on it." Lincoln smiled. It was clear that he had mastered Euclid at least this far. "There are squares and rectangles, triangles and circles, parallelograms, trapezoids and rhomboids. And tom boyds." She gazed saucily at Lincoln. "I was not a tom boyd," she said.

He smiled. "Why did you want to get away from home?" he asked again. His inflection, emphasizing "you," suggested that he might also have wanted to get away.

She appraised him. Had she misjudged? Could he actually be interested in that? "I was the third child in our family," she said, testing his interest.

"Christened Mary Ann. The third daughter of a father who wanted sons. Then Levi came. And Robert, who died at fourteen months. Then another girl. My parents named her after my father's sister: Ann."

"Ann and Mary Ann?" asked Lincoln.

"I became plain Mary."

The conversation stopped at the news she been dispossessed of her name. Molly could see Lincoln about to tell her that she was not plain, but he couldn't get it out. He did say: "Was that like having your tail end cut off?"

She laughed. She had heard of Lincoln's backwoods witticisms, usually reserved for men. He smiled. "Begging your pardon, ma'am," he said. "Had they run out of names so soon?"

"I'd've asked my mother," she said, "except she died the next year after having her seventh in twelve years. She was only thirty-one. I was six."

"My condolences, Miss Molly." He did not say that he had lost his mother before he was ten.

"My father was out looking for a new wife before my mother was hardly buried. Miss Betsey joined us a year and a half later. She started having my father's children almost as fast as my mother had. So she was busy with them."

"That left you out," Lincoln said. Molly nodded. "Did you and your stepmother get along?" Lincoln did not mention that his stepmother had seemed to save his life.

Molly smiled sheepishly. She shook her head. She thought she should not be boring this caller with family history and determined to get off the subject as quickly as possible. She did not want to sound whiny. "Once Elizabeth married Ninian," she said, "I was sent off to school. I stayed during the week, off on Monday, home Friday. That's how I came to study Euclid."

Lincoln nodded, giving her nothing to build on.

"Did you want to get away from home?" she asked. "It sounded as if maybe you did."

"Oh, a man wants to strike out on his own," he said.

Molly wished a young woman could do that. In a different kind of world, she thought, she might make a good lawyer. But she did not tell Lincoln this. "Is that why you ride circuit?" she asked. "To strike out on your own?" He shrugged. "I suppose that's how one learns the profession, isn't it?"

Lincoln nodded.

"And do you get interesting cases? Conspiracies? Murders? Or is it all 'That varmint stole my cow'?"

Lincoln smiled. "There's a good bit of cow practice, I reckon. Another feller and I are handling a murder case next week up in Carthage, Hancock Circuit Court."

Molly brightened. Now that she had stumbled on Lincoln's subject—she might have known this would be it—perhaps he would prove himself a talker. "I could have guessed, Mr. Lincoln, that you'd be handling other murder cases after your summation snatched Henry Truett right off the gallows." He shrugged. "Don't be modest," she teased. "Will you add another acquittal to your belt?"

"It's the evidence that acquits, Miss Molly. Not the summation."

"How modest you are, Mr. Lincoln." He looked at the floor. The sadness that sometimes came across his face settled there now. "Is this more difficult than the Truett case?" Molly asked. "That seemed difficult enough."

"Dickey and I—Lyle Dickey's the other attorney—got the case moved out of Schuyler County, where the murder was committed, to Hancock County, thinking we had a better chance there." After a moment he added, "Sometimes the folks upstate aren't too happy to have Springfield lawyers try their cases. Especially when they've made up their minds the defendant's guilty."

"Did your client actually—" Lincoln nodded and Molly did not need to go on.

"He's twenty-one years old. Couldn't get along with a feller he worked with, stabbed him to death. Says it was self-defense."

"Isn't that what they always plead?"

After a moment Lincoln said, "It's easier to defend a feller when you're pretty sure he's innocent."

"And this young man is—" Molly let the question hang in the air.

"The prosecution will say he snuck up on the victim." Lincoln shrugged. "It'll be difficult. The victim's widow is likely to be in the courtroom."

"You'll have to let me know how it comes out."

"Don't put any money on the defense."

"Do I look like a wagering woman, Mr. Lincoln?" She asked, "What's the other book you brought?"

"Poetry."

"You like poetry? I *love* poetry. What's the book?"

"Robert Burns."

"Will you read me a poem?"

"If you'll read me one."

They read poetry to each other and as he gave himself to Burns, the sadness left Lincoln's eyes. They discussed the poet's artistry, his use of words, his rhythms, his common touch. Lincoln acknowledged that he tried to write poems now and then, but was no good at it. It was hard enough to write speeches, he said, to give them humor—audiences wanted to laugh, after all—but also to give them substance, to use words that held emotional weight but not to misuse them by turning them into clichés.

Molly thought how surprising it was that this man who said so little, whose words had to be painstakingly drawn out of him, should have more interests than Stephen Douglas, who could talk endlessly and wittily. But only about politics.

CHAPTER

4

Renting a horse at the livery stable, Abraham Lincoln threw across his saddle the large leather bags that carried legal papers and texts. He rode out of town on Jefferson Street, headed toward Carthage, some one hundred fifteen miles distant. On Monday the Hancock Circuit Court would convene there. On Tuesday he and Lyle Dickey would defend Billy Fraim on a charge of murder. Riding along, he thought fleetingly of Molly Todd, of her vivacity and wit. Most of the time he thought about Billy Fraim. The young man had worked as a laborer on steamboats until the night fourteen months before when, drunk, he had stabbed a man to death. It would not be easy, Lincoln knew, to convince the Carthage jury that a young drunk with a long-bladed knife was acting in self-defense.

If he had appeared at Elizabeth Edwards's ball in a satin waistcoat and silk tie, this Saturday morning he wore pantaloons that rode well up his calves when he sat in the saddle. His coat and vest were too loose. His coarse black hair, customarily in rebellion against whatever comb he had recently pulled through it, was hidden by a rust-colored hat. The hat itself looked as if its owner had sat on it continually since its purchase. His expression was melancholy. Fraim's case worried him.

Leaving the town, Lincoln noticed a haze of green enveloping the trees. Buds were beginning to open on twigs. Grass shoots obscured the dead gray-brown vegetation that had lain across the prairie all winter. A hint of coming warmth was in the air, a taste of spring, but only hints and tastes of it this early in the day. Barely two months beyond his thirtieth birthday, Lincoln huddled into his coat and pulled the woolen muffler tighter around his neck.

Seven years before when he had captained volunteers from the village of New Salem in the Black Hawk War, the prairie had seemed wilderness. Peopled by savages. Hostile in its silence, in its deceptive emptiness. It had harbored unknowns, all the dangers and threats of violence that people who had lived in wilderness knew from their struggles, victories, failures.

It was no longer wilderness now, no longer silent. It was purged of savages. Now its grasses sang. Its birds and insects gave forth music. Its emptiness was only illusion, for the prairie had been surveyed. Lincoln himself had done some of the surveying. Lines that no one could see, but were nonetheless real, divided the prairie into counties; they platted parts of the counties into town lots.

Lincoln looked across the prairie. Its dark loam, black as a man's hat after rain, lay a foot and a half thick beneath him. Sometimes it was three feet thick. The soil seemed to cry out: "Buy my plots. Make me farms. Lay roads across me. My soil is the richest in the world. It will give you food; it will give you fortune!"

On Coterie Hill this Saturday afternoon James Shields called at the Edwards mansion. Molly and her friend Julia Jayne had just finished baking a cake in Elizabeth's kitchen. Molly invited Shields to join them and gave him the frosting pan and a spoon to scrape it clean. Once the cake was frosted and sitting on the sill of the kitchen window to cool, the threesome went next door to fetch Merce Levering and Jim Conkling for a walk into the countryside. They strolled under the spring buds beginning to clothe the branches in green. They talked about the places they had come from: Merce from Baltimore, Conkling from New Jersey, Shields from the Emerald Isle far across the sea. They agreed that Illinois, with its deep, rich soil, its prairies as expansive as anyone could wish for, its abundant opportunity, was the place to make their lives.

It came Molly's turn to talk about her birthplace. "What can I say about Lexington, Kentucky?" she asked in mock complaint. "Half the citizens of Springfield hail from Kentucky."

"And what can I say?" asked Julia. "I've lived here all my life." Her father, Dr. Gershom Jayne, had come to Illinois in 1819 after fighting in the War of 1812, the first medical doctor to practice so far north in the state. "I hope I'm not stuck here forever," said Julia. "I want to see the Atlantic Ocean. And New York."

"New York I've seen," said Shields. "From a hospital bed." He told them about fleeing Ireland and repeated the story he had told Molly of a mast falling during a storm outside New York harbor and crushing both his legs.

Shields was amusing, Molly thought, full of funny and outrageous tales about the Auld Countrie he was so glad to have left behind. Even if the tales gave credibility a mighty stretch, they must contain some germs of truth. He kept them up when the five of them had cake and lemonade with Ninian and Elizabeth back at the house. But even as he made her laugh, Molly kept thinking of the words the Lord spoke to Samuel when the prophet looked at Jesse's sons: "I have not chosen this."

Late in the afternoon Lincoln arrived in Beardstown and presented himself at the local tavern. "I don't think I've got a bed long enough for you," the tavernkeeper said.

"I sleep crosswise mostly," Lincoln replied. "Sometimes I use a chair for my feet." The tavernkeeper said it promised to be a slow night for a Saturday. If his luck held, the young attorney might find a bed upstairs he could occupy alone.

At dinner there were five men sitting at the table. Lincoln told them, "I was in this town seven years ago today."

"Why was that?" asked a traveler from the East. He appraised Lincoln as if he was a type peculiar to the West.

"I come to Beardstown for the Spring Season," he told the traveler. "This metropolis is noted for its Spring Season."

The traveler smiled. The Westerner was pulling his leg.

"Black Hawk War?" asked the tavernkeeper.

"Yep," said Lincoln. "I shed blood for my country." The traveler examined the young man, interested in this fact. "Of course, mostly it was to mosquiteers," Lincoln added with a slow grin. The traveler was not sure how to react. The other men laughed. "In '32," Lincoln went on, playing rural for the traveler, "oh, did we have the skeeters! And the rains! Remember?" The tavernkeeper nodded.

"Who's this Black Hawk?" asked the traveler.

"Trickster redskin," grunted a man who had come up river from Meredosia. "Chief of the Sauk and Fox. We taught him a lesson."

"The way I recollect it," Lincoln said, "Black Hawk and his people had agreed to stay west of the Mississippi. Treaty'd been signed."

"Injuns agree to something one day and change their minds the next," said the man from Meredosia. "'Course, what can you expect from savages?"

"Frightening time," said the tavernkeeper.

Lincoln leaned back in his chair, ready for a tale. "When word reached the village of New Salem, where I was living then," he said, "that Black Hawk and four hundred warriors and fifteen hundred women and children had crossed back—"

"Women and children?" asked the traveler. "That doesn't sound like war."

"Coming back to raise corn on the Rock River, they said," explained the man from Meredosia. "Repudiated the treaty."

"Claimed they'd been tricked," said the host.

"Like children claiming they didn't know they couldn't give back the candy they chose and had already stuck in their mouth," said the man from Meredosia. "Them savages."

"When word came," Lincoln went on, "that the Governor wanted volunteers, the village boys threw down their hoes. I closed up the store I was tending. Fighting Injuns! That was the greatest excitement we'd been offered in years!" The young man pushed his chair back from the table, the better to gesture as he talked. He crossed one long leg over the other, his eyes sparkling, his high-pitched voice rising with enthusiasm. "We met on Dallas Scott's farm on Richland Creek," he continued. "We formed ourselves into a company, told our sweethearts—those of us that had them—

not to worry, we'd kill the Injuns, they wouldn't kill us. And we marched over here to Beardstown."

The men shoved their plates to the center of the table and leaned back in their chairs to listen.

"When we got here, of course, we weren't the only company of volunteers. No, sirree! Villages all over Sangamon County were sending boys. We got into a dispute with another company. Had our eyes on the same campground." Lincoln turned to the tavernkeeper. "There're houses standing on that ground now," he said. "I walked out there before supper."

"Town's growing," said the host.

"Did the dispute get settled?" asked the traveler from the East. "What'd you do: flip a coin?"

"We were farm boys, mister," said Lincoln. "I doubt there was a single coin in either company."

"So what'd you do?"

"We did just like in the Bible," said the young man. "David and Goliath. Each company chose its champion and they wrassled for the ground."

"You must've been the Goliath from your company," said the traveler. "I haven't seen a bigger man than you for some time."

"Yep, I was the champion of the New Salem boys," Lincoln acknowledged. Smiling with pride he added, "They'd elected me captain to take care of just such business. So I had to do my duty. Well, big as I was, Lorenzo Dow Thompson was bigger. Stronger. Even Goliath was a midget next to him. On the plains of Jordan the little feller won with his sling. On the plains of Beardstown the slinging was done by Lorenzo Dow Thompson. We wrassled twice. He slung me both times. The second time I thought he might toss me right across the Illinois River."

The traveler from the East laughed and asked, "Why didn't you settle the dispute with Black Hawk that way?"

"We'd've offered to," Lincoln said, "if we'd ever seen the Injuns." He grinned. "We spent a month running around Illinois, chasing Injuns we never saw. We went short on rations and shot the hogs of farmers we were protecting. Which they objected to. We took souvenirs from villages the Injuns had escaped from. We met fellers we liked a lot—I'm in partnership with one of them right now—and, all in all, we had such a fine time that, when we were sure we were never gonna meet the enemy, we re-enlisted. And all the time we were shedding blood to the skeeters."

When Lincoln arrived in Carthage the next day, he put up at Artois Hamilton's tavern. It catered to the legal trade when the Hancock Circuit Court was in session. Between conferences to line up cases to defend, other lawyers pestered him for details about the acquittal of Henry Truett. At supper Judge James Ralston, who would preside at the Fraim trial, asked Lincoln to sit beside him and queried him about Truett's trial. Lincoln shrugged, said he'd learned a good deal by observing his betters. He thought it wise to be modest because the people of Hancock County might sense themselves as being on trial. They might feel obliged to show that, while jurors might let murderers walk in Springfield, they meant to hang them in Carthage.

As the lawyers were finishing supper, a man entered the dining room and approached the men. "Is one of you Mr. Lincoln?" he asked. Lincoln identified himself. The newcomer hesitated, as if surprised by the young lawyer's appearance. Then he said, "I'm John Taggart. I have a store across the road."

"How d'ya do?" Lincoln replied. He stood.

The man continued to appraise him, the roomful of lawyers looking on. "The store's doing real well," he said. He offered his hand. Lincoln shook it. "Mr. Lincoln," he went on, "I understand you're one of the brightest young men in Illinois."

This statement flustered Lincoln. As he stood, uncertain how to respond, his lawyer colleagues laughed at his predicament.

"I've heard I'm one of the homeliest," Lincoln said.

"You're the feller that saved Henry Truett from the gallows, aren't you?" the merchant asked.

The lawyers watched; they waited to hear how Lincoln would answer.

"With you staring at me like that, Mr. Taggart," Lincoln said, "I feel like the ugly man who met a woman on horseback. Woman says: 'Well, for land sake, you are the homeliest man I ever saw.' To which the man replied: 'Perhaps I am, ma'am, but I can't help it.' 'I suppose not,' the woman observed, 'but you might stay at home.'"

The lawyers laughed.

"Are you looking for counsel, sir?" Lincoln asked. "Maybe we should talk across the room."

"I'm looking for a husband for my daughter," Taggart said.

The crowd of lawyers whooped. They clapped and hooted. Lincoln blushed and took a step backward. Taggart pursued him. "She's nineteen," he said. "Healthy. Intelligent. Been to school some."

"What's she look like?" someone called.

"She's good-looking!" Taggart replied. He carefully pulled from his pocket an ivory miniature of the girl and showed it to Lincoln. "Painted last year," he said. "She's a joy to look at." The miniature showed an attractive, dark-haired girl.

"She is a fine-looking girl," Judge Ralston said. "I've met her. If I were your age, Lincoln, and single, I'd ask Taggart to invite me to dinner."

Lincoln glanced at Ralston. Was he serious or making fun?

"Come to dinner tomorrow," said Taggart.

"I'm in court tomorrow," Lincoln replied.

"Your case isn't till Tuesday," the judge interjected. "Dickey can handle anything that'll come up tomorrow noon."

Lincoln did not know what to say. Men around the table continued to watch, amused at his discomfort.

"She draws some," the girl's father continued. "Sings. She's a good cook; her mother's seen to that. She's got a strong body, wide hips. She'll give you all the children you want."

"I hadn't thought about wanting children," Lincoln said.

"You must be thirty," Taggart said. "What do you think about in your spare time?"

Lincoln himself laughed. The others roared taunts.

"Your invitation honors me," Lincoln finally managed. "But your daughter can do better than me."

More taunts filled the air. "False modesty! Tain't so! It's a lie!"

"My daughter won't be happy, marrying some farmer," Taggart said. "You've got quality, Lincoln. My daughter knows that. You were smart enough to get Henry Truett acquitted—"

"The evidence acquitted him!" jeered the lawyers.

"—but you speak the language of the people. My girl can make you happy."

"I can't make her happy," Lincoln replied. "And the way you speak of her convinces me she deserves better'n me."

Taggart put his fists on his hips, irritated by the young attorney's refusal.

"I don't talk well to women," Lincoln explained. His colleagues cackled. "The prettier they are, the more my tongue goes shy." Whistles. "I'm a happy bachelor." Taunts. "I board free in Springfield." Hoots. "I don't pay for my lodging."

A lawyer cried, "Lincoln, what else are you getting free in Springfield?"

The men howled. Lincoln cackled, his gleeful laughter sounding above the others. But he was also embarrassed. He began to blush. "I owe money the size of the national debt," he told Taggart. "I couldn't give your daughter a place to rest her head. She wouldn't be happy with me."

"Let her be the judge of that," suggested Taggart. "Come to dinner."

'Sir, I guarantee that, if she and I married, five years down the line if I were fighting with a bear and people came to help, she'd cry, 'Let them fight. I don't care which one gets whipped." The lawyers laughed. Taggart shrugged. "If I ever get solvent," Lincoln said, "I'd like to meet her. But she'll have children by then."

"Well," said Taggart, preparing to leave, "I know why you convince juries. You certainly convinced me!"

On a morning that was fresh and fragrant with the first spring blossoms, breezes gently stirring the air, Lincoln met Lyle Dickey at the Carthage town hall. He'd been a schoolteacher urged to follow the law by Cyrus Walker, one of the lead attorneys on the Truett case. "You got any thoughts about putting our client on the stand?" Lincoln asked.

"Risky," said Dickey. "Terrible risky. What do you think?"

"Juries like to hear a defendant speak for himself."

"Lawyers don't. I'm edgy about what he might say."

"Let's take a look at him."

The two men went to the basement of the jail where the cells were and took seats at a table. The sheriff unlocked Billy Fraim's cell and brought him out. Fraim walked toward his lawyers, rolling his shoulders, carrying an almost visible chip on each one of them. As Fraim watched them through narrowed eyes, Lincoln wondered if the swagger and hostility were defenses. It might be that behind them was a scared young man, possibly an innocent one. But behind them might be a bully. Dickey glanced at Lincoln as if to say, "See: risky."

Raised on a farm, Fraim was strong, stocky and rawboned. From what witnesses said when he had liquor, he was a hard drinker. He wore threadbare pantaloons and a shirt badly in need of washing. His jaw carried several days' growth of beard. He was charged with stabbing and killing fellow laborer William Neathhammer at Frederick, four miles north of Beardstown. He was exactly the sort of man on whom Merchant Taggart did not want to waste his daughter.

The men shook hands. Out of earshot the sheriff took up a position to prevent Fraim from trying to escape. Dickey asked Fraim how he was being treated. How was the food? Was he sleeping at night? Was he ready for tomorrow?

"I've been ready for tomorrow for more'n a year," he said. "Neathhammer swore he'd kill me. Was I supposed to let him?"

The lawyers explained the mechanics of the trial. They emphasized that his fate lay with the jury. "Ever seen a play?" Lincoln asked. Fraim watched him. Why this question? Then he nodded that he had. "Trial's rather like a play," Lincoln explained. "Audience starts making judgments about a character the minute he walks on stage."

"The same thing happens with a jury," Dickey said. "It starts making judgments about you the minute you enter the courtroom."

"I'm content to have them see me as I am," Fraim replied.

"How you carry yourself is a kind of evidence," said Lincoln. "Let them see an innocent man."

"Shave and wear a clean shirt."

"Where'll I get a clean shirt?" Fraim demanded.

"We'll try to make sure you have one," said Dickey. "Trousers, too."

"Since I'm having my day in court, I want to tell my side of it."

Dickey glanced at Lincoln. Fraim noticed the glance. "I've been sitting in that cell for fourteen months," he said, striking the table with his open palm. "I want people to hear my story. From my lips. Not the story told over back fences or in the papers. He was intending to kill me."

If the breezes outside blew warm and fragrant, the air in the basement room did not move at all. It was close, dank and a little chilly. It smelled of tobacco and unwashed bodies and piss buckets that had not been emptied. Lincoln wondered what it had been like to live for more than a year in this cave, this hole in the ground, shivering in the winter, sweating all summer, your muscles crying out for exercise, your soul for human contact. Probably Fraim's mind had turned over the story of Neathhammer's death so often it no longer knew what was true and what false.

Dickey said, "We can talk about you taking the stand."

"I want to," Fraim said.

"We want to win this case," Dickey said. "We want to save your life. To do that you're going to have to let us make the decision about your testifying."

"We've done a lot of this," Lincoln pointed out. "We know the kind of questions the prosecutors will ask you."

"Like what? That don't scare me."

The lawyers explained. "The prosecutors will try to put in the minds of the jury a story about how you committed the crime," Lincoln explained. "They'll ask, Did you plan to kill him?"

"And that puts the idea of a plan in the jury's mind," said Dickey. "They'll ask, Did you sneak up on him?" Fraim shook his head. "That puts in the jury's head the notion that you did."

"Did you plan to kill him?" Lincoln asked.

Fraim hesitated. Then he blurted, "He planned to kill me."

"Wrong answer," Dickey said. "The right answer is 'No, sir! I never did!' And they better believe you when you say it."

When they finished discussing the questions Fraim might be asked, Lincoln advised him, "Whatever you feel, you want to appear remorseful."

"I ain't remorseful."

"How you look is part of the evidence the jury will weigh," Dickey said. "Don't walk into the courtroom looking like the toughest man there."

"Don't look like you want to take a swing at someone."

"If you'd been sitting in that cell all this time, you'd want to take a swing at someone, too. At the whole world."

"Surely you're remorseful this happened," Lincoln suggested. "Look at all the time you've spent here as a result."

Fraim said, "Neathhammer got what he deserved. If I hadn't of killed him, he'd of killed me."

"But you had a knife," Dickey pointed out, "and he—"

"If he'd of had a knife, he'd of stabbed me." Fraim shrugged. "If this is what I deserve . . . Well, so be it. Death can't be worse than sitting in this jail."

As Fraim walked back toward his cell, the sheriff beside him and his shoulders rolling again, he turned back to shout, "Maybe I should of let him kill me. Then he'd of been sitting in jail all this time and I'd of been somewhere else."

Lincoln breathed deeply as soon as they got outside the jail. He was glad to stretch his legs, to see sunlight and people. As they walked back toward the tavern, Dickey said, "Not an ideal client. He must've gotten drunk to do it." Lincoln said nothing. "We've got our work cut out for us."

"You ever want to work on a steamboat?"

"I was teaching school at his age."

"When I was twenty," Lincoln replied, "I had a powerful urge to have a job on a steamboat."

They walked a bit further in silence. "If he takes the stand, he's a goner," Dickey said. Lincoln did not deny it. "He justifies himself. That's no defense."

"If he doesn't testify, he'll curse us if he hangs."

The four ladies—the three Todd sisters and Merce Levering, who'd come over from next door—sat in the garden of the Edwards home, wearing sun hats and sewing. The sun was high, almost the first afternoon when it was warm enough to sit outside. They were chatting about the invitations to Fanny's wedding. Elizabeth said, "I told Ninian, 'It's one thing to have them here for parties. But not for Fanny's wedding.' " Without really consulting Fanny, Elizabeth had demanded the exclusion of all self-taught attorneys, men of more ambition than learning who read just enough law to become licensed. Such men really intended to launch political careers. "And I've insisted that we hold back on political cronies. After all, this wedding is not a Whig meeting."

Molly put down her sewing. "Do you realize," she asked, "that most of the men who've called on me are self-taught lawyers? The interesting ones anyway."

"There are graduates of colleges in this town. Anson Henry, Elias Merryman. Jim Conkling went to Princeton College in—"

Merce busied herself with sewing, staring at the frame that held her embroidery. Molly glanced at her, amused. "Jim Conkling is spoken for," Molly said.

Merce pricked herself with her needle. She gasped, blushed. "He's not spoken for," she declared.

Molly laughed. "Then why did you just prick yourself? You may not know you're going to marry him, Merce Levering, but I know. I'm never wrong."

"There are other college men, Molly," Fanny remarked.

Elizabeth said, "If college men know you enjoy seeing Douglas and Shields and, God forbid—"

"As you well know, Lincoln is partnered with our own cousin," Molly interrupted. She did not want her access to gentlemen regulated by her sisters. That would be almost as bad as Miss Betsey doing it.

"Elizabeth is right," said Fanny. "If you see only self-taught men—"

"Oh, please!" said Molly.

"We have a certain place in town," Fanny insisted. "It's important to maintain our standards."

Molly rolled her eyes and looked to Merce for support. Merce was too well trained to offend anyone. She lowered her eyes and said nothing. Molly wanted to speak her mind, but one of the Irish girls appeared to announce that Mr. Webb was in the parlor, wanting to know if Miss Molly would walk out with him. Molly glanced at the others. Webb? Who was Webb? She may have danced with him at her launching party, but she had no recollection of him.

Fanny whispered, "He's a legislator friend of Ninian's."

Merce leaned close beside her, whispering as well. "He's middle-aged. With two children. He's looking for a mother for them." Because her advice might breach decorum, she mouthed the word, "Beware."

The prospect of walking out with a man seeking a nanny/housekeeper appalled Molly. She started to shake her head.

Elizabeth reminded her, "When a girl's new in town, Molly, she can never have too many beaux."

Molly could not deny the truth of this. Furthermore, it was well for the town to know that a number of men were calling. She excused herself, certain that her natural flirtatiousness would carry the day, and started into the house with the Irish girl. It was only when she and Edwin Webb left the house and started down the lane that she realized how short, stout and very middle-aged he was. She felt herself tongue-tied. Fortunately, Mr. Webb did his utmost to be charming.

That night, awake in a bed too short for him, ignoring the turnings of the man who shared it and trying not to hear the snores of the twelve men sleeping in the tavern room, Lincoln stared at the darkness. Dickey would examine the witnesses; he would do the summation. Now he was hoping to find some angle on the Fraim case that might save his client. Mulling the predicament of Billy Fraim, who had stoked engines on steamboats, he thought of that Indiana farm boy, almost a man, who had yearned to live his life on the Ohio River, but had not been given that opportunity.

When Lincoln was seven, his father had taken the family from Kentucky to Indiana. The country was not open prairie like Illinois. It was wild forest, the home of bears and big cats, so heavily wooded and untamed that Tom Lincoln had had to hack a path through trees so that his wife and two children could reach the land he'd marked out for their homestead. Their first winter in Indiana the family lived in a three-sided structure, roofed but open on the fourth side. A fire had to be kept burning at all times. Tom Lincoln needed the help of another man. Abe, at eight, became that man. At ten his mother died. For a year the boy, his sister and father lived more like savages than settlers. Then, leaving the children, his father disappeared into the forest, headed back to Kentucky. Often the boy and his sister wondered, Had he abandoned them? Would he ever return? One day his father came back with a new wife, a widow he'd known as a young man. He'd paid her debts and she'd married him. They brought with them her three children. The work on the farm was harder then because more people had to be fed. An axe was so often in Abe's hands that it came to feel like an extension of his arms. He spent the next years plowing, harvesting, helping to make a farm out of forest.

That was when he would think of the river. Of life on a steamboat. Maybe he would be a steamboat pilot, a king of the river, a man in fancy clothes who worked with his head, not his back, a man admired by all. At sixteen Abe and two friends sawed logs to sell for firewood on steamers. But there was little demand. He hired out to a man who ran a ferry across the Ohio. One day he rowed two men out to a passing steamer. When each man threw a half-dollar into the bottom of his craft, Abe could hardly believe that in less than a day he'd earned a whole dollar.

The next spring he and a friend floated down the Ohio bound for New Orleans on a flatboat carrying a cargo of corn, flour and meat. The Ohio felt swift, rising to floodtide. At Cairo the clear Ohio met the turbulent, swirling Mississippi with mud so thick he thought he might be able to plow it. With a current so swift that it swept before it entire trees and the carcasses of cattle. It tested his prowess with an oar.

Sometimes the river was lonely. Hours would pass when Abe saw no sign of humanity: no other craft on the river, no sign of habitation on the shore. But often the river was alive with traffic: steamboats, rafts and flatboats like their own. Now and then they hitched alongside other craft to swap news and tales. They were warned never to fall into the river. The mud was so heavy it would drag them under. Now and then they docked at plantations to trade. The river men they met and the landsmen, too, applauded Abe's way with jokes. The hours of floating and trading, starwatching and storytelling rushed past. Here was freedom at last. Given the comradeship of the river, Abe wondered if he could find work in New Orleans. Maybe he could make a place for himself there and never go back to the farm. Why should he be his father's hired man when he could hire out for himself and keep the wages he earned?

One night they were docked at a plantation, close enough to the Gulf to smell salt on the air. After dark seven men came on board, black men, escaped slaves, desperate for food, money and a boat. The two youths drove the men off the flatboat and made a getaway. And Abe wondered if he was really ready to light out on his own. What if he became desperate for food and work? So he returned north by steamboat to collect what he was owed. Not yet twenty-one, he obediently turned his wages over to his father. A chance to live on the river never came again.

Lincoln sat on the edge of the bed, seeing through the interstices in the floorboards the dying embers in the tavern fireplace below. As the snores of his fellow counselors reverberated around him, he wondered if he could explain to a jury about the river. That life on the river could sometimes be tough. Sometimes men had to fight for their lives. Sometimes in those fights one man killed another; it could be a matter of survival. The trouble was that Billy Fraim had been drunk. Lincoln would argue that it was drink that had killed Neathhammer, not Fraim. That the man who sold Fraim the whiskey was as guilty as Fraim himself. But it was known that Lincoln did not drink, not since coming to Illinois. Jurymen might take him for a temperance man. That would not help Fraim. They liked to get drunk. They deserved to, working as hard as they did. They got drunk without killing anyone. Why couldn't Billy Fraim?

Late the following morning Fanny took Molly to see the Globe Tavern, where she would be living in a mere matter of days as the bride of Dr. Wallace. Before they reached the Globe, however, Fanny insisted on walking Molly through the nearby State House square where the new Illinois capitol building was under construction. Dr. Wallace's drug store happened to give onto the square, and the tour with Molly would happen to give Fanny an excuse for "looking in." When Molly first saw the State House cupola, she stood stock still. It rose above the prairie like one of the cathedrals of Europe. "It's so high!" Molly exclaimed.

"If angels don't pay attention," agreed Fanny with an excited laugh, "they may fly right into it."

"How this town has grown since my last visit!" said Molly. "It's practically civilization!"

Fanny smiled, demurely proud of the place she had chosen to make her life.

"What we kept hearing of in Lexington was cholera epidemics and economic downturns."

"Not half of it true," Fanny assured her. "You know how much dust news gathers when it travels!" She guided Molly along the north side of the square past ramshackle shops with wooden awnings stretched out over wooden sidewalks. This was "Chicken Row" where vendors sold country produce. On the edge of the square itself squatted long stonecutters' sheds and rows of blocks of buff limestone. The girls admired the majesty and height of the capitol and agreed that the sturdy, fluted limestone pillars at its entrances would give it strength and grace and last a thousand years. An enormous hog wallow lay close by the sidewalk and beyond it a sow nosed at one of the sidewalk timbers, grunting, trying to dislodge it, sending mud mist into the air. Fanny picked up a piece of limestone debris and flung it at the animal. When it hit its mark, the sow snorted, looked up momentarily and returned to work.

Moving along the east side of the square, Fanny pointed across Adams Street to a new, three-story brick building. "The American House," she said. "A real ornament of the prairie, built just last year so that Ninian's brother legislators have a place to stay when they come here to decide the fate of the state." Among its run-down surroundings the American House looked like a shiny gold coin amid tarnished coppers. "There's carpeting and wallpaper and furnishings to rival anything in St. Louis or Louisville," Fanny bragged. "Your husband can take you there on your wedding night."

Molly jabbed her sister lightly with her elbow. "I have not come here to find a husband."

"You're sure to find one, though," Fanny insisted. "Every available unattached woman in this town finds ten bachelors or widowers waiting to form an alliance."

The women moved to where the drug store, just opened by her sweet doctor and his partner, was located. Waiting outside while Fanny said hello, Molly saw signs for the law offices of Cousin John Todd Stuart and those of the town's faithfully Whig, weekly paper, the *Sangamo Journal*, edited by Elizabeth and Ninian's friend Simeon Francis. She also noticed the emporium of James C. Bell & Co., managed by the handsome Joshua Speed; it, too, was on Hoffman's Row. She grew aware of sudden silence and realized that the masons had stopped cutting stone in order to gaze at the new girl in town. She lowered her eyes to her folded hands and took refuge in the drug store, examining bottles of home remedies while Fanny flirted with her fiancé.

When they returned outside, the masons' hammering, cutting, and sawing had resumed. Despite that noise, Molly could almost hear the buzz of contentment that Fanny exuded. They headed now for the Globe Tavern, and Fanny happily sang its praises. She felt certain it would be an ideal way to start married life. Because she would not have to contend with the problems of running a household, she could give herself entirely to the adjustments she would face as a bride.

The tavern was a long frame two-story building stretching along Adams Street. As they approached it, stepping along the boardwalk, elevated slightly above the level of the muddy street, Fanny observed, "I'm not sure what Father would think of one of his daughters starting married life in a boardinghouse."

"Miss Betsey would not allow it," said Molly.

"Dear Miss Betsey would be horrified. But the thing is, Cousin John Todd Stuart took his Mary there when they were first married."

Molly glanced at the sow and piglets oinking down Adams Street and wondered what Fanny would think of them as neighbors.

"If Cousin John Todd could start his marriage there—it was called the Eagle Tavern then; it changed managements this very month—Dr. Wallace and I think it will work just fine for us," Fanny continued. "Especially while he and Mr. Diller are getting their drug store started. I mean, we can't build a home just when Dr. Wallace is starting his business, can we? The new managers at the Globe will make certain everything's nice, you know."

Fanny chattered on, pleased for once to be the person who held forth, for etiquette demanded that she do more listening than talking with the older Elizabeth, Ninian and her "sweet doctor."

"The City Hotel charges only three dollars a week, lodging and board," she prattled on. "So when the Globe charges four dollars a week, it is a bit more expensive. For transients it's thirty-seven-and-a-half cents for breakfast and supper, twenty-five cents for the room, a dollar for stabling and feeding a horse for a day and a night. So paying weekly is an ever so much better arrangement. Not that I need worry about any of it. Finances are my sweet doctor's charge, not mine."

They reached the tavern's entrance, swung open the heavy door and went inside. The reception area was empty and dark, the atmosphere close, the air too long shut in. Fanny beckoned Molly upstairs to the second floor. They hurried along the corridor, skipping like naughty schoolgirls, and entered the room where Fanny would begin her married life, a room already occupied by Dr. Wallace. Stepping into it, Molly felt overwhelmed. The double bed loomed enormous in the room. Molly put her hand to her throat. In that bed Fanny would learn about love-making, perhaps become proficient at it, even skilled, for certainly proficiency would enhance the happiness of her marriage, though not so skilled as to become dissolute. Babies would be conceived in that bed; babies would be born in it. The bed looked lately slept in, the coverlet pulled up to a pillow. Fanny gaily ran to it, jumped onto the mattress and smelled the pillow. "It's him!" she exclaimed. "His smell." Both girls giggled. Molly had never seen Fanny like this; the excitement in her laughter delighted her. She glanced about the room, at the armoire, the table beside the window, heavy chairs drawn up to it, and the oil lamp resting upon it.

"What do you think?" Fanny asked. But before Molly could answer, she exclaimed, "Oh, we're going to be so happy here!" She withdrew a vial of perfume she had secreted in her dress, opened it and, giggling, poured a drop or two on the pillow. "I told him we were coming here. Now he'll have whiffs of me all night in his dreams."

When the girls returned to the first floor, who should they find in the reception area but Colonel George Washington Spottswood, who had greeted Molly when she arrived in town. He turned his abundant figure toward them with a smile. "Two elegant ladies from Kentucky! The Globe Tavern is indeed honored." Fanny explained that she and Molly had peeked at the room she would occupy with Dr. Wallace after their wedding. The Colonel joined the explanations by revealing that he had just bought the establishment and aspired to make it the best lodging of its kind in town. Certainly having a lady of the Todd family, the most renowned lineage of Kentucky, would act as an inspiration to the entire staff. He invited the ladies to stay for dinner; if they lingered for an hour they would find the dining room filled.

"Thank you, Colonel," Fanny said. "We cannot stay, but I will show Molly the room. It's so commodious."

She led Molly into the dining room, spacious enough for large entertainments, now being set up for noonday diners. Servant girls wiped tables to a fine sheen and placed cutlery on them. At the far end of the room two young women, residents, sat in the sunlight of the window seat gossiping together. Fanny gave a delighted cry and hurried toward them, gesturing Molly to follow. "These are my new friends," Fanny said. Molly trailed behind, glancing at the landscapes on the wall and breathing in the aroma of the roasts being prepared for dinner.

Molly was introduced. By way of greeting, one of the women offered hard candy from a pill box. Molly took a piece; she let its sweetness invade her mouth. As the women's conversation turned to local matters, Molly noticed the greening trees outside the windows, a breeze rustling the branches. Fanny's soon-to-be fellow lodgers were not, Molly knew, likely to be invited with their husbands to Fanny's wedding. Elizabeth felt that women found happiness in running their own establishments, keeping them tidy, procuring provisions, creating family homes. Young women who lived in boardinghouses with their husbands—and sometimes young children—did not have enough to occupy them, Elizabeth thought. A woman without sufficient occupation in her own home was likely to make an occupation either of religion or dissipation. Fanny seemed likely to succumb to neither, Molly thought, although Elizabeth regarded gossip of the kind just now being exchanged as the first way station on the path to dissipation. With too little occupation, trapped in a single room however spacious, a woman might grow bored. If her husband kept spirits, she might imbibe them. Gossip with fellow lodgers might lead to revelations of a couple's secrets or, even worse, to conversations with traveling men who did not need, like the lodgers' husbands, to go to the law office, the counting house or the drug store. Such a man might ask to borrow a book; he might enter a woman's rooms to retrieve it. And then what?

Elizabeth took an even dimmer view of children being raised in boardinghouses. How could proper training be given in such a place? Proper food could not be provided. How could a child learn manners while eating at table with dozens of others, many of whose manners would be quite uncouth? A shy or frightened child might not eat at all. Bold children might become unruly. Elizabeth could not, of course, dictate what Fanny should do. She wanted her happy and launched on her own marriage. But she would maintain the standards of Quality Hill as long as she could.

The next afternoon at the trial in Carthage, Dickey handled the witnesses and decided that Billy Fraim speaking in his own defense carried too many risks. As Lincoln rose to give his summation, the jury was watching Billy Fraim for evidences of contrition and remorse. His manner did not show them.

"When a young feller grows up on a farm," Lincoln began in summation, "more'n likely he's never known anything else. Never known that a landscape can change. You prob'ly know what I mean. Then he sees a river. And, why, it's magical to him. Flowing constantly. Changing every moment. If you're a young feller who's been imprisoned by forest or endless prairie, cut off from the rest of society, a river promises escape. And escape, freedom. If you were a feller raised on a place where nothing happened except one season following the next and each one with its own particular drudgery, the river life calls out to you. Moving water makes your blood race. It's exciting. Sometimes it's dangerous. There are paddle wheelers and rafts, flatboats, even canoes. And people on them, all going somewhere."

Lyle Dickey watched Lincoln addressing the jury and wondered if his partner was talking about himself. He had never heard Lincoln mention his boyhood. He thought a river promised escape only if a boy really yearned to get away from home.

"That's how Billy Fraim saw things," Lincoln continued. "He wanted to escape, to join that life. Sure, he wanted excitement; he was hardly twenty. He did a lot of hard work, helped the development of this great state of ours. But he also did some things he prob'ly shouldn't have done. He drank more liquor than he should have. He learned to take offense when it would have been better to learn to get along. But it's hard to get along with a feller who bullies you.

"William Neathhammer was older than Billy. Married. He knew more about the world. But he bullied Billy, picked on him. Gave him the impression he was going to kill him. A fight for survival was at stake. We all know what happened. Billy killed him. He sits before you wishing he hadn't. Wishing more than anything that things had turned out differently.

"You've all been twenty. Most of you have done things you wish you hadn't done. In that sense Billy's no different from you.

"The question before us is this: Should that mistake, which Billy acknowledges was wrong, for which he's deeply sorry. Should that mistake cost him his life? We don't believe it should."

Lincoln reviewed the case and the evidence. Neathhammer's widow, now remarried, sat in the courtroom. As Lincoln spoke, she stared at the jurymen demanding that Billy Fraim's life be given for her husband's. Lincoln searched the faces of the jury for men who might be with him. Sometimes they nodded, but their jaws were set.

In the Edwards home in Springfield, Fanny's fiancé, Dr. Wallace, came to dinner with the family. Elizabeth and Ninian, Fanny and William Wallace chatted about preparations for the wedding. Molly's attention drifted. She remarked the way Dr. Wallace watched Fanny, a little the way wolves looked at their prey before pouncing and devouring them. Fanny seemed very taken with the doctor. She declared that she was in love with him and had all the symptoms: giddiness in his presence, palpitations when he entered the Edwards home, burning sensations where he touched her. Molly did not find him attractive. He was too old—thirty-seven—and had already passed beyond youth. And, however much the family maintained that he was a doctor, in fact, he was a druggist. After exposure at her father's house to men who discussed the issues of a growing nation, and the excitement of conversing with them, Molly could not quite understand how Fanny could settle for a druggist.

She wondered, too, when Dr. Wallace would "devour" Fanny. On their wedding night? She wondered exactly how it would happen. How would Fanny feel? Exalted? Repelled? Disappointed? Maybe it was something you had to get used to.

Certainly Molly had little specific information about what happened. Several nights before, she and Fanny had made inquiries of Elizabeth, who was newly pregnant. "My heavens, what a thing to talk about!" she exclaimed. "You make me blush."

"But what happens?" Molly asked. "Why won't you tell us?"

"Because what happens between a man and his wife is no one else's business. Mr. Edwards would scold me for weeks if he thought I said anything to you."

"Does it hurt?" Fanny asked. "I'm sure it doesn't—at least not much—because I know Dr. Wallace would never hurt me." Again, after a pause: "Does it hurt?"

"If it hurt, do you suppose women would keep on having babies?"

"Having babies hurts," observed Molly. "Mama died of it. Grandmother Parker says that if women and men took turns having babies, men would make women go first and no family would ever have more than three."

"We're blessed to have children!" Elizabeth exclaimed. "I look at Julia and feel how fortunate I am. When I gave her suck, I always felt—well, positively exalted."

"I can't wait to have a baby," Fanny said.

Molly felt herself in the presence of two madonnas. Their ooohs and ahhs excluded her. "I wish I'd asked Mammy Sally about this before I came west."

Her sisters screamed, scandalized.

"Mary Todd, you are a limb of Satan!" Fanny exclaimed. "Miss Betsey's right!"

But they were all laughing. Finally Elizabeth became serious. "Don't ever think it's the same thing for white folks that it is for darkies," Elizabeth chastised. "It's something very different, I assure you."

"What happens exactly?" Molly persisted.

"These questions!" Elizabeth cried. "You've seen horses, haven't you?"

Molly and Fanny both looked surprised. "Horses?" said Molly. "A stallion mounts a mare from the rear."

"I declare!" shouted Elizabeth, reddening. "You've seen your brothers. You know where things are located. I doubt it will happen to you from—I can't say it!" Elizabeth put her head in her hands, too mortified even to express her embarrassment in laughter. After a moment she said, "You will find out soon enough, Fanny. It may hurt a little at first. But very soon you may find that it's not entirely unpleasant."

"Does that mean I'll enjoy it?" Fanny asked. "Do you enjoy it?"

The question obviously astonished Elizabeth. "Oh, my heavens!" she said. "Mr. Edwards would skin me alive if he knew we were talking this way!"

The jury in the Fraim case did not take long to deliberate. When it returned, silence filled the room. The jury foreman pronounced a verdict: Guilty. No one spoke. Lincoln filed a motion for arrest of judgment. Two days later he argued it. Judge Ralston listened, overruled the motion and sentenced William Fraim to be hanged within a mile of Carthage within two weeks.

Returning to Springfield on horseback, Lincoln fell to brooding. The day was dark with low hanging clouds. Rain had fallen during the week and the road was deep in mud. He had defended few capital cases and had never before lost one. He trusted the jury's judgment in rendering its verdict. He did not think Billy Fraim would die because of anything he or Dickey had done or failed to do. Still, it was no easy matter to think of a client so young being hanged.

When he returned, he thought, perhaps he would call on Miss Todd; she had expressed interest in the trial. But the prospect of seeing her did not lift his gloom. Given his debts, Lincoln wondered, Could he ever marry? He wanted a wife. The thought of having one excited—and terrified—him. But he brought only three things to the game of courtship: homeliness, debts, and a tongue tied in knots.

His attempts at courtship ended in failure. No sooner had he and Ann, the New Salem tavernkeeper's daughter, realized they loved one another than, in that summer of endless rains, she died. For a time he'd thought constantly of ending his life and joining her. Fate seemed to be playing with him.

A year later he was courting Mary, a large, somewhat older but very handsome woman from Kentucky, wealthy by the standards of New Salem. Their courtship was a continual testing to see who would dominate. Did he want her? He could not decide. Whenever he spoke or wrote to her about marrying, he enumerated his shortcomings. Eventually she rejected him. Then he was heart-sick and humiliated and ever more conscious of his poverty and homeliness, his lack of prospects.

As he got off the horse and walked to stretch his legs, this question haunted him: Would he want to marry any woman who'd be willing to marry him?

CHAPTER

5

Molly Todd walked solemnly into Elizabeth's parlor and made her way through the assembly of guests. Dr. Wallace grinned at her, obviously pleased with the prospect of shedding his bachelorhood. Molly reached her position, turned back and gazed at Elizabeth moving toward her. Then in a moment Fanny herself would appear, her hand linked into the arm of Ninian, who would on behalf of her absent father officially present the bride to her husband.

Molly glanced over the roomful of guests. Even though she had not been long in Springfield, most of the faces were familiar. When anyone caught her eye, she gave that person a smile appropriate to a bridesmaid: demure, all sweetness. For right now she would keep her wit and tartness hidden. Apart from the times when her children would be born, these were the most important moments of Fanny's life.

Or were supposed to be.

Now and then Molly wondered if a wedding were not really an elaborate livestock exchange. The rights to a dumb animal were shifted from her owner/father—or in the case of Fanny from her owner/guardian, Ninian—to her new owner, her husband. A little like a promising heifer. Properly cherished, properly bred, the heifer would give milk and calves. So would the young bride. And this, it was supposed, would make her happy.

If she could not yet put names to all the faces, Molly felt certain these were the "best people" of Springfield. Fanny would want them in attendance in order to meet her doctor, the better to learn that he was available to treat them, the better for them to learn—if somehow they had not heard—that he and Mr. Diller had opened a drug store in Hoffman's Row. And Elizabeth would settle for no less than the best people; neither would Ninian. The best people always came to the ceremonies of the Todd and Edwards families. "Never forget that you are a Todd!" Elizabeth frequently admonished her sisters. "We are the first family of Kentucky, and the Edwardses are the first family of Illinois."

Like the Edwardses and the Todds, most of those present had originally come to Illinois by way of Kentucky. In the veins of a number of them Todd blood flowed. It was an article of faith with Elizabeth that this blood gave evidence of itself in the fineness of the faces. It was true that Cousin John Todd Stuart, whose mother, Hannah, was Molly's father's sister, possessed both presence and fine features. So did Cousin John Hardin, who had brought his wife, Sarah, and family over from Jacksonville. As did Cousin John Todd, to whom Elizabeth always referred as the "best doctor in town." She would probably say that less often now that Fanny was marrying Dr. Wallace, but she would go right on thinking it.

Other best people included the spiritual guardian Parson Dresser and his wife as well as two land-wealthy early settlers, regarded by Molly as the "landed nobility." Also Dr. Gershom Jayne, his wife, and his daughter, the attractively fresh-faced and uncomplicated Julia, Molly's friend. Also tall, fat, and jovial Simeon Francis, the editor of the

Sangamo Journal, the Whig newspaper published weekly, and his wife, Eliza; they might also become friends, Molly thought, for the Todds and the Edwardses were ardent Whigs.

Catching Julia's eye, Molly cocked an eyebrow and pursed her lips in mockery of the solemn ceremony toward which they were both headed. She saw a smile quiver on her friend's mouth. Although a friend, Julia might also be a rival for young men's attentions. But Molly did not want to think about rivals. She was not in any contest to catch a man. Still, she concluded that no other belle possessed her wit and sparkle and her talent for conversation. Of course, wit and a teasing tongue ill served her with young men attracted to demure, quiet girls. Those men wanted child brides, girls who lacked the education she had received, who never conversed with their husbands nor were allowed to mature into women, who received pretty dresses and sweet candies as rewards of the marital state. Well, they were welcome to them!

As her sisters took their positions for the ceremony, Molly saw in Elizabeth a woman who always did as her husband requested. She took no interest in affairs outside the circles of her home and friends. Undoubtedly Fanny would follow her example, especially since Dr. Wallace was fifteen years her senior.

Molly thought once again—for it was not a new thought to her—that, if she ever married, she did not want to have that kind of relationship with her husband. She would marry only for love.

While Molly Todd watched her sister Frances exchange vows with her groom, Abraham Lincoln sat with his legs stretched out on a narrow bed that constituted part of the furnishings of the law office he shared with John Todd Stuart. His arms were folded across his narrow chest. He stared across the room, not at the table that served as a desk nor at the sorry excuse for a bookshelf that held the firm's legal library. He was thinking about Billy Fraim. And about Molly Todd.

A few days before he had visited the offices of the *Sangamo Journal* where he regularly read newspapers from around the state. He had come this afternoon to see if there was news of Billy Fraim's fate. He was reading the *Illinois State Register*, Springfield's Democratic paper, when he heard the door open. The laughter of young women floated into the room. He looked up to see Molly Todd entering the anteroom of the office with her sister Fanny. Lincoln jumped to his feet.

"Mr. Lincoln," Molly said.

"Miss Todd," he replied. Then, nodding to Fanny, he again said, "Miss Todd."

"What a surprise to see you here." Molly flashed him a teasing smile. "I thought attorneys were always deep in law books."

"I'm reading about cases around the state."

"And keeping abreast of politics, I have no doubt." Lincoln shrugged and put his large hands holding the paper behind his back. "Fanny and I have come to make sure the announcement of her wedding is in the paper."

"Dr. Wallace is far too busy to handle such matters," explained Fanny.

"Of course, we poked our noses into his drug store," Molly said, "as long as we were in Hoffman's Row. And we checked on the progress at the State House." Simeon Francis entered the anteroom. Fanny moved to him. "Do sit down, Mr. Lincoln," Molly urged. Lincoln returned to his chair. "I may sit beside you," Molly warned and did so. "What are you reading?"

Lincoln showed her the copy of the *Register*. Molly looked disdainful. "I prefer the gospel according to St. Whig."

"St. Whig has got to know what the Devil is thinking," Lincoln replied. He felt more relaxed in the anteroom of the newspaper office than in Ninian Edwards's home.

"I grant there's wisdom in that." Molly looked at him saucily. "And our friend Senator Euclid? Is he offering comprehensible axioms these days?"

"Some more so than others."

They sat side by side for a moment in silence, watching Fanny and Francis parley. Molly did not think she could invite Lincoln again for a lesson in Elizabeth's parlor, not without seeming forward, especially since they had not really studied Euclid. "The last time we talked," Molly said, "you were about to venture to Carthage. It was Carthage, wasn't it? Was Hannibal there?"

"He'd gone to the Alps."

"How like him not to wait. As I recall, you told me about a difficult case you had to defend in Carthage." Lincoln nodded. "How did that go?"

"Badly."

Molly was uncertain how to react. "I believe you said your client killed a fellow worker with a knife." Lincoln nodded again. "I've thought about him several times." She paused for a moment as Lincoln watched her. "How amazing to be controlled by that kind of passion."

"It happens now and again."

"Does it?" It was obvious that Molly had had no experience with this kind of man. "When you parleyed with him, were there still traces of that passion?"

"Because of it we didn't dare put him on the stand."

"Badly means . . ."

"He was sentenced to hang."

"Gracious!"

After a moment Lincoln observed, "Gracious, I'm sure it wasn't." Molly looked almost startled at these words. Lincoln wondered if any man of her acquaintance had ever discussed such things with her. They said nothing for a moment. At length Lincoln asked, "Have you ever attended a hanging?" Molly shook her head, astonished at the idea. "Well, if you're ever invited to one, send your regrets."

"I declare, Mr. Lincoln, why would I ever be invited to a hanging?" Molly watched Fanny talking to Simeon Francis across the room. At last she asked, "Have you attended a hanging?"

Lincoln finally said, "There was a hanging outside Springfield some years back. Folks still talk about it. A blacksmith named Van Noy killed his wife in a drunken rage."

"This was in Springfield?" Lincoln nodded. "Did you see it?"

"Heard about it from people who did."

The conversation lapsed. Fanny finished her talk with Simeon Francis and approached the bench where the couple sat. "I expect we must be getting along," Molly said. She looked disconcerted. She and Lincoln rose. He noticed Fanny raise an eyebrow to her sister. He could not see Molly's reaction. She called farewell to Francis. Lincoln said goodbye to the ladies and held the door as they departed.

Now in the office in Hoffman's Row Lincoln thought about Van Noy's hanging and about Billy Fraim. Stuart had advised him repeatedly not to brood about losing a case nor about the destiny that awaited Fraim. Instead he had suggested that Lincoln write and file the declaration for their clients Kerr & Co., who were trying to collect a debt of $2600 from David Prickett of St. Louis. Or read newspapers. Or take his favorite book of poetry—Bobby Burns or Lord Byron—walk out onto the prairie and spend the day reading aloud. Lincoln had taken care of the declaration.

By now Billy Fraim had met his destiny. Probably he had swaggered to the gallows. Staring across the darkness of the office, Lincoln could not stop imagining how it had been. Apart from a traveling circus or the Fourth of July fireworks, a public hanging provided people of the prairies one of the few spectacles they would ever see. It also offered them an opportunity to break the monotony of their existence. Being an occasion no one would miss, it allowed them to come together in town, share gossip and take a close look at one of life's mysteries, death itself.

Van Noy was drunk when he murdered, just as Billy Fraim was. He had been tried and convicted within two days. Longtime Springfield residents still dated happenings in their lives from the hanging. "It was before Van Noy went to perdition," they would say. Or "about the time the blacksmith got strung up."

Van Noy was hanged in late November, Lincoln remembered hearing. Harvests were in, leaves had gone from the trees and winter was about to lay its cold hand across the land. No crowd would gather again in town before the following spring. So women bundled their children into warm clothes; men loaded their families into wagons and drove the necessary miles. With leaves off the trees townspeople could see, for miles out against the horizon, wagons full of blanket-wrapped and quilt-clad prairie families. Although the countryside was only sparsely settled then, Springfield was crowded with people that day. They gathered outside the jail. They built fires to warm their hands, smoke thick in their nostrils. Women huddled together, taking delight in the mere sight of other women. In dread and in anticipation of what they had come to see, men passed jugs of cider around and told stories and laughed louder than they should have.

When Van Noy was brought out, a silence fell over the crowd. He looked at his former neighbors, people whose horses he had shod, whose tools he had made or repaired. He was loaded into a wagon, bound hand and foot. The wagon started off. No one spoke. Sitting in family wagons, women and children watched him pass. A procession formed. Wagons creaked west on Jefferson Street. Riders followed on horseback. Excited boys ran beside the wagon in which Van Noy rode. They dared one another to touch the wagon or jump high enough to look Van Noy in the eyes.

The procession turned south on First Street. It escorted the condemned man to a hollow south of town where withered leaves lay ankle-deep. There a gallows stood. From the gallows hung a noose. Some of the last birds of autumn twittered about it.

When the crowd moved as a procession, it was excited, almost jovial, families shouting to one another. When it arrived at the hollow and found the sheriff's wagon beneath the gallows, another hush fell over it. The sheriff lowered the tailgate. He and a deputy climbed into the wagon. The deputy pulled Van Noy to his feet. His knees were so like taffy that the deputy held him upright. The sheriff placed the noose around his neck. "Go meet the devil, Van Noy!" someone yelled. Others took up the cry, especially women who had known his wife.

The sheriff and the deputy jumped from the wagon. The sheriff took a whip and slapped the horse. It broke into a gallop. Van Noy's knees buckled. His body swung off the wagon. The crowd fell silent. The body pitched. It rolled. It swayed. At last it hung, twitching in death. People continued to watch. Boys ran up to touch the dead man's boots. The sheriff shooed them away. Gradually the wagons left, heading back to town. Some people stayed until the sheriff's wagon was brought back to the gallows. They watched as the sheriff cut down Van Noy's body and the wagon drove away.

Sitting on the narrow bed in the office on the second floor of Hoffman's Row, Lincoln thought about the hanging of Billy Fraim, about the crowds that gathered to watch his body swing from a rope and fight the rope and then hang lifeless.

At the wedding supper that followed the ceremony, Elizabeth had carefully seated Molly with guests from the Coterie, between James Conkling and Elias Merryman and opposite the Byronic, though fickle-hearted Joshua Speed. If Elizabeth considered Conkling, the Princeton graduate, a man fit to adorn the Todd-Edwards family circle, she acknowledged Mercy Levering's prior rights by seating Merce beside him, on the opposite side from Molly. Dr. Merryman was sure to find Molly enchanting. Her dress showed her hair to advantage as well as her lovely neck and sloping shoulders. It accented the color of her eyes. If one or two young women at the table were more classically beautiful than Molly, none possessed her vivacity, wit and sparkling conversation. Ninian Edwards always claimed that Molly could make a bishop forget his prayers—and privately contended some less flattering things about her as well. Elizabeth was certain she would please Dr. Merryman. She was sure that he would talk about her throughout the town and help make her reputation.

Molly had insisted that young women she liked also be placed at the table. In addition to Merce, Julia Jayne sat directly across from her beside Speed. Anna Rodney, one of Springfield's demure and obedient young ladies with whose father Ninian did business, was on the opposite side of Dr. Merryman. Molly quickly made her impression on the doctor. She enjoyed chatting across the table with Julia. When she turned to converse with James Conkling, she found him so taken up with Merce that he quite forgot that a gentleman converses with both of his partners. Conkling and Mercy talked almost exclusively—tête-à–tête— about the East. Finally, realizing that Molly wished to join their talk, Merce included her— with such sweetness and sincerity that Molly forgave the couple's absorption with one another.

In the house on the southwest corner of Madison and Third, Bill Butler, clerk of the Sangamon County Circuit Court, sat at the head of the table. Gathered about him, supper over, were his son Evan, brother-in-law Noah Rickard and his Black Hawk War pal Abraham Lincoln, who had joined them for supper. Two years before when Lincoln had come to town with hardly a penny, Butler invited him to take his meals at his table. Butler's wife, Elizabeth, did the cooking, aided by her teenaged sister Sarah Rickard. Stories to swap, a full stomach and the presence of Sarah, who slid into the chair across from him, helped Lincoln throw off the spectre of Billy Fraim's hanging.

"Remember that farmer-preacher up in Monroe County?" asked Butler. "Made horse collars for his team by braiding straw together. One day, breaking stubble with a son, he left the harness on the beam of the plow when he went to dinner." Butler's listeners nodded their heads. He continued, "Now the son didn't take to farming—"

"Sounds like somebody I know," said Sarah, giving Lincoln an impish look.

Lincoln grinned. Sarah was turning into a fine-looking woman.

"So after the farmer went off to dinner," Butler went on, "the son hid the horse collar, hoping to have a nap while his father braided a new one."

"That sounds like somebody I know," said Lincoln, fixing Sarah with an intense stare. Sarah blushed.

"Well," continued Butler, "the farmer wanted to get the job done. So when he couldn't find the horse collar, he just pulled off his britches, stuffed the pant legs with stubble, rigged up his horse with this improvisation and plowed the rest of the afternoon as barelegged as when he came into this world."

"I'll bet his legs itched when he put those britches on again," said Sarah. Lincoln laughed appreciatively. He liked a woman who made a good audience for a story.

"Nice to see you laughing," Butler remarked. Lincoln shrugged. "That client up to Carthage been haunting you?"

Lincoln shrugged again. Sarah watched him with a sudden seriousness.

Butler grinned. "This isn't a case like that mob over in Coles County, is it?"

"Which mob was that, Dad?' asked Evan.

"Why a mob went to the jailhouse one dark night to take vengeance on a man convicted of murder. Sheriff tried to stop them, but they rushed the place. They took the prisoner from his cell and hurried him to a tree. The prisoner kept insisting they'd taken the wrong man. He hadn't killed anybody. 'Course, that's what every murderer says. So they strung him up. Next morning they saw the feller was right. They'd hanged the wrong man. So they went to the sheriff, full of remorse, and told him, 'Guess the laugh's on us.' "

Lincoln laughed, his high voice squealing. "Let's pray that's what happened up in Carthage," he said. "And if they did it, they let my boy go free."

Noah commenced to tell a story about a farmer outside of Jacksonville who was afraid the railroad would scare his cows so much they would give no milk. Sarah crossed one leg over the other and laced her hands about her knee. Lincoln did the same, imitating the way she sat, the way her head was cocked. Knowing immediately that she was being mocked, Sarah became self-conscious, sought to ignore Lincoln and sat more upright in her chair. Lincoln sat erect in his and pursed his lips with mock self-conscious annoyance. Sarah turned her head to look at him, her eyebrow cocked. Lincoln turned to look at her and cocked his eyebrow in exactly the same manner. Sarah stuck her tongue out at him. He stuck his tongue out at her.

Sarah looked over at her sister in the kitchen. "He's doing it," she said. "I told you he would."

Lincoln looked toward Butler's wife. "He's doing it," he said, mimicking Sarah's intonations. "I told you he would."

"Pay him no mind," advised Elizabeth Butler.

"How can I?" asked Sarah, staring fiercely at Lincoln, sticking her tongue out at him once more.

Mrs. Butler came to the table and set plates on it.

"How can I?" asked Lincoln, staring even more fiercely at Sarah than she was staring at him. He stuck his tongue out.

Sarah took a plate.

"He's such a big, ugly gorilla!" said Sarah, breaking into laughter, still staring.

Lincoln took a plate without looking at it, still staring at the girl. "He's such a big, ugly gorilla," he said, using Sarah's intonations. He mimicked her laughter, still staring, never taking his eyes off her.

"Gorilla!" Sarah accused. She made a prairie version of gorilla grunts, hunched her shoulders and began to rub her plate, still staring at her adversary.

"Gorilla!" Lincoln mocked. It took all his concentration not to laugh at her. He imitated Sarah's gorilla grunts, rubbed the plate, still staring at her.

Sarah rubbed the plate, then rubbed her face, never taking her eyes off Lincoln.

Lincoln rubbed his plate, then smeared his face, never removing his eyes from the girl.

The spectators at the table began to chuckle at this tomfoolery.

Sarah rubbed the plate against her face.

Lincoln rubbed his plate against his face.

"Look at your plate!" Sarah said. She looked down at her plate.

"Look at your plate!" Lincoln mocked. When he looked down at his plate, he saw that Sarah had prepared it especially for him, holding it over a candle until it was dark with soot. The plate was streaked with soot where he had transferred it to his face. Everyone was laughing now. Lincoln looked at the hand that had rubbed the plate. It was covered with soot.

Sarah showed him her plate and hand. They were clean. Once more she stuck out her tongue at him. "That plate soots you, Abe Lincoln!" she laughed.

Lincoln grinned at her. Then he rose, went to look at his face in a mirror and gasped, "What a big, ugly gorilla!"

Scanning the wedding guests, Molly wondered if she was destined to marry one of the men now in the room. Probably. That probability distressed her. Not that there weren't acceptable men in the room. Probably some man here could make her feel as Fanny claimed Dr. Wallace made her feel: short of breath and palpitatey. You did not have to confer with Mammy Sally to understand that people were made that way.

But perhaps it had been a misfortune for her to grow up in a family where her father was a man of consequence. To be so closely acquainted with senators and governors and her father's neighbor Senator Henry Clay. Molly did not want to marry just anyone of the Ninian Edwards circle. She wanted a man fired by ambition. A man who intended to make a reality of a vision he now had of this growing state and this new nation. A man who wanted to influence events. If a woman was to cast her lot with someone, why not someone who dreamed of being as prominent as Henry Clay?

That was not Ninian. Molly understood that he had already lost the fire of any ambition he once possessed. It was now enough for him to claim a noble lineage—at least noble for the prairies—and increase the family wealth.

Glancing across the assembled men, Molly sensed that the most ambitious men—except, of course, Cousin John Todd Stuart and Cousin John Hardin, who fairly dripped with both ambition and skill—were the men Elizabeth had carefully excluded. The prairies offered opportunity to men who had the hunger to seize it, men already in the process of creating themselves. Shields and especially Douglas possessed that kind of ambition. Webb did not. Speed did not. Nor did Anson Henry or Elias Merryman. Did Lincoln? He had not talked about himself enough for her to know. Liked poetry and had a way with a jury. Lacked elegance and refinement, oozed rusticity. In stature and style he was a complete contrast to Douglas and the handsome Shields. Their every move exuded confidence and the expectation that women would fall at their feet. At least Lincoln was a Whig.

Out behind the Butler house Lincoln pulled a bucket of water from the well and began to wash his face. A large spring moon rode overhead. Sarah Rickard watched him.

"How long's it been since you washed that face?" she asked in her mocking, flirtatious tone.

Lincoln dipped his hand into the bucket and tossed water at her. She danced out of the way. "Didn't get me!" she sang. "But I got you!"

"You got me all right," Lincoln agreed. Rinsing off his face, he made his hands into a scoop, dipped them into the bucket and started after her. "Now I'll get you."

Sarah laughed and circled away from him. He hurried after her. She danced around the well, raced to the bucket and picked it up. As she did so, Lincoln tossed water at her, lunged for her, took her by the back and wrapped his arms about her. She laughed and squirmed. He tightened his grasp. She threw the bucket toward his feet. He stepped back, still holding her, raising her off the ground. He felt her body tight against him, the softness of her breasts against the inside of his forearms. He smelled her hair, went dizzy for a moment and had to step backward to keep from falling. He still held the girl off the ground, his lips right next to her ear.

"You ever been kissed, Sarah Rickard?" he asked.

"No!" she cried, struggling to make him hold her tighter. "You kiss me, you gotta marry me!" she warned.

He kissed her cheek and put her down. She took several steps backward and stared at him across the moonlight. They looked at one another.

"The Bible says Sarah shall cleave unto Abraham," Lincoln told her.

"You asking me to marry you?" she demanded.

"You want to live your life like a good Christian woman? I'm telling you what the Bible says."

Sarah looked at him for what seemed an eternity. He wondered if she would come to him to collect her kiss. Instead she ran away.

Lincoln realized he was panting. His head felt on fire. He picked up the bucket, lowered it into the well and brought it up again. He placed it on the side of the well. To bring the fire under control, he plunged his head into it.

When he returned from the Todd-Wallace wedding, Speed found Lincoln sitting on the open windowsill, staring at the enormous moon. Lincoln turned to him. His face wore a mournful expression. He spoke with a stutter.

"My God, Speed," he said. "What have I done?"

Speed did not know how to respond. Lincoln's look of sadness became one of terror. "I think I asked Sarah Rickard to marry me."

CHAPTER

6

Spring turned into summer. Heat settled over Illinois. The trees grew heavy with leaves and provided refuge from the sun. As Elizabeth Edwards's pregnancy progressed, Molly Todd took over more care of Julia. Lincoln rode out with other lawyers hoping to find clients needing help in the circuit courts. Stephen Douglas continued, with the help of Jim Shields, to refine strategies for the electoral success of the Democracy in the year ahead. And all of them happily participated in the social life of the small prairie town. Young people of the Coterie entertained themselves with musicales and masquerades, balls and banquets. There were picnics and parades and political speeches on the Fourth of July. There were outings by the river and the occasional wedding. Hostesses offered dancing parties and ice-cream socials. Theatrical troupes passed through town. The young men called on ladies and walked out with them. Molly strolled with Douglas and Shields and Bat Webb. She read poetry with Lincoln. Douglas also walked out with Julia Jayne, and Lincoln continued to tease and occasionally roughhouse with Sarah Rickard, once it became clear that he had not, after all, asked her to marry him.

One Saturday at an outing by the river, Will and Fanny Wallace, established marrieds by midsummer, acted as chaperones to guarantee the safety of Molly, Merce Levering and Julia Jayne from those famous rakes Jim Conkling, Lincoln and Joshua Speed. The men threw horseshoes while the women arranged their picnic hampers. Speed had brought his banjo and led them in song.

After eating, while the Wallaces and Jim and Merce strolled by the river, Speed and Julia challenged Lincoln and Molly to a game of horseshoes. Lincoln watched, amused, as Speed suavely circled his arm around Julia, pressing his body to hers as he showed her how to pitch a shoe. Julia seemed flattered with his attentions, charmed by his smile and his dark good looks. Since she meant little to him, except for the pleasure that contact with young women always gave him, Speed easily returned that pleasure by delighting her. When Molly seemed not to look for similar instruction, Lincoln felt bashful about offering it.

Later he and Molly skipped stones across the river's surface. Molly proved a failure at this pastime until Lincoln undertook to instruct her. First he explained that she must select skippers with the same care King David used in selecting stones for his scrip. Second he took her hand and her arm, put his arm about her and bent her close to the ground. In this position they released several stones together. Each enjoyed the touch of the other, and Molly began to get the hang of stone-skipping.

After a time she asked, "Do you think the Whigs can beat the Democrats next year and take the White House?"

Lincoln would not say "I do" to her, not after the teasing she administered when they first met. So he told her, "Why not? I'll surely do what I can to see that the Whigs take Illinois."

"What'll you do, speechify?"

"Give more speeches than a preacher, I expect. Write articles, edit a paper."

"You'll be so busy folks will hardly see you."

"I hope not," Lincoln said. He felt himself blush at releasing those words and sent a stone bouncing across the river's surface. It skipped four, five, six times. Lincoln grinned and Molly watched him admiringly.

"You make a stone fly," she said. "I doubt King David did it better and he had a sling."

To cap the summer festivities the Coterie organized a costume party. At the instigation of Molly and Merce, it was to be held at the Lawrason Leverings and all the guests were to appear incognito, in costumes and masks. Preparing for the party one afternoon, Molly sat on the Edwardses' porch weaving a wreath for her costume. Stephen Douglas appeared and suggested a walk. "I'll be happy to walk with you, Mr. Douglas," Molly told him. "But you'll have to wear my wreath."

"I look even more distinguished in a wreath," said Douglas.

Molly finished the wreath and set it jauntily on his head. As they walked together, Douglas fairly strutted, pleased with himself, delighted to be strolling with the wittiest, most popular girl in town, picking wild blackberries for her, staining his hands, tasting the berries' thin, rich juice. For her part Molly was not unhappy that this energetic young political operator would recognize her at the upcoming party, if not for her size, her wit and her gaiety, then for the wreath that she had put on his head. Recognize her he did and he monopolized her dances.

When Lincoln called on Molly to read poetry with her, they offered each other passages from Lord Byron's *Childe Harold's Pilgrimage*. Then they debated the question: Was Byron himself Childe Harold? How much of the poem was based on fact? How much was exaggeration?

One afternoon as they strolled together—summer was turning to autumn, the evenings growing colder—Molly read aloud from Shakespeare's sonnets. When she finished, Lincoln asked, "Who do you suppose his Dark Lady was?"

Molly laughed and declared, "A home wrecker. A husband stealer."

"Maybe," Lincoln acknowledged. "But what a poet! How did he write so much and so well? He produced these sonnets when he was relaxing."

"Mr. Shakespeare ought to have been ashamed," Molly said. "He left a wife and children in the countryside and danced off to London to be in the theater."

Lincoln suppressed a smile. He would not get drawn into this. Shakespeare was undoubtedly an errant husband and neglectful father. But, oh! Could he write!

"That's a little like chasing the circus out of town," Molly continued.

"You want your husband to stick around?" asked Lincoln, chuckling.

"Well, if he's running off, I want him to take me with him!"

The crisp days of autumn came. The leaves changed color and began to fall. Molly spent more time inside. She wrote letters to family and friends back in Lexington, did mending, joined Elizabeth and Fanny in receiving ladies who came to call. Life around the headquarters of the Coterie grew quiet. Due to Elizabeth's pregnancy, she and Ninian entertained less and less. Molly did more of the cooking and housework, the supervising of the Irish girls and looking after Julia. She kept busy making baby clothes for Elizabeth and also for Fanny who shared her secret with her sisters that she, too, was expecting.

One autumn afternoon Molly and Douglas strolled out toward the country. For a man who always had ideas and projects fulminating out of his head, he was strangely silent. He thrust his hands deep into his trouser pockets and kicked at fallen leaves, trampled them, releasing the thick odor and tiny motes of their crumpling. Molly walked with her hands warm in gloves, wondering what was on her friend's mind.

Finally he asked, "You ever think about marriage?"

Molly grew suddenly alert. She laughed silently to herself. Think about marriage? Of course, she thought about it. Didn't Douglas know that females thought about marriage starting at the age of five? "Oh, I suppose," she replied.

"Going to parties is an awful lot of fun for a girl, isn't it?" said Douglas. "Why get married when you're having so much fun?"

Was Stephen Douglas fixing to ask for her hand, Molly wondered. Gracious! What would she say? "Do you think about it?" she asked.

"I suppose," he said. "It's where we're all headed, isn't it?" He walked on, pulverizing leaves.

"Oh, look at this!" Molly exclaimed. She picked from a tree a maple leaf and held it up to the sun. It glowed red, yellow and orange. "The leaves in Lexington aren't as brilliant as these." She expected him to say that the leaves in Vermont were the most glorious of all. That's what she had heard.

Instead he said, "What do you think about it?" She gazed at the leaf, wondering at his persistence, then turned from it as if she had not heard. "About marriage."

She looked back at the leaf. Finally she said, "I think a woman better love the man she marries." After a moment she added, "Of course, there are plenty of reasons to marry that have nothing to do with love. But if a woman commits her life to a man, she better be sure she loves him."

"How does a woman know she loves a man?" asked Douglas. "Or a man that he loves a woman? He sees her mainly at parties or when he calls on her. That's a time when she devotes herself to being fascinating and finding him interesting."

"Interesting won't do," Molly said. "She needs to find him riveting."

"There can't be many riveting men around Springfield."

Molly knew that she was supposed to exclaim: What do you mean? You are! But she did not say it. "She needs to find him irresistible," Molly declared. "And she needs to be sure he loves her. She doesn't want to find out she's just a means of giving him his children. And his dinner."

"And he doesn't want to discover that he's only a provider of home and victuals and all the rest." They walked on farther. "I guess you know when you're in love," Douglas remarked. "That's what everyone says."

"Fiddlesticks!" replied Molly. "There's a fellow in town who knows he's in love three or four times a year."

"And who would that be?" Douglas laughed. They both knew she was talking about Joshua Speed.

"The night I arrived here I saw four men throw the shoemaker into a trough for beating his wife. They got her to beat him."

"He's a drunkard. That's the problem there."

"Well, I'd rather stay a spinster than want to beat my husband."

"A big house," said Douglas. "Is that important to you? A barn and a carriage and horses?"

"My husband doing work that satisfies him: that's important. And his being good at it." They both knew that he liked his work and was good at it. That meant she might be talking about him.

They stopped in the path and looked at one another. Molly thought he was going to kiss her. He'd kissed her before and certainly that was on his mind. A light sparkled in his eye. Suddenly he was teasing her. "A contented husband," he said. "And a little land speculation on the side won't hurt?" He laughed at her.

She slapped his shoulder with the back of her hand. He caught her hand, pulled her quickly to him and kissed her. Releasing her, he grinned like a boy who'd robbed the cookie jar. Then he regarded her seriously. "I couldn't marry anyone till next year's campaign is over. When it is, I'll want to marry you."

Molly did not know what to say. Was this a proposal? Or more of his teasing? And how did such a tease as he know how he'd feel a year from now? "You flatter me, Mr. Douglas," Molly told him. "And I must confess: you confuse me. What just happened? Was that a proposal?"

"Are you suggesting a kiss is a contract?" He leaned forward to kiss her again, as if to test her kisses' availablity. Molly turned away her head.

"You are the lawyer, sir. I'll know you're offering me a contract when I see you down on your knee."

"If you can wait a year, Miss Molly, that's where you'll find me."

"I'll make sure the parlor carpet's clean."

They started back toward the house, teasing one another, talking less about intentions than enjoying the distinct pleasure of flirting. Molly wondered if Stephen Douglas tried out proposals on young women just to hear how they sounded, the way he might try out political passages he could use in a speech.

"When I was a little girl," Molly told him, "I used to say I was going to marry a President of the United States.

"A sitting President or a fellow on his way there?"

It was a moment when Molly could have told him that he had the makings of a President. He might even be expecting her to say it. But they had been teasing one another and she sensed that, if she said that, he would want to believe she was serious. So she did not say it. Stephen Douglas was self-confidence personified. Telling him such a thing would be like throwing herself at him.

"President of the United States," he said. "That's setting the bar awfully high." He raised his hand as high above his head as he could reach. He let the hand circle her head, suddenly dropped it to the middle of her back, pressed her to him and gave her another kiss, a teasing one, hardly more than a peck, as if to assert his right to kiss her. She screamed in mock horror, slapped him on the chest and ran away. When he caught up with her, he took her hand. They walked back hand in hand to the Edwards house.

The next afternoon while she was sitting with Elizabeth, she asked, "How did you know you were in love with Ninian?"

"Are you wondering if you're in love with Stephen Douglas?" her sister asked. "Because I've been wondering myself."

"He's talked about marrying me," Molly confessed.

"When?"

"Maybe in a year."

"A year! Why so long? Was it a proposal?"

"It doesn't matter," Molly said. "Because I'm not in love with him." The excitement in Elizabeth's eyes drained away. "He always has to be the center of attention," Molly explained. "That does get tiresome.

"Mr. Douglas is going places. Don't be too hasty in turning him down."

"You called him a parvenu."

"Did I?" Elizabeth gave a little laugh. "I don't remember that. Anyway, he's the best of the bunch that call on you. You could go anywhere with him."

"How did you know with Ninian?"

"I just knew. My heart beat fast when he was around. I was flattered that he noticed me. My knees began to go wobbly. I wanted to laugh and sing all the time."

Molly was doubtful that she would ever feel that way. But then Elizabeth had been very young when she had decided to marry Ninian. Hardly eighteen. Ninian was handsome and rich, had been a dashing figure at Transylvania University, son of a man who'd been both Governor of Illinois and a United States Senator. Of course, it was easy to fall in love with someone like that. Have your knees go wobbly, but not even know who he was.

As autumn progressed, the Coterie had get-togethers and outings. Sometimes Molly was with Stephen Douglas, often enough so that gossips in town thought they were a match. But frequently she was with someone else. Occasionally members of the Coterie took the train to see friends in nearby Jacksonville, Springfield's sister city only twenty-five miles away across the prairie. There were visits from relatives: Todds from Missouri, Edwardses from Alton on the Mississippi just north of St. Louis.

That fall Stephen Douglas did not mention marriage again to Molly Todd. If he loved her, he loved politics even more. This was not the time for Stephen Douglas to think about marriage. As the political year he had told Molly about started to unfold, he had one goal in mind: carrying the state of Illinois for the Democrats.

Molly also had a goal: to be seen around town with as many different escorts as possible. That way people would know that she and Stephen Douglas were not yet, and maybe never would be, a match.

CHAPTER

7

Late that fall while the Edwards household awaited the arrival of a new baby, Molly Todd and Julia Jayne, Anna Rodney and Merce Levering met in the afternoons to think about parties that would keep the Coterie occupied into winter. Meanwhile, political fever gripped the young men of Springfield. They often met in the evenings at the back of Joshua Speed's store. Before a fire of logs pulled from the stack out back, they discussed the issues of the day, often amid laughter, sometimes amid shouting and name-calling. Occasionally young men dipped a ladle into the barrel of corn liquor that Speed kept for customers, drinking from it and passing it from hand to hand. The Whigs included Speed himself, Lincoln and most of the other men, even on rare occasions Ninian Edwards. Although outnumbered, the Democrats, particularly Stephen Douglas and James Shields, possessed the bravado to hold their own. Advocates of the common man, they did not hesitate to call Whigs "silk-stocking, ruffle-shirt men."

There were also those, less consumed by politics, who gathered around Speed's fireplace for fellowship, men like Charlie Hurst, who clerked and lived at the store. Jim Conkling joined the others when he did not call on Merce Levering or after his call ended. The same was true of Billy Herndon, the store's other clerk, who, not yet twenty-one and without resources, was determined to marry the sweetheart he saw almost every evening. Herndon had been exposed to anti-slavery views during a year at strongly abolitionist Illinois College in Jacksonville. His father, a Democratic state senator, one of the Long Nine, had brought him home because of it. To demonstrate independence from his father, Billy had recently become a Whig. He also bunked upstairs with Speed, Lincoln and Hurst.

The men discussed the role of the West in the young nation's future. They debated ways to increase its influence. They cursed paper money that kept losing value and bemoaned the fact that legal or medical clients generally paid in paper. They argued about land speculation. All of those who could afford them owned town or prairie parcels and were distressed that their value was not increasing faster.

The men also debated slavery. Many of them shrugged about it, resigned to it as constitutionally sanctioned, while others considered it morally objectionable. Some regarded it as the wrong road economically. Most of them roundly condemned abolitionism; they saw it as the work of meddlesome extremists. "Personally I don't hold with slavery" is how most of these men explained their position. "But the constitution permits it and abolitionists are looking for trouble."

Most of the men agreed on the need for internal improvements, without too much worry about how they could be financed. James Shields as Illinois State Auditor insisted that the improvements were overextending the resources of the Illinois bank, that they threatened to make its notes worthless. His warnings led to bitter wranglings about the national policy toward banks. President Andrew Jackson, whom excited Whigs labelled a "tyrant," a "backwoods Caesar," had killed the Bank of the United States. Martin Van Buren, his successor, wanted an independent treasury; he envisioned a complete divorce between government and banks. "The people run this country," the Democrats cried, "not Nicholas Biddle in Philadelphia!" "But the currency's been undermined!" replied the Whigs. Jacksonian policy, they insisted, would damage the credit on which rested the internal improvements system and expansion in the prairie states.

Up on the Hill at the Edwardses or the Leverings the young women also discussed politics, but in their special way. "How can men gather every night at that store and talk politics?" Anna Rodney wondered.

"It's not only politics," Molly assured them. "They pass around jugs of corn liquor and tell racy stories."

"They argue endlessly about the Bank of the United States," said Merce. "About Andy Jackson and Matty Van Buren."

"In a hundred years who'll care?" asked Julia Jayne. "You just know that eventually this whole business will get sorted out, maybe even in a way that will help the poor buy food."

"And the rich get richer!" said Anna. The women laughed ruefully. Yes, that was how men would sort things out.

Molly did not think that the controversy over the Bank of the United States was inconsequential. In fact, she felt strongly that Andrew Jackson and the Democrats were all wrong on that issue. But this was not the time to say so.

One late autumn evening at the Edwards house, the young women drank tea and knitted neck scarves for the cold weather ahead, discussing pumpkin pie recipes and how beautiful the reds and oranges of the autumn leaves had been, about snow flurries ahead and Christmas not far off. They decided to organize strolling carolers and announced the plan to Elizabeth when she came in to sit with them. Ninian was down at Speed's store.

As odors of tobacco and corn liquor scented the air at the store, flames in the fireplace threw flickering light on contending men. Short, squat and big-voiced Stephen Douglas shouted at the tall, thin clown, Abraham Lincoln, who was mimicking him. "Stop playing the fool, Lincoln, and argue like a man," shouted Douglas.

Lincoln bent his long frame down toward Douglas's mouth and held a hand to his ear. "Louder, Steve," he said. "Cain't hear ya."

Douglas dropped his voice to a whisper. "Why should I argue with the likes of you, Abe?" he asked. "Let's have a public debate. Let the voters hear what we have to say." He looked around at the assembled men. "We're going into a big political year. Next year about this time we'll be electing a President. Let's start that year with a public debate in the courthouse."

"Make it a series of debates," Lincoln suggested, no longer the clown.

"I don't want to skin you fellers more than once," Douglas said. "But I'm up to it if you are."

And so it was decided that there would be a series of debates, at least three. They would be held in the courthouse, starting the Tuesday of the week that the Sangamon County Circuit Court began its three-week session in mid-November. The men shook hands on this decision and passed the jug of corn-whiskey.

Douglas took a swig and burst out laughing. "Once I get through with you," he boasted, "you silk-waistcoated Whigs will be the laughingstock of the new state capital."

Up on the Hill the women were talking about babies, Elizabeth's due in mid-December. "Ninian is hoping for a boy," she said.

"Men always want boys," observed Anna. "Why is that?"

"They chase girls to get boys," said Molly. "It doesn't make sense."

"If they could find boy babies by the roadside, it would save us a heap of trouble," Elizabeth said. "Not that I object to children," she quickly added. "My baby Julia is the best thing that ever happened to me. After Ninian, of course."

"Oh, of course!" the women all agreed.

At breakfast the next morning Ninian told Elizabeth and Molly about the debates. "I assume the ladies are invited to see men demonstrate the superiority of their intellects," Molly said. "I wouldn't miss it for the world." She told Merce about the debates later that morning, and they made plans to attend.

When they approached the courthouse on the afternoon of the first debate, Molly noticed Merce scanning the square. "Looking for someone?" she asked.

"I might be," Merce acknowledged, giggling. "We wouldn't want to be seen without escorts, would we?"

"Perish the thought."

Jim Conkling made his way across the square to greet them. "I've got Jim Shields saving seats for us inside," he told them. "He's sure it'll be a

Democratic day. The Little Giant is going to work his magic."

Shields stood and waved the threesome to their seats. He took Molly's hand in greeting and, as was customary with him, squeezed it so affectionately that Molly wondered when she would get it back. She sat between Shields and Merce and folded her hands, as Miss Betsey had taught her, keeping them very close to Merce. "The prairie whirlwind goes on second," he told Molly.

She smiled. "That would be Mr. Douglas."

'He's been looking forward to this. Any time Douglas is trolling for votes, he's at his best." Molly was amused at Shields's confidence that his whirlwind friend would blow them all away. "Lincoln speaks tonight."

"And that's the long and short of it," Molly said.

"Exactly."

Molly found her thoughts wandering almost as soon as Whig orator Cyrus Walker started to speak. She sensed that Merce would have left had not Jim Conkling been beside her. Molly set herself to listen. A plodding frontier sage, middle-aged, medium height, Walker had bored so many audiences that he seemed like a wind-up toy. Shields leaned close to Molly. "Douglas will blow this fellow to Kansas," he whispered. Molly smiled tightly, her eyes narrowed at his grin. Surely Jim Shields knew she was a Whig! But he was right. She thought of Walker twisting over Springfield, his coattails flying, in the tornado of Douglas rhetoric that would toss him to Wichita. She glanced around to see if Lincoln was in the room. To save Whig pride he would have to do better than this! She did not see him. It was possible that he was at work in the Springfield circuit court; it was in session, after all. But she doubted that he would miss hearing from Douglas what he would have to answer that evening.

When Walker finally concluded to tepid applause, Molly and her friends stood. Merce and Conkling were whispering, wrapped up in each other. Molly turned to Shields. "Mr. Walker did not fire these hustings for the Whigs," she observed.

When they resumed their seats, Douglas was introduced and began in a gentlemanly tone with courteous bowings to the ladies among his listeners. Once he got into the rhythm of his talk, his tone and gestures grew more forceful. He showed an uncanny mastery of facts and proved himself to be vigorous and persuasive. He was energetic in refuting Walker's points, at first in a dignified manner, later in scornful terms. "The man can speechify!" Shields whispered to Molly.

She nodded in admiration for it was clear from the outbursts of applause that Douglas had his audience with him. When he stripped off his coat and yanked open his cravat, Molly wondered what it would be like to live with a man who expressed himself so forcefully. He spoke with such passion that she wondered if he would prove to be combustible. Would he talk like this, she wondered, if his dinner were late? If he was angry, might he truly catch fire? He had tried to bite off Cousin John Todd Stuart's thumb, had he not? Would such a man bite his wife?

When she walked back up the hill with Merce and Conkling, she easily remembered his arguments. But she realized there had not been a single felicitous turn of phrase. There was nothing she could quote to Ninian and Elizabeth.

That evening she returned to the courthouse, accompanied by her brother-in-law. So close to the birth of her baby, Elizabeth would not venture from the house. As they took their seats, Ninian pointed to a trapdoor in the ceiling. "Cousin John Todd Stuart's law offices are just above that trapdoor," he told Molly. "If he's not busy, he can monitor what's happening in this courtroom."

"How strange," said Molly.

"In winter he and Lincoln warm themselves on hot air."

As the auditorium began to fill, Bat Webb approached the seat beside Molly and asked her permission to take it. She gestured him to it. "How's our tall drink of water going to do tonight?" he asked. "I need some tips from the master."

"Lincoln's the master?" asked Molly. "I thought the master spoke this afternoon."

"That's the pretender," said Webb with a grin. "Lincoln and I will be talking our heads off in another few months, rallying the faithful, trying to convince the doubtful."

"You're a Whig elector, I believe," Molly said.

"That's what electors do."

When Lincoln took the platform, he seemed so tall to Molly, so elongated, that she thought he might be able to touch the trapdoor leading to the offices he shared with Cousin John Todd Stuart. Douglas had seemed to fill the platform when he spoke. Lincoln was a much larger man, but oddly, when he began to speak, there still seemed space around him. He started off in the plainest manner, speaking in a tone that lacked conviction. Patting the pockets of his coat as if hunting for a speech he'd left behind, he seemed to Molly very much the man she had welcomed in the Edwards parlor, with whom she had walked under the trees in their yard. Only now it was his job to speak, whereas when they were together he always left the speaking to her.

He noted apologetically that the debates had gone on and on. He hoped the audience would bear with him. The whole enterprise, he said, reminded him of a certain Joe Wilson who built a henhouse for his chickens to protect them from skunks. Still sustaining losses, he went out one night with a shotgun to keep watch. "Soon he saw half a dozen skunks running in and out of the henhouse," Lincoln said. "Thinking to exterminate the whole tribe at one swoop, he blazed away, but only hit one. The rest ran off. Being asked why he didn't give chase and finish off the rest, he said, 'Why, blast it, it was eleven weeks before I got over killing the one. If you want any more skirmishing after skunks, you can just do it yourselves.' " Lincoln paused and grinned at the audience. "And that's the way you must be feeling about our speechifying."

The audience rewarded this story with laughter, even with scattered applause. Molly watched the audience settle. Its welcome gave Lincoln confidence; he relaxed. The tension went out of his high-pitched voice; it found its natural timbre. He began to restate the arguments that Walker had made, but with phrases Molly found she could remember. Commenting on the Democratic party's fiscal policies, he claimed that Jackson and Van Buren were like the Irishman with new boots who was afraid he would not be able to get them on until he had worn them a day or two to stretch them. The audience laughed at that, at least the Whigs in the audience did. When Lincoln said the Democrats had worn their policies through two administrations and they still didn't fit, the Whigs applauded him.

"These fellers who see nothing but bugaboos in the United States Bank," Lincoln went on. "Reminds me of an old bachelor I knew in the Hoosier State who went out hunting one day. His brother heard him firing away and went to investigate. 'What're you doing?' the brother asked. 'There's nothing in that tree you're shooting at.' 'If it's the last thing I do,' said the old bachelor, 'I'm going to kill that squirrel up there.' The brother examined the old bachelor closely and discovered the problem. 'Now I see your squirrel,' he said. 'You've been firing at a louse on your eyebrow.' "

This story rather embarrassed Molly. It was so rustic, a story neither her father nor Ninian would ever tell. But the politician's job was to connect with his audience, and Lincoln had done this. His audience was laughing. Molly laughed too, amused less by the story than by Lincoln's manner of acting it out. His delivery grew ever looser. She could hardly believe that the Lincoln she knew, so tongue-tied and awkward around women, was the speaker now before her, so animated and quickened by his audience's response. This Lincoln seemed more a comic spielman on a circus midway than a politician. Molly felt certain that what she'd heard rumored about Lincoln's racy stories and witty short poems, designed exclusively for male audiences, must be true. She wondered if, while they sat together in Elizabeth's living room, she could ever induce him to share some of these stories. She realized, of course, that this could never happen.

As she rode back up the hill with Ninian, warm inside the carriage after the crisp air of the November evening, he observed, "Bat Webb is quite taken with you."

"Bat Webb? Bat? Where'd he get that nick-name?"

"His middle name is Batterson. He had that look in his eyes," Ninian said.

Molly pondered: What look? She wondered if Ninian wanted her out of the house. There was plenty of room and she could be helpful once the new baby arrived. Hmm. "The Bat has two young children for his next wife to raise," Molly said. "After Miss Betsey everything that has to do with step-mothering terrifies me."

After they rode a bit farther, she asked, "What do you know about Lincoln's background?"

"Nothing," said Ninian.

"Nothing?" asked Molly. "We recite our family heritages hereabouts as if they were pedigrees. You're the son of a Governor and Senator. My parents— Well, you know my family. We all trot out these credentials. Why not Lincoln?"

"Because Lincoln has no background," said Ninian. "Isn't that obvious? All I know is a few years ago he walked out of a village in Menard County. He'd been newly elected to the Legislature and was wearing what I assume was the first suit he ever owned. I imagine he succeeded electorally because he told the best stories of the Clary's Grove boys who voted for him." As they rode on, Ninian added, "And in a country that's done away with property qualifications for voting, that's all you need to get elected."

"Tell me one of his racy stories."

"Never." After a moment Ninian said, "You shock me, Molly."

"Then tell Elizabeth and she can tell me."

"I would never tell that fine lady such stories."

After a moment she asked, "How long has he been in Springfield?"

"Two or three years."

"He runs the Whig party in Illinois?"

"With Logan and Baker. He's not that gawky scarecrow that sits, tongue-tied, in the parlor with you."

"But he is that man."

"Not for long then. He's ambitious. Means to get some place."

"With a wife, I wonder?"

"You volunteering for the job?"

"I hardly think so."

"My hunch is he'll stay a bachelor. He can't fuse those two characters: the gawky scarecrow in one society and the ambitious operator in the other. He'll find a wench somewhere whom he doesn't have to honor with marriage. He'll visit her occasionally and that will take care of what he needs from a woman."

"Now you shock me," said Molly. They rode together in silence the rest of the way home.

On the evening of the second debate Molly stayed home with Julia while Elizabeth rested. The event was to be a rematch between Douglas and Lincoln; the previous debate had been judged a draw. Lincoln was undoubtedly the more entertaining speaker, Molly thought, and political debate in front of large crowds was decidedly a form of entertainment. But one could not deny the force of Douglas's arguments. She was sorry to miss the occasion and waited up for Ninian's return to get his opinion. "A disappointing evening," Ninian reported. "Lincoln stumbled. I spoke with him afterwards. He was clearly upset."

"And how was Douglas?" Molly asked.

"As always. Energetic. Forceful. He's a steam engine, not a man. Lincoln's missing the mark shows at least that he's human. I'm not sure Douglas is."

Brushing her hair the hundred strokes that night, Molly realized that she felt sympathetic to Lincoln. That he was a fierce competitor she did not doubt. She was certain that a bad performance would distress him, especially since he was likely to meet Douglas in debate repeatedly throughout the state in the coming months. But he had never been boastful, at least not in her presence, whereas Douglas, whatever his virtues, was overwhelming in his self-confidence.

Molly and Merce went to the courthouse the next day to hear the final debate. Once again Jim Conkling greeted them, this time with Douglas, the hero of the previous evening, in tow. "I understand you were most impressive last evening, Mr. Douglas," said Molly, tilting her head and assuming a skeptical expression. "I will not say 'astonishing' for fear it will go to your head." She realized she was flirting. Something about Douglas brought that out in her.

"My opponent was humbled," Douglas acknowledged modestly. "I'm not sure how much I had to do with that."

As they moved into the courthouse, men kept approaching to shake Douglas's hand. Molly glanced about for Lincoln, but did not see him. "If you're looking for Lincoln, I don't think he's here," Douglas said. "His tail's between his legs." Molly was surprised that he read her so easily.

"I was just looking for Julia Jayne," Molly said, having just caught sight of her friend. "She's going to join us." Molly waved to Julia, who moved toward them. The affection with which the Little Giant greeted her made Molly aware that he must also be a regular caller at the Jayne home. Fortunately, Bat Webb arrived at that moment, causing Douglas to place a proprietary hand on Molly's elbow.

As they all entered the courthouse, Molly whispered to Webb, "I understand our Whig disappointed last night." He nodded, looking grim. "Was it awful?"

"His stories fell flat," Webb told her. "The audience wasn't with him."

"Is he here today?"

"I'm told he's in court. A man does have to make a living."

As if to compensate for Lincoln's poor showing, the day's Whig speaker deliberately chose to be provocative. He was Ned Baker, one of the three-man Whig junto. The Whig partisans cheered him raucously, pleased that party men were showing fire. Those who disagreed with him started a murmur of objection. When he spoke about land speculation, invective tumbled from his mouth. He charged collusion between land speculators and certain newspapers. "Wherever there is a land office," Baker charged, "there is a Democratic paper to defend the corruptions in that office."

Douglas, the former Registrar of the Land Office, bristled. "Is he calling me a thief?" he muttered under his breath. He sat at the edge of his seat. The opposition murmur grew louder. An editor's brother stood. He shouted, "Pull him down!" Men began to stand throughout the auditorium. Others shouted, "Enough of that, Baker! Take him down!" Baker looked uncertain. He gestured to quiet the crowd. "Hold on! Hold on!" he said. But the commotion grew louder. Next to Molly, Douglas smiled, enjoying Baker's discomfort. Suddenly he stood; he joined the shouting. Molly wondered if he would rush the platform. She looked around for a way to escape.

Suddenly a hole opened in the ceiling. A man's feet appeared. Molly gasped. The commotion hushed. Legs followed the feet, very long legs. They seemed to go on forever. The commotion revived. Baker and his opponent stood back. Throughout the hall people rose to their feet. They laughed. They shouted. They began to throw things. In the ceiling a man's waist appeared. Then his narrow chest. Molly watched, amazed. The man's arm strength seemed incredible as he lowered himself through the trap door. Everyone in the hall was watching. The man dropped to the floor, a large man, tall, yet agile as a cat. Molly gasped. It was Lincoln.

He scowled at the audience. He gestured with his hands for silence. Shouting continued. It grew louder. Lincoln reached for a stone water pitcher on the speaker's table. He brandished it. "I'll break this over the head of the first man who lays his hands on Baker," he announced. The commotion continued. "Who's first?" As the tumult subsided, Lincoln shouted, "This is the land of free speech, friends. Mr. Baker has the right to speak. So does his opponent. We ought to hear them out! I'm here to see we do!" A few men still shouted. "I'm here to protect Mr. Baker!" declared Lincoln. "No man's going to take him from this stand unless he takes me first."

At last the hall calmed. Order was restored. The debate continued, but Molly could think of nothing but the sight of a very long man descending from above. It was the sort of thing you heard about in church. You didn't expect to see it at the Sangamon County Courthouse.

There was a family dinner that evening at the Edwardses. Lincoln's performance was extensively discussed. "It shows you why the Clary Boys over in New Salem elected him in the first place," observed Will Wallace.

"Everyone will forget his poor showing the other night," said Ninian. "What they'll remember is today."

"I'm afraid it's too backwoods for me," said Elizabeth.

"Give the man his due," insisted Molly. "He can swing an axe like a rail-splitter, but loves poetry. So he has a soul. He tells witty yarns and tall tales."

"Not for mixed company," said Elizabeth.

"So he has a sense of humor," said Fanny.

"He defends friends and insists on the right of free speech," said Molly.

Wallace raised an eyebrow and teased, "That's marriageable material, Molly."

"For a scullery maid," quietly commented Elizabeth.

Tobacco smoke thickened the air that night around Joshua Speed's fireplace as shouting and raillery bounced off the rafters. Always an abstainer, Lincoln was the only man who did not partake of the corn-liquor that flowed freely. The Democrats were in high spirits because they had won the debates, they felt, on the issues. The Whigs were equally joyful knowing that politics was showmanship, much of it, and that, well after they'd forgotten the issues, voters would remember a long man's descending through the ceiling. "You really didn't need to protect me, old boy," Ned Baker insisted to Lincoln. "You know I'm quite capable of fighting my own fights." Baker was, in fact, captain of the local Sangamo Guards.

"But when would I get another chance to drop in on such a meeting?" Lincoln asked. "After my showing last night, I had to redeem myself!"

As the men laughed and drank in the back of Speed's store, up in the big house on the hill Molly Todd lay in bed waiting for sleep to come and thought once again of Lincoln. She had been right, defending him at dinner. He had wit, a knack for showmanship and a sense of humor. He had masculine strength, lowering himself through the ceiling like that, and, determined to safeguard his friend, he had a mothering instinct. Suddenly Molly understood that, although her brother-in-law, Dr. Wallace, had been joshing her, he was right: Lincoln was marriageable material. He was a man out of which the right woman could shape a kind of greatness. Imagine that.

The next time he called, *Childe Harold's Pilgrimage* under his arm, Molly said, "The last time I saw you, Mr. Lincoln, I thought it was God coming through the ceiling. Then I recalled, of course, that God does not have such long legs."

CHAPTER

8

Molly and her sisters were invited to have tea at the Leverings to meet their friend Mrs. Parker from central Massachusetts. She had come to Illinois to see what the frontier was like. Elizabeth declined the invitation. She and Fanny were both pregnant now, Elizabeth well along, modesty preventing her from leaving the house even to go next door to join a party of women friends. Fanny, not really showing yet, especially if she covered herself with a shawl, was happy to leave the confines of the Globe Tavern. She and Molly hurried to the Leverings through the bleak winter sunlight, running in small steps through musty fallen leaves, shivering in the wind that blew off the prairie with a kind of moaning.

It was warm inside the Levering parlor, a fire roaring in the fireplace. At the first sight of Mrs. Parker it was obvious to Molly—from the silk of her dress, from the slimness of her waist and the perfection of her skin—that she was a rich man's wife. She was quite handsome. She carried herself well and wore the latest fashion. The Coterie women examined her apparel carefully to see what they would be wearing when fashion came west. Molly whispered to Fanny that Elizabeth would be sorry not to have seen Mrs. Parker's dress. The woman proved to be a cousin of Lawrason Levering, perhaps ten years older than Mercy Ann, who had returned to Baltimore for Christmas.

Molly soon realized from the conversation that the visitor's husband must be close to thirty years older than his wife. By some miracle of travel possible on the eastern seaboard, Mrs. Parker, though raised in Maryland, had met and married an industrialist from Lowell, Massachusetts. He owned a textile mill that employed thousands of young women, most of them between seventeen and twenty-four, daughters of Massachusetts, Vermont and New Hampshire farmers.

The Coterie women asked what sorts of labors these girls performed. As Mrs. Parker detailed their work—spinning, weaving, preparing weft, and pasting—Molly felt a sudden, quite unaccountable envy of their lives. Those young women were useful! Every day their labor accomplished something. It was valued and remunerated. But her envy was something she dare not express. As they lifted cakes and teacups to their mouths, the Coterie women watched Mrs. Parker with a kind of astonishment. "These girls," the women asked, "are they happy? Are they safe?" And as they let pastry sweeten and milky liquid warm their bodies, they wondered, "What are their morals?"

Mrs. Parker reassured them on all scores. They lived in boardinghouses, supervised there by matrons, usually widows. They must be of good character, in their speech and acts exhibiting a praiseworthy love of temperance and virtue; they must be sensible to their moral and social obligations and keep the Sabbath in a praiseworthy way. Girls found to be dissolute or lazy, gamblers, drunkards or dishonest, were dismissed and sent home. The prudent worker could save up to a dollar and a half a week. After four years of textile work, a careful girl's savings might amount to $250.

"That's a tidy sum for a dowry," said Mrs. Levering.

"Indeed," agreed Mrs. Parker. "It's a fine life for most of these girls, certainly preferable to living on a farm. But I must confess it would not be the life for me." Her eyes flashing, she smiled mischievously and confessed, "I have never been the soul of prudence. I could say, 'regrettably never,' but the truth is I don't regret it for a moment."

Some of the women tittered; others, Fanny among them, looked a trifle shocked.

"Piety, purity, domesticity and submissiveness: those," said Mrs. Parker, "are regarded—at least by males—as the cardinal virtues of the American woman. But not by me. My husband's first wife possessed those virtues. When she passed to her reward, he wanted something different. I came out here hoping to find that women in the West were smarter than their Eastern sisters. I hoped they would not be shackled to these supposed virtues."

The women gathered in the Levering parlor laughed uneasily. If they did not all embrace these virtues, they would never admit to it publicly. Purity they prized, but they knew that piety could get out of hand. Had they not seen frontier women, worn out by work and childbearing, appearing to be fifty when they were thirty, giving vent to excessive emotion in churches or at revivals where emotionalism was sanctioned? That emotionalism expressed itself in shrieks and violent howlings, in bodily convulsions, even sometimes in a kind of ecstasy. Some clergymen encouraged this rapture and during it touched the transported women with a tenderness their husbands never showed. As for domesticity, it was women's lot. If not domesticity, there was for them only the sewing trades, dressmaking or millinery, governessing or keeping hotels or boarding-houses, all of which were more or less domestic trades. Their submissiveness, Molly knew, was shown in their acceptance of this condition.

"Why did you marry your husband, Mrs. Parker?" one of the guests inquired.

"I could say," she replied, mischievous again, "that I married him because he asked me. Or because all the interesting young men had gone west to seek their fortunes." She smiled wickedly. "But because I am far from home, I can tell you frankly that I married him because he was rich. Just as he married me because I was young—and enticing. He had gold and houses. And I had a sense of myself different from what his wife's had been. I was more educated than his wife. Less submissive. Also less pious." Again the naughty smile. "And I suspect less pure."

A few of the women giggled embarrassedly; others tried not to gasp aloud.

"The marriage works," Mrs. Parker said. "Both of us are realists. We each knew what we wanted from the other. The first time he kissed me, I put my tongue in his mouth. That's the way the French kiss. He responded and I knew I had him."

Now some of the women did gasp aloud. They could not imagine such a kiss. It was a courtesan's trick.

"We sleep in separate bedrooms," Mrs. Parker revealed, "and he visits no oftener than I want." The Springfield women seemed a little shocked and that pleased Mrs. Parker. "Women must shake off their enslaved condition," she said. "We must become educated and mentally active. And, if possible, self-sufficient."

Molly did not know what to think. Mrs. Parker was probably being intentionally provocative, enjoying her chance to shock women who even in their idleness did not want to change the course of their lives. "What did you think of that?" Molly asked Fanny as they hurried back to the Edwards house. The wind had grown cold.

"I kept thinking," Fanny said, "that I had taken my unborn baby to an immoral atmosphere. I'm not sure I should tell Dr. Wallace what I've done."

"She's certainly living comfortably and well," Molly acknowledged.

"I suppose most courtesans do," Fanny replied. "I'm so glad I married for love."

Molly said, "That's what I mean to do."

Later, before it grew dark, Molly walked down the hill, accompanying Fanny to Globe Tavern, both girls wrapped in heavy woolen cloaks against the evening chill. Although they did not speak of her until they were in town, the aura of Mrs. Parker walked with them.

Eventually Molly gave voice to a question she had been mulling. "Do you suppose Mrs. Parker is happy in her marriage?"

"I wouldn't be surprised," Fanny replied. "After all, she got what she wanted, gold and houses." Molly felt the cold settle on her cheeks as she breathed in the scent of wood fires warming the houses. Smoke curled out of chimneys, dissolving into clouds that the sunset colored orange. "But I'd rather be one of those girls working in her husband's mill than do the kind of work she does."

Molly smiled at this and pulled the cloak tighter about her.

"She's so modern," Fanny said, "that I'm sure she'd say we all do that kind of work, we wives. But we don't." She turned to her sister and stopped walking, observing Molly primly, ready to drop on her a verity that she had learned from her greater experience of life. "And don't you ever for a minute think we do."

Molly said nothing, but Fanny was sure she sensed what Molly, that bundle of contrariety, was thinking: that Mrs. Parker had a point, that all women faced the challenge of making their men happy, sometimes through their stomachs, less often through their minds, but always in their "wifely duties." The difference was that Mrs. Parker became rich doing it while other women were content to be poor.

"It's all a matter of values, Molly," Fanny went on. "Values are happiness. She's got hers; I've got mine. When I meet my Maker, you won't find me saying, 'Dear Lord, you ought to see my house. It's the envy of the town.'"

Molly wondered, but only for a moment, what she would say to her Maker. Probably it would be "Why can't women vote? And do important work?" To her surprise she heard unexpected words coming out of her mouth articulating thoughts she hardly knew were in her head. She found herself saying, "Do you and Dr. Wallace— Do you kiss the way she said French people kiss? Tongues in each other's mouths?"

She sensed Fanny stiffen just as the women in the Levering parlor had stiffened and fallen into silence.

"Could that be . . . pleasant?" Fanny walked quickly along as if trying to outpace Mrs. Parker's aura. "It sounds revolting at first." Fanny said nothing. "Just the way it seems revolting to a child," Molly went on, "to eat the little piggy she's played with in the barnyard. But when you grow up, you realize little piggies can taste ever so succulent." Molly hurried along beside Fanny. "So—

do you and Dr. Wallace kiss that way? And do you like it?"

Fanny looked at her sister across the gulf of experience that separated them, Molly still a virgin and she not only a wife now and an expectant mother, but the love-object of a man who had led her, reluctant at first, down a garden path of unimagined physical encounters, most of them eventually— Well, if she could not yet acknowledge them as delightful, they were certainly not repugnant.

"A strange silence fell over the women when Mrs. Parker mentioned thrusting her tongue into Mr. Parker's mouth. The first time they—"

"We're almost at the Globe," Fanny interrupted. "I'm worried you'll be walking home in the dark."

"Did you notice that silence?" Molly insisted. She would not lose her way going up the hill, but if she had not felt a little lost about this other, the unexpected words would not keep jumping out of her mouth. "Was that because the women were shocked that people did such things? Or because someone dared to talk about them? Tell me. You must know. Do you and Dr. Wallace—"

"Molly dear, you must understand." She felt Fanny's grip on her arm and heard the chiding tone, Miss Betsey's tone, that seemed to come to her from out of a different generation. "There are things married women never discuss— I can't tell you about my— My intimate relations with— Oh, please! You're embarrassing me to death."

"But then how does an unmarried woman ever know these things? How did Mrs. Parker know about—"

"Indeed!" Fanny huffed. "As I said: it's values." She hurried along. When they reached the entrance of the Globe, Fanny took Molly's hands, squeezed them and kissed her cheek. "Run on home," she said and went inside.

Molly walked pensively back through town and up the hill, wondering if her tongue would ever touch a man's tongue. If it did, she was sure she would shudder. But would it be a shudder of repulsion or one of ecstasy?

When the Legislature first convened in Springfield, half a dozen of the town's up-and-coming young men celebrated the state capital's move to Sangamon County by hosting a cotillion. In his satin waistcoat and ruffled shirt, Abraham Lincoln stood in the lobby of the American House, the town's best hotel, greeting guests with fellow hosts Joshua Speed, Stephen Douglas and James Shields. As the dancing began, the hosts moved into the ballroom. While the others danced, Lincoln stood as was his wont at the edge of the dance floor, ungainly as a stork. Although his expression suggested melancholy, he nodded to people, smiled and shook hands with men. He danced with the wives of fellow legislators: Sarah Hardin from Jacksonville and Eliza Browning from Quincy. He looked around for Molly Todd, who made a party an occasion. He did not see her anywhere.

When the cotillion was in full swing, Molly arrived, escorted by Bat Webb. "We do apologize for being so late," she told Lincoln. "But Elizabeth is about to have her baby. Ninian sends his regrets even though he's on the invitation as a host." She put a hand on Lincoln's wrist. A tingle went up his arm. He smiled. "I should probably have stayed home myself," she acknowledged. Her eyes flashed with joyful wickedness. "But when a girl's got dancing feet, it's impossible to miss a party.

So I'm being naughty." She glanced to make sure that Webb was still talking to friends and whispered to Lincoln. "You're going to promise me a dance, aren't you, Mr. Lincoln?"

When he watched her dancing, first with Webb, then with Douglas, Shields and Speed, Lincoln felt lonely. He looked around the ballroom for Sarah Rickard, but knew that she would not have come to a cotillion at the American House.

When finally Lincoln asked Molly to dance, she said, "I'm dying of thirst." She took his hand and led him to the punch table. Lincoln was aware that his large hand entirely covered her small one.

"I keep hearing," Molly said as they stood drinking punch, "that what we're really celebrating tonight are your political skills."

Lincoln gazed down at her, her sparkling eyes, her teasing smile. A sweet fragrance rose from her as it might from a blossom. He felt she was casting a spell on him as he was sure she did on every man she spoke to. "Political skills?" he asked. "Are we at the same party?"

"Your modesty is one of those skills, isn't it?" She cocked her head as if she could see through him. "You're slim and crafty as a . . . hmm." She hesitated, hunting for a metaphor. "I certainly won't say 'as a serpent' because I've just had that compliment paid to me. And I was not pleased." She smiled. "I'll just say you're obviously a man who knows his business. I admire that kind of man."

"Thank you, Miss Molly."

"Don't you want to know what I heard?"

Lincoln shrugged. Molly made a face. "Ma'am, you're embarrassing me."

"You were the one who wrote the bill to have the whole legislature vote to move the capital.

That's what I heard. You knew every legislator who wanted the capital in his own town would vote for that. From Jacksonville, Peoria, Podunk. Then once that vote was taken you set the trap for Springfield. Superb."

"I can't imagine who told you that was my doing. It just—"

"It was you. You know how I know?" She stood erect on her little frame and almost reached his shoulder. "I know because three different men have told me they gave you the idea."

Lincoln laughed and shook his head.

"Success has many fathers, Mr. Lincoln. But I think you did the deed."

Molly sparkled. When they finished their punch, he danced around the floor the most exciting and attractive woman at the cotillion.

Later that evening Speed and Lincoln sat in their ruffled shirts, watching the dying embers in the fireplace at the back of the store. Charlie Hurst was with them, wearing homespun. As a store clerk he felt he had no place—and certainly no money—to go to a cotillion at the American House. They heard someone push into the store, listened to the footfalls as he made his way to the back. It was Billy Herndon, returned at last from the long farewells that were a regular part of his courtship with Mary Maxcy. He joined the others with a sigh of frustration.

"I guess I can hold out till I'm married," he said, shedding his waistcoat and tossing it across a barrel. "But it won't be easy."

"Miss Mary won't allow you liberties?" asked Speed.

"If she did, I wouldn't tell you," said Herndon.

"We could smell it on you," Lincoln remarked. "A skunk gives off an odor when it's excited and so do you."

"If I was a skunk," said Herndon, "I wouldn't be waiting."

"How was the cotillion?" asked Charlie Hurst. "These fellers think it was the best party they've ever been to. Of course, they were the hosts."

"Maybe the best party I been to this month," allowed Herndon, laughing at Lincoln and Speed. They clearly expected superlatives to drop from his lips.

"An excellent cotillion," declared Speed. "There'll never be another one to celebrate the state capital coming to Springfield."

"What wasn't wonderful about it?" Hurst asked Herndon.

"Got my head bit off by Miss Molly Todd," he said.

"Her sister's about to deliver," said Lincoln. "Maybe she was antsy about that." He gazed at Herndon with a critical eye. "It's also true she doesn't tolerate fools. She might have looked you over and taken you for one."

"Must've smelled that odor of the skunk on you," said Speed.

"Not me," said Herndon. "I was on my best behavior when I danced with her. Held her firm, but not close. Made polite conversation. Ended by complimenting her. She took offense and hustled off. Left me in her dust."

Lincoln laughed, recognizing the Molly Todd he knew.

"What did you say?" asked Hurst.

"She's a spectacular dancer. No other woman in Springfield dances like her. So we smoothed along and she talked with me, flirty like."

"She's always flirty," said Speed. "Don't suppose she thinks you're special."

"I know she doesn't," Herndon went on. "So after we danced, I said: 'I apologize for being so awkward, Miss Molly. You are a wonderful dancer. You glided through that waltz with the ease of a serpent.'"

"A serpent!" cried Lincoln. His high-pitched giggle—heeheehee—filled the room with glee. Speed laughed as well. "You compared Molly Todd to a serpent?"

"I was trying to compliment her."

"That's one of the better compliments. What did she say?"

"She said, 'Mr. Herndon, comparison to a serpent is rather severe irony, especially to a newcomer.' Her eyes were flashing darts and she huffed off."

Lincoln leaned back in his chair. "I'm sure she slithered upstairs, coiled up and cried." As he laughed, tears ran down his cheeks.

"You can have your aristocratic Kentucky girls," said Herndon. "I'll take my homegrown Mary any day." He gazed into the embers with an expression of dazed silliness, obviously thinking of his beloved, a small smile on his lips. "I cannot wait to be married," he said. "Married! Me!" He looked at the others and asked, "Why aren't you fellers married? It's easy as falling off a log."

"I reckon you have special talents with women, Billy," Lincoln teased. "I've always suspected you did."

"That's why you're clerking in this store," said Hurst. "To draw the girls."

"Like bees to nectar," said Speed.

"Like bears to honey," said Hurst.

"Like the serpent to Eve," said Lincoln. "plucking that apple in the garden."

"Why aren't you married, you three?" asked Herndon. "Most fellers marry at my age, twenty, twenty-one. You're thirty, Lincoln. You're pushing it, Speed."

"Takes money to marry," observed Hurst. "I'm saving to buy a store."

"Store can't wrap herself around you at night," said Herndon.

"Like a serpent," remarked Lincoln. He began to laugh again.

"Why aren't you married, Lincoln?" asked Herndon. "The ladies skeer you?"

"I'm choking in debt," said Lincoln.

"The right girl doesn't care about debt. If she loves you—"

"If you love her, you won't stick her in poverty."

"You're not in poverty, Lincoln," said Hurst. "Must be something else."

"You don't know it," said Speed, "but Lincoln *is* married. To the Legislature. She's a wife he had to ask five thousand fathers to marry."

"She's a wife who turns me down a lot," added Lincoln. "You make a proposal. She discusses it till you want to choke her. Then she turns you down."

"Billy doesn't want a wife who turns him down," teased Hurst.

"What about you, Speed?" asked Herndon. "Why aren't you hitched?"

"Because he falls in love every other day," said Hurst.

"Speed should be a Mohammedan," suggested Lincoln. "Those fellers can take as many wives as they want. One for beauty. One for brains. One who's good in the kitchen. One who's good in bed." The men grinned at one another.

"Yes!" cried Herndon.

"Mary Maxcy's going to be well worked over by you," observed Speed.

"She can't wait," said Herndon gleefully.

When the others turned in, Lincoln stayed before the dying fire. Billy Herndon's enthusiasm for marriage must be infectious, he thought. Because he, too, was thinking about it. And about Molly Todd. She was intelligent, charming, spirited, a little plump, but he had always liked that in a woman. He'd grown up around women whose lean, labor-worn bodies and gaunt faces showed the difficulty of their lives. A little plumpness in a woman suggested a comfortable, well-fed station in life. Molly talked flirty to men, just about all men as far as he could tell. When she talked flirty to him, he tingled. She'd talked so flirty to Billy Herndon that he'd forgotten where he was and compared her to a serpent. Lincoln chuckled at that. He liked it that she said what she thought and left Billy in his tracks, his mouth hanging open as she disappeared.

Molly must have come to Springfield expecting to find a husband, he thought. Her sister Fanny had found one right quick. Ninian Edwards had patrician airs now that he was two generations from ancestors who had busted the soil. But Will Wallace, Fanny's husband, had no pretensions to being an aristocrat.

Lincoln wondered whom Molly Todd would marry. Not him certainly. A man who came from where he came from could not aspire to marrying a Todd. The Little Giant? Douglas was even a greater schemer than he himself, a more devious

164

manipulator. If she wanted him, she was welcome to him. They were more of an age, more of a height. Those advantages might work for Douglas. But he thought Molly had more sense than to choose him. Douglas would want a woman subservient to him, one who sat at his feet listening to his interminable talk. That was not Molly's role. Jim Shields? No. Jim Conkling? Maybe, if he were free, but he wasn't. Joshua? No. He fell almost immediately for the women who attracted him. And he hadn't fallen for Molly. Bat Webb? No. Stepchildren to raise. Too lacking in distinction. Molly did not want the kind of distinction that her sister Elizabeth had chosen, wealth and family background. And she would not be satisfied as Fanny was with a man who meant well, but lacked drive. She wanted distinction.

So whom would Molly marry?

Could he dream of marrying her? They were the very opposite of each other. But opposites were said to attract. Hmm.

The woman a man married determined the kind of life he led. He was finally getting where he wanted to be. Five years ago he would not have thought it possible. He'd managed to get where he was because he wasn't married. If he'd hitched up with Ann Rutledge—he thought of her rarely, but never without regret. With her he might still be a surveyor. He'd have a few acres to plow and some stock to feed and two or three young'uns already. And if he'd married Mary Owens? He shook his head. That wasn't even a romance. Just two unmarried people, looking at the possibility of pairing off. And Sarah Rickard? Could he be happy with her? She was too young yet to have the kind of ambition that Molly had. Ambition was something a man who was trying to get ahead needed in a wife. He was ready to love a woman. Could he make Molly fall in love with him? Not if she knew his background. Could he even kiss her if she'd let him? They were so different in height. He had no idea how to do either of those things.

Molly Todd. What an incredible thought!

Christmas came. In the big house on the hill the Edwardses celebrated the arrival of a son, Albert, born December 16. Always one to enjoy children, Molly was delighted at Bertie's arrival and at sister Fanny's pregnancy. But there were times when she felt like a girl brought in from Ireland to cook and clean and be a nursemaid. She wondered when she would have a family of her own.

The new year began: 1840, a presidential election year. Men continued to gather around Joshua Speed's fireplace to laugh, tell stories and argue politics. In the long winter months Stephen Douglas used the discussions at Speed's as practice sessions for upcoming debate. Speed dreamed of girls and wondered if he might not find more to choose from back home in Kentucky, where the ratio between men and women was more favorable to him. Like Molly Todd, he wondered if marriage, which might be a bondage or a joy, would be right for him. Billy Herndon spent the weeks courting Mary Maxcy, pushing his romance as far as she would allow and holding himself in check the rest of the time.

Abraham Lincoln practiced law (divorce cases, estate matters, real estate and indebtedness disputes), deliberated with the town board and sat on committees of the Legislature. In his leisure time he warded off loneliness for a woman, reading newspapers at the offices of the *Sangamo Journal*. He studied the speeches and literary style of Henry Clay, Daniel Webster and John Calhoun.

Both Lincoln and Douglas, as well as Bat Webb, paid frequent calls at the home of Ninian and Elizabeth Edwards. They came not to see newborn Bertie, but to have the pleasure of the company of Molly Todd. Molly, who celebrated a birthday on December 13, had just turned twenty-one. That was an age at which most young women in Springfield were already married. So Molly wondered what in the world would happen to her.

CHAPTER

9

A dreary beginning to February. Snow and rain for days. Molly felt like a prisoner in the house. She did housework until she could stand it no longer. She read books until she wanted to throw them against the walls. She played the piano until her fingers were tired. Now Merce Levering was with her. They had pasted invitations and dance cards into their scrapbooks, read to each other poems they had written, and admired the pressings of spring flowers made months ago. They had talked about what their weddings would be like and who they'd invite and who they'd shun until Molly thought that if marriage was as imprisoning as the weather maybe she would prefer to be a spinster. "I have got to get out of this house," she told Merce. "If I don't, I'll scream and the babies will wake up and Elizabeth will be so cross she may send me back to Lexington."

"We could go to my house," suggested Merce.

"For once it's not raining. Let's walk someplace!"

"There's mud everywhere!"

"Don't get prim on me, Mercy Ann Levering. I couldn't stand it."

Merce laughed. "Where could we walk?"

"To St. Louis," said Molly. "We'll amble along the waterfront and meet riverboat gamblers who want to buy us dinner."

Merce laughed again. "We'll ruin our dresses. We'll sink to our knees in mud."

"Let's wear pantaloons!" offered Molly. "And workmen's caps. We'll pass ourselves off as men." Molly clapped her hands. "We'll smoke cigars."

"We're both too rounded to pass as men."

"Well, I have got to get out of this house." Molly made a face.

When they had donned their capes, bonnets and boots, hoisted their dresses up and ventured as far as the road winding past the Edwards house, they saw that, indeed, there was mud everywhere. "We can't do this," said Merce. "The mud is so deep we'll disappear."

"I am walking to the courthouse," announced Molly. "There are wood shingles in the basement. We'll get a stack of them and step from one to the other. We'll pick up the ones we've used and toss them in front of us until we get to the square."

"What'll we do there?" asked Merce.

"Go to the office of the *Sangamo Journal* and read newspapers from all over the state." Molly slapped her hands together in joy. "We'll tell Simeon Francis what we've done and he'll put us in the next issue of the *Journal*."

"My brother will send me back to Baltimore," said Merce.

"Nonsense. We'll be famous in town as the female Lewis and Clark. Men will call on us incessantly!"

Merce looked uncertain, but Molly turned and hurried back toward the house. She returned in a few minutes, carrying a stack of wood shingles so high that she could barely see over them. "Take some of these and start walking on them."

Merce took several shingles and laid them out before her. She stepped gingerly from one to the next, certain she would land in the mud. She squealed, then laughed. Finally she cried, "This is like hopscotch with moving squares. This'll be fun."

The two girls started out, Merce laying the shingles before them, Molly picking them up as they went.

At his office in Hoffman's Row on the courthouse square Lincoln lazed on a narrow lounge, reading the latest edition of the *Illinois State Register*, his legs stretched out before him, his feet resting on a hard wooden bench. Nearby his friend Jim Matheny sat on a chair containing a buffalo robe and thumbed through the first number of *The Old Soldier*, the Whig campaign paper. It had appeared several days before. Lincoln looked up from the *Register*. "How do you like *The Soldier*?" he asked.

Matheny nodded. "You edit this?"

"Edit some of it. Write some of it."

"I recognized a piece of yours," Matheny said. He held up a Whig circular that the central committee had sent around the state to rally support for William Henry Harrison, the party nominee for President. Even though the Whigs thought Andrew Jackson had pursued disastrous policies, they were trying to replicate the factors that had made him a popular President. Jackson's being a general was considered an undeniable ingredient and so the Whigs nominated a general. Harrison had defeated Tecumseh and the Shawnee Indians at the Battle of Tippecanoe thirty years before. Thirty years was, admittedly, a good while back. Jackson had popularized the West and, fortunately, Tippecanoe was in the West, western Indiana. "Old Hickory" had been the name affectionately assigned to Jackson, because hickory was tough, and so the Whigs were popularizing for Harrison the nickname "Old Tippecanoe." Jackson had launched an era of the common man, and although Harrison had grown up in Virginia, the son of a signer of the Declaration of Independence, Whigs portrayed him as a simple farmer who lived in a log cabin in western Ohio and drank cider from apples he grew himself. They denounced "Matty Van," Martin Van Buren, Jackson's successor as President, as an aristocrat who lived in splendor.

"Did you write this circular, too?" Matheny asked.

"The committee wrote it: Speed, Ned Baker, Anson Henry, me."

"I don't recognize the Lincoln style in it."

"*The Register* disagrees," Lincoln said. "They denounce the . . . Let's see . . ." His finger moved along the relevant column. "The secret circular of Messrs Baker, Lincoln & Company. Of us they say, 'They prefer darkness to light because their deeds are evil.' " Lincoln giggled joyfully, tossed the *Register* aside, unfolded his legs, rose and stretched.

He went to the window and looked into the courthouse square. Below him the square was empty. "Wicked out there," Lincoln observed. "You ever have mud fights as a boy? Soon as we have a real thaw it'll be a prime mud fight pitch out there."

"Where'd you grow up as a boy?" Matheny asked. Lincoln shrugged. Matheny watched him, amused. His friend talked little about his past. His reticence was not unusual. Men coming west often arrived in town, leaving their pasts behind and happy to keep them at bay. "Where?" Matheny repeated. "On a farm?"

Lincoln continued to watch out the window. "On farms here and there," he finally said. "Glad it's my mind working these days. And not my body." He turned back toward the room. "I better get back to it before I forget how."

Some time later, giggling while vigilantly maintaining her balance, Merce stooped slowly, carefully placing a shingle into mud as Molly bent over to—slurp!—retrieve another out of the muck. She held the rescued shingle well away from her body. The girls' labors met with success. They achieved the courthouse square with their boots, dresses and bonnets mainly unsullied.

"This is the longest it's ever taken me to walk down here," said Merce.

"You'll never forget this outing," Molly assured her. "You'll tell your grandchildren about it."

"If I ever get home." After a moment Merce asked, "How do we get home?"

"We'll ask when we get to the *Journal.* Simeon Francis has good ideas."

As the girls made their laborious way across the square, Molly glanced up at the office of Stuart and Lincoln. Was Lincoln there? Or in court somewhere? How would she ever get that man to kiss her? Jim Conkling kissed Merce. Douglas kissed her. But the kiss she wanted was the one that was withheld: Lincoln's.

Alone now in his office Lincoln stood at his desk, stretched and glanced out the window. He stooped toward the glass. A couple of ten- or twelve-year-old girls were crossing the square on shingles. Suddenly he laughed aloud, for they were not children. They were the town's most attractive young women. "Molly Todd! Molly Todd," he thought, "what are you doing?" He watched the young women until they disappeared from sight.

Lincoln began agitatedly to pace the office. He knew where the agitation would lead. No, he told himself, he would not appear suddenly at the *Journal*. What would Simeon Francis think? He had read papers there just yesterday. Still he could not forgo a chance to see Molly Todd at a place other than Ninian Edwards's house. He would figure out how to explain himself on the way to the *Journal* office. He slipped the gray shawl over his shoulders and locked his door.

Outside the *Journal* offices Lincoln found mud-encrusted shingles leaning against the building. When he entered, he saw Francis chatting with the two young ladies. They were warming themselves at the potbellied stove. Hearing the door open, Francis turned. "Lincoln!" he said. "What are you—" He caught himself in mid-question. He did not need to ask what Lincoln was doing. Attractive young ladies drew men to newspaper offices just as advertising drawings of young ladies drew readers to newspapers blessed with sufficient circulation to have advertisers.

"Mr. Lincoln!" exclaimed a voice Lincoln happily recognized. "You are not defending the innocent in court today?" Molly smiled at him. Merce Levering continued to warm herself at the fire.

"I come here sometimes to seek the wisdom of Simeon the Wise." Francis chuckled at this nonsense, knowing well enough what Lincoln came seeking.

"We came here to get warm," said Molly.

"Quite a day to be out. I saw two children from the office window." Lincoln grinned, teasing. "They were shingle-walking across the square."

"That was not children, Mr. Lincoln," said Merce Levering.

"That was us!" Molly proclaimed.

174

"The belles of Springfield," said Francis. "Shingle-walkers!"

Francis excused himself. He had a *Journal* to get out. Lincoln busied himself pretending to look through papers from around the state. The women whispered to one another, Merce murmuring she should leave and Molly insisting that she should do no such thing, taking her wrist to restrain her. "I'll pop into my brother's office," Merce announced. "It's just down the way. He'll be surprised to see me!" She pulled her arm out of Molly's grasp and went to the door. "Goodbye, Mr. Lincoln," she said over her shoulder as she disappeared.

"Did she flee because of me?" Lincoln asked.

"I expect she's gone to ask her brother for a ride home. It was my idea to go shingle-walking. I'm sure she'd rather ride back up the hill."

Alone with Molly, looking at her, Lincoln felt a strange elation, as if it were springtime inside him, even if it was winter outside. He kept wanting to grin. He confessed that he had recognized the girls and wanted to make sure they did not get swallowed up by mud. Molly, who kept wanting to grin herself, said she feared she might stumble into a pig wallow and disappear forever. "If you did, I would rescue you," Lincoln said.

"You'd reach your long arms right down into that wallow and pull me up, would you? My, how gallant!"

"I would," Lincoln assured her. He felt a blush rise on his cheeks, betrayed by sentiment he could not control. It was like being naked before her and he was sure she would tease him about it. Instead, she looked away, afraid he might go shy on her when they were talking so well. Lincoln recovered. He said he would write a poem called

"Childe Molly's Pilgrimage" even though he lacked Byron's knack for rhyming. Molly saw that he talked more easily away from Elizabeth's house. She wondered how she could "happen" to meet him here more often.

They chatted for a time, standing near the stove. A couple passed by on the wooden sidewalk. "Who's wearing a hat like that on a day like this?" Molly asked.

Lincoln went to the window. "Those sidewalks are slippery as goose grease, Miss Molly. Be careful when you start back." Molly joined him at the window, standing close beside him. They watched a man and a woman step carefully along the wooden planks. The woman was dressed as if central Springfield were central London, her large hat adorned with plumes that trembled behind her.

The couple hesitated at the edge of the sidewalk before venturing onto the muddy road. As the man reached for the woman's elbow, she slipped, her feet flying out from under her. She landed on her backside in the mud; her companion fell onto his stomach. "Oops!" gasped Lincoln. Molly began to laugh. She leaned against him and put her face into his sleeve to muffle the sound of her chortling.

Lincoln's arm tingled where her face pressed against him. He felt his heart beating faster and wondered if she could feel it. She continued to laugh.

Finally she pleaded, "You must never tell a soul what I've just done, Mr. Lincoln. Laughing at mud-splattered souls when we should have gone to help them." She tried to control her laughter.

"That lady reminds me of a duck," said Lincoln.

"A duck?"

"Feathers on her head. And down on her behind."

Molly let out another burst of merriment. She leaned again against Lincoln's sleeve. He placed an arm about her, patted her gently. "You have a disrespectful tongue, Mr. Lincoln," she chided. She was genuinely amused and strangely elated at the touch and strength of his arm, but also a little appalled at the backwoods witticism spoken in her presence. Now she blushed. She pulled away from Lincoln and playfully slapped his arm, in appreciation and in reprimand.

After a time they returned to the potbellied stove to receive its warmth. They spoke of Lincoln's cases, of the new Edwards baby and how its arrival had changed the patterns of work in the house. Finally Lincoln said, "I wish I had a carriage to take you back up the hill, Miss Molly. I could get a horse from the livery stable."

"Nonsense, Mr. Lincoln. I came out for a walk and I will walk!"

Lincoln stood awkwardly for a moment, gazing at her, as if wanting something more: a smile, the promise of another meeting, her head against his sleeve once more. "I should be getting back," he said. Molly wondered if he would kiss her. Douglas might kiss her in the *Sangamo Journal* office just to boast that he'd done it. But not Lincoln. "Goodbye," he said. He gazed at her affectionately and disappeared.

Outside Lincoln did not feel he needed the shawl around his shoulders. He whistled, hurrying back to the office.

Molly glanced at the *Journal's* collection of Illinois newspapers so that it did not appear that she had come to town merely to flirt. After a time she started back across the square alone, still walking on shingles. She picked one up—bwapp!—turned carefully, holding it well away from her body, and laid it down. She placed her foot onto it—ooze!— and was careful about transferring her weight. She wondered how long it would take her to reach home. She might not arrive till midnight. Ninian might call out a posse. Elizabeth would scold her.

Soon Molly heard the clop-slurp-clop-slurp of a horse behind her. Turning, she saw a horse-drawn dray approaching. Molly recognized the driver. He slowed the cart. "Afternoon, Miss Todd," he said. "I'd be honored to drive you home if you can stand riding on a dray."

"I would love a ride, Mr. Hart. I've had my fill of shingle-walking."

Hart helped Molly onto the dray. There were no sides to the cart, and as they started moving, she held onto Hart's shoulder. As they rode along, Molly knew that people gazed at them from their windows. She giggled and thought, "Let the gossips wonder if I've run off with Mr. Hart. This is better than 'down on my behind.' "

Lincoln paced back and forth across the office, reliving that fleeting moment when he might have kissed Molly Todd. Speed would have done it; he was a stealer of kisses. Lincoln thought maybe Molly wanted to be kissed, but how did a fellow ever know? What if he tried and she'd rebuffed him? If that happened, he'd want to jump into a mud wallow and let it swallow him up. Would he ever have the nerve to kiss her? And if he did, where would kisses lead? Might he fall in love with her? And feel what the poets sang about?

Although his arm still lightly tingled where she had put her face against it, he could not believe that the feelings the poets lauded were meant for him. And if by chance he did feel love for her, he could not imagine asking her to marry him. Him married to a Todd? Linked to the Edwards house on Quality Hill? Unthinkable. When his father had needed a helpmate in birthing a farm, a mother for two motherless children, and a cook, he went off to Kentucky. He did not go looking for high-flown feelings of rapture. He went to find a woman and he did: a woman he'd known long before. She needed a provider for her and her family, a father for her three fatherless children, and someone to settle her debts. He paid her debts and brought her to Indiana as his wife. Lincoln had loved his stepmother. But did his father love her? Had his arm ever tingled when she set her head against it? Probably not. Poetic love was for rich folks, not for them.

As winter hung on, Molly was glad that 1840 was an election year, for she was ready for changes in her life, for things to happen, for the ousting of President Martin Van Buren even if "Matty Van" lived a thousand miles away. Out shopping one morning with her sister, she began to hum a melody. "What is that you keep humming?" Fanny Wallace asked. "I hear that tune a lot."

Molly laughed. "You'll be hearing a lot more if it." She sang:

> What has caused this great commotion, motion,
>   motion,
> All the country through?
> It is the ball a-rolling on, on and on
> For Tippecanoe and Tyler, too.

"Is that a campaign song?"
"It is." Molly sang it again, prancing along the plank sidewalks of Courthouse Square, as if she

were dancing a Virginia reel, swaying to "motion, motion, motion."

"Have you become a dancing girl for the Whigs?"

Molly delighted in dismaying a sister determined to become a matron. She trilled a tune assailing Van Buren for aristocratic airs:

> Let Van from his coolers of silver drink wine
> And lounge on his cushioned settee.
> Our man on a buckeye bench can recline.
> Content on hard cider is he.

As Fanny took refuge in disapproval, Molly saw tall, heavy-set Simeon Francis standing outside the *Sangamo Journal* office and waved. He waved back, smiled and rotated his shoulders as if he were dancing, too.

"What would Miss Betsey say to your flouncing?" Fanny asked.

"I couldn't care less!" Molly declared. "Come dance with me," she urged. "I'll teach you the song."

"Molly, I'm a married woman." People passed the two Todd girls, men raising their hats, women smiling at Molly's exuberance. Fanny looked mortified at her sister's behavior. Molly laughed. "You can swish your skirts in the center of town as you please," Fanny said, "but please remember my delicate condition."

"Oh, Fanny! Honestly! Your 'delicate condition' is hardly observable."

"Well, I feel as big as a house. This may be my last outing until the blessed event occurs. There are standards I must observe."

"You are so proper I can hardly stand it." Molly sang another snatch of song. "'Van, Van is a used-up man.' I lullaby Elizabeth's babies with these songs."

She caught sight of Stephen Douglas across the way and assumed a demureness she did not feel. Since Douglas still called on her now and then, perhaps it was not necessary for this Prince of the Democrats to observe her chirping Whig campaign songs.

Douglas did not see her. Looking neither to the right nor left, he marched single-mindedly toward Simeon Francis. Though he had no need of it, he walked with a cane, slamming it into the wooden planks at every other pace.

Molly put her hand on Fanny's arm and stopped to watch the Little Giant. Carts and horsemen passed before them on the muddy street. Douglas strode off the sidewalk into the street. A hog wallowed before him; he gave it a solid whack with his cane. The hog squealed, but did not move. Douglas jumped onto the walkway and headed toward Francis. The editor watched him with an amused expression, his arms folded across his chest.

"Damn you, Francis!" Douglas shouted. "Enough of your scurrilous lies about me!" He lifted his cane and started toward Francis. When he reached him, Douglas began to pummel the taller, heavier man with the cane. Francis raised an arm to fend off the blows. He grabbed Douglas by the hair, pushed him into the street and against a wagon. A teamster jumped down beside the adversaries. With the help of others who ran into the street, the teamster managed to pull the two men apart. The shouting continued as they were separated.

"What in the world is that all about?" asked Fanny.

"It's an abomination what's printed in that *Journal*," answered a man standing nearby. Molly looked up and saw Jim Shields. He raised his hat. "Mrs. Wallace," he said, "Miss Todd." Then he continued, "A man's got a right to defend himself against slander. His reputation's his most valuable possession." He tipped his hat again and headed into the street to comfort Douglas.

Molly turned her back to the street and began to laugh. Fanny looked shocked. Molly covered her mouth with her hand and laughed harder. Fanny led her away. Once they left Courthouse Square, Fanny gave her sister a shake. "What are you laughing at?" she asked. "Grown men fighting in the streets! It's an outrage."

"But it's so comical!" Molly protested. "Like a Punch and Judy show in the town square. These men trade terrible insults in the papers all the time." She laughed again. "Douglas is a little tornado. He's got a lot more vinegar in him than sense."

Fanny said, "I am certainly glad Dr. Wallace is not in politics."

Later in the week Lincoln visited in the evening both to consult with Ninian, who was an important backer of the Whig party in Illinois, and to pay a call on Molly. When Lincoln handed him the latest copy of *The Old Soldier*, Ninian said, "Been a busy month for you, hasn't it?" He rolled his eyes. "For you fellers who prefer darkness because your deeds are evil."

"We're trying to organize the state," Lincoln said. Addressing Ninian, but speaking for Molly's benefit, he noted that he was both writing and editing *The Old Soldier*, making sure that it got distributed, helping to form Whig clubs and rally support for "Old Tippecanoe." Lincoln noted that he'd spoken at an all-day Whig meeting—"festival, they called it," he said—in Peoria, the first of one hundred or more speeches he'd give before election day.

"Are you organizing Whig glee clubs, Mr. Lincoln?" Molly asked.

"If we got one going in Springfield would you sing in it?"

"I would, sir, if you would."

"If I was singing, Miss Molly, you'd find an excuse to miss rehearsals."

"You are too modest, Mr. Lincoln."

"Modesty has nothing to do with it. Sometimes as a boy I'd go sing in the forest. Bears and skunks and wild turkeys, they'd all holler for me to stop."

"Who is writing these campaign songs?" Ninian asked. "Molly's teaching them to our Julia and I'm not sure they're the thing for a child's education." As Ninian was leaving, a copy of *The Old Soldier* in his hand, he remarked, "Molly saw the famous altercation in the courthouse square."

"Francis is writing it up for the *Journal*," Lincoln said. "He claims the cane was too heavy for so small a man as Douglas."

"*Old Hickory*, the Democratic rag," Molly said, "is calling Francis 'a compound of goose fat and sheep's wool.'"

"If you find out what that means, Molly," Ninian said as he departed, "let me know."

"You read *Old Hickory*, Miss Molly?" Lincoln asked.

"It's not nearly as well written as *The Soldier*," said Molly.

"Indeed, it's not," Lincoln agreed. He smiled.

The smile made Molly hope that Lincoln would linger. Perhaps they could regain the rapport they'd found in the *Sangamo Journal* office. But as he took a seat beside her on the settee, she could see him withdrawing into taciturnity. She realized that it was partly a matter of being in Ninian's house.

"I'm flattered that you spend a minute with me, Mr. Lincoln," she told him. "You must be the busiest man ever. Next to God, of course."

"Next to God. Gracious," said Lincoln.

She sat with her knees close to his knee and placed her hand within easy reach. "Will you really give a hundred speeches?"

"A good many more, I wouldn't be surprised."

"Goodness," said Molly. She gazed at him with admiration, smiled shyly and thought, My hand's just waiting there for you. Don't you see it?

"It tends to be the same speech over and over," said Lincoln.

"Do you come through the ceiling on any of these speeches?"

He chuckled and took her hand. He wrapped his fingers tenderly about it and felt a warmth he could carry with him when he left the house. He gazed at her. Would he kiss her? She leaned closer to encourage him. He looked back at her hand.

"We've talked about poetry," she said. "What about the poetry of the campaign?"

"I hadn't thought of campaigns being poetical. Just hard work."

"Van, Van, Van the used-up man. That's not poetry?"

Lincoln smiled.

Molly sang softly, "'Farewell, dear Van, You're not our man. To guide the ship, We'll try old Tip.' Will you sing with me, Mr. Lincoln?"

"You won't start caterwauling if I do?"

"Only in my mind," she said. "I've got more manners than bears and skunks and wild turkeys."

So they sang Whig campaign songs together, starting with:

> The times are bad and want curing
> They are getting past all enduring.
> So let's turn out Martin Van Buren
> And put in Old Tippecanoe.

In church the next Sunday Parson Dresser inveighed against liquor, laziness and licentiousness. He slapped the pulpit with the flat of his hand every paragraph or so, to keep Satan away from the church, and his parishioners attentive. Aware of their position in the congregation, Elizabeth and Ninian sat erect in the Edwards family pew. They listened devoutly. Molly knew that to uphold Todd family honor she must not nod off or even give Elizabeth some excuse to pinch her just above the knee. She detected the buzz of a fly and watched it circle in the dead air that carried the pungency of bodies that had foregone the weekly bath. She tasted the dryness of her throat; she wished for a cup of cold water in Christ's name. The cup's coldness against her wrist: that would keep her awake.

She appraised the congregation, the women with their bonneted heads, the men attempting to keep their shoulders thrown back as a way of staying awake. She noticed that the Jaynes were there, the Leverings and the Rodneys as well as a sprinkling of Todd relatives. Simeon and Eliza Francis were there. So was Stephen Douglas; Molly wondered if he had brought his cane. She pondered if it were comical or merely Christian that these two men, so lately adversaries, could worship the same God—but was He the same to them?—in the same place.

She did not see Lincoln in the congregation although Joshua Speed with whom he bunked was there. Perhaps Lincoln was Presbyterian, Methodist or Congregationalist. Perhaps he did not believe in God at all. Molly rejected that notion. Perhaps he was a freethinker and had developed personal notions of the Deity's being and activity. But surely he believed in God. Everyone in her circle believed in God, some truly, out of conviction, like Ninian and Elizabeth, others out of convention and social pressure. Which was she? Hmm.

She must ask Lincoln what he thought of God. Surely he would know how to answer, for no man who sought the endorsement of his fellows in the form of votes could confess to not being Christian. That was death at the polls.

Parson Dresser struck the pulpit with a daydream-breaking thud. Elizabeth pinched her. Molly gave her a defiant glance. She had not been nodding. Elizabeth pointed straight ahead with her index finger, cautioning that Molly must give her thoughts to liquor, laziness and licentiousness. Not to Lincoln.

When he returned to his home on the hill late on a Saturday afternoon in mid-March, Ninian Edwards was visibly upset. He handed his horse over to the stable hand without a word. Little Julia, now almost three, greeted him excitedly at the door. He left his hat and gloves on a table, lifted his daughter off her feet, saying, "Hello, my princess," gave her a perfunctory kiss on the cheek and handed the child to Molly, who with Elizabeth had just arrived to greet him.

"How was the convention?" Molly asked.

Ignoring his sister-in-law, Ninian told his wife, "I need to speak with you." He hurried upstairs. Elizabeth glanced at Molly with a baffled expression, whispered, "See to Julia, could you, please?" and obediently followed her husband upstairs.

"What's wrong with Daddy?" Julia asked.

"Nothing, darling," her aunt assured her. "He's just had a long day, that's all." The Whigs held their first statewide convention that day, allowing delegates to nominate candidates, something that previously had been done by the three-man Springfield junto. Something had happened to displease Ninian.

Molly took Julia upstairs to the nursery where she could look in on Baby Bertie. There they played with Julia's blocks. The child was learning her letters from them.

After a time Elizabeth entered, a look of strain on her face. She tiptoed to the crib to peek at the baby, leaned over to kiss her daughter's head and signaled to Molly. "Where you going?" asked Julia.

"Aunt Molly and I are just going to talk a minute in the hall."

"Is Daddy all right?"

"Of course, darling." Molly could hear Elizabeth trying to keep tension out of her voice. The child heard it, too, and looked up. "We'll talk and I'll come back in just a minute to nurse Baby."

Out in the hall Elizabeth said, "The Whigs went crazy at their convention. The junto's lost control of things." She paused for a moment, then blurted, "Ninian's lost his seat in the Legislature. The Whigs did not renominate him."

Molly looked dumbfounded. Ninian's father had been Governor before statehood and both Governor and United States Senator afterwards. Ninian had been a legislator for years. He brought valuable continuity of experience to the House.

"Can you imagine?" said Elizabeth. "Passing him over? The effrontery!"

"How does he feel?"

"Insulted, of course. How else could he feel?" Elizabeth's hands were knotted into fists. "His pride's been deeply wounded. And justifiably. When I think of the service he and his family have given this state."

"How is this possible?" Molly asked. But she knew well enough how it was possible. Ninian was an aristocrat. That he considered himself superior to other men, a moneyed patrician, he made evident by everything about him: the clothes he wore, the way he walked, the look in his eye, the words he used, the people he chose to associate with. But the people entering Illinois on foot or in wagons or on flatboats were not patricians; they would not vote for people who considered themselves their betters. The Founding Fathers had expected people like Ninian to play a special role in guiding the country, some of them anyway, but the country was fifty years old, and the common men who voted now wanted to choose people like themselves.

"He's a proud man as well he ought to be and he feels humiliated." Elizabeth shook her head and bit her lower lip. "Oh, how could they? He's the most distinguished man in the whole state, the leader of Sangamon society." She began to cry. Molly put her arms about her to comfort her. But Elizabeth was patrician, too, and not one to allow herself to show weakness. She pulled away, wiped the tears from her eyes and stood erect.

"Would you mind staying with the children during dinner?"

"Of course not," said Molly. She felt a little degraded by this request, but on this evening she did not look forward to the ceremony of dinner with Ninian.

"He's too mortified," Elizabeth said, "too embarrassed, to face anyone but me. He'll be all right tomorrow, but—"

"The two of you be together," Molly said. "That's fine."

Molly and Julia had dinner in the kitchen with the cook from County Mayo and the serving girl from County Cork. Afterwards the serving girl came to the nursery to announce, "Mr. Lincoln's come, he has, to see Mr. Edwards. I thought you'd be wanting to know, Miss."

Molly stood. "Thank you. Would you mind staying a spell with Julia?"

Molly got a cloak, descended by the back stairs and hurried along the back corridor to the entry hall. She slipped out the front door and waited against the walls of the house where there was no breeze. In the brisk evening air she gathered the cloak about her.

Finally Lincoln stood in the doorway. He shook hands with Ninian and started into the darkness. The door closed. "Mr. Lincoln," Molly whispered.

"Molly?" he asked. "Miss Molly?"

"Over here."

He came to her and there was just enough light from the house for them to distinguish the outlines of their faces. "You must be frozen." He reached out to her, with more familiarity than usual, took her by the shoulders and chafed her arms. "That better? It's nice to see you."

"I heard what happened to Ninian," she said. "But are you all right? You've been renominated, haven't you?"

"Baker and me, both," he said. "We're debating Douglas next Wednesday in Jacksonville. They couldn't very well toss us out without compromising the ticket."

"They toss you out, they'll lose the election."

"May lose it anyway." He took her hands in his. She stepped closer. "This is nice, seeing you here."

"You can hardly see me, Mr. Lincoln," she teased. "Is that why it's nice?"

He dropped her hands, and she thought she'd overreached with such a shy man, teasing him. Gently his large hands with their enormous fingers slid onto either side of her face. At the tenderness of his touch she thought she might swoon. He kissed her.

"Finally," she said. She thought, Why did I go and say that?

"That's why it's nice," he said.

"You're bold in the darkness." She thought, Again!

He laughed softly. "Can we meet here more often?" He took her hands again.

"Can you come inside and sit a spell?"

"Another number of *The Old Soldier* is supposed to be out Monday. I have to write up what happened today and look over the rest."

They looked at each other through the darkness.

"I'll call on you in the next few days."

"Yes, do. Before Jacksonville."

He opened his hands to release hers, but she held on. "Kiss me again," she said. "If you can find me."

"I can find you," he said. He kissed her, his long arms about her, holding her to him. He moved off, feeling elated, as if he could jump over the trees in the yard.

Molly watched him disappear into the darkness, then slipped back inside the house. She heard Ninian and Elizabeth in the parlor. She tiptoed through the door into the back hall. She ascended the back *stairs*, hardly breathing, tossed the cloak into her room and returned to the nursery. "Thank you," she said to the serving girl. "Everything all right here?"

"Yes, Miss," said the girl. "And with you?"

"Fine, thank you," Molly replied, hoping that her voice did not betray the pounding of her heart.

CHAPTER

10

Spring came. Breezes brushed by softly and tasted as sweet as nectar. The days grew longer. Birdsong welcomed the dawn and sun warmed the land. Rain beat down on disheartened, yellow-brown remnants of grass and turned the prairies green. Dogwood and redbud burst into bloom— along with Johnny-jump-ups, purple coneflowers and lamb tongues, bluebells, black-eyed Susans and pink and white cornflowers. Gooseberries hung in clusters. Oaks and ashes and maples began to leaf. Squirrels played in the trees. Lilacs perfumed the evenings while buzzing insects— bees and flies, mosquitoes and June bugs—gave them sound.

Politics swept across the land, sweet as the scent of blossoms if it seemed intriguing, as undeniable as a swarm of locusts if it seemed a plague. For Whigs the spring was a season of joy. They felt themselves riding a wave of public approval. Whig associations sprouted across the state. Whig singing clubs sang campaign songs; barbershop quartets rendered them in four-part harmony. The public grabbed up copies of *The Old Soldier*. They snapped up copies of *Old Hickory*, too, for how else could they argue the merits of issues and candidates? Men argued about them at stables and mercantile establishments, in fields, outside courthouses and inside taverns.

Not four more years of Van Buren! the Whigs contended. Matty Van was a New York Tammany ward heeler who'd become a plutocrat on entering the White House. He was no friend of the Western man. He courted economic disaster, played havoc by reducing tariffs. Hadn't he opposed western internal improvements? And the Cumberland Road, the Illinois and Michigan Canal grant and the reduction of the price of public lands? Not Van Buren! Whigs went about singing, "Van, Van, Van, the used-up man." He must be turned out of office.

Not Harrison! cried the Democrats. That old codger, that coot. The Battle of Tippecanoe had happened ages ago, before the War of 1812. Harrison's men had faced hungry Indians armed with tomahawks, not the sort of British regulars that the Democrats' hero Andy Jackson had defeated at New Orleans. Harrison was too old to campaign, said the Democrats. His operatives kept him caged in a log cabin in a tiny Ohio town— "You ever heard of North Bend?"—where a committee of Whigs spoke and thought for him. If people claimed that his running mate, the slave-owning Virginian John Tyler, wasn't even a Whig, Whigs would snort derisively and sing out loudly the chorus of a song that ended:

> And we'll vote for Tyler therefore,
> Without a why or wherefore.

Whigs were delighted to have their opponents portray their candidate as a mere man of the people. That's what he was! And, no, Old Tippecanoe was not, definitely not, in a cage. He spoke and thought for himself. And, yes, he did live on a farm in a simple log cabin. He did not drink fine wines, like Matty Van, or dream of becoming king. No, Harrison drank hard cider and wore a coonskin hat. Whig clubs began to construct log cabins in honor of their standard bearer. Whigs drank hard cider, at work and at play, at Whig club meetings and glee club concerts, and quite a few of them began to wear coonskin hats.

But the campaigning was not exclusively about presidential office. There were local issues to discuss as well as local candidates to assess. Weekly small-town papers covered local political debates like sporting events. This was one of the ways Molly Todd kept up with the doings of her friend Abraham Lincoln. She read accounts of him in papers at the Whig *Sangamo Journal,* where editor Simeon Francis was a friend or, with less feeling of ease, at the Democratic *Illinois State Register,* where she passed herself off as an admirer of Douglas and Shields.

When Lincoln called on her between out-of-town rambles, she learned little. "Doesn't it anger you, the things they say about you?" she asked. "Stephen Douglas went after Simeon Francis with a cane. I saw him do it." Lincoln just shrugged. She grabbed a paper she had put on the table beside the settee. "Look here!" she exclaimed. "The *Register* calls you 'clownish'! Here it says,"—she read the passage to him—"that you 'left the stump literally whipped off it!' And by Douglas, which is preposterous."

Lincoln only laughed. "That's the way the game is played," he explained. "Maybe that's why it's not generally a game for ladies."

Molly fumed.

"I've written some pretty nasty things about fellers myself," he told her. "Usually I do it anonymously. Everybody understands it's just wrestling with words. If you get thrown, you get right back up, ready to throw the other feller."

If getting Mr. Lincoln to talk in a social setting was a challenge, he could certainly talk on the stump! When he got going, he was easily good for two hours. He traveled to Belleville for a Whig rally, speaking with nine other orators. Reading the *Missouri Republican,* which termed his speech "lucid, forcible and effective," Molly recognized that description as befitting her friend. But when the Belleville *Advocate* reported the same speech as "weak, puerile and feeble" and said, "Poor Lincoln!," she wondered if the reporter—who might be a stableboy for all she knew—had mixed up the names of the orators. After a Whig rally in Carlinville the Democratic *Register* labeled Lincoln "the lion of the tribe of Sangamon" and added "and judging from outward appearance, originally from Liberia." The enormity of this insult infuriated Molly. How dare some farm-town editor allow her friend to be slandered in this fashion, even if it was just "wrestling with words"? She had to march for an hour in the country to walk off the sting of that insult. When the Quincy *Whig* reported that Lincoln was "going it with a perfect rush in some of the interior counties," she grinned with pleasure. When it continued, "Thus far the Dems have not been able to start a man that can hold a candle to him in political debate. All their crag nags have come off the field crippled or broken down," she burst out laughing and clapped her hands. She went home to the piano, played Whig songs, taught them to Julia and sang them at the top of her voice.

Lincoln's friend Billy Herndon got married in late March. Molly did not attend the wedding, but Lincoln reported to her that Billy whistled a lot around Speed's store these days so the marriage must be well launched. He just wondered how long the whistling would continue. "Billy's got less money than a beggar," Lincoln said, "and no woman's happy when poverty sets in."

"If you're in love," replied Molly, "better to be poor than apart."

Lincoln looked at her askance. "Living on love," he said, "that's meager rations."

"In a marriage the important thing is love," Molly declared.

Lincoln did not reply. They were strolling through a meadow dotted with bloodroot and wild prairie rose, the sun warm on their backs, the air silent except for the occasional call of a lark. Molly picked a pink-magenta rose and smelled its sweetness. She held it out to him. He took it, touching her hand, scented it and put it behind his ear.

After they walked a bit farther, Molly said, "I was at a tea party with a group of ladies. Late last fall. A young woman was there, the wife of a much older man, a widower. Someone asked what had attracted her to her husband and she said, 'Gold and houses.'"

Lincoln laughed. "That was frank." He pulled the prairie rose from behind his ear and tossed it away.

"I was appalled," Molly said. She stood erect, full of righteous indignation. Lincoln suppressed a smile. "That woman was no better off than Mammy and Chaney in my father's house. She was a comfortable slave owned by a man she didn't love."

"Do they fight, I wonder?" Lincoln asked. "And can love last if you're poor?" They walked on a bit farther, Lincoln kicking at dirt clods. Finally he said, "I'm afraid that marriage yokes you together like oxen, and all your lives you drag your burdens behind you." He shrugged. "Unless your burden's yoked beside you."

Molly did not like the sound of this. "Are wild strawberries out yet?" she asked. "Let's see if we can find some."

Douglas also called now and then. He was even busier than Lincoln, he assured Molly, canvassing and debating for the Democrats, trying to solidify the vote of the Irish canal diggers. He mentioned that he and Lincoln had joined forces to defend a man accused of murder in Clinton. Lincoln had not so much as mentioned the case to Molly. "Did he do it?" she asked.

"I doubt it," said Douglas. "Lincoln's no good if he knows a client's guilty."

"Did Lincoln get him acquitted?"

"We both did," Douglas emphasized. "We were co-counsel. Lincoln actually argued the case, but I did my share." Douglas preened a bit. "I got quite a good fee for my work: $200. Got it before the trial. If you lose a murder case and you haven't gotten paid, you're not likely to collect your fee." Douglas clapped his hands and laughed. "Lincoln took a ninety-day note from the client. He'll have trouble collecting."

Molly smiled to flatter Douglas's self-assurance, but it irritated her that he always had to be smarter than the other fellow. In this case it sounded as if Lincoln's argument had brought about the acquittal. Lincoln's heart was as wide as the stretch of his arms, she thought. Douglas's was hardly a hand's breadth.

The next time Lincoln called, she asked about the case. Lincoln shrugged as if he could hardly remember the details. "Will you get your fee?" she asked. "Douglas got his before the trial took place."

"Douglas was thinking about the fee. I was thinking about the case." Lincoln said he reckoned the man would settle the fee when he had the money to pay. If he didn't, Lincoln could always sue for it.

"If a man's going to get ahead in this world," Molly told him, "he needs to think about his fees."

Lincoln smiled and said nothing. Molly wondered if he would ever marry. If he would marry her. At this moment she felt certain that would never happen. A bachelor could be casual about his fees, not a married man.

As the campaign dominated Springfield's thoughts, its conversation and calendar, Molly was at a loss to know what to think of it. As entertainment and a source of gossip she enjoyed it. She felt a fascination in watching politicians engage one another, the way she supposed athletes did in the sometimes violent sports—wrestling and pugilism—each feeling out his opponent's style, studying his approach and tactics, looking for his weak points.

Douglas sought to win debates through aggressiveness, through force of will and personality. His carriage bespoke solidity. His voice, low, loud, strong, hammered home his message. To win, Lincoln relied on anecdote and commonplace speech, sometimes on mimicry and ridicule. His gangly carriage, his extra-long limbs, his ready laughter, high-pitched voice and storyteller's skill all made the anecdotes work. Lincoln was not above stooping to trickery, to playing the former village boy who, retaining village boy mischievousness, could prick the pretensions of opponents.

Molly had heard of Lincoln's contest with Colonel Dick Taylor. No audience missed the contrast between them. On one hand there was the speaker from the party deemed to represent the business elite, the Whig party, a lanky young man with gray eyes and unruly black hair, without claim to military title, who told funny stories and presented himself as the common man embodied. On the other hand, from the party of the toiler, the Democracy, came a colonel wearing his worldly success—fine clothes and other adornments—offering himself as the people's friend, denouncing the lordly manners and aristocratic pretensions of the Whigs. Hearing this twaddle, Lincoln had finally had enough. Sidling beside the speechifying colonel on one occasion, he reached over, grasped the lower edge of his vest and tugged it open. Out popped a ruffled shirtfront, a watch chain with a gold watch, seals and jewels. The Colonel looked aghast. The audience roared with laughter.

Molly knew what Lincoln had said when the laughter subsided: "While Colonel Taylor was making these charges against Whigs, as he rode in fine carriages, wearing kid gloves and flourishing a gold-headed cane, I was a poor boy, hired on a flatboat at eight dollars a month. I had only one pair of buckskin breeches. Now when buckskin gets wet and the sun dries it, it shrinks. And my breeches kept shrinking. Whilst I was growing taller, they were growing shorter and tighter." Molly imagined Lincoln's voice getting higher and more strangled as he built to "If you call this aristocracy, I plead guilty to the charge."

This was all great fun, especially when your friend was racking up victories. But when it came to substance . . . Was there substance in the campaign? Douglas bemoaned the lack of ideas; the Whigs, he said, offered only circuses. Molly suspected he would have presented circuses if he had thought of them. Ninian complained that the Whigs had become a party of pandemonium. Reason had fled from political discourse; madness ruled. Of course, Ninian was still nursing the wound of the party's failure to nominate him for the Legislature. When Molly asked Lincoln about substance, he only grinned and cocked an eyebrow. "Unmasking Dick Taylor," he said, "you don't think that's about ideas?"

"But are you talking issues?" she persisted.

"You think I can talk for two hours and never mention an issue? I'm not a hound chasing its tail." He shrugged. "I'm not partial to circuses, but we've got to fight the devil with the devil's fire. We must beat the Democrats or the country will go to ruin."

The first week in June the Whig circus came to Springfield. Delegations poured in from all over Illinois for the Young Men's Whig Convention. They arrived on foot, on horseback, in wagons and carriages. They came from every direction, those from as far away as Chicago walking for three weeks beside teams of oxen. The oxen came—fifteen yoke, twenty-five yoke, thirty yoke—pulling log cabins erected on wheels, complete with raccoons, coonskin hats and kegs of hard cider. They came singing songs—"Without a why or a wherefore/We'll go for Harrison therefore"—with banners flying, with singing clubs and barbershop groups, with fiddlers and Jews harpists, washboard players and saw players. They came by the thousands. They camped wherever they could. Their fires lit up the night sky. Molly could smell their woodsmoke when she brushed her hair at the window before she went to bed.

Molly joined friends for the procession the next day. First came soldiers of the Revolution, most walking slowly, even infirmly. Spectators applauded service rendered to a nation in its birth pangs more than sixty years before. Next, veterans of the War of 1812 paraded past, followed by Whig delegations from nearby states: Iowa, Missouri, Indiana. After these marched delegations from fifty-nine Illinois counties. Cook County's delegation had a band and a brig thirty feet long.

The next day, barbecue. And speeches by some of the best orators in the land: a son of the great Daniel Webster, and local men as well, Ned Baker and John Hardin. They assailed Matty Van and hailed Harrison—as a fighter for the toilers, as a plain man who could ride, shoot and look danger in the eye. Abraham Lincoln spoke to the crowd, standing at the back of a wagon. Molly saw him for a moment after his speech, her eyes sparkling with pride. She told him his speech was the best one of them all.

Molly began to frequent the offices of the *Sangamo Journal*. They served as an informal Whig club. She read newspapers from around Illinois, heard the Tippecanoe Singing Club in concert and happened often to see Abraham Lincoln there. She told him that, come July, she was off to visit relatives in Missouri. He told her he would miss seeing her around town.

Before she left, he called more often at the house on the hill. He and Molly would sit together on the black horsehair settee and talk about poetry and politics. If Elizabeth was not moving around the halls or Ninian did not join them to inquire how things were going with the Whigs, Lincoln would take her hand. And when they parted, he would bend his long frame down to kiss her.

Lincoln stood on the back of a wagon, told stories and touched on the points he always made when speechifying. Watching his friend's performance, Bill Butler worriedly stroked his chin. The men who stood below the wagon responded without enthusiasm to Lincoln's stories; they seemed less persuaded than usual by his arguments. Butler had a hunch he knew what the problem was. When Lincoln jumped down from the wagon, Butler pulled him aside. "How's it feel up there?" he asked.

Lincoln shook his head. "This used to be fun." Formerly he would feel that he held an audience in the palm of his hand. He could make them laugh; he could convince them of the correctness of his side of the issues.

"What's gone wrong?" Butler asked. "The longer you're at this sort of thing the better you ought to get."

Lincoln knew Butler well enough to know that he had hunches he wanted to share. "What do you think it is?"

Well, Butler admitted, he was no politico. But it seemed to him the electorate was changing. More settlers were arriving every month. They were the kind of voters the Democrats appealed to, men of the earth, hardscrabble men struggling to make good on the bargain that had brought them to Illinois, that hard work and a little luck would assure a better life for them and their families. They were men with no patience for pretensions.

"Those are my kind of people," Lincoln assured his friend.

"Are they?"

"What do you mean? You know they are."

"This is a small town," Butler said. Folks knew that Lincoln had fought in the Black Hawk War, that he'd learned the law not at a university like some men, but by teaching himself, keeping observant eyes open, studying human behavior and reading law books. They knew he bunked in the loft above Speed's store. They knew he took his meals with the Butlers. "What else do you suppose they know?" Butler asked.

"What're you getting at?" But Lincoln knew well enough. Voters did not like Ninian Edwards. Despite his experience there, the Whig Convention had rejected him as a candidate for the Legislature. No ruffle-shirt candidates for them! Edwards lived in a big house on the hill, kept servants and carriages, owned tracts of land that were gaining in value every day. Lincoln did not claim Ninian Edwards as a friend; Edwards certainly did not claim him as one. Still, people knew that he visited Edwards's house every week. They did not see him walking with girls like Sarah Rickard, who were of the people. Neither did they see him walking with Molly Todd, but they knew he walked with her. Since he called on her so regularly—he tall, struggling and self-taught, she small and attractive, well-educated and from wealth—they figured he must have aspirations to advance himself through connections, to join Edwards's family, to turn his back on his background and be different from ordinary folks. He must have pretensions.

Butler did not blame the young man for being attracted to Molly Todd. If not as beautiful as some, she was bright and intelligent, merry and

204

lighthearted. "Shall I spell it out for you?" he asked.

"No need."

"Are you hoping to be one of them? That's what voters want to know."

"I'm as much like them as the man in the moon."

Butler half laughed at the obviousness of this. "They know that."

"Spill it out. What're you getting at?"

Butler looked off at nothing and shuffled his feet. "I feel real awkward sticking my nose in your business."

"Well, you've done it. So what's on your mind?"

"The voters are going to punish you for what they think."

Lincoln told himself he did not care what voters thought. He liked the girl and he would not stop seeing her to win elections. Still . . . the political arena was a place he could achieve distinction. Like any normally ambitious man who came from nothing, he wanted opportunities for distinction. There were not many avenues open to him for that.

"Let me tell you what I think," Butler said. "This idea keeps hounding me. You marry Sarah. In another year she'll make you a fine wife. She's just people. She'll work hard for you, give you children, do anything you ask." Lincoln said nothing. Butler wished the ground would open so he could disappear.

"Sarah wouldn't have me. She knows me too well."

In frustration Butler blurted out, "Don't think you can marry Molly Todd."

Lincoln was not sure he had ever thought he could. But if that was the case, why did he keep calling on her? He looked blankly at Butler.

"Ninian Edwards will never let you marry her," he said. "Neither will Elizabeth. They're too high and mighty for us." He took hold of Lincoln's arm and stared him in the eye. "I hate myself for interfering. But Ninian Edwards won't let that happen. If Molly should agree, you'll rue the day you have to ask him for his blessing. 'Cause he won't give it." Still glaring at Lincoln, Butler said, "Voters want a man who understands how things are. They'll punish you for wanting something you can't have and not knowing you can't have it." Butler threw up his hands in self-disgust and walked away. Lincoln caught up with him. "Forgive me," Butler said.

"What should I do?" Lincoln asked.

"I hate myself for—"

"Stop hating yourself. Spit it out."

"Stop seeing her. Make up your mind to marry Sarah or some other girl off the hill. There are hundreds who'd be happy to accept you."

Lincoln laughed at the foolishness of this. "You looked at me lately? I'm no Beau Brummel."

"Promise them you'll get better looking as you grow older."

"Well, I haven't so far."

"Tell them you're Beau Brummel in the dark." Lincoln laughed heartily at this, the sound of his laughter churning in his body, ascending his long throat and spilling into the air with merriment. If a fellow was ugly, it was better to laugh about it than hide.

If Lincoln was chortling, Butler thought, maybe he would listen to him. "The campaign has got you soul and body just now," he said. "So now's the time to break with the Hill. You campaign as a man of the people." Lincoln had stopped laughing and was listening. "Show folks you are one. You'll have forgotten her in a month." Lincoln shrugged; he was not at all sure about that. Butler said, "Any man who hasn't slept with the woman ought to be able to get over her in a month."

Molly knelt on the hard wood of the floor, taking folded garments from the bed and placing them into the trunk that would accompany her to Missouri. The house was quiet. Lincoln had paid a final call before she left; he had seemed preoccupied about the campaign. She wondered if they would still see each other when she returned. If there was a time to break things off, this was it.

Candles lit the room and the interior of the trunk. A breeze stirred the curtains at the window, carrying with it the scent of lilacs. Molly heard a step outside her door, then Elizabeth's light tap on it. The door opened. Carrying a taper, Elizabeth slipped into the room, smiling maternally, and sat on the edge of the bed. She gazed at the chemises, petticoats and corsets and smoothed the folds on some. When in the glow of the candlelight she felt a sisterly warmth, she ventured, "You know it's possible you'll meet a man you're taken with in Missouri." She gazed out the window where dreams of romance lay. "A doctor, a lawyer, a banker. There are as many men seeking their fortunes in Columbia as there are here in Springfield."

Molly sat back on her ankles, wishing the packing were accomplished. "Dear sister, you talk as if I were going off prospecting for marriageable beaux." She took several chemises and ordered them in the trunk.

"I just want you to be aware of opportunities that may arise. If Cupid shoots his bow at you, don't be surprised."

A candle sputtered. Molly continued her packing without replying.

"You're at an age when these things happen."

Molly wanted to say, "You mean I'm at an age when if these things don't happen soon, people will think me an old maid." But she held her tongue, leaning against the leather that covered the pine base of the trunk and felt the metal at its edge press against her waist.

"You're the most attractive young woman in six counties," her sister told her, using the crisp tones that reminded Molly of Miss Betsey. "You come from the best people. You're a superb dancer, a brilliant conversationalist with an infectious laugh."

"I'm a stubby pineknot," Molly said, still leaning over the trunk.

"Nonsense. You're an ornament in any society." Elizabeth smiled as Miss Betsey might have if she wanted her out of the house.

"Dear Elizabeth," Molly replied, facing her finally through the candlelight, "you know I know how this game is played. I have no objections to falling in love. Truly falling in love." She pulled herself to her feet and stretched, feeling the pleasant sensation of muscles extending themselves.

"Sometimes a woman makes an advantageous match and only afterwards falls in love with the man she's married." Molly rotated her back and gazed through the half-light at Elizabeth, contentedly imparting life lessons. "In the best of circumstances most of us don't know the men we marry very well. Only later—"

"Only later is too late for me, especially in a slave state." Molly refolded a corset, feeling the stiffness of the stays and catching a slight scent of the powder she'd used when she'd last worn it. "But I'll keep my eyes open in Missouri."

"Good," Elizabeth said. "I know you'll have a good time." She gave a mischievous laugh and added, "I won't say 'Happy hunting!' "

Molly was not amused, but she smiled. Elizabeth rose and went to the door. Before opening it, she turned back, as if a thought had just crossed her mind. "Your political friend Mr. Lincoln calls rather frequently." An index finger rode her chin, a gesture of her thoughtfulness. "Is it wise to encourage his calls?"

"I'll be gone for several weeks." Molly touched her chin, mimicking Elizabeth's gesture. "That's hardly encouragement."

Elizabeth disregarded the mimicry; probably she was unaware of it. "Lincoln has a way of getting what he wants," she said. "A canny operator. He's very shrewd behind that hayseed exterior."

"Fine political instincts make him interesting," Molly replied. She took the rest of the clothes and placed them in the trunk; she would arrange them in the morning. "But he's inexperienced with women. Vulnerable, too. He's done nothing to make me think he has intentions toward me."

"No? He does call." Molly leaned over the trunk, keeping her back toward Elizabeth. "Lincoln is in his thirties," her sister said. "He's undoubtedly thinking of marriage." Molly did not reply. The breeze stirred. The candles fluttered. Silence, pregnant with import, reverberated in the room. "Look at me," Elizabeth said. Molly turned to gaze at her with an expression of defiance. "No!" Elizabeth cried. "You can't be thinking that! Not with him!" Then she became Miss Betsey. "Be careful. Don't be so unwise as to send signals he may mis-interpret."

"My dear sister," Molly said, trying to hold her sharp and witty tongue in check, to suppress all traces of annoyance from her voice, "Lincoln is so reticent with women that I—"

"Even the reticent overcome their shyness," observed Elizabeth.

"Lincoln has no intentions. He's a friend, not a beau."

"They are all beaux—until you marry."

The sisters regarded one another across the stillness that was now so different from the quiet Molly had enjoyed before her sister entered. She wondered if Ninian had sent Elizabeth to warn her off Lincoln. Or was it a message she wanted to convey herself? No longer able to control her tongue, Molly said, "Don't be too sure I'd object to having the man ask for my hand."

"But," Elizabeth objected, "you've said yourself that you'd have to love the man you marry. And—" She began to laugh. Molly found herself extremely annoyed at this. Elizabeth exclaimed, "Sister, you can't! " She laughed even harder, then controlled herself. "If the poor man screwed up his courage to ask you, think what your refusal would do to him. A man as awkward as him. You just called him vulnerable." Elizabeth approached, took Molly's warm hands in her cold ones and looked into her eyes. "Let him find someone of the same background. There must be women of humble background for whom he'd be perfection."

"Shall I introduce him to your Irish servant girls?" Molly asked, letting her irritation show. "No, I think I'll let you do that, Elizabeth." Though rebuffed, Elizabeth still held Molly's hands. "Don't worry," Molly said, tired now of advice and solicitude, but aware yet again that she was a guest in her sister's home. "I'm going away. He's making speeches all over Illinois. Fathers will trot out their daughters for him to inspect." She glanced about the room that seemed just now like a prison. She sat on the bed. "The truth is I have decided to let this separation put an end to it."

"Really?" Molly wished Elizabeth did not look so gleeful.

"Yes. An end to whatever it is." Truth to tell, she did not know what it was. Not a friendship because men and women did not really have friendships across gender boundaries. And yet with their similar interests in politics and poetry, what was it if not friendship? Not a courtship because . . . well, Lincoln did not know how to court a woman. Despite the nobility she sensed in him, the people he came from did not court the way members of the Coterie did.

"Will you write him a note?"

"No." Molly stared across the room, seeing nothing. "If it hasn't been a courtship—"

"What else can it have been?"

Molly wondered how long she could stay in this prison house. Elizabeth had such limited notions of what was possible. "If it wasn't," Molly said, "I don't want to presume that it was. If it was a courtship, I don't want to hurt him."

"No, don't. As you say, he might be quite vulnerable."

If it was a courtship, Molly thought, Lincoln had to let her know. She didn't think he ever would. He had taken great risks, she could sense that, to move from where he'd come from to where he was now. She did admire him. But if his background had not taught him how to make known his intentions, hers had not taught her how to make the moves that were his to make. She knew how to flirt, but she had no intention of mischievously inquiring, "Do you intend to marry me?" Giggle, giggle. "It just occurred to me you might." Other flirts might do that, but not her. She would not throw herself at a man, even a man she might love.

"I will be gone more than a month," Molly reminded Elizabeth. "He has plenty to do and will forget about me." She hoped that this was not the case, but would let Elizabeth think it was. "I will try to fall in love in Missouri." She did not explain the compelling reason for this: that while there were advantages to being connected to the Edwards family of Springfield, there might be even greater advantages to being connected at a distance. "When I come back, even if I have not managed to find an attachment in Missouri, if Mr. Lincoln calls, you can tell him that I'm resting. Or not at home. Or busy with the children. The man is perceptive. Soon enough he will understand."

Elizabeth looked approving of the rupture, but not of the way Molly intended to effect it. "Write him a note," she advised. "That's the kinder way."

After Elizabeth left the room, Molly sat on the bed for a long time, feeling sad. Finally she rose and went to her table. She took a piece of stationery and a pen and began to write: "Dear Mr. Lincoln, Tomorrow I go to Missouri. I know not when to return." Ordinarily when she wrote to friends the words almost ran ahead of her pen, leaving her hardly any time to mark a period. Not now. Her thoughts were coming slowly. What capital letter to form now? "While I am gone," she wrote and paused and continued, "you will travel this state giving speeches. Perhaps this separation will afford us time to—" She paused again. To what? She dipped her pen in the ink well.

She wrote the word "consider—" Consider what? She made herself continue: "not only the fate of the country, but also our own. Fate is something we do not control ourselves—" She wondered if she believed this. The whole idea of America was founded on the notion that people could determine their own fates. Lincoln seemed to embody that notion. "At least we do not control it if we are women," she wrote. "In Missouri I will come to terms with the hand that Fate has dealt me and which I must play." She would not be more obvious than that. She read over what she had written and finally continued: "Dear Friend, I'm sure you understand what I mean. You must know that I wish things were different. But I have been told since earliest childhood never to forget that I am a Todd. I have at last resigned myself to being what I am." She stopped writing. Tears obscured the sight of her words. She continued, "Please know that I will always think of you with warmest affection."

For a long moment she stared pensively across the room. She reread the note, stared again. At last she folded the note and slipped it into an envelope. She addressed it. Tomorrow she would give it to Elizabeth to see that it was delivered.

CHAPTER

11

When Molly visited the Missouri branch of the Todd family in Columbia, she was introduced to men seeking a wife; men who might interest her were paraded before her. She did not fall in love. To her surprise, however, she spent more time than she would have expected contemplating Elizabeth's advice. She enjoyed Missouri. The Columbia Todds were most hospitable, and if she was to settle among them, there would still be the advantages of family connections, but without the close supervision of Elizabeth and Ninian. There was also a young man, scion of a notable Virginia family and very agreeable, who paid repeated calls. Molly liked him well enough. With the proper encouragement, which she knew how to give, he might ask for her hand. She thought often about Elizabeth's saying that most couples did not really know one another when they married; they fell deeply in love only afterwards. She knew that she was moving through, but not yet past, the time when most young women on the frontier got married. She understood, too, that infatuation did not last. She wondered if love bloomed only after a couple lived together for a time, made babies together and raised their children through the trials and small happinesses of daily living. The scion was pleasant enough, and she had promised Elizabeth that she would try to fall in love. But the spark was not there. And did he possess nobility of character? Somehow that had begun to seem important, and it yet was a dimension of the man she could not know.

Now she sat writing a letter to her friend Merce Levering, who had returned to Baltimore. It was late July. Her visit to Missouri had lasted several weeks. It was now time to return home. But the visit kept getting extended. Was her Missouri family expecting something to happen? Or was it just that hospitality followed in her wake? Whenever she met Missourians, she found them pleased to greet a pretty new face, delighted to welcome a young woman of background, good manners and fine education, one who conversed with such wit and intelligence. Molly enhanced the Todd reputation. Wherever she went, invitations followed. There were mothers who wanted her to meet their sons. Or young widowers who might offer a good match.

Now after being unrelentingly charming, it was pleasant to be alone in her room for an hour, communing with a friend who demanded no pretensions. She wrote almost as fast as she thought. Of course, she knew that sentences should not run on endlessly. In school she had made the acquaintance of periods and the practice of capitalizing the first word of a new sentence. She knew about commas, too, but let them take care of themselves. Her thoughts ran too quickly to bother with such things. Merce would understand; she would forgive ampersands. Frequent underlinings would help her pick out ideas Molly deemed of special note.

"You will readily credit me Dearest," she wrote, her pen scratching at the paper, "when I tell you my time has been most delightfully spent, this portion of the state is certainly most beautiful, and in my wanderings I never encountered more kindness & hospitality, as my visit was particularly to my relations & did not expect to remain for any length of time, I was not anxious to mingle with the strange crowd, and form new associations so soon to be severed, yet every lady almost that called extended an invitation to us to spend an evening with them, so I have necessarily seen more society than I had anticipated, on yesterday we returned from a most agreeable excursion to Boonville, situated immediately on the river and a charming place, we remained a week, attended four parties, during the time, one was *particularly* distinguished for its brilliancy & *city like* doings, the house was very commodious, four rooms & two halls, thrown open for the reception of the guests, in two, dancing was carried on with *untiring vigor,* kept up until 3 o'clock, however, Cousin A & myself were more genteel left rather earlier *Your risibles* would have undergone a *considerable state of excitement,* were you to have seen the 'poetry of motion' exercised in the dance, had our grandfathers been present in the festive halls of mirth, they would undoubtedly have recognized the familiar airs of their youthful days, all the old Virginia reels that have been handed down to us by *tradition,* were played, your Cousin Sep methinks would have enjoyed the danse, no insinuations meant, save his extreme fondness for this fascinating amusement, and the rapid manner they hurried through the figures, at the end of each cotillion. I felt exhausted after such *desperate exertions* to keep pace with the music."

Molly dipped her pen in the inkwell, wondered what more to write, possibly news from Springfield—although Jim Conkling would be reporting that for Merce. She scribbled on, the pen moving almost in automatic writing.

"The mail comes in to day, and I am on the wing of expectation, hoping to hear from my dear sister Fanny. Dr Wallace I hear has been sick, & Fanny I fear is unable to play the part of devoted nurse at *this time,* to both child & husband—"

Molly paused. What about her Springfield beaux? Merce would want to hear about them. "Every week since I left Springfield, have had the felicity of receiving various numbers of their interesting papers, Old Soldiers, Journals—" Merce would wonder if Elizabeth had sent them or someone intentionally unnamed—"& even the *Hickory Club,* has crossed my vision." Merce would assume that Douglas had sent the Democratic *Hickory,* so she would not be coy about that. "This latter, rather astonished your friend," she wrote, "*there* I had deemed myself forgotten—"

She would not tell Merce that she had received, quite unexpectedly, letters from Abraham Lincoln. Was it a courtship after all? Even if it were, wasn't ending it the wiser course? She had not given Elizabeth the note she had written Lincoln the evening before she left Springfield. She had brought it with her to Missouri. She had assumed that he would be too busy with cases and writing and giving speeches all over southern Illinois to have occasion even to think of her, much less to write her letters. So why send the note she had written? Then his letters had come. She had told Elizabeth that Lincoln had no intentions with regard to her. Kisses were not intentions. Might letters be a shy man's way of stating his? Might it not be better never to send the note? To see how things played out when she returned? She must never forget that she was a Todd. But Todds did

218

what they wanted, didn't they? Hadn't her father gone seeking a new wife hardly before her mother was buried? She was not sure what would happen with Lincoln. Very likely nothing. It was his job to declare himself; he might never do that. But she would not send the note. She might hint of something to Merce, because it pleased her to think there was something to be hinted at. But it was too early and too risky to be definite, especially since merely hinting might be rash. Why risk the possibility that Merce would react as Elizabeth did?

"When I mention *some letters,* I have received since leaving S- you will be somewhat surprised, as I *must confess* they were entirely *unlooked for,* this is *between ourselves,* my dearest, but more of this anon." That was enough.

She stopped writing, mulling her most recent news about Lincoln. She knew Jim Conkling would write Merce the news she herself had just heard. It showed Lincoln's cleverness in debate, his capacity to best an opponent, but still it was worrisome news. It was one thing to best an opponent, something else to destroy him. At a campaign meeting Jesse Thomas had joked about the Long Nine, especially Lincoln, who was not present. Friends told Lincoln what was happening, and he rushed to the meeting to take the platform when Thomas finished. Perhaps it was a matter of turnabout being fair play. Thomas had poked fun at him; he would return the compliment.

But Lincoln did not merely poke fun. He mimicked Thomas's voice, his inflections, his gestures. He imitated his opponent's walk, exaggerated the movements of his body. The crowd guffawed and hooted and cheered. Lincoln's ridicule increased, grew more scathing. Poor Thomas had to witness this humiliation. Tears began to run down his cheeks. The town was calling it "the skinning of Thomas." Molly had heard that Lincoln was almost immediately remorseful. Even if he did not feel sympathy for Thomas, Lincoln's political instincts would tell him he had gone too far. Springfield was still a small place. But Molly felt certain that Lincoln's better nature would commiserate with Thomas. Lincoln had apologized. Even so, an apology could not put flesh back on a man who'd been skinned. She hoped Lincoln would not suffer a rebuke at the polls. The Illinois election day was only three weeks away.

Molly stared at the inkwell for a moment. When Lincoln called on her at the Edwards home, he was always bashful, slow of speech, lacking in confidence. Each visit required some time before he felt comfortable with her. She had seen him be virile, funny and forceful in debate. Even eloquent. But the man who could reduce an opponent to tears—and would not hold back from doing that? She did not know this Lincoln. She wondered if she knew him at all.

She went back to the letter. Her hand wrote on, telling Merce how much she missed her company, making an oblique reference to Jim Conkling. And as she did, she thought about Lincoln. She wondered whom she would marry. Wondered where they would live. Would they live in Missouri? More than once Merce had said she might.

Cousin Anne called to her. Her father had returned from the courts and wanted to take them for a drive. Molly hurried to finish her letter.

"If you conclude to settle in Missouri," Molly wrote, "*I will do so too,* there is *one* being here, who keeps urging my return, an agreeable lawyer

& grandson of *Patrick Henry—what an honor!* Shall never survive it—I wish you could see him, the most perfect original I had ever met, my beaux have *always* been *hard bargains. A*t any rate, Uncle and others think, he surpasses his *noble ancestor* in *talents,* yet Merce I love him not, & my hand will never be given, where my heart is not— Cousin A has a most devoted hero who watches her every look, with a *lover's eye,* and I have long told her she was a coquette in a *quiet* way—and they are said to be the most dangerous ever—Be as *unreserved* as you find me, I forget myself writing to you, pass my imperfections lightly by, and excuse so miserable a production from your most attached friend

Mary"

When Molly returned to Springfield, Lincoln ignored Butler's advice and went to call. Elizabeth Edwards had the Irish girl tell him that Molly was resting. "Mrs. Edwards said to tell you . . ." the girl told him. Lincoln was puzzled. He had written Molly letters in Missouri. True, he had not received letters in return, but she was undoubtedly busy and he had been outside Springfield a good part of the time. He wondered if Molly was sick. Or had she formed an attachment to a man in Missouri? He didn't know what to think.

The second time he called, Elizabeth Edwards herself came to explain that Molly was involved with the children and could not be disturbed. Her manner was patrician, cordial but without warmth. Lincoln stood before her, baffled, wanting to ask questions but sensing that they would not be welcome. They would be evaded and he would be dismissed.

Walking back to town, he realized that being prevented from seeing Molly made him want to see her even more. Did she want to see him? If she had not formed an attachment on her travels, then Butler's warning was proving true: Ninian and Elizabeth Edwards were not permitting the connection to continue. Was this what Molly wanted? Did she know that he'd called? Probably. The Irish girls would tell her. Lincoln stayed away for a week. This was not easy to do, but if Molly was interested in seeing him, she could send a signal.

Then he heard that Bat Webb was calling at the Edwards home. Bat Webb! Molly could not be seriously interested there! Moreover, his welcome indicated that Molly had not met anyone in Missouri.

The third time Lincoln called, he hoped Elizabeth Edwards would not be at home. Molly saw him approaching from a window. The attentions of Bat Webb had made her realize she felt a real affection for Lincoln. She ran downstairs, fearing that if he sustained three rebuffs, he would never call again. She concocted an errand she must do outside and bumped into him "quite unexpectedly." "Mr. Lincoln!" she exclaimed. "How nice to see you. What a surprise!" She thanked him for the letters he had written her and, since a young lady was permitted a little white lie to a gentleman caller, asked, "Did you get a letter from me?" Lincoln said he had not. Molly said, "Really? Hmm." They walked out together, chatting about his speechifying in southern Illinois and her being feted in Missouri. He hoped that what Butler had warned him voters thought was not true, but he would not be deterred. She realized that she had missed him. When they had walked far enough into the countryside to be alone, Lincoln kissed her in the broad daylight before God Himself. They both wondered where this connection was headed.

When the ballots were counted in the Illinois polls, held in mid-August, Lincoln won re-election to the Legislature, but with the smallest vote of the elected candidates. Lincoln realized that Butler had warned him about a real concern of voters. Molly wondered if his skinning Jesse Thomas had played a role in his lowered vote count. Thomas and his law partner had parted ways. Had Lincoln's humiliating him provoked that rupture?

When he called at the house, Ninian congratulated him. "Seems I found favor with fewer voters this time," Lincoln said.

"Things are changing," Ninian remarked. Ninian was pleased, Molly sensed, that voters had diminished Lincoln's stature as a vote-getter. This was balm on the wound Ninian still nursed. Lincoln said that the important thing was that the Whigs should win the national election in November. Ninian agreed. If the voters failed to elect Harrison, the country faced an uncertain future. Lincoln was leaving almost immediately to campaign throughout the southern section of the state.

Lincoln and Molly strolled again into the country. Despite the tall escort beside her, she felt as if she were walking the path alone. She glanced at Lincoln. He had been so glad to see her when she had returned. Now he seemed some stranger she had never met who was merely keeping pace with her along the lane. She did not attempt bright conversation; there was no point in that. He had entered that place of melancholy he seemed to carry with him, a place he entered alone, never inviting her to follow.

Finally he asked, "Where do you suppose we're all headed?" He might have been talking to himself. Molly knew that pondering metaphysics was contrary to his mode of thought. "Is what I'm doing preparation? And if it is, for what?" They strolled on, Molly's hand in the crook of his elbow. "Or are we on the river of life, doing our best, avoiding the sandbars and trying not to let the currents capsize us?"

"Don't be discouraged," Molly said. She wondered if she could follow her own advice. So many possibilities were open to him. A young woman could only wait for some man to ask for her hand. She did not want to marry the grandson of Patrick Henry. However noble he was. Or Bat Webb. "I'll tell you, I wouldn't mind giving all the speeches you do."

"The same speech over and over?" He chuckled. "Telling the same stories, leading up to the same jokes, hammering away at the same issues."

"I'd campaign for women's suffrage," Molly declared, trying to lighten things. "If we can raise your children, we ought to be able to vote for our leaders."

But he seemed not to hear her. "I feel like a runt pig," he said, as if talking to himself again, "trying to eat at two troughs. The big pigs push me out of both troughs and I can't get any slop." They walked on. "When I do politics, I neglect the law, which is where the money comes in. When I do cases, I neglect politics, which is where I think I can distinguish myself. And yet when I do it, I don't seem to make any headway."

They walked on. They entered a grove of trees. She wanted to stop him and say, "Kiss me." That would catapult a lot of men out of their melancholy. But not Lincoln. He was not a demonstrative man; certainly not when he was melancholy. He might not even kiss her. It was likely that he would look at her, surprised, and not know what to do.

CHAPTER

12

Celebrations broke out in the offices of the *Sangamo Journal* when the news arrived from the state of Maine: the results of the country's first national poll. The Whig ticket swept the state. Those joyfully present immediately started singing:

> Farewell, dear Van,
> You're not our man.
> To guide the ship,
> We'll try old Tip.

They paraded around the office, shouting at the top of their voices, and spilled out into the street.

When the Coterie next got together for a dance, Molly and Lincoln and other Whigs in the crowd, which meant most of those assembled, burst forth with the latest Whig song. They stomped the ballroom floor to its undeniable rhythm:

> And have you heard the news from Maine,
> And what old Maine can do?
> She went hell-bent
> for Governor Kent,
> And Tippecanoe and Tyler, too,
> And Tippecanoe and Tyler, too.

As they circled the ballroom, stomping, they pointed at Stephen Douglas and grinned with triumph. Douglas covered his ears. Jim Shields came up beside him and put his arms around his shoulders. Together they and their fellow Dems bellowed out a party anthem:

"The Paper Plague afflicts us all,
Its pains are past enduring.
Still, we have hope in Jackson's robe,
Whilst it wraps around Van Buren."

The Whigs began to stomp closer and closer around Shields, Douglas and their Democratic allies like Indians on horseback, attacking a wagon train of settlers with wagons drawn into a defensive circle. They stamped till the floor shook. They raised their arms out to the heavens. As far as the Coterie was concerned, Douglas and Shields were vanquished.

Although, of course, she could not vote, Molly felt an extraordinary excitement on election day. She rode to the courthouse with Ninian, holding young Julia on her lap. She sat, watching from the buggy, while Ninian presented himself to the appropriate official, spoke the name of the candidates he preferred and so cast his vote. A large crowd of men waited outside the courthouse. Even many of those who Molly thought had the look of Democratic voters were talking about General Harrison. Several, already tipsy, were singing "Farewell, Old Van." When Ninian returned to the buggy, Molly left Julia and walked over to the offices of the *Sangamo Journal*. There she would be among Whig partisans and could join in savoring the likelihood of a Whig victory.

None of the men who danced attendance on her would be there. Douglas and Shields were out encouraging Irish canal diggers to vote. Bat Webb was off in White County, his constituency. Lincoln was at Lawrenceville, not ten miles from where Old Tippecanoe had negotiated with Tecumseh, chief of the Shawnees. He would not vote at all. Instead he would officially deliver the Lawrence County election returns to the Secretary of State in Springfield. Lincoln had been campaigning in the southern part of the state for weeks. Molly longed to see him.

When he returned to town, he called at the Edwards house. There Whigs, in a state of euphoria, had been in and out all day, celebrating Old Tippecanoe's victory. The merrymakers chatted excitedly, as if by voting they had contributed to the achievement of a great change, perhaps even a revolution. The White House was now back in Whig hands! They did not talk about the downside of the election, the Whigs' failure to carry Illinois. The state had gone Democratic.

Lincoln was not in a mood to socialize. Molly took him into the kitchen, got him refreshments and sat with him at the kitchen table. "At least Whigs took the main prize," she said, trying to see the bright side. "The first President from both the north and the west." Lincoln nodded. She had never seen him look so tired. The fatigue distressed her; she knew a victory in Illinois would have energized him. The planning and organizing, the writing and speechifying, the traveling over bad roads in rain or shine, the tasteless food, the nights in overcrowded inns: all that now seemed to have been for naught. Like it or not, the results called into question the political skills of the organizers. The Democratic victories for the governorship and in the Legislature meant that Whig ideas would not be implemented in Illinois, that the party would face setbacks, that Lincoln would once again lack the votes to become House speaker.

"Maybe Tippecanoe will appoint me an Indian agent somewhere," Lincoln said.

Indian agent! thought Molly. She was appalled.

"Or to a consulship somewhere: Venezuela maybe. Peru or Guatemala."

"Venezuela? You'd actually consider that?" Molly was not sure exactly where Venezuela was; it sounded like the ends of the earth. England was one thing, maybe even France. But Venezuela? Guatemala? "Why would you go there?"

"To flee politics." He leaned his chair back, rested his head against the kitchen wall and smiled exhaustedly at the alarm that showed in her face. "Governor Carlin's called a special session of the Legislature," he explained. "The internal improvements bill of a few years back is bankrupting the state. I voted for that bill."

"Of course, you did!" she exclaimed. "We need turnpikes, canals, railroads."

"Too bad we can't pay for them."

Lincoln did not stay long. When she said goodbye to him at the door, she examined the sky, wondering if there'd be snow. He told her, "Sangamon Circuit Court goes into session this week."

"Can't you take some time off? Get some rest?"

He shook his head. "The only money I've made in weeks is the nineteen dollars for bringing the returns in from Lawrence County." He smiled at her exhaustedly. "I missed you. Prairies can be lonely. I'm sorry there wasn't time for letters."

She gave him a forgiving smile. "I missed you, too."

"I thought about you every day." He took her hand for a moment; that pleased her. Since there were people coming and going, he did not kiss her.

With some rest, Lincoln bounced back. Once again his fellow Whig legislators chose him as their floor leader. However badly his political confidence was shaken by the Democratic victory in Illinois, his political talents were needed to stave off further defeats. And the defeats came. The most notable one took place at the end of a special session of the Legislature, called to deal with the near-bankruptcy of the state. It involved a subterfuge devised by Lincoln. Molly learned of it at dinner the night before the trick was to be sprung.

The special session brought to town Ninian's uncle Cyrus Edwards, a state senator, and his daughter Matilda. Since the special session was likely to be followed immediately by the regular one, the two visitors from Alton would be Ninian and Elizabeth's guests for the close of the year and much of the winter. This prospect delighted Molly. Cyrus's presence at the dinner table promised lively political discussions, and the beautiful Matilda, three years younger than Molly, was likely to prove a most pleasant companion, especially now that Merce Levering had returned to Baltimore.

At dinner that evening the men discussed the state's near-bankruptcy. The legislators included not only Ninian and Cyrus, but also Cyrus's young protégé, Joseph Gillespie. Ordinarily Matilda's beauty and demure manner left young men breathless. But as they sat around the table analyzing the sacrifices required in the state's internal improvements schemes, Molly realized that Mr. Gillespie glanced repeatedly, not at Matilda, seated across from him, but at the intelligent and witty young woman beside him, a young woman who found politics, even state politics, fascinating. Molly smiled at Gillespie engagingly while Matilda and Elizabeth looked bored by the political talk.

The notes of state banks in Illinois had lost so much value, the men explained to their companions, that the governor wanted to require that all state debts, chiefly taxes, be paid in gold and silver coins, not in increasingly worthless notes. The Legislature, however, had voted to retain payment in banknotes until the end of the next session. If the Democrats could adjourn the special session, their majority would allow them to require payment in coin, not paper, immediately. By preventing the special session's adjournment, the Whigs could force it to merge with the regular session. If that happened, they could hold off until spring any requirement for specie payment, thereby putting off misery and ruin for people without coin.

"The Democrats have us in a tight spot," said Cyrus Edwards.

"Surely Lincoln will come up with something," declared Ninian. "The man is wonderfully devious." Molly could not tell if he said these words in admiration or condescension.

"Lincoln does have a plan," said Gillespie. He glanced around the table and smiled at Molly. "I'm not sure I should reveal it."

"Oh, do!" encouraged Molly.

"We may not even understand it," remarked Elizabeth.

"Some of us surely will!" Molly put her hand lightly on Gillespie's forearm. "We'd die before we'd divulge it." Gillespie grinned conspiratorially at Molly. "Boycott the session," Molly suggested, almost too quickly.

Gillespie grinned. "Some Whigs will have business elsewhere tomorrow."

"If there's no adjournment tomorrow," Cyrus explained to Elizabeth and Matilda, "we'll go into regular session Monday and the sessions will be merged."

"Lincoln and I will make sure there are never enough Whigs in the chamber to constitute a quorum," Gillespie said. Pleased with himself, he sat back and smiled.

The idea that Whigs would foil Democrats, who had so often foiled them, delighted Molly. She glowed with pleasure. "Come to dinner again tomorrow," she told Gillespie, "and report what happened." As the family was about to leave the table, the Irish serving girl entered to announce that Mr. Lincoln and Mr. Speed had arrived to call on Miss Molly and Miss Matilda. Molly noticed the disappointment on Gillespie's face. "Do come and join us," Molly suggested to Gillespie. "You can make sure that Matilda and I say nothing of the secret plan."

When Molly, Matilda and Gillespie joined the two callers, Molly said, "Please respect our delicate conditions, gentlemen. Mr. Gillespie has been telling us political stratagems and we have promised to die rather than divulge them." The look of surprised betrayal on Gillespie's face made the women laugh. Knowing Molly's appetite for mischief, Lincoln smiled. But he cast a scrutinizing glance at Gillespie. "You must not press us, Mr. Lincoln," Molly said flirtatiously. "Our lips are sealed."

"Nor you either, Mr. Speed," teased Matilda.

When they settled themselves, Speed sat beside Matilda. His eyes kept darting toward her as if they had never before beheld such beauty.

When the gentlemen ended their call, Molly and Matilda walked them to the door and followed them into the night air to look at the sky. While Speed stayed close to Matilda, Lincoln pulled Molly aside. "A bunch of us in the Legislature are getting up a party to go over to the Hardins in Jacksonville for Christmas. Can you come with us, Molly? It's never a party without you."

"If I say I'll come, will you kiss me?"

"In front of these others?"

"Follow me into the house," she instructed. To the others she exclaimed, "There's something I meant to get." She hurried into the house. Lincoln followed her. Once inside the entry hall, they closed the door and kissed.

"So you'll come?"

She stood on tiptoe and he kissed her again. When they broke the kiss, she said, "That's what I had to get." Lights danced merrily in her eyes. "It's too cold out there for me," she laughed, giving Lincoln a shove. "Tell Matilda she'll catch her death outside."

The next afternoon Lincoln and Gillespie stood at the entrance of the Legislature, greeting friends, feigning camaraderie while actually counting members who entered the house. Enough Whig members were attending to refute any charge that they were boycotting the session. There were still too few members to achieve a quorum, exactly what Lincoln intended. Moreover, good luck had come his way. Several Democratic members had taken ill and could not attend. "I was nervous for

234

a moment last night," Gillespie said, "when Miss Todd was teasing us. Are we safe?"

"She's a better Whig than most of our members," Lincoln said. "But it's hard keeping a secret in politics." He scanned the chamber. Only a moment or two remained before the session would be called to order. "Let's take a quick check inside. Maybe we can stay ourselves."

Lincoln led his deputy into the chamber. They stood against the wall close to the door and scanned the room, counting members. Lincoln suddenly felt a cold flush of alarm. Democratic members who were reported sick were present in the chamber. "Quick!" he whispered to Gillespie. "Let's get out of here."

As they started from the room, the sergeant-at-arms closed the door. "Excuse us, please. Excuse us!" Lincoln demanded. The sergeant-at-arms paid him no attention. He locked the door and placed himself before it as a guard.

"The Dems have caught us," Gillespie said.

"No, they haven't. Follow me."

Lincoln headed across the room to a row of French doors. He forced one of them open, mounted the sill and jumped. Gillespie followed him. They landed, hands and feet in mud. As they hurried away, a Democratic legislator came to the window. "Too bad, Abe," he called. "We've got the votes we need."

When they reached the end of the building, Gillespie laughed and said, "That was exciting. Like playing hooky from school."

"We're going to look like fools," Lincoln said, "if they really have the votes."

That evening when the same group gathered around Ninian's table, Molly informed Gillespie,

"Matilda and I had an excruciating day keeping your secret. Did your plan work?"

Gillespie looked shamefaced. "What a fiasco!" he said.

"Were you discovered? Honestly!" Molly cried. Poor Lincoln, she thought, then wondered if he would think they had revealed his scheme. "We told no one," she insisted. "We've been with the children all day."

"The Democrats discovered the plan," Gillespie reported. "Several pretended to be sick. They suddenly appeared and caught too many Whigs in the chamber. They had the sergeant-at-arms lock us in."

Although she was sorry for Lincoln, Molly could not help laughing and clapping her hands.

"That wasn't the worst," Gillespie admitted. "We panicked. Dove out a window."

"Out a window?" Molly roared with laughter. "Did you land in the mud?"

"We did." Gillespie seemed pleased that Molly was so amused. "It's humiliating. The special session was adjourned after all."

Molly kept laughing, thinking of Lincoln, down on his behind. "Did anyone break a leg?" she asked. Then she repeated, "Really, we didn't tell a soul."

Around the fire at Speed's store Lincoln's friends ribbed him mercilessly. He said, "I'm in mind of a Black Hawk War military strategist who boasted of his cunning. But as soon as arrows flew, he turned tail and ran. Caught out, he said, 'My stratagems are as cunning as Caesar's. But if the enemy tricks me, my legs take flight.' And that's what happened to me. My cowardly legs went right out the window."

The men laughed, and Lincoln rescued himself, as he so often did, with a story. But later upstairs with Speed he seemed depressed, "How could I have gotten tricked so bad?" he wondered. After a moment he pressed, "What do you think?"

"Sorry," Speed said. He finally confessed, "All I can think about is Matilda Edwards. Isn't she the most beautiful—"

Lincoln shook his head. "You in love again?" After a moment he said, "It must be that infernal Douglas, don't you expect? Someone must've told him. He's got spies everywhere."

Both men stared at the floor. Finally Speed confessed, "I'm hankering to ask Matilda to marry me. What do you think?"

Lincoln had hardly heard his friend. He grumbled, "People will be talking about my jumping out that window for the rest of my life."

When Stephen Douglas next called on Molly, the governor had named him Illinois Secretary of State. It was a plum of a job, bestowed on Douglas because of political services. When she entered the parlor where he awaited her, Molly felt herself enfolded in the aura of Douglas's self-satisfaction. It was late afternoon. He stood before the fire, warming his legs, even more pleased with himself than usual. "Congratulations, Mr. Secretary," Molly said. She gave an ironic curtsey. Douglas guffawed, knowing that she was mocking him, but delighted nonetheless.

"I'm surprised you have time to make social calls," Molly told him.

"I've come to recruit you to the Democratic Party."

"Indeed," she said. "Is it a cotillion? You know I love parties."

"The Dems have suffered a small setback in the national election," he told her. "But I assure you that Old Tip-the-Canoe will make an undistinguished president. In one hundred years our citizens will have no idea who he was. The Democratic Party owns the future."

Molly wondered if Douglas ever flirted with a woman, as he was flirting with her now, without mentioning politics. "Will you Democrats give women the vote in Illinois?" she asked. "If you will, I'll fetch my dancing slippers."

"Join the future, Miss Molly. The Whigs are done for." He grinned at her. "I guess you heard they've started jumping out windows."

With mock severity she replied, "Sir, you are in a Whig home!"

"Now that we control the Legislature," Douglas confided, "we'll expand the supreme court. Democratic justices will be in the majority." He held Molly's hand in both of his. "Join us, Molly. The day has passed for ruffle-shirt Whig aristocrats."

"Not every Whig wears a ruffle shirt, Mr. Douglas."

"I know who you mean," he said. "But I'll get to the Senate and he won't. The ruffle shirts won't let him." Douglas smiled at her. Molly thought he might lean toward her to kiss her. Instead he implored, "Come join us."

He was very persuasive. Molly wondered: Exactly what affiliation was he seeking? Did he require the political one before any other could be contemplated? "You'll have to let me consider this, Mr. Douglas."

"Don't wait too long." Now he did kiss her.

After he left, his magnetism faded. Molly knew for certain she was not interested in a romantic affiliation in which both she and he would love the man.

Billy Herndon was tending store when Lincoln entered Speed's emporium in the middle of the afternoon. "Lincoln! Land's sakes!" he exclaimed, looking alarmed and flustered. "What're you doing here?"

"I live here," Lincoln said. He held up a pile of laundry he had picked up from Elizabeth Butler. "Just taking this up—"

"Don't go up there," Herndon said.

Lincoln circled over to the counter Herndon stood behind. "What's wrong, Billy? Is having a pregnant wife making you nervous?"

"Talk to me a spell. What's new with you? I hardly see you anymore." Lincoln smiled at this curious talk and headed for the stairs. "Don't go up there," Herndon said. His voice possessed a warning tone. Lincoln had never before heard Billy use it.

Lincoln stopped moving toward the stairs and looked around. Charlie Hurst was not in the store. Were he and Billy hiding a runaway slave up there? Billy had abolitionist principles, but Lincoln had not heard of his helping the Underground Railway. Lincoln smiled. "What's going on, Billy? You hiding an escapee?"

Billy looked at the counter. "Nothing's going on up there."

Lincoln wondered if Billy— But why would his wife be there? Would Charlie Hurst take a—

"Don't go up there." Lincoln moved back to the clerk and set his laundry on the counter. "You fellers ought to get married," said Billy.

Lincoln grinned. "What in the world is happening up there?"

"Nothing. I hope nothing."

"Is Charlie there with a girl?" Speed was the one with the good looks and the silver tongue. But was it Charlie that took the girls upstairs? Speed was too cautious, afraid he'd get trapped into marriage. But not Charlie, hunh? Lincoln chuckled. He'd just peek in, scare Charlie and later tease him. The girl could hide under a pillow. "I'm going up there," Lincoln said.

"Don't." Billy stared at the counter.

"If he's not careful, Charlie's gonna find himself married." Lincoln could not help grinning. "Why doesn't he take her out in the country?"

Finally Billy whispered, "It's Speed up there."

Lincoln's jaw dropped. Speed? Risking marriage? But with whom? Lately he was in love with Matilda Edwards. That rascal! If he'd gotten her to climb the stairs with him, she was not the vessel of purity she pretended to be. Lincoln had to know.

"You fellers ought to get married," Billy said again. "When you're married, there's no sneaking around. You've got a way to handle these . . . urges." He smiled sheepishly. "The Good Book says better to marry than to burn. I can tell you: it's better for me."

Lincoln glanced around the store to make sure that he and Billy were alone. He dropped his voice to a whisper. "They doing . . .? You know . . ." He gestured with his hands.

Billy shrugged. He assumed they were.

"Is she—" Discretion prevented him from speaking Matilda's name. Billy stared at the counter, wishing the interrogation would end.

"Who is she?" Lincoln's voice was barely audible.

Billy shook his head.

"Do I know her?"

"Can't tell ya."

"We're old friends, Billy. We trust one another."

"Won't tell ya."

They heard a woman's footsteps on the stairway. The footsteps stopped. They heard air catch in a throat as if someone was crying. The footsteps resumed. Out of courtesy the men turned their backs. The woman hurried through the store. She paused inside the doorway to smooth her dress and put on her bonnet. Lincoln stole a glance at her. He recognized her lithe form, her walk as she started out the door.

He turned back to Billy. "Sarah?" The clerk said nothing. Lincoln reached across the counter and grabbed Billy's shirt. "Was that Sarah Rickard?"

"I'm a gentleman, Abe. I don't know who that was."

Lincoln seized his laundry and hurried up the stairs, taking them two at a time. Speed was at the window watching the retreating figure. Lincoln halted, studying him, and breathed deeply to scent the air, testing it for a musky telltale odor. But the room smelled as it always did. Lincoln said, "Tell me you did not compromise that girl." Speed hung his head, but did not turn from the window. Lincoln glanced at Speed's feet; he was not wearing boots. He wondered what else Speed had taken off while Sarah was with him. "She was crying," Lincoln said. "What happened up here?" Speed did not reply. "Answer me, Joshua. What's a good girl like her doing here?" Speed turned to face Lincoln. His face was drawn with emotion. "You been keeping company with Sarah?" Speed nodded. "Last I heard you were marrying Matilda Edwards."

"It happened sudden."

"It's always sudden with you." Lincoln turned to scrutinize the bed. Because they rarely smoothed it in the mornings, it held its secrets. He saw two pillows drawn close together. They had not been that way when he left for the office.

Speed watched Lincoln studying the pillows. "Nothing happened," he said. Lincoln examined his face. Had he been crying, too? "It could've happened, but it didn't."

"Were you on the bed with her?"

Speed would not look at him. "Nothing happened," he repeated. He reached over, grabbed one of the pillows and held it to him as if it were a woman.

"Then why was she crying?" Speed did not reply. "Is it Matilda?"

"I told her I'm going back to Kentucky," Speed said at last. His father had recently died, and his mother had asked him to return to direct the work of the plantation outside Louisville. "I guess she understands. Hope she does." Speed sat on the side of the bed. "She asked me to take her with me." He shuddered. "I just wanted to take her." Speed agitated his head as if he were shaking off a persistent fever. "Oh, we came close. She was taking off her dress." He kept moving his head. After a moment he added, "Knew I mustn't."

"Indeed, you mustn't. She's very young."

"I was scared if I did I'd have to marry her." He drew the pillow away from his body and tossed it to the far side of the bed.

"I'd have made sure you did."

"I figured you might." Lincoln watched Speed, wondering exactly what had happened. He set his laundry on a stool.

"Having to marry her. That frightened desire right out of me." Speed stretched out on the bed, staring at the ceiling, listening for sounds of patronage in the store below. There was only the silence of the early afternoon, the sun beating down on the roof. Finally he reached over, took the pillow again and embraced it. "She'll make some man a fine wife." After a moment he confessed, "Right now I wish it was her standing there the way she did. And not you."

Lincoln said, "Billy almost had a cat fit, thinking I'd catch you two at it."

Speed stared unhappily at the ceiling. "She cried. Her dress was half off when she saw it wasn't going to happen. She was so ready and I was afraid to let it happen." He pushed the pillow down to his groin and pressed it against him.

"That better be your pillow," Lincoln said.

Speed threw the pillow at him and sat up. "She cried when I told her I couldn't see her again." Speed reached under the bed for his boots and began to put them on. "I was powerfully taken with her. With Matilda, too." They were silent for a long moment as Speed pounded his feet into his boots and thudded them against the floor. Finally he asked, "Abe, am I ever going get hitched? The thought of it scares me to death. But I want a woman bad." Lincoln smiled. They both knew what that was like, looking at women but not too obviously, wondering what it would be like living with one, having one in your bed every night. "But what if she turns out to be the wrong one and I'm tied to her for life?" Lincoln sat beside him on the bed. "I feel these overpowering urges. What's the matter with me?"

"Billy says, 'Better to marry than to burn.' "

"I'm burning right now." After a moment he said, "Wish we'd done it." He reached for a pillow and embraced it yet again, chewed the ticking, oblivious to its taste. "When I'm an old man, I'll sit on a porch somewhere in a rocker, thinking, 'One fine summer day Sarah Rickard had her dress half off in the loft of my store and I shook my head.' I'll wonder, 'What was the matter with me?'"

"You old coot. Won't remember whether she took it off or not."

"Maybe not," Speed said. In his voice there was a note of finality, a closing out of the memory. Ready to return to the store, he went to the water barrel, dipped cool liquid into his cupped hands and threw it onto his face. "I couldn't make Sarah happy. Not in Kentucky." Toweling off, he surveyed the room and shrugged, baffled. "I have Sarah up here," he confessed, "and I can't stop thinking about Matilda. Something's wrong with me."

"Are you really going back to Kentucky?"

"Charlie's buying my interest in the store."

Lincoln said, "I thought I'd asked Sarah a while back to marry me. Remember? She was just a sprout."

"She's a woman now," Speed said. He stared at his hands. "She wanted it bad as I did." Lincoln wondered if he'd had his hands inside her dress. "Let me tell ya: it was a close thing."

When Lincoln went back downstairs, Charlie Hurst had returned to the store. He and Billy were both helping customers. Lincoln left without speaking to them.

Again Molly wrote Merce Levering in Baltimore. In her inimitable style, being sparing with periods, profligate with commas, she wrote, "I know you would be pleased with Matilda Edwards, a lovelier girl I never saw. *Mr. Speed's* ever changing heart I suspect is about offering *its young* affections at her shrine, with some others, there is considerable acquisition in our society of *marriageable gentlemen,* unfortunately only 'birds of passage.' *Mr. Webb,* a widower of modest merit, last winter, is our *principal lion,* dances attendance very frequently. . . ."

Molly wondered what Merce would make of her reference to Webb. The widower kept dropping hints that with a bit of encouragement a proposal could be had. Molly was careful to withhold that encouragement. Still, it was useful to have Webb around. He was a convenient escort when Lincoln and Douglas were out of town, as they frequently were. Even when Lincoln was in town, his work sometimes distracted him from remembering social obligations, and it was useful for whatever beaux found her interesting to know that there were other horses in the race.

She resumed her letter to Merce, writing: "I suppose like the rest of us *Whigs*—though you seem rather to doubt my *faith* you have been rejoicing in the recent election of Gen Harrison, a cause that has excited such deep interest in the nation and one of such vital importance to our prosperity—This fall I became quite a *politician,* rather an unladylike profession, yet at such a *crisis,* whose heart could remain untouched while the energies of all were called in question?"

Molly paused to wonder what dear Matilda thought of her political interests. Though her father was in the state Senate, Matilda was more pious than political. Piety had made her refuse attendance at some social occasions since her arrival. Molly thought that her "Strong attachment" to a certain young Mr. Strong back home in Alton motivated some of this piety, especially with swains like Joshua Speed falling all over themselves in admiration of her.

Molly continued, "Once more, allow me my dear friend to wish you were with us, we have a pleasant jaunt in contemplation, to Jacksonville, next week there to spend a day or two, Mr. Hardin & Browning are our leaders the van brought up by Miss Edwards my humble self, Webb, Lincoln & two or three others whom you know not, we are watching the clouds most anxiously trusting it may snow, so we may have a sleigh ride—Will it not be pleasant?"

She ended the letter with a reference to Merce's brother's family and with love from her sister Fanny Wallace and news that Elizabeth was suffering a cold. "I am still the same ruddy *pineknot,*" she wrote. "I must close, write very, very soon if you love me—ever your attached friend

Mary"

Molly was bathing Julia in the small metal tub that the stable boy had carried into the kitchen and set on the kitchen table. Cold water direct from the pump outside had been warmed by water boiled on the stove. Julia was cooing and splashing when Elizabeth entered the kitchen; she had just nursed Bertie—her bodice was still only half-buttoned—and put him down for the night. "I have a little something I want you to take to Sarah Hardin," she told Molly. "Don't let me forget it." Molly and Matilda were leaving the next day for Jacksonville.

Elizabeth stood beside the metal tub and finished with her daughter, dribbling water over the child, the light of the oil lamps glinting on the droplets, the child's newly-bathed scent filling the air. Elizabeth laughed with her as she splashed. Molly prepared to receive Julia inside a warm towel when Elizabeth lifted the child to her.

"Mary, you'll be journeying with three men who find you attractive," said Elizabeth in maternal mode, using her given name. "When your smiles are beaming encouragement to these swains, please shower them on Joe Gillespie and Bat Webb."

Molly took wet and slippery Julia, her body child-soft, and began to towel her off. "Mr. Webb is too old for me and Mr. Gillespie I hardly know."

"You've been flirting shamelessly with him. Get to know him better."

"I flirt shamelessly with everyone. You know that," Molly said. "I expect to have a gay time with all the men, watching them drool over Matilda. She's so beautiful and modest they can hardly resist."

Elizabeth glanced up to measure her sister. She shook her head in warning. "I sometimes suspect that you believe it would be an interesting project to make Abraham Lincoln into something— At least socially acceptable."

"Mr. Lincoln has many fine qualities," Molly said. She set the naked child on the cold floor. Julia gave a cry, shivering, and before either woman could stop her, went running down the hall, crying, "Daddy! Daddy!" She disappeared into her father's study. When the women arrived to rescue the child—mid-December was no time to go running naked around the house—they found her sitting on Ninian's lap, cuddled in his arms.

Elizabeth slipped a nightgown over Julia's head and a robe around her shoulders. Ninian pulled her feet inside his coat. Elizabeth let Julia stay on her father's knee.

Out in the hall she warned Molly. "Please don't play Pygmalion to Lincoln's Galatea."

"Galateas don't often jump out of windows. Though it strikes me as a quick-witted thing to do. If I'm in a house on fire, I'll stick with Lincoln."

"But if it's your heart that's on fire, I fear he'd make a very poor choice."

As they stood in the hall, the women heard the stable boy spilling water on the kitchen floor as he took the metal tub back outside.

"Must you talk about him this way?" Molly asked. "Lincoln's my friend."

"I give credit where it's due," Elizabeth said. "Lincoln got the capital here. But since he's been the Whig leader, Whig representation has declined in the Legislature. Whig influence has declined in the state. Now this trick that went wrong has resulted in his jumping out a window. A fine example of what it means to be a Whig."

Both Molly and Matilda were showered with attention on the excursion to Jacksonville. Sarah Hardin teased them, saying, "It's certainly different having young ladies in the house again. These men are on their best behavior. Some are preening, of course, and being charming. Even the husbands."

Late the second day of the excursion Lincoln went outside behind the house to chop firewood. As if it were a lark Molly said she would help him. She had not been alone with him the entire trip. As she loaded wood into his arms, she said, "Mr.

Webb tells me you two campaigned together in Carmi."

"We did," said Lincoln, adjusting split logs on his arms.

"What's White County like?"

"It's rural."

"Sangamon County's rural, most of it. Is it like that?" Lincoln said nothing. Molly put on more logs and looked at him. "Is White County a place I'd like to live?"

"Maybe if you were a chipmunk."

Molly laughed. "Do I look like a chipmunk to you, Mr. Lincoln?"

"Not when you're loading wood."

"But sometimes I do? You're full of compliments."

"I'm full of wood. How much more you going to put on?'

"Till your arms drop," Molly said sassily. "Mr. Webb says you two drove his daughter Patty over to Wabash County to start in secondary school."

"She rode on my lap. Mine's more capacious than his."

"Would I like Patty?"

Lincoln cocked his head and scrutinized her. She hoped he would find this as curious a question as she meant him to.

"I expect you'd like her," said Lincoln. "Why do you ask?"

If he recognized her bait, he certainly wasn't taking it. "Why do you suppose I ask?" She swallowed hard and plunged ahead. "Mr. Webb keeps hinting about offering me a proposal of marriage."

Lincoln said nothing. Molly leaned down and took two large logs. As she rose to load them on Lincoln, she felt like throwing them at him. She glanced at him and he was grinning.

"You're not going to marry Webb," he said.

"Oh?" She slammed the logs down hard on his load.

"You're going to marry me." She looked at him. Had she heard him correctly? He looked back at her, as if he were not quite sure he had heard the words that had come out of his mouth. For both of them, as they gazed at one another, this moment seemed to last an hour.

Finally Molly said, almost in a whisper, "I am?"

"Yes, ma'am."

She regained her sense of herself. "Without being asked?"

Lincoln began to laugh as if the wood in his arms were weightless. "Don't get up on your high horse now, Molly."

"Are you asking me?" She looked peeved. "That's no way—"

Lincoln was still laughing. "I guess I am."

"You're such a jokester! How am I to know?"

"I am asking you."

Molly straightened up to her full height. "I don't see you down on your knee."

"You want me on my knee here? I'm carrying a load of wood."

"I wouldn't object."

Lincoln struggled to get to one knee without dropping the logs. When he was kneeling, he opened a hand. Molly put hers in it. Lincoln laughed. "This is an uncomfortable way to make a life commitment."

Molly pulled her hands away. She gave Lincoln a push. He fell on his side, spilling the wood. "You are the most exasperating man!"

Lincoln stood. "Can I kiss you?"

"Certainly not!" She picked up the split logs and reloaded them on Lincoln's long arms. He watched her eyes, but she would not look at him. When she was finished with the wood, she said, "When you want to be serious, I'll listen to your proposal. And you better make it before Mr. Webb makes his because I'll be listening to his, too."

"I'm serious right now, Miss Molly." But there was laughter in his voice. Molly stood erect and turned her back on him. He watched her march off, her back ramrod straight, her head held as high as she could lift it, the motion of her hips causing her skirt to sway delightfully.

Lincoln entered the house and delivered the wood beside the fireplace. Molly was in the kitchen. He went to her and said, "Miss Molly, I could use some more help getting another load of wood." She shot him an irritated glance. Under it her lips were trembling, trying not to smile. She followed him out behind the house to the woodpile. There Lincoln turned to her. "I don't want to exasperate you, Molly. I want to excite your warmest affections."

"You have, Abraham."

"I've wanted to blurt that out about marrying you for months."

"You've done a very good job of hiding that fact."

"I could hardly let myself believe our marrying would make any sense for you."

"Why not let me decide about that?"

He looked down at her and smiled. "You think for yourself. I like that." He shivered not from the cold winter day but from what was happening to them. "Are you cold?" he asked. He reached out, took her upper arms and rubbed them warm. She looked up at him. He kneeled before her on one knee and took her hands in his. "I love your intelligence, Molly. I love your spirit. Your beauty. The blue of your eyes. The fire in them when you're amused or angry."

"I don't get angry."

Lincoln shrugged. "You sometimes take offense. There's fire in your eyes then. That fire, I love it. I love you. I want to make you happy—always." He stared into her eyes for a long moment. "I really wonder: Can I do that? We're so different."

"I can be happy with you, Abraham. I love you."

"Will you marry me?"

"I will." She leaned forward to kiss him. He held her close to him.

"Can I kiss you whenever I want now?"

She kissed him. "Not when people are around."

He rose from his knee and brushed off the leg of his pantaloons. He took her hand and looked at her. She saw a sudden sadness in his eyes and reached up to stroke his cheek. "For months I've wondered about this," he said. "Could it happen? Could we possibly be happy together?" He looked at the ground, too shy with his emotion to hold her eyes with his. "Every day traveling around I've been thinking of you, wondering . . . Could this be?"

"Yes! It can! It will be!"

He glanced down at her, smiled shyly and looked away again. "'Scuse me, but I can hardly believe this. Abraham Lincoln, coming from where I've come from, marrying you." He glanced at her. "Oh, I hope we're happy."

"We will be. We love each other."

Lincoln grinned. "If we don't get some wood in the house, folks will wonder what's going on."

"When can we tell people?"

Lincoln gathered wood into his arms. "Let's wait a couple of weeks. I've got to get used to this idea."

"I was certain you loved me, Mr. Lincoln. But I would not have wagered on your actually asking me to marry you."

He handed her a couple of logs. "You go inside with these. I'll stay out here a spell to get acquainted with this amazing turn of events." She took the logs and smiled at him. He leaned down to kiss her.

She started for the house, humming. Watching her go, Lincoln realized that it was now his job to care for her and the children they would have for the rest of his life. This prospect elated him. It also made him wonder: What have I done? What have I done?

CHAPTER

13

As she walked back into the Hardin house, leaving Lincoln at the woodpile, Molly felt like dancing. Engaged to be married! Was she singing? She thought she must be. How could she hide her elation? Why should she want to? Could she take Matilda aside and tell her the news? Somehow she would manage. When she entered the house, Matilda and Sarah Hardin were busy in the kitchen. The men were talking politics with such absorbed interest that they paid her no attention.

Outside at the woodpile Lincoln dealt with his delight by splitting logs into kindling, humming to himself as his axe flew.

Until the party returned to Springfield, Molly, perhaps more joyfully than usual, showered flirtation upon Webb, Gillespie and Lincoln. Only the closest observers would have noticed a special twinkle in her eye when, after flirting with Webb and Gillespie, she glanced at Lincoln, enjoying their secret. Lincoln tried to keep his jealousy in check as his beloved paraded before his rivals an availability that she did not possess. He contented himself with the fact that she declined to take walks outside with the other worthies, complaining of the briskness of the air, but agreed to risk the oncoming winter with him. Sitting beside her before the fire after dinner, Lincoln felt relaxed enough to tell stories in the presence of ladies.

They were rustic rather than risqué, and everyone laughed.

After a full day at the Legislature Lincoln took Joshua Speed for a farewell dinner at the Globe Tavern. In less than a week Speed would sell his interest in the James C. Bell store to Charlie Hurst and soon thereafter start back to Kentucky. "Speed, I hate to see you leave," Lincoln told him. "You're the best friend I ever had."

"Come to Kentucky," Speed urged. He had been working on that idea for several weeks.

Lincoln knew why he could not move to Kentucky. Molly Todd had no intention of returning to the state inhabited by her stepmother. Their engagement was a secret—even from Speed. But as Lincoln looked at the friend he trusted implicitly, he said, "I'm going to tell you something I agreed not to tell anyone, not just yet." A smile spread across Lincoln's face. He bent toward Speed and Speed bent toward him. He whispered, "I asked Molly to marry me."

"You rascal!" Speed shouted.

Lincoln grabbed the lapel of Speed's coat and gave him a warning look.

His friend laughed. "Don't worry," he whispered. "I'm not going to shout it. When did this happen?"

"In Jacksonville," Lincoln confided proudly. "The words just tumbled out. I couldn't quite believe that it happened."

"She said yes?"

"She said, 'I don't see your knee on the ground.'" Speed laughed at this confirmation of the lady's identity. "When I put it to her officially, down on my knee, she said she didn't think I'd ever screw up the courage to ask her."

Speed offered congratulations. "You talked to Ninian?" he asked.

"I figure we can start married life right here in the Globe. Like the Wallaces did."

"You talked to Ninian?" Speed asked again.

"I'm sure Molly figures living here's going to be different from living in her brother-in-law's house." Speed started to speak, but Lincoln stopped him. "Don't ask again," Lincoln said. "No, I haven't talked to him." Then he added, "I'm going up there as soon as we finish here." He stared at the tablecloth a long moment, then grinned. "You wouldn't want to go up there for me, would you?"

"Thank you, no." They were silent for a time, contemplating Ninian Edwards. Speed advised, "Be who you are. That's who she wants to marry." He patted his friend's shoulder. "I'm sure he'll consent."

Lincoln nodded. "God has only one *d*," he noted. "But the Todds have got to have two."

Molly Todd stood outside the closed door of Ninian's study. "Come away from there," Elizabeth said.

"He hasn't come to talk Whig business," Molly said.

"Come away from there," Elizabeth repeated. "If the door opens quickly, you'll be mortified about it the rest of your life."

Molly considered this and walked down the hall, Elizabeth following. She went to the kitchen, entered it and moved to the stove, holding her hands over it to warm them. They were trembling. She knew Elizabeth had followed her into the room. She hoped they would not talk. Silence. Elizabeth was wondering if she should speak.

Then as her sister left, Molly heard the door swing closed. She exhaled a sigh. The warmth, silence and lingering aromas of dinner should have comforted her, but she felt too on edge even to be aware of them.

In the den Abraham Lincoln and Ninian Edwards stood side by side before the fire, warming the backs of their legs. Lincoln wondered where Molly was, what she was doing. "You know why I've come," he said.

"Not officially, no." Ninian moved away a step as if to separate himself from the business at hand. "You better tell me."

"I've asked Molly to marry me and she's agreed." Ninian took another step away. "We would like you to give us your consent."

Ninian was now standing so that Lincoln looked at his back, at the fine woolen cloth across his shoulders. Ninian said nothing for so long a time that Lincoln grew aware of the crackling of the fire, the smell of his host's tobacco. He waited, wondering if he had spoken in a dream and not out loud. Finally Ninian said, "Would you like some whiskey?" He left the fireplace and opened a cabinet in which sat decanters and a tray of glasses.

"No, thanks," Lincoln said.

His back still to Lincoln, Ninian took a glass, poured a healthy shot of bourbon into it, the sharp scent of it suddenly released to the room. He took a swallow. Savoring the bourbon on his tongue, whirling it in his glass, he turned back to Lincoln. He gazed at him for a long moment. "Let me talk to you like a brother," he said. "Would you like to sit down?" He gestured toward a chair.

"I'm fine here," Lincoln said.

"I feel that we are brothers, Lincoln, brother Whigs." Ninian took another sip of bourbon. This was going, Lincoln thought, as he feared it might: Ninian's aristocratic tongue professing kinship while his feet bespoke estrangement, his throat and his soul needing whiskey to survive this interview. If their talk was to be cordial, Lincoln thought, the business would need only a handshake. "We've fought some Whig battles together," Ninian said, "and won our share, thanks, I might say, to you." He increased their separation, walking behind his desk as if he would sit. But he remained standing. "Is this marriage really what you want?" he asked.

A strange question, Lincoln thought. "Of course," he said. "I'll do my best to make Molly happy." He felt awkward saying the words, but he got them out. Ninian made no reply, let the words wander around the room, bumping into things, displaying their ineptness. Lincoln felt obliged to chase those words with others. "I'm aware that my best may not be what she's accustomed to, but I will do my utmost."

Still Ninian said nothing. He sipped more whiskey, held it on his tongue, watched Lincoln. "If this marriage is what you both want," he finally remarked, "then it's what I want for you." He tried to smile, didn't quite manage it. "Molly's a wonderful girl, bright and intelligent." These pro forma declarations seemed false to Lincoln. Ninian shrugged. "She's maybe a little willful. You know that." He accomplished a smile, a chuckle. "Frankly, I'm glad to get her off my hands. It's time she got married. Unless she does, before you know it, she'll be an old maid."

Lincoln watched from the fireplace without speaking, surprised at this frankness. Ninian took another sip of bourbon and sat at his desk. He leaned back in his chair, feigning ease, and set his feet on the *Sangamo Journal* at the edge of the desk. "You know you're welcome here," he said, raising his glass slightly in salute, "and always will be."

"Thank you," Lincoln said, even though the words were not true.

"But let me remind you— " Ninian shifted his legs, rose again from his chair, leaned back against the bookcase behind him. "Country folks look at us as an— " He shrugged as if embarrassed to tell a country man like Lincoln about "country folks." "Excuse me using the word 'aristocracy,' " he said. "But it's true. Country folks regard us here on the hill as an aristocracy. Do you want people to think of you as an aristocrat?"

Lincoln smiled. "I don't think that's likely to happen, Edwards," he said. "I'm as plain in looks and manner as a pile of manure. Country folks know manure."

Ninian laughed and nodded, acknowledging Lincoln's superior knowledge in this matter. "You're a born politician, Lincoln," he said, as if in this matter as in all others Lincoln was acting the politician. Lincoln's eyes narrowed. Ninian raised his hands expansively to signal that he was not being insulting. "And you're a comer." Ninian took another sip of whiskey. "You arrived here— What? Hardly more than three years ago? You were so burdened by debt that you sold your own horse out from under you. Bill Butler paid your debts."

Lincoln did not try to hide his distress at hearing these words, and Ninian stood more erect, more self-confident, seeing Lincoln ill-at-ease.

"I've made some inquiries," he acknowledged. Lincoln nodded. "Discreetly, of course. I'm her guardian. I could do no less." The men studied one another. Ninian seemed to feel stronger now that he had taken the offensive, surprising Lincoln with what he knew. He slouched now, sat casually on the side of his desk.

Lincoln stood erect, hoping to appear in control of himself.

As if to explain, Ninian added, "Inquiries were necessary. You've never been forthcoming about your background."

"I've never pretended to be more than I am," Lincoln replied. "Or to have more than I do."

"I admire that in you," Ninian remarked. "We all do. You don't put on airs like that Irish upstart Jim Shields, who walks around town like a dandy. As if he were the handsomest man in Sangamon County."

Lincoln wondered if Ninian meant what he said about admiring him. Or was he being patronized?

Ninian continued, "It's never mattered to you that you carry the backwoods on your back. Like a badge. That your manners are unrefined. That you're awkward in the best company. Especially around women."

Lincoln now understood that these professions of admiration were, in fact, insults. That was how aristocrats handled these things. The fire crackled. A light scent of smoke rose from it. Even so, as Ninian stared at the liquid stirring in his glass, there seemed a stillness in the house. Lincoln knew that somewhere Molly was listening to it just as he was.

Again Ninian raised the glass to him. "You don't mind me saying this, do you?" He smiled engagingly. "That all the education you've ever had, you've gotten yourself. We esteem you, Lincoln. You're intelligent. You're canny and you're certain-

261

ly going to get where you aim to go." Once again he shrugged. "Men of my background value that. Do you know why? Because sometimes we lack the grit to drive for what we want. Often, in fact." Ninian took another sip of bourbon.

Lincoln understood that Ninian now felt so confident of being in charge of the interview that he could admit his own weakness: that he lacked grit. But an aristocrat did not require grit, whereas it was crucial if the countryman were to succeed.

"After three years here," Ninian continued, "you've made yourself into a well-known lawyer and a skilled politician. I've watched you on the stump. I've seen you in the Legislature, maneuvering men to your will, greasing them sometimes and swallowing them at others. I've wished I had your skills. Your leadership was the reason we got the capital transferred to Springfield."

This praise embarrassed Lincoln even though he knew it cut two ways. "We all did that together, Edwards," he said, "the whole Long Nine."

"You're skillful and modest," Ninian went on, as if delighted that Lincoln was jumping through hoops for him. "And from what I've seen you're not that interested in money. Good for you! That means you can't be bought."

Lincoln said nothing. Was this another insult? He assumed so. Aristocrats disparaged money because they'd always had plenty of it, whereas the countryman chased it, sometimes cravenly, because he knew he needed it to survive. Lincoln determined to let the insults roll off him. He would stay focused on his goal, the consent.

"But I have noticed," Ninian continued, "that you're interested in position." Lincoln tried not to react. Ninian had appraised him accurately, demonstrating that aristocrats were capable of reading the lower orders. "You want to move into a place where folks can look behind your appearance and your manner to see who you really are. You're chasing distinction. Am I right?"

Now it was Lincoln who shrugged. "Aren't we all chasing distinction?" he asked.

"But if a man comes from nothing, it's—" Ninian did not finish the thought. "Don't think being an aristocrat clothes a person in distinction," he went on. "Except maybe among other aristocrats. I know what folks in town think of those of us living up here on the hill. You're on your way off the hill to achieving distinction already. As a politician. As a leader." Lincoln felt that these were not insults. Could Ninian envy him these skills? "That's over for me," Ninian said. "I'm the son of a Governor of this state, of a Senator. But I'm out of politics."

"You know I was awful sorry that happened, Edwards."

"I can't say I wasn't." Ninian looked at the floor, not able to let Lincoln see the humiliation he still felt. "But I accept that when the state convention fell into the hands of country people, there was likely to be some feeling against the gentry up here on 'Quality Hill.' " He said the words "Quality Hill" with a scorn that made Lincoln realize Ninian had his problems, too. He pronounced them as if they were an insult, a failure on his part to embrace the egalitarian ethic of the country.

"They reject me because they consider me an aristocrat. So I want to warn you, Lincoln: if you marry Molly, they'll think you aspire to the aristocracy. That you come from them, but aspire to think yourself better than they are." Lincoln shook his head because, even if Ninian assumed he aspired to that, he did not. He and Molly would not be living in a manner that suggested pretensions to anyone. "Right or wrong," Ninian said, "country people will not forgive you for those aspirations. Just as they cannot forgive me for being who I am. Their small-mindedness and jealousy may keep them from giving you a chance to be the leader you have all the skills to be: a Congressman, a Governor, maybe even a Senator from Illinois."

Lincoln weighed Ninian's words and knew he had a point. Still he said, "Marrying Molly won't change who I am." Ninian gave him a disbelieving smile. "Voters know who I am. Anyway, I won't always be in politics."

"Lincoln, you're political to the bone."

Lincoln smiled. Now it was he who looked at the floor.

"Consider something else," Ninian said. "In another twenty-five years—you'll be in your middle fifties then, at the height of your powers as a politician—there's bound to be a national crisis over slavery." Lincoln nodded. "The Union may be severed, the North moving toward an industrial, free-labor economy, the South trying to maintain its agrarian, slave-labor way of life. Your destiny's with the North. As a politician you'll have to oppose slavery."

"I already do. You know that."

Feeling comfortable now with his part of the interview, Ninian poured himself more bourbon and pressed close to Lincoln. "What I know," he said, "is that you're thinking of marrying into a well-known family from a slaveholding background. Molly grew up in a slaveholding household. From the windows she could see the Lexington slave markets. Hasn't she told you about Mammy and

Harvey, Pendleton and Chaney? She loves those people—but as servants, inferiors." Lincoln knew this was true. But so what? He loved her, wanted to live with her. How could it matter what people might think in twenty-five years?

Ninian watched him. "If you marry Molly, her slaveholding background will dog your political career. 'She used to own slaves.' " He mimicked grumbling voters he had once represented. "That's what folks will say, whether it's true or not. 'Her family still does!' " Again the mimicry. "They'll say that, too. It'll hold you back." He shrugged. "Maybe she's worth it."

"I love her." These words were hard for Lincoln to get out. As he listened to them, they sounded trite and obvious.

"I take you at your word. Still," Ninian advised, "think about it before you jump."

The men fell silent. The fire had died in the fireplace. The logs had turned to embers, the red glow flaring and receding like the breathing of a living thing. Standing in the study, his legs no longer warm, Lincoln wondered what would happen in twenty-five years. Would he still be in politics? He expected so. Would the issue of slavery have become a national crisis? One could hardly doubt that. The North and the South were headed in different directions, and the extension of slavery had to be opposed. Would Molly's slaveholding background pose a problem?

"Molly's a fine girl," Ninian finally remarked, breaking the silence. "Clever. Attractive. Rather pampered. You know that." He smiled a little shamefacedly, as if he were responsible for the pampering. Lincoln watched him without replying, recalling that Molly described her upbringing not as pampered, but fraught with comfortable neglect. "She has a wicked and witty tongue," Ninian continued. "Accustomed to getting her way. A bit given to extravagance." Ninian let these negatives sink in. When they had, he went on with positives: "She can also light up a room. She's got the vivacity to charm the scowl off an angry constituent's face. And the best education of any woman I've ever met." He seemed to be reaching a conclusion. "I'm sure she'll dedicate herself to making you happy, giving you children and gladdening your home." He smiled and raised his glass to Lincoln.

He took a sip of the bourbon, tasted it on his tongue and seemed to decide he owed Lincoln further warnings. "But don't go into a marriage without realizing that she will be expensive to keep," he said. "She's been waited on all her life. I know she sees herself as one of the middle children of a large family, often overlooked. Still, her father could give her whatever she wanted. She likes fine things and money slips through her fingers." These words put an image in Lincoln's mind of gold coins falling through Molly's small hands that he felt so honored to hold. "Be aware of that," Ninian stressed. He smiled like the real brother he was proclaiming himself to be. "You'll tell yourself that all of that can be worked out. Probably it can. But," he shrugged, "she hasn't been able to work out all her problems. She came to Springfield, fleeing from a stepmother she couldn't stand. Has she told you about Miss Betsey?"

"I left my family, too," Lincoln said. "I have no problem with her doing that." Although he had fled his own family, he could not quite understand what Molly's differences were with Miss Betsey. His own stepmother had been one of the best

266

people he had ever known; she had always supported him.

"I'm glad we talked," Ninian said. "Will you
build a house for her?"

Lincoln swallowed. He still had debts; he had
neglected his law practice stumping through the
southern part of the state for a victory the Whigs
had not achieved. He could not possibly build
Molly a house.

Ninian grinned. "You weren't thinking of lodging her in Speed's store, were you?"

Lincoln smiled at this attempted witticism. "I
thought to start we'd live at the Globe Tavern.
Like Fanny and Will Wallace."

"Babies come pretty fast. That's what Fanny
discovered."

"We'll manage somehow," Lincoln assured him.
He requested what he had come for. "Edwards,
may I have your blessing?"

Molly remained alone in the kitchen, standing
now across the room from the stove beside the
swinging door. She held it ajar with her foot so
that she could hear when the men left the study.
She had folded her arms across her chest. Their
skin was stippled with gooseflesh, and she tried to
rub warmth into them. What could be taking them
so long? If the interview was going well, it should
be over. If it was going badly, it should have concluded by now. So what was happening? Was Ninian offering advice about how to conduct a marriage? How to please a woman? These were not
things Lincoln would discuss with him. Nor was
he any expert. Elizabeth was so submissive in
most things that Ninian would not have known if
he pleased her or not.

Molly paced back and forth to get her blood moving. She hummed to herself, the tune sounding plaintive when she needed something joyous. This was a woman's life: waiting, waiting, waiting for men. Intolerable! Someday women would— She heard movement. She rushed forward to listen. Silence. Was it her imagination? Or someone walking upstairs? What was taking so long?

For a long moment the two men stood across the study, staring at each other in the dim light of the oil lamp. Lincoln began to realize that consent was something Ninian would not give. "You don't need my blessing," he said. "Everything you've done, Lincoln, you've accomplished on your own. Why not this, too?"

An aristocrat's way of saying no. Lincoln tried to mask how much this refusal disconcerted him. "Will you stand in the way of our marrying?" he asked.

"No," Ninian said. "I've learned my lesson. Folks don't want us aristocrats forcing our way of doing things on others. Even our own family doesn't want that." He took refuge once more behind his desk, sipped at his glass for fortitude. "I know how resolute you can be. And Mary's very headstrong. So . . ." He shrugged. "Far be it from Elizabeth or me to stand in your way." He paused a moment, as if uncertain he should say anything more.

"Go on," Lincoln said.

"I really do want us to have talked like brothers." He opened his hands as if in supplication. His face assumed an expression of openness and sincerity. "If you marry her, we will be brothers." He paused, torn by a struggle inside him. "I'm

268

loath to say this to you, Lincoln. I've wondered for some weeks how I could."

Lincoln steeled himself. "Say it. I suspect I've heard worse about me than you'll say."

Ninian shrugged, submitting to Lincoln's advice. "There are people in town, in the state, who will never accept you. The real Kentucky aristocrats." He looked abashed at what he was saying, but he repeated, "They'll never accept you." This assertion demanded an explanation. "When they look at you, they don't see a man who's worked unstintingly to make something of himself." Now the stiletto, Lincoln thought. He prepared himself for the thrust. "They see a fellow consumed with ambition. A fellow who's ungainly, awkward—"

"Homely," added Lincoln. He knew the list.

"Yes, since you've mentioned it." Ninian smoothed the velvet lapels of his coat. "A man who smells of the earth and the common herd. A man completely without finesse. A man who wears his background on his back – just as we all do."

"Yes, let's be frank," Lincoln said. "So I'll ask: Is that how you see me?"

Ninian hesitated a long moment, then shrugged. "It's how my wife does." The man was no aristocrat, Lincoln thought. No aristocrat would assign to his wife opinions that he lacked the courage to acknowledge as his own. "Elizabeth will be polite to you, of course," Ninian said. "Because of her upbringing. She also wears her background on her back." Ninian stopped to let Lincoln taste his words. "The people who won't accept you will always say, 'He married a Todd to connect himself to an influential family.' They will say, 'He married a Todd, but if he'd had to, he'd have married a toad.' "

The sting of these words made it hard for Lincoln to speak. Finally he asked, "Your wife thinks that?"

"I should not have mentioned my wife. The jury will disregard . . ." Ninian tried to smile. "These people will say, 'Mary Todd couldn't get Stephen Douglas to ask for her hand . . .'"

The words were like a whiplash to Lincoln, to be compared even in this matter with Douglas. He tried not to react.

Ninian went on, "'. . . so she settled on Lincoln.' Then they'll laugh up their sleeves and ask, 'Was that really better than being an old maid?'"

Ninian sat on the edge of his desk, like a warrior wounded after striking a fatal blow. Lincoln wondered if he loved Molly enough to live with this all his life. He wondered if she loved him enough—if it was going to be like this.

Ninian said, "Since we're talking as brothers, as a brother let me say, I think you're making a mistake." The two men looked at one another, both spent now. It was as if they had gotten beyond contesting with one another. Now Ninian could merely state the truth. "When it comes to committing matrimony," he said, "it's a mistake you'll carry with you for the rest of your life. The people you were brought up with may have divorced or run off. But you're marrying a Todd. If you have any decency, you know that means forever." They stared at one another. "Forever," Ninian repeated. Lincoln nodded. Neither man lowered his eyes. "I give you this warning mainly, of course, because I don't want unhappiness brought into my life. Or my wife's. Or my children's." He opened his hands to indicate that he withheld nothing. "But neither do I want it brought into yours. I have no doubt that if you two marry, that's what will happen." He shrugged. "But I won't stand in your way."

Ninian drained his whiskey glass and set it on the desk. He stepped from behind it, starting to offer his hand, then put the hand behind him. "I'm glad we had this talk," he said. "Would you like to see Molly now?"

"It's getting late," Lincoln said. "I'll see her tomorrow or the next day."

Ninian opened the door for Lincoln and showed him from the house. Molly heard the men from the kitchen and hurried into the hall, expecting to see Lincoln. Ninian came from the entry. "Where's Mr. Lincoln?" she asked.

"It was getting late. He said he'd see you tomorrow."

Molly looked stunned. Surely she was supposed to see Lincoln before he left. "Why didn't he stay? What did you say to him?"

Ninian put an expression of reasonableness on his face. "I assured him that Elizabeth and I want you both to be happy." He looked at her carefully. She stared at him, wide-eyed. "Don't you believe me?"

"If that's what you said, then why did he leave?"

"I said, 'We want you both happy.' " He gave another of his shrugs. "I also said I thought the match was a mistake." Molly gasped. Ninian regarded her reaction wavering on a knife edge between acceptance and an anger that would lead to shouting. "I told him why I thought that."

"Did you insult him?"

Ninian looked as if he'd been offended. "People in our position don't insult each other."

"Did you list his deficiencies? I'm not Martha Washington, you know."

"Mary, you're shouting," Ninian said quietly. "Do you want Matilda to think you're an Irish scullery maid?"

Elizabeth came into the hall with a look of reprimand on her face. "The babies are sleeping," she said.

Molly hurried upstairs, tears in her eyes. She could not go to her bedroom for she was sharing it with Matilda, and she did not want to have to explain the tears. She went to the nursery. She could be alone there with the two sleeping children, but she must be sure to muffle her crying.

As Lincoln walked back down the hill to Speed's store, the air was cold. When he breathed, a chill filled his lungs. It spread throughout his body. He felt the chill, even in his overcoat, and a great relief that the interview was finished. For several days he had felt elated. Something had happened to him that he had not really thought ever could: he knew the happiness of being loved and making a woman happy by returning that love. The taste of that had buoyed him for several days. But as he walked down the hill in the cold, he felt the old melancholy settle down on him. By the time he reached the courthouse square his elation had turned to sadness.

The next evening there was one of a succession of year-end parties that bedazzled the Coterie. A number of young people gathered beforehand at the Edwardses. Joe Gillespie and Bat Webb, Jim Shields and Stephen Douglas were there, drawn like bears to honey, by Molly and Matilda. Speed arrived to vie for Matilda's smiles. Lincoln was not with him. Molly danced up to Speed gaily and whispered with concern, "Is everything all right?"

"I expect so," Speed said. "He's been at the Legislature all day."

"How was he when he got home last night?"

"I didn't see him. I was already asleep."

Molly made herself smile. Either Speed was covering for Lincoln, telling a white lie, or Lincoln had walked around town a good deal after leaving Ninian.

"He'll be along," Speed said. He gave Molly's arm a pat and made his way to Matilda. Molly put on her party smile and circulated among the guests, checking new arrivals every minute or so. Lincoln did not appear.

Finally it was time to leave. Molly could not stay behind, waiting for Lincoln, without revealing to the others that which they had decided to keep secret. So when Douglas and Shields offered their arms, she took them and left the house, laughing at Douglas's witticisms, but looking for Lincoln, wondering what kept him.

When Lincoln appeared at the party, he seemed distracted. Molly was dancing with Bat Webb. She disengaged herself as soon as she could and went to him. He looked as if he had not slept the previous night. "Are you all right?" she asked. "I'm worried about you." She took his hand and led him away from the dancing.

Alone in a hallway, he said, "I couldn't face entering Ninian's house."

"Was it awful?" she asked.

Lincoln shrugged. He tried to smile.

"Let's go back to the party. You'll feel better."

"No. I came to see you for a minute." He took her hand and kissed it.

"Kiss make well?" she asked. He smiled. She stood close to him.

He glanced about. "Someone's going to see us." He kissed the top of her head. "That person will tattle to Elizabeth. That'll give her the fantods."

"Come back inside."

Lincoln shook his head. "I wanted to see you." He did not dare to kiss her again. He squeezed her hands and smiled and left the party. Molly watched him go, wanting to run after him, to go wherever he went. But that would throw both Elizabeth and Ninian into a tizzy. She would never hear the end of it. Once again she put on her party smile and went back inside.

CHAPTER

14

When he called on her on the first day of the new year, the sight of Lincoln took Molly's breath away. She saw him walking toward the house, with the slow steps of a man twice his age, his hands thrust deep into his overcoat pockets, the wind lifting the knitted scarf off his neck. He did not look at her when he entered. When she kissed him, he was perfunctory. She tasted the cold on his lips, felt them chapped. She helped him out of his coat and, smelling agedness, was not sure whether the odor came from the coat or the man. She had seen him before in the grip of melancholy, but now he wore an expression of infinite sadness. His posture was stooped. His flesh seemed pasty and weighed down with troubles. "My dear," she asked, "what is it?" She took his hand and led him to the horsehair settee in the parlor. She shut the doors, stoked the fire and returned to sit beside him. Once again she took his hand. He did not seem the Lincoln she had last seen and certainly not the one, so full of humor and good spirits, who had asked her to marry him at the Hardins' woodpile only a week before. "What's happened?"

He gazed at her despondently, then leaned forward, his elbows on the thin knees, and stared at the fire.

"Abraham, what is it?" she asked again.

"I've been thinking," he said.

"They must be doleful thoughts," she replied, trying for a bright and playful tone that might cheer him. "But this is supposed to be such a happy time for us." She slid close beside him and linked her arm in his.

"I'm like a peasant. That's what I've been thinking." He paused. What could he be talking about, Molly wondered. He seemed hardly able to go on.

"You're not a peasant!" she told him cheerily. "We don't have peasants in America." She put her head against his shoulder and gazed up at him. "I thought you were a lawyer. Have I let the wrong man into my parlor?"

"I've been thinking," he said, not looking at her. Finally he finished the thought: "that I'm a peasant who wants to marry a princess."

"The princess intends to marry you."

He stared at the floor, his head held in his hands as if it would hang limply on his neck if he did not prop it up. "Or maybe it's more accurate to say—" He glanced at her woefully. She reached up to kiss his cheek.

"There, there," she said. "Whatever it is, it'll be all right."

He continued to stare at the floor. "Maybe it's more accurate to say . . . I'm like a plantation slave in old Kentuck . . ."

"A slave? What nonsense you're talking!"

He glanced at her quickly, shaking his head, then looked again at the floor. "We know what that situation is like," he said. "We've both seen slaves, lowly, humble, without prospects." He sat back disconsolately and glanced about the room. "You suppose there are slave boys who dream about marrying the daughter of the folks at the Big House?" What preposterous thing was he talking about? She did not know how to answer. "If there are, I'm like them."

"Abraham, what are you saying? You're not a darky. How could—"

"I'm not a darky," he said, "but I'm marked."

Molly sat back. What foolishness this was!

He stood and began to pace the room, a tall, thin figure slowly walking back and forth, spreading the smell of agedness and defeat, his head hung toward the floor, his hands in his pockets. "I'm marked," he repeated, "just as clearly as any slave is marked. Aristocrats of old Kentuck look at a black man and immediately put him into a box labeled Slave. They look at me and put me in one labeled Bumpkin."

"You're no bumpkin!" Molly exclaimed. "You're the best young attorney in Springfield. You're the leader of the Whigs in the Illinois House of Representatives."

"Bumpkin," Lincoln repeated, pacing. "Aristocrats look at me and, though I'm white, they know I'll never belong among them." He was talking, as if to himself, and Molly knew that he must have paced his office, telling himself the things that he was now telling her. "They can say to each other and even to me that, for a bumpkin, I'm quite an amazing fellow." He laughed hollowly. "I educated himself, became a lawyer and a politician. I make a decent, if precarious, living." He paced on, as if rehearsing a summation. "That's how some Springfield folks see me. How I try to see myself. But that's not how they see me. They see an 'ungainly fellow.' That's how Edwards expressed it."

"Who cares about Ninian!" cried Molly, astonished that such a man as Lincoln should care what Ninian thought. "He's accomplished nothing on his own."

"Awkward," Lincoln went on, moving back and forth before the fire. "Homely. I provided that word. Social pariah." He let the words reverberate around the room and seemed to be listening to them. "I don't blame Edwards," he went on, still pacing. "Because I am ungainly and awkward."

"It's not true," insisted Molly. "You've got a nobility about you that these so-called aristocrats can never match."

"Homely."

"You have nobility!"

"I am homely," he said, turning to her, inviting her to inspect him. She saw bone-deep weariness. "I'm homely and I wish I weren't. If I came from a long line of book-reading people, I'd look different. If my people had owned vast acreages and thousands of slaves—"

"If you had," she told him sneeringly, "I wouldn't look at you twice. I've known men like that. They're the reason I came west."

"If I'd been taught to use the right soaps and the right combs." He went on, almost automatically, reciting the self-depreciation he had been piling on himself. "If I'd gone to dancing school and Transylvania University like Edwards and given the graduation speech in Latin like he did."

Molly rose and took him by the arm. "None of that means anything!" She wondered if she were shouting.

"If I could greet my guests in French." Molly dragged him back to the settee and pushed him down. "If I knew how to choose the right fork and hold a teacup on my knee."

"You can hold me on your knee," Molly said, moving onto his lap. He let his forehead sink to her shoulder and lightly put his arms about her waist. "There," she said. "That's what I care about."

"I don't wear the right clothes," he went on, as if in a kind of trance. "I'm not charming to women."

Molly gazed at the top of his sad head and smiled. "I think you're wonderful," she said. "Does anything else matter?"

He leaned back, no longer in his trance, and crossed his arms over his narrow chest. "Of course, it matters," he said. "I can't have the woman I love being mocked by her own class of people." His hands and shoulders moved; his face contorted itself into that of gossips. He mimicked, "That poor Molly Todd. Had such prospects. Then she went and threw herself away on that rustic scarecrow." Molly laughed at his mimicry, but Lincoln shook his head. He was not seeking to entertain her, but to report what would be said. "Assured her he could provide for her, but he can't."

"Is that the problem?" Molly asked. "You think you can't provide for me?"

Lincoln lowered his eyes and said nothing.

"And for our children?"

"Children come fast, you know."

"You'll be able to provide for us," Molly said patiently, beginning to refute all that he had said about himself. "You're a man of talents and capacities and promise. You'll be going to Congress one of these days. John Todd Stuart won't want that office forever." Lincoln listened to her, staring into space, and Molly did not know if he was merely tolerating her or if he heard her words. "You could be a Senator. Maybe even President." She spoke with conviction. Those words might seem far-fetched to most people, but Molly Todd believed them.

"Senator, maybe," Lincoln said. "I'd need someone helping me get there."

"I want to give my life to helping you, Abraham. I really do see nobility in you."

"Stop, Molly." He lifted her off his lap and set her lightly on the settee beside him. He put his head in his hands. "We're talking fairy tales here." He rose and stood before her, looked down at her out of his sadness. "I'm trying to tell you. This can't be." He glanced at her, then looked away. "I can't let this be . . . for you."

"Do you love me?"

At first he did not reply, gazing at the floor. He looked older than her father, older than Henry Clay, who also possessed nobility. "That's not the question to ask."

"What is the question to ask?" she said quietly.

"Could you love me if I never made anything of myself?"

"But you will. I see it in you."

Lincoln said nothing.

"Have you lost confidence . . . in what we can be together?"

He turned his back on her and started pacing again. Now he turned back to her. "I've seen more of the world than you, Molly. I've seen . . . failures. Reverses. I spent the autumn stumping for a Whig victory in Illinois and it didn't happen. Sometimes you work and work and it still does not happen."

He seemed infinitely tired to her.

"And after talking to Edwards, I understand better how his people see me."

"I'm his people!" She was not being submissive. Lincoln could not want her to submit, not to these lies about him. "I do not see you that way!"

"I mean the men from old Kentuck . . . the aristocrats, as he calls them."

Molly thought of the energy he had expended in campaigning, the intellectual strength and vitality, the showmanship, that each of the speeches required. The bad roads between towns. The trudging on, even in rain. The inns where he'd stay, sharing beds with strangers. At the end of all those roads was disappointment. And debts. No wonder he was tired. "Together we will be all right," she said. If she won the argument, she wondered, would it be true?

"You say that, my sweet Molly. But what do you know about me?"

"All I need to know."

He got down on his knees before her and took her hands. "You know nothing about me," he said. "I've been careful never to talk about what I've come from."

"I don't care where you come from. I care what you are!"

He spoke now as if making a confession. "A lot of folks are aware I never trot out my background. Edwards pointed that out to me. It's true."

"Tell me then." She looked into his eyes and smiled. "Am I going to be shocked?" The question surprised him. "Am I going to run from this room, screaming, 'Save me, Ninian! Save me!' "

Lincoln smiled, shook his head. She grinned at him.

"I am waiting to be shocked."

He lifted himself off his knees and sat beside her. He leaned against the back of the settee and stared at his hands. "Have you any idea the kind of work these hands have done?" Gently she touched those hands. He dropped them beside him. "I was born in a one-room cabin in Hardin

County, Kentucky. My grandfather—another Abraham, I was named for him—was killed by Indians. My father was just a boy then, eight years old. All my grandfather owned passed to Mordecai, his oldest son." He smiled resignedly. "Uncle Mord ran off with all the talents in the family. And all the money. So my father had to fend for himself. Got himself a few acres of land. Married my mother. Had a daughter."

Learning of Lincoln's people, Molly suddenly realized that he came from white trash. Molly's father regarded poor whites as a pestilence on the land, hardscrabble land-grubbers who undermined slaves' respect for their masters. Certainly in Lexington she had never considered marrying into a white-trash family. It seemed hard to accept that Lincoln's Uncle Mordecai was a member of her father's class while his father, Mordecai's brother, was a man the Todds would scorn. Their scorning him: she had sensed this, she supposed, but had never thought of it in these terms. No wonder he said he was like a slave wanting to marry the daughter of the Big House. She wondered again if the marriage would work.

Explaining who he was, Lincoln wondered if he should acknowledge to this daughter from the Big House how little he knew about his mother's family. He'd heard his mother was not legitimate. Probably she was the daughter of some Virginia planter, a young aristocrat, who had put his grandmother in a family way. He sometimes thought that his ambition, his ability to analyze, and any nobility of character he actually possessed must have come from that aristocratic forebear. It seemed impossible that it could have come from people who scratched the soil for a living like his father. But he would not tell her these things. Nor would he say that his sister had come cross lots, conceived before the marriage. Nor that his father could hardly read. If he told her such things she might truly run screaming from the room.

"After I came along," he said, "my father kept moving us to different small holdings, trying to find better land." Molly realized his really was a white-trash family, living more precariously than many of her father's slaves. Everything the family owned could be loaded into a wagon. There really was nobility in Lincoln's character if he had risen out of that. "Finally we moved to Indiana," Lincoln continued. "It was a free state and my father didn't hold with slavery. Also the government had surveyed the land, unlike in Kentucky, and it was possible to get clear title to a holding. The land he chose in Perry County was plumb in a forest. He had to hack a trail to get there."

Telling Molly this, Lincoln wondered what her family's holdings had been. Undoubtedly they had slaves working land; that was his impression from Ninian. His father did not like slavery partly because he did not want to compete with slave labor. By the time his father was farming, vast tracts of Kentucky's best land were owned by men of wealth, like Molly's father, who employed gangs of slaves to till their holdings.

"I was seven when we went to Indiana," Lincoln went on. "We lived in another one-room cabin." Molly glanced at the room in which they were sitting. Had the cabin the Lincolns lived in been no bigger than this? "At night you could hear panthers screaming," Lincoln said. "Bears would come out of the forest and make off with the swine. When I was ten, my mother took milk-sick and died. We were still clearing the farm. It wasn't producing much to speak of. We lived on what we hunted."

Molly turned to Lincoln and threw her arms around him. If she found it hard to connect with poor whites, she knew what it was like to lose a mother. When her own mother had died— What a terrible time! And yet she had at least been so-laced by a well-established home and by slaves like Mammy, who gave her comfort. How dreadful for Lincoln to lose his mother when the family was living in the wilds. Maybe that accounted for his moodiness, the sadness so often in his eyes.

"My father knew we couldn't survive alone," Lincoln continued. "So after about a year he went back to Kentucky. He found a widow he'd known as a boy, paid off her debts and married her."

What a way to marry, Molly thought. Marriage as a business arrangement. "Did they—" She hesi-tated to ask. "Did they love each other?"

"They needed each other," Lincoln explained. "She had three children. He brought her and her children to us in Indiana."

"Was she awful?" asked Molly.

"She was wonderful to me." Lincoln paused for a moment thinking of Sarah Johnston Lincoln, remembering the wealth she and her children had brought to his father's homestead: bedding, a spinning wheel, a table and chairs, a walnut bu-reau and a habit of cleanliness. How dirty he and his sister must have looked to her the first time she saw them! Lincoln said, "We survived because of her. Once she came, we weren't just a misera-ble threesome fighting the wilderness anymore. She helped me get what schooling I could. It wasn't much. She let me read by the fire at night when my father wanted me doing chores." Lincoln gazed at Molly and smiled. "You didn't run off."

"Did you think I'd admired you all these months," she asked, "wondering how I could land you, without wondering where you came from?" But the truth was it had taken a while to perceive his virtues, to penetrate the awkwardness. And if she, like so many others, had at first considered him a bumpkin lawyer, she had never thought of him as white trash.

"Have you been back to see the family?" Molly asked.

Lincoln shook his head. Family life had been for him a kind of oppression. Except for his step-mother. He had not really connected with his own kin. His people were content to live scratching the ground, never escaping the soil. Having never felt deeply connected to family, it seemed an uncertain thing to try to form one now—and with this woman of privilege and education who had known nothing of his background. With no model to emulate, the odds of failing were better than those of succeeding. Did he know how to get close to a woman? This one would want to be a partner. It would be different with someone like Sarah Rickard, who had no better education than he did and was so much younger. Molly would make a claim on his life. She'd want children, but his experience of fathers had not been good. Could he please her in the process of fathering their children? Would she be disappointed with him? What he knew of that process had been learned around the farm. He would be a bumpkin in that, too.

"Just like I'm not going back to Lexington," Molly said finally. They were two people, she realized, who had left their families behind. She wanted to leave Elizabeth and Ninian, too.

"I wanted to use my head, not my hands. Not my back."

"I'd like to use mine, too," Molly said. "Not much chance for a woman there."

They both had capacities beyond their place, Molly thought. Their world would allow Lincoln to strive to use his, but hers must still be hidden.

Lincoln told her about keeping a store and being a postmaster in New Salem, contracting a debt for provisions that had not yet been settled. He told her about meeting people who later helped him in the Black Hawk War, about getting himself elected to the Legislature and reading law. "The rest you know."

"Thank you for telling me," Molly said. "You're not the man my father expected me to marry. Or Elizabeth or Ninian. But you're the man I want to marry. Intend to marry. That's all that matters to me."

"Thank you for saying that."

"I mean it."

He looked at her for a long time with a kind of infinite sadness. There was wetness in his eyes that he tried to blink away. Finally he said, "You haven't understood what I've been saying." He lowered his eyes. "I should not have spoken to you as I did in Jacksonville." He glanced at her, seeing the uncertainty in her eyes. "We say we're the land of the free. But we're not free. In real life the peasant doesn't marry the princess. The slave, who knows he's not free, does not marry the daughter of the folks at the Big House. I should not have spoken as I did."

"But it can happen!" Molly said. "We are free to marry. Who's to stop us?"

"I've got debts, Molly." He glanced at her, then looked at the floor. She did not care about his debts. Why wouldn't he look at her? He said, "I can't provide for you."

"That's nonsense. I'm not a princess. I'm a woman who wants to be with you."

Lincoln looked over at the fire, avoiding her eyes. "I don't love you," he said. He glanced up. Molly looked stunned, as if he'd hit her. Tears flooded her eyes. She bit her lips.

Lincoln stared awkwardly at the floor, knowing he'd hurt her. After the interview with Ninian he had known he had to do this. But he had not wanted to do it this way. Those terrible words were the ones that Speed insisted he must say. They had discussed it the night before when he had shown Speed the letter he intended to have delivered, and Speed, who had so much experience in these matters, assured him it could not be done that way. Now he glanced up at her, his words still reverberating in the room. "I don't love you enough if this goes bad," he said. If he did not love her, why did he feel tears rushing into his eyes, a lump forming in his throat? He reached out to take her hands. "Just a month ago when something wasn't working the way I'd planned, I jumped out a window. But I couldn't do that with this." Tears were running down his cheeks as they were down hers. "I couldn't stand to see you miserable. And you probably would be."

She stood, trying to maintain her composure, looking mystified, betrayed. Lincoln reached out to her, drew her to him, lifted her onto his knee and kissed her. They held one another, trying to control their emotion, kissed one another.

Lincoln lifted her from him. He rose, his sadness almost more than she could bear. He stepped back, looking at her, went to the door and was gone.

CHAPTER

15

As Lincoln left, Molly burst into sobs. Tears streamed down her cheeks. She thrust the side of her hand into her mouth so that Elizabeth would not hear. Although her body was shaking with sobs, a kind of paralysis seemed to grip her. She felt rooted to the settee, staring at the door through which Lincoln had departed. She could not think. She could only wonder: What just happened? "I don't love you," Lincoln had said. Then he had lifted her to his knee—he was crying—and kissed her. So he did love her! But she was alone now. He had gone. What just happened? she asked herself. Had something shaken his confidence in himself? Or had the campaigning of the last months broken him with exhaustion? Could he mean what he'd said? Was the engagement off? No! He did love her!

A knock sounded at the door. Molly had no idea how long she'd been alone. She brushed the tears from her cheeks, tried out a maniac smile, sought to compose herself. Another knock. Elizabeth opened the door, peeked inside. "Did I hear Mr. Lincoln leave?" she asked. Molly nodded, biting her lips. "Aren't you chilly?" Molly saw that the fire had died to embers. "You'll catch your death of cold in here." Elizabeth stirred the embers with a poker, bent to take another log and placed it on the coals. She turned and examined her sister, noticing the redness of her eyes, the wetness of her nostrils, detecting her nervousness and shame. "Is everything all right?" She sat beside Molly, took her hands and chafed them. "Are you all right?"

Molly bit her lips and did not look at Elizabeth. Finally she asked, "What did Ninian say to Mr. Lincoln?"

Elizabeth scrutinized her. If something had happened—and there was no other explanation for Molly's behavior—Elizabeth did not want the blame to fall on her husband. "What do you mean?" she asked. "They talked together like gentlemen."

"He must have said—" Molly felt emotion churning inside her. She did not want to appear vulnerable to Elizabeth or seem an object of pity. She controlled the upheaval inside her, but she could not look at her sister. "Now Lincoln wonders if it's a good idea."

"My dear, we've all wondered that."

"What did Ninian say?"

"Did Lincoln break the engagement?"

"Did Ninian tell him that he was like a peasant wanting to marry a princess? Did he say that Lincoln would never be accepted by you two?"

Ah, Elizabeth thought, we've escaped. She found it difficult to mask her relief. "This is probably not the time to say this," she acknowledged. "But if the match is off, you can count yourself a very fortunate girl. That marriage would have been disastrous." She patted Molly's hands happily, her mind already planning how to manage the announcement of this news. Molly watched her with the same distaste she had felt for her stepmother. Miss Betsey had also tried to arrange her life.

"Fortunately, not many people know there was an engagement. Isn't that so? You two weren't telling people till you both had worn the idea a bit. Now you realize it doesn't fit well." In her head Elizabeth began to list the things that must be done. "First, you must write a letter, releasing him from any obligation. Then we'll quietly tell a few people that he realized he'd overreached himself. You took pity on his aspiration and impulsively accepted."

"No," said Molly. "I love him. He hasn't overreached. I won't have you saying that about him."

"You're thrilled by the idea of shocking a few people," Elizabeth said, as if Molly were the limb of Satan that Miss Betsey always claimed. "We'll say you considered the proposal and refused him."

"No. Because if he returns here tomorrow with his confidence restored, I'll be ready to run off with him."

"Mary, please."

"I'm not even sure the engagement's broken."

"You must consider what the town will say. You're its brightest ornament. A sparkling belle cannot go begging a bumpkin to declare for her. How ignoble!"

"You will not say anything that belittles him. You understand?"

"The main thing is . . . you're out of it. You must write that letter." Molly shook her head. She would not write a letter of release, not just now. Elizabeth smiled at an idea that pleased her. "We'll say that he became infatuated with Matilda. That won't belittle him. It will just show that he doesn't know his way around better society."

"Yes, say that, dear sister," agreed Molly scornfully. "No one will believe you. Lincoln hasn't had

291

a minute's conversation with Matilda. Everyone knows it's Speed who swoons after girls, not Lincoln. But understand this: you will not say anything derogatory about Lincoln. Whatever it was Ninian said did damage enough."

When Lincoln returned to the store, Speed was arranging the fire, about to go upstairs. "I thought you might be gone an hour," he said. "But you've been gone half the night."

Lincoln sat down and stared at the embers.

"Well?" Speed asked. Lincoln said nothing. For an hour he had been wandering around Quality Hill, where no one would see him crying. He was dealing with a confusion of emotions he'd never known before. His body felt hollow. Shame and the humiliation of inadequacy had swallowed his innards, leaving only pain. He imagined that Molly was feeling even worse than he was—if that were possible. "Well?" Speed repeated.

Lincoln pulled off his boots. "Did you sell your interest in the store to Charlie?"

"All taken care of. He's the proprietor now and I'm on my way back home." A silence. Speed scrutinized his friend. It was clear from Lincoln's posture and his doleful face, barely visible in the last glow of firelight, that the interview with Molly had not gone well. "Did you make the break like we discussed?"

Finally Lincoln said, "I guess."

"You told her you didn't love her, right?" Lincoln made no reply. "I know it's hard to say. But . . ." Speed's voice trailed off.

"I should have done it by letter." Lincoln had written Molly a letter unequivocally ending the engagement. But Speed had objected that these matters were not handled in this way. He should know; he had handled them often enough. Women kept such letters, Speed explained. Written words were an eternal monument against a man. But Lincoln had not thought he could manage it any other way. "If you won't deliver it," Lincoln told him, "Billy will. He hasn't liked Molly since she took exception to being compared to a serpent." Speed threw the letter into the fire. Together they had watched flames consume it.

Now Speed repeated what he had said the previous night. "No fellow with any manhood does it with a letter." He asked again, "What happened?"

Lincoln extended his feet toward the fire and rested his chin on his collarbone. He folded his hands across his chest.

"You told her frankly, right, that you didn't love her?"

"I did. Through tears."

Speed shook his head. "You weren't crying."

"I was. She was. It was like Niagara."

"But you got out of there, right?"

Finally Lincoln said, "I took her on my knee and kissed her."

"For God's sake, Abe! It's not done that way."

"I don't have your experience breaking hearts."

"You made a bad lick of that last."

"Am I out of it?"

"Maybe she'll release you. Then you'll know."

Discussing it with a man who knew about these things, Lincoln felt his emotions begin to settle. He would hurt for a while—Speed acknowledged that—but basically he would be happily free and relieved that the deed was done. He wanted to be married. Every man did. Speed certainly did. But the prospect of marriage was terrifying. Especially with Molly Todd. How could he provide for her? And fit in socially? He thought he loved Molly, but what did he know of love? Probably after two weeks of marriage they would realize they had made a mistake.

"Why is this so complicated?" Lincoln asked. "Billy Herndon, who's underfoot around this place, is asleep right now curled up against the little wife he's had a good time making pregnant. And here we are, fellers who know a lot more than Billy ever will, and this business completely flummoxes us."

"Some fellers jump off the cliff," Speed said, "and pure bliss catches them. Others howl all the way to the bottom and go crash."

Lincoln sat by the fire after Speed went up to bed. He wondered how Molly was feeling, wondered if she thought it was over. Now that Speed was gone, he could admit to himself that he hoped it wasn't over. Molly made him feel alive. When she entered a room, he wanted to smile; his heart stopped beating for a moment, then got all warm. She made him feel important and fascinating, maybe even noble. That was her word. It astonished him that she wanted to smile when she saw him. This was a woman of discriminating tastes. If he fascinated her, if she saw nobility in him, he could not be dismissed as awkward and homely. He loved Molly. She could take him places he wanted to go. She could be a comfort to him as they journeyed.

He stared at the fire, which had now died, and felt cold. All this emotionalism, he thought; it was like a malady. The strain of trying to please another being, of being responsible for a woman's happiness: that was probably more than he could handle. He felt queasy. Maybe it was better that it was over.

Throughout January Molly made a pretense of high spirits around the house in order not to arouse the curiosity of the Irish girls or the Edwardses from Alton. Despite her duties as the mother of a newborn, Elizabeth watched her as carefully as a nurse with a fragile patient. She urged Molly to write Lincoln a letter of release, as if doing that might work as a kind of medicine. As much as possible Ninian avoided his ward. He feared that Molly's quietude around him might unexpectedly burst into screeching accusations of driving Lincoln away. To avoid these at the table he often invited other out-of-town visitors for dinner. Matilda did not ask about the abrupt end of Lincoln's visits; she associated them with the departure of the ever-attentive Joshua Speed. Acquaintances no longer came to coo over Baby Bertie, and the Coterie enjoyed a respite from parties. Hostesses still concocted afternoon entertainments for ladies. Attending these, Molly feigned the vitality and playful wit universally expected of her. She and Matilda assumed the roles of the town's reigning belles. Molly happily allowed Matilda's beauty to take center stage.

When Molly was alone, she daydreamed that Lincoln laid siege to the house. He overturned the social order of Quality Hill. His confidence revived, he defied Ninian and the Kentucky aristocracy. Sometimes he invited Molly to set the date of their wedding. Sometimes, sweeping her away on the back of a steed, they eloped.

But Lincoln did not come to call. She dared not ask friends for news of him. Nor could she go to his office or the Legislature or Speed's store, hoping to see him.

For his part Lincoln moved through the days like an automaton. He woke and dressed from habit. He took his meals at the home of Bill Butler. He checked in at the office and spent hours staring at the walls. Congressman Stuart, long off in Washington, had not visited the place for months. Lincoln sat through sessions of the Legislature, voting on measures, hardly knowing what they provided. After Speed left for Kentucky, Charlie Hurst put the barrel of corn liquor off-limits. Few men gathered around the store's fireplace at night. Lincoln had always been content with his own company; now he felt lonely, abandoned. He packed his few belongings and moved to the Butler house. Sarah Rickard was often there, still a teenager, but ever more womanly, ever more marriageable. They treated each other like siblings.

Lincoln thought constantly of Molly, wondering how she was, wishing he could see her. He knew that Napoleon would have stormed the house and taken her away with him. What would Washington have done? He knew that Elizabeth would urge her to send a letter of release. He daydreamed that she refused and, instead, sent word vowing defiance of her family. This she did out of noblesse oblige; it was the princess, not the peasant, who must reach out. He mused that she appeared at his office seeking legal counsel. A friend had received a proposal of marriage, she revealed, only to have the swain express reservations about the match. What was her friend's legal position? As they discussed this dilemma, he set her on a stack of law books and kissed her. She persuaded him of his unusual goodness, and they resolved to marry.

At the end of his days in the Legislature he would go by his office, hoping to find a note she had slipped under the door. But no note was left. He sat at his desk until dusk, to be present in case she came. But she did not come.

When day after day passed and Lincoln did not call at the house, Elizabeth insisted that Molly do what etiquette required. She must write the letter of release. After these sessions with Elizabeth, Molly would throw on a cape and walk through the cold January air, trying to clear her head. She hoped she would encounter Lincoln taking a solitary ramble on the Hill. When she did not, words of the letter began to form in her mind.

At last she wrote the letter. Tears ran down her cheeks as she dipped her pen in the inkwell. Her words released Lincoln from all obligations of a contract. Her own feelings had not changed, she wrote. She afforded Lincoln the privilege of renewing the courtship whenever he wished. To put an end to her badgerings, she showed the letter to Elizabeth and asked her to have it delivered.

When Lincoln received the letter, a fog of blackness enveloped him. He had always been healthy. Now he took to bed, felt himself pulled ever deeper into sadness and melancholy—the "hypo" he called it. Friends thought that he might not revive, that he had gone insane. Some of them feared that he would take his own life. They removed knives and razors from his room.

Gossip buzzed through Springfield. Molly had thrown Lincoln over. No, no! Other way around. John Hardin's sister wrote her brother inquiring if Lincoln had suffered "two cat fits and a duck fit." "Poor Lincoln," Jim Conkling wrote Mercy Levering. "How the mighty are fallen! He was confined about a week, but though he now appears again he is reduced and emaciated in appearance and seems scarcely to possess strength enough to speak above a whisper. His case at present is truly deplorable."

When Molly heard reports of Lincoln's collapse, she wanted to go to him. Elizabeth and Ninian absolutely forbade her to see him.

Toward the end of January Lincoln wrote his partner John Todd Stuart, "I am now the most miserable man living." Although he was back at work in the Legislature, his spirits would not recover for months. His letter went on: "If what I feel were equally distributed to the whole human family, there would be not one cheerful face on earth. Whether I shall ever be better, I cannot tell."

CHAPTER

16

Pleased that Molly Todd had rejected the Whig leader just as Illinois voters had rejected the Whigs, Douglas and Shields began paying calls again at the home of Ninian Edwards. Molly charmed them with sparkling conversation while Matilda's demureness delighted them. The men preened and chuckled. The long fight had begun in the Legislature to change the composition of the Illinois Supreme Court from Whig to Democratic. They wanted to share battlefield tidbits with Molly. Douglas acknowledged that he was leading the fight. "From the lobby, of course," he said. "I'm not a member of the Legislature. But the general doesn't need to be in the trenches."

"Our Democratic majority is going to change Illinois," Shields promised. "We're going to expand the Supreme Court from four justices to nine. Would you ladies like to be justices? We're taking names."

"Justice will not become the plaything of politics, will it?" asked Molly.

"No more than it was," Douglas assured her. "The old Whig majority was blindly Whiggish."

"We will also pass a measure, granting aliens the right to vote."

"That is an outrage," said Molly. "Why should Irishmen vote in our elections?"

"We don't vote in theirs," noted Matilda.

"*We* don't vote in ours either," said Molly.

"Do politics interest you, Miss Edwards?" Douglas asked, trying to draw her attention to himself.

"Not really," Matilda replied, not looking up from her crocheting. "If I had the vote, I'm sure I wouldn't know what to do with it."

"If Irish canal diggers were voting Whig," said Molly, "you'd both be working hard to pass a measure preventing them from voting."

"But until they do," said Douglas, "we'll champion their right to exercise the franchise." He giggled. "And that, my dear ladies, is the beauty of politics."

Molly learned quickly enough at the dinner table that the Democrats had succeeded in doing precisely what Douglas and Shields had outlined. Before she knew it, the two gentlemen had returned with more good news.

"Douglas has been appointed a Supreme Court justice!" Shields proclaimed. "He really is a comet crossing the prairie sky."

"It's remarkable," agreed Molly. "Quite astonishing, I would say."

"Have you ever known a man who accomplished so much at twenty-seven?"

Hoping that a change of scene might jolt Lincoln out of his "hypo," John Todd Stuart wrote Daniel Webster, Old Tippecanoe's incoming Secretary of State, recommending that Lincoln be named the American *chargé d'affaires* at Bogota, Colombia.

Late one afternoon in early April, while he was studying the particulars of a case, Lincoln heard urgent footsteps running along the corridor to the office. A knock sounded at his door and the door flew open. A boy stood in it, panting heavily, his cap in his hand. "Mr. Francis says to come right away. He got a telegram from Washington. The President's dead."

Lincoln ran with the boy to the *Sangamo Journal* offices. Simeon Francis handed him the telegram. As he read it, the boy went off to round up Ned Baker, Stephen Logan and others at the courthouse.

"A month in office to the day," Francis said. "This is a catastrophe. Tyler isn't really one of us."

Lincoln handed the telegram back to Francis and took a chair.

"You want to write something for us?" Francis asked.

"Who'd have thought an Indian fighter would die of pneumonia and job seekers," Lincoln said. "I wouldn't know what to write."

William Henry Harrison, for whom Lincoln had campaigned so tirelessly, had been inaugurated as the country's ninth President on March 4. Although the inaugural ceremony was held in a cold drizzle, Old Tippecanoe had insisted on delivering his address without overcoat or hat. Whigs had laughed about it at the time. Old Tippecanoe was sure full of beans, they said. But he had contracted pneumonia. Office seekers pestering him for positions had complicated his recovery. Now he was dead. He would be succeeded as President by John Tyler of Virginia, a slaveholder who was not a Whig at all, but a maverick, anti-Jackson Democrat put on the Whig ticket to attract southern votes.

"Always some new crisis in politics," Francis said.

Lincoln nodded and returned to his office. But he did not want to work. He went back to the Butler house. Sarah Rickard was there, peeling potatoes for the evening's stew. When she saw Lincoln, she felt alarmed. He looked a little the way he had in January when he was in bed for a week. "Are you all right?" she asked. "Can I get you some water?"

"Come take a walk with me," he said. "The President has died."

"Wasn't he just elected a while ago?"

"Come walk with me. I'll tell you about him."

They strolled out into the country, talking not about the President, but mainly about flowers coming into bloom and leaves starting to unfold on the trees. Lincoln did say that because a new President would be taking office, a job he might have had in South America would not be offered him. Sometimes they did not talk at all. Sarah realized that the President's dying signified things to Lincoln that she could not even imagine. She understood, perhaps for the first time, that now and then a man just wanted a woman to be with him.

For his part Lincoln took stock of his life. The last months had been an up-and-down time: up with great hopes about Molly and for the election, down with the voters' rebuke of him and the Whigs' failure in Illinois; up with Molly's agreeing to marry him, down with Ninian Edwards's making it clear that he had overreached; slightly up with the prospect of getting out of Illinois for a consular job overseas, down with Harrison's death, a non-Whig slaveholder's entry into the White House and the end of any hopes of a consular posting.

Lincoln knew that politics was the art of the possible. Perhaps living happily, usefully, also partook of that art. It was time, he thought, to be realistic about where he was headed and his prospects for getting there. He would never succeed with the Coterie; he had already set himself on a path away from Quality Hill. Since his practice of the law was beginning to succeed, it made sense to leave politics and focus on the law. He wanted a wife. Molly Todd could talk about marrying only for love. But he would be realistic. Affection and partnership would have to be enough to win a young woman, perhaps the younger the better. They would sustain a marriage across decades; interest in their children would hold them together. Sarah Rickard was in love with Joshua Speed, but would never see him again. Would she marry his best friend? Lincoln decided to find out.

Months passed. Molly and Lincoln did not meet. Although the town saw Molly and her cousin Matilda Edwards as embellishments of gaiety to its civic life, and Molly assiduously acted this part, inside she felt hurt, lonely, uncertain of her prospects.

In June, almost six months after the breakup with Lincoln, she once again wrote Mercy Ann Levering. "My late silence would doubtless lead you to imagine that you were only occasionally remembered," she wrote. "I have been much alone of late and my thoughts have oft been with thee, why I have not written oftener appears strange even to *me*, who should best know *myself.* That most difficult of all problems to solve, my evil genius Procrastination has whispered me to tarry til a more convenient season & spare you the infliction of a letter which daily experience convinces me would be 'flat, stale & unprofitable.' " Pausing, her pen at her inkwell, she wondered how much Merce would read between the lines of her letter, surmising, as before, that Jim Conkling had given her the gossip of the town.

"The last two or three months have been of *interminable* length," she continued. "After my gay companions of last winter departed—" She hesitated. Would Merce understand that this was not a reference merely to Matilda? She continued, "I was left much to the solitude of my own thoughts, and some *lingering regrets* over the past, which time can alone overshadow with its healing balm, thus has my *spring time* been passed."

She realized that some account of her social life must be offered. "We have an unusual number of agreeable visitors, some pleasant acquaintances of last winter, but in their midst the *winning widower is not.*" It was necessary to deny any link with Bat Webb. She mentioned that Joshua Speed had gone to Kentucky, but was expected to return shortly for a visit. "*His* worthy friend deems me unworthy of notice, as I have not met *him* in the gay world for months, with the usual comfort of misery, imagine that others were as seldom gladdened by his presence as my humble self, yet I would that the case were different, that he would once more resume his Station in Society, that 'Richard should be himself again,' much, much happiness would it afford me." She felt a lump forming in her throat as she wrote these words about Lincoln. Was he seeing no one? Was he as lonely as she?

She closed her letter by mentioning mutual friends who were marrying—William Anderson, Miss Whitney—and sadly penned the words, "Write very, very soon to your ever attached friend."

In late July Lincoln and Sarah strolled in the countryside as they now did almost every week. Sarah felt quite grown-up, walking with a man almost twice her age. Lincoln seemed unfathomably deep to her. Sometimes he talked of things she knew nothing about, and sometimes he said nothing, walking with his head lowered, his sad eyes watching the path. This evening, however, he seemed cheerful and carried his coat over his arm.

"I was thinking about my stepmother," he said. "Another Sarah. I've been lucky with the Sarahs in my life. They're good women."

"Was she pretty?"

"I thought so because she was good to me. Not as pretty as you." Lincoln thought of his father, realizing he needed a woman and going back to Kentucky to find one who needed a man. Courtship rituals were not always necessary.

"Do you remember making a fool of me at your sister's dinner table months ago? You beat me playing muggins. Remember?"

Sarah laughed. She had not forgotten her triumph over Lincoln, who thought he was so smart mocking her. She wiped her face elaborately with her hands to prove that she remembered. When Lincoln grinned, she giggled and bent over.

"Afterwards when I washed off at the pump," Lincoln asked, "do you remember what I said?"

"About what?"

"Sarah and Abraham. Bible says they're to cleave together."

Sarah said nothing, her giggles suddenly gone. She did not look at him and kept walking.

"What if we got married?"

His father had probably said something as simple as this when he found Sarah Bush Johnston in Kentucky. This Sarah knew she would never marry Speed, for whom she had felt a passion. So why not marry his best friend? He knew he would never marry Molly Todd. So why not Sarah, whom he had always liked?

"We've known each other a long time," Lincoln said. "We've done things together. We get along. Why not get married?"

Sarah stopped walking. She said, "You want to marry me? You've never even kissed me."

Lincoln leaned forward to kiss her.

"Don't!" She turned her head away, put her hand to her cheek. "Oh, I'm sorry," she exclaimed, stepping away from him. She started to walk again. "I like you. Really, I do." She hurried along. Lincoln trailed behind her. "It's just— I couldn't marry you. I think of you as a brother, Abe, not a husband."

CHAPTER

17

A year passed. During it Lincoln took stock of his life. He withdrew from the society of the young people who amused themselves at parties on Quality Hill. He reassessed the advances he had made and reverses he had suffered in politics; he studied his position as a Whig leader of declining popularity in a state increasingly voting for the Democracy and decided not to stand for re-election to the Illinois Legislature. He examined the prospects of the Stuart & Lincoln legal partnership. If the law did not excite him in the way that politics did, still it was where his future seemed to lie. He dissolved the association with Stuart and went into partnership with the state's ablest attorney, Stephen T. Logan. He did not know if he would ever marry. Considering the surplus of single men on the frontier and musing on the death of Ann Rutledge, whom he had once loved in New Salem, the rejections of Mary Owens and Sarah Rickard, and his own feelings of inadequacy with the milieu of Molly Todd, though with the lady herself, he realized that bachelorhood might be his fate. Perhaps he had no choice but to resign himself to this prospect.

For Molly Todd the year that passed was one of contradiction. Her inclination was reclusive, to reduce her involvement with what social busyness the small town offered. But Elizabeth would not allow her to withdraw. Molly must continue to play her role as Springfield's "brightest ornament." Although she constantly reviewed what had gone wrong in the romance with Lincoln—her family's aristocratic pretensions, Lincoln's feelings of inadequacy, her own failure to understand the depth of support he needed—she did not want to discuss that romance with anyone. Members of the Coterie had watched its progress with curiosity and astonishment. Its destiny seemed to be rupture, and when that rupture occurred, gossips in the Coterie and in the town itself wanted to relish the particulars. Had there truly been an engagement? Which party had broken it off? What failure of the soil-scratcher-turned-lawyer had doomed the connection? Or was it Molly's tongue that had severed the attachment? Gossips waited to hear her savage the yokel who had reached beyond his grasp. She did not indulge them. She did not disparage Lincoln; she did not discuss him. Her family's opposition only made him more attractive, only increased Molly's inclination to rebel. But rebel against what? As children came along, her sisters were increasingly involved in their own families. She foresaw a future of being an old-maidish aunt whose failed romance would be whispered about the prairie town as she and Lincoln lived out their solitary lives.

And then one day when summer again smiled across the prairie and new leaves turned the town green, Lincoln and Simeon Francis were talking in the offices of the *Sangamo Journal*. "We are having a little gathering at the house," said Francis. "I hope you'll join us. You need to get out more into society." Lincoln was not much for society, but he agreed. Eliza Francis always put on a good spread.

308

During a visit to the Edwards home, Eliza Francis mentioned to Molly that she and Simeon were having a small gathering at their home. "A little garden party to welcome the summer. It's so nice outside just now. Would you like to come?" Molly said she would.

When Molly arrived, a little late, at the Francis home, Eliza embraced her. "How lovely you look," she said. "Everyone's out back. Shall we go through?" They started through the house. "I think you'll know everyone."

As they came onto the back porch, the chatter of the party died into silence. Molly glanced about. Why the sudden quiet? Then she saw Lincoln. As everyone was doing, he turned to gaze at the porch. Molly saw him put down his punch cup, as if to flee, and noticed him restrain that impulse. Molly made herself smile at her surprised friends. Molly and Lincoln at the same party? That had not happened in months.

"I think you know everyone," Eliza Francis said again. Molly smiled at people she saw practically every week. Eliza took her hand and led her, pulled her, toward Lincoln. He looked like a startled deer, uncertain whether to bound away. But he merely put his hands behind his back. "You know Mr. Lincoln, I'm sure."

"Mr. Lincoln," said Molly. She did not trust herself to offer her hand. But she did gaze into his eyes. She had often seen them sparkling with merriment or listening to her with intelligence and wondering at her. She had also known them to be dark with sadness. They were not sad now. They were curious to see what would happen.

"Miss Todd," said Lincoln. He bowed slightly toward her.

Eliza reached out to pull one of Lincoln's hands from behind him. Holding both their hands, she smiled at them and said, "Let's be friends."

"Of course," said Molly. She glanced at Lincoln and turned to her hostess, forcing a smile. She was vaguely aware that the other guests, who had ostensibly returned to their conversations, were, in fact, watching them.

"My dears," Eliza said to them quietly, "the town is too small for you not to be friends. It is very hard for a hostess to gather a party and leave one of you out. So be friends. Springfield hostesses will be grateful to you."

Molly and Lincoln smiled. They both felt nervous, awkward, their hearts beating faster, and they were aware of being both ignored and watched. Eliza excused herself, saying she was needed in the kitchen.

"You are looking well," Molly said at last. Lincoln nodded, the impulse to flee still apparent in his eyes. "I heard you're no longer a member of the Legislature."

"A man can't do that forever."

"Have you done with politics?"

"Hard to be done with it."

"In your blood?" He shrugged. "Hard to be a Whig in a Democratic state?"

"Hard to concede the state to Democrats."

Suddenly Molly had run out of conversation. She glanced about, feeling awkward, knowing that Lincoln would let the conversation lapse.

"Are you traveling to Missouri again this summer?" he asked, surprising her.

"Not this summer." For a moment they both stared at the ground. She glanced up at him. "I've thought of you so often." He nodded. "I heard you were sick. I guess that was a while back. Beginning of last year."

Lincoln shrugged and looked at the punch cup he held in his hands.

"Too much campaigning, I suppose. In a losing cause."

"I guess maybe."

"Did you drop out of society? I heard your name so rarely. I wanted to know that you were all right." She felt emotion clogging her throat. She had to look at the ground a moment to maintain her composure. "So it's good to see you again. You look wonderful." She tried to smile.

"So do you." The expression in Lincoln's eyes was softer now as he watched her fight to control her emotions.

"And you are now partnered with Stephen Logan?"

"The best lawyer in the state."

"Second best," Molly replied quietly. Lincoln shook his head. "And things with Stuart are fine?" Lincoln nodded. "He won't run for re-election?"

"It's your cousin John Hardin's to win or lose for the Whigs."

"You're the better man."

"There weren't enough who thought so."

They were talking politics again, and as that engaged his attention, Lincoln grew more relaxed.

"I see from the papers that you've been giving temperance talks."

"Just one. For the Washingtonian Society on Washington's birthday." He examined her face. "How have you been?"

"As always. Nothing much changes in my life." She did not want to talk about the parties at which she acted the gay belle and even less about the loneliness she felt. "Your friend Mr. Speed got married, I understand."

"In February."

"And he's happy?"

"He was so nervous about it he took sick."

Molly smiled sympathetically, but she thought: These men who are nervous about marriage. Honestly! It's the woman who should be nervous. After all, she commits her whole being to a marriage while a man has a professional life completely apart from his family.

"Speed's fiancée took sick, too. He was afraid he might lose her." Lincoln grinned. "That's when he discovered he really loved her."

Molly laughed. "And the marriage is a success?" Lincoln nodded, as disinclined to say much as ever. "Have you met the wife?"

"I have. Fanny Henning's her name." Lincoln thought it perhaps best not to rhapsodize about her beauty, her striking black eyes. "I went to visit Speed at the family plantation outside Louisville." His eyes grew merry. "Shall I tell you a story?"

"Please do."

"Speed had been calling on Fanny long enough to know he wanted to marry her. But every time he went to see her, her guardian uncle, a violent Whig, stayed with him and Fanny to talk politics. Poor Speed could never be alone with the girl. So when I was there, he took me along when he visited her and I pretended to be a Democrat."

"A Democrat!" said Molly with mock horror. "How could you?"

"It wasn't hard. I know their stump speeches about as well as my own." He grinned at her. How pretty she was in her summer dress. He realized he'd missed her. "So while the guardian and I are arguing politics, Speed slips away with Fanny and asks her to marry him. She accepts. And by the time I tell the old gentleman that he's made some points I'll have to consider, his niece's future is sealed."

As they talked, their hostess brought them cakes and punch. The afternoon slipped away without their being aware of it. Questions played in their minds. Molly wondered, Is this connection worth renewing? Yes, she thought, but not with the whole world watching. Lincoln asked himself, Do I want to get back into this? He had been lonely and felt unappreciated by women who looked only at surfaces. Molly had always perceived more deeply than that. So, yes, he did want to pursue this. But did Molly? They had not spoken in eighteen months. Well, she seemed perfectly willing to talk. If he did pursue it, how would they handle it? Knowing how Elizabeth and Ninian felt, he could not call at the house on Quality Hill. His pride would not let him.

For her part, Molly wondered: How can I arrange to see him? Will he ask to see me again before we leave? He hasn't always known how to manage these things. Will he send a note? Or will we not speak again for another year?

At the end of the party Eliza Francis took them aside. "Nice to see you together as friends again."

"Everything is always so lovely here," Molly said.

"Sometimes friends need a place to meet," Eliza observed. "Simeon and I are always happy when friends meet here. And when you're in the newspaper business, you know both how to publicize things and how to keep things secret."

Molly and Lincoln began to meet at the Francis house. At first these meetings were tentative, neither person certain of the other's feelings. But Molly's willingness to meet him in secret quickly reassured Lincoln on this score. She was flirtatious, coy and coquettish. Lincoln could not doubt that her feelings of old had not changed. He sensed that she understood what had motivated him so many months before and harbored no resentment. He knew that she was meeting him in defiance of her family and away from the environs of Quality Hill, where he was not comfortable. He began to see that this might be right, after all.

Often their meetings were brief, less than an hour. One of those very few intermediaries who were in the know—Julia Jayne or Anna Rodney— would call at the Edwards house and slip Molly a note. Molly would excuse herself, read the note and return, the blue of her eyes more intense, a shine of anticipation on her face. "This is so exciting!" the go-between would whisper. "So romantic! Meeting a man in secret. Your family not knowing a thing."

"Who says I'm meeting a man?" Molly would whisper, giggling. "You just gave me a note. You don't know what's in it." The girls would stifle their laughter so that Elizabeth would not get suspicious. "Don't say anything to anyone. You've got to promise."

The intermediary would nod, place a finger across her lips and make a cross over her heart. Secretly the intermediaries wondered: What happened at these clandestine meetings? Were there mad kisses? Passionate embraces? Did Molly's noble beau, disparaged by her guardians, kneel before her? Did he pledge undying love? Were plans discussed for an elopement?

Near the appointed hour Molly would concoct an excuse and slip from the house. Through back

314

lanes, where she was little noticed, she would fly to the Francis house. There she would find Lincoln. He had concocted a reason to absent himself from the offices of Logan & Lincoln. They would say breathless hellos to Francis or Eliza, for one of them was always present in the house. There could be no suggestion that Molly met a man unchaperoned. Alone in the parlor, Molly might sit on Lincoln's lap. They would giggle and laugh, whisper and speak quickly, words they needed to say to one another tumbling out, their hands intertwined.

Sometimes they would talk politics—and with good reason. Not only did the subject fascinate them both, but a financial crisis gripped the state. In February the catastrophically mismanaged State Bank of Illinois failed. Sound money fled Illinois. State Bank notes became virtually worthless. But these notes were the currency of most of the people. They had to resort to barter. Economic activity slowed to a standstill.

To keep the state government operating challenged the state's Democratic administration. Due to its overambitious program of internal improvements, the state was deeply in debt. As a result, it could not borrow. Financiers feared that Illinois would repudiate its debt. As one of several measures to deal with the problem, James Shields, the State Auditor, published a proclamation prohibiting the payment of taxes in paper money; they had to be paid in silver and gold. Although unavoidable, this decision worked terrible hardships on citizens.

This crisis for Democratic state officers afforded their Whig opponents an opportunity to ridicule and berate them. Lincoln and Molly recognized that opportunity. Moreover, the target was irre-

315

sistible: Shields. His resourcefulness and aggressiveness were surpassed only by those of his great friend, the recently appointed State Supreme Court justice, Stephen A. Douglas. "He's a talented lawyer," Lincoln said of Shields. Molly giggled because Lincoln was suppressing a smile. "Hardworking and energetic." Molly snickered because Lincoln was imitating the over-ornate manners that Shields had brought with him from County Tyrone. "He's witty, reputable and handsome."

"This is the way he holds a young woman's hand." Molly took Lincoln's hand and began to rub and squeeze it as if to remove the skin.

"Oh!" whispered Lincoln, as if succumbing to passion. "Oh! Oh! That sets my heart aflutter."

Molly laughed aloud. "He considers himself Springfield's most eligible bachelor, quite a darling of the ladies."

"I must learn to squeeze hands," said Lincoln. "To meet the competition."

"Here's a pity," suggested Molly. "There's no political satirist in Springfield who can do justice to the man." She grinned wickedly at her friend. "And there's no paper in town that would publish the piece if he did."

"Indeed, it's a pity," agreed Lincoln.

When Molly read the August 19th edition of the *Sangamo Journal,* she saw a letter signed by Rebecca, a farmer's wife. It was headed "Lost Townships." Beginning the letter, Molly grinned. Although it contained Rebecca's vernacular, any politically savvy reader could recognize it as a statement of Whig campaign points. Rebecca bemoaned the State Auditor's proclamation that taxes must be paid in gold. "We've got no gold," she complained.

Lincoln often contributed unsigned pieces to the *Journal*. That was why Molly had flirtingly challenged him to satirize Shields. When they were next together—Julia Jayne was with them this day—Molly said, "I laughed myself silly over that piece of yours about Jim Shields in the *Journal.*"

Lincoln grinned and said, "That piece wasn't mine. It lacked my signature style."

"Then Rebecca is stealing your signature stories," Molly declared, "because I've heard out of your own mouth the story about the man with the patent leather leg."

Lincoln laughed. "In my story," he said, "the man has a cork leg."

"I'm glad to know it's not your work," Molly told him, "because whoever wrote that piece was much too easy on Jim Shields."

"Oh, I agree," said Lincoln.

"If you were to write such a piece," asked Julia, "how would we recognize your signature style?"

It would be funnier, Lincoln said, more satiric. He'd do more to develop the character of the letter writer. He'd be a denizen of the Lost Townships.

"He!" cried Molly. "This letter writer's a she, Rebecca. Is that because it makes the real writer harder to trace?"

"Good question, Miss Todd," Lincoln said. "Someone might think you'd written that letter yourself."

"Maybe I did," said Molly cheekily. "In my next letter I'd call her . . . Aunt Rebecca."

"Aunt 'Becca," suggested Julia, delighted with the game.

"Aunt 'Becca, she should be," agreed Lincoln.

"And what's going to happen?" asked Julia.

The threesome decided that Aunt 'Becca would step over to her neighbor's place and find him reading the Democratic *Register*. He would have just learned that taxes must be paid in gold and silver. "Let's call him Jefferson for our Democratic friends," declared Molly giddily. "Jeff and 'Becca will complain that officers of the state want taxes paid in gold so that they can pay themselves in gold."

"Maybe the next letter will take a swipe or two at Shields just for fun," suggested Lincoln. "Like saying he was appointed by old Granny Harrison when everyone knows he won the office by election." They were having a fine time laughing at what Aunt 'Becca would write. "And she'll assume he's a Whig," added Lincoln.

"A cur-sed British Whig," said Molly. "That will get his Irish dander up."

"A lying Whig," suggested Lincoln. "On account of those Whigs, aristocrats though they be, are always lying."

He wished he could write such a piece, Lincoln assured them. But he was too busy, certainly too busy to write it short. He declared with mock importance that he was up to his ears solving serious problems for serious people.

When Molly and Julia walked home together, Julia said, "Molly Todd, I have never seen you so flirty. I declare you're the queen of flirty." Molly laughed and did not deny the charge.

When Lincoln handed Simeon Francis a sheaf of handwritten pages that began "Dear Mr. Printer," the editor asked, "What's this?" Lincoln only grinned. Francis read "I see you printed that long letter I sent you a spell ago." He smiled as Aunt

'Becca explained that printing this new letter would not only give her the benefit of being known by the world but would bestow on the *Sangamo Journal* respectability. "How have you had time to write all this?" asked Francis.

"Molly Todd and I sort of worked it out in your parlor," Lincoln said.

"So that's what goes on in our parlor. I've been wondering."

"That first letter was such a good statement of Whig positions, I thought we ought to keep up the fun. It's harmless stuff, just a little sticking it to the Dems for the financial mess we're in."

Francis looked through the copy. "You're saying Shields is a Whig?"

"That's part of the joke. Them damn Whigs, they're always lying." Lincoln chuckled. "And the idea that Tyler appointed Shields. That'll set him off."

"All right, I'll use it, Aunt 'Becca." He shook Lincoln's hand, understanding that printing the piece would advance Lincoln's courtship. He wanted to see that succeed. "Readers like jokes. Better to laugh about the fix we're in 'stead of weeping about it."

"Don't tell Molly it's gonna be in. It's a surprise."

When Molly looked through the September 2nd edition of the *Sangamo Journal*, she burst out laughing. If she was the queen of flirty, as Julia Jayne contended, then Lincoln was the king. There it was: "Letter from the Lost Townships." Once again it was signed by Rebecca, Aunt 'Becca. The letter made Molly feel unique. She had never heard of a woman being secretly flirted with, courted and nudged with jokes in newspaper columns.

Lincoln's drolleries made her guffaw. The wife of neighbor Jeff had just had a baby. When 'Becca visited him, Jeff complained, "I'm mad as the devil!" and 'Becca asked, "What about? Ain't its hair the right color?" She laughed aloud when 'Becca identified Jim Shields as a Whig. But the next bit took her breath away. "Shields is a fool as well as a liar," she read. "With him truth is out of the question; and as for getting a good, bright, passable lie out of him, you might as well try to strike fire from a cake of tallow." She wondered what Jim Shields would think about that.

"You scoundrel!" she said to Lincoln when she next saw him. "That was a roguish letter you wrote in the *Journal!*"

"You mean Aunt 'Becca?" Lincoln asked. "Wonder who that is. Not me."

"Abraham Lincoln!" Molly declared. "That's a good, bright, passable lie!" Lincoln flicked his eyebrows. Molly laughed. "Which is more than you can get out of Jim Shields, that British Whig!" They grinned at each other, pleased with one another and the mischief they were sowing together.

"It's just some cockeyed Whig poking a little fun," Lincoln said.

Molly told him how much she had laughed at 'Becca's letter. "I hope Jim Shields is as amused as I was."

"If he can't take a little ribbing," Lincoln assured her, "folks will just think he's more ridiculous than they already do. Don't worry about it." He gave her a kiss—Eliza Francis was busy in the kitchen—and said, "You look pretty today."

320

Julia Jayne told Molly, "This is the most exciting thing I ever did see: a man writing you love letters in the *Sangamo Journal*. Now you've gotta write him back to show him you're interested."

"You think?"

"No doubt about that in my mind!"

James Shields halted his buggy outside the offices of the *Sangamo Journal*. He left it, passed through the anteroom and entered the editor's office. Francis stood. Since Stephen Douglas had attacked him on the street, he determined to keep a desk between them. Shields said, "I'm on my way to Quincy on state business and I see scurrilous slander about me in your paper."

"A few jokes," Francis said mildly. "It's not slander."

"Who wrote it?"

"Aunt 'Becca. She wanted to tease you about being a Whig."

"The state's in a severe financial crisis," Shields said. "And I'm a little too busy to find this fun. This is personal vituperation."

Francis tried not to smile at this elaborate phrase. Shields was obviously irked. "No offense meant, Mr. Shields," he said. "I thought readers who have to dig around for silver to pay their taxes might enjoy a laugh or two. The letter is political, not personal. It's satire, not an attack."

Shields sought to control his exasperation. "Ever since coming to this town," he said, "I've endeavored to conduct myself, I have, at a level that shuns personal abuse. Amongst both political friends and opponents. But a man can't ignore it when it's thrown at him, can he?" He told Francis, "I demand to know the identity of 'Rebecca.' "

A little harmless fun," Francis insisted. "I wouldn't print slander or personal abuse in the *Journal*. This is part of the political game, that's all."

"Who wrote these articles? I demand to know."

"What did you think of them?" Francis asked, trying to divert the conversation. "You know, specie payment hurts a lot of folks who are—"

"Being called a liar by your paper hurts people, too. I am not a liar. I demand an apology from the author of that scurrilous piece." When Francis made no reply, Shields said, "It was Lincoln, wasn't it now? He writes pieces like that. Everyone knows it."

Francis tried to keep it light. "Perhaps you'd like to write an answer for us—"

Shields interrupted, "I demand an apology, I do. Or satisfaction on the field of honor."

"You Democrats get very hot under the collar, Mr. Shields. Douglas attacked me in broad daylight and for what? A little harmless name-calling. The *Old Hickory* called me 'a compound of goose fat and sheep's wool' and it didn't bother me."

"Your reputation apparently means nothing to you," Shields replied. "Mine means everything to me. I am not a liar." Francis said nothing. "Lincoln wrote that, didn't he?" Shields again demanded.

Francis shrugged. "He wrote the letter that's got you so excited."

"When I return from Quincy, I mean to have an apology. Or satisfaction." Shields turned and left the office. Through the window Francis watched him get into the buggy and start off to Quincy. As soon as he had gone, Francis wrote Lincoln a note, warning him that Shields was demanding "satisfaction."

Lincoln was surprised in opening the next edition of the *Sangamo Journal* to find another letter signed "Rebecca." He would leave shortly for the Tazewell County Circuit Court at Tremont and had had no time to write more satires. He certainly would not have done it after receiving Francis's warning that Shields was furious about the first letters.

In the new letter, in a feat of literary transformation, Rebecca had become a widow. She contemplated marrying "Mr. S———." Moreover, she revealed that, if it came to dueling, she always chose her weapons carefully: "broomsticks or hot water or a shovelful of coals." The Lost Townships had also produced a poem, announcing Rebecca's marriage to "Erin's son" and taking revenge on Shields for the way he squeezed young women's hands. It concluded with these lines:

> And hands that in rapture you oft would have pressed,
> In prayer will be clasped that your lot may be blest.

There was no time for Lincoln to arrange to see Molly. He went by the *Journal*. "Molly must've written the poem," he told Francis. "I know she writes some verse now and again. Did she write the letter?"

"Julia wrote it."

"Why did you print it? It'll only inflame Shields's anger."

"The lady's interested in you, Lincoln. Shields be damned. I wanted you to know that."

With the dust of the road still on him, Shields found Lincoln in Tremont. What had begun merely as a demand for an apology with some menacing references to "satisfaction" had escalated into the probability of a duel. Accompanying Shields was his second, Colonel John Whiteside. In addition, Bill Butler and Dr. Elias Merryman had ridden to Tremont to serve as Lincoln's "friends."

Shortly after arriving, Whiteside presented Lincoln with a letter from Shields. It complained of "slander, vituperation and personal abuse" and took "the liberty of requiring a full, positive and absolute retraction of all offensive allusions." Whiteside informed Lincoln that he would call later for Lincoln's answer.

Lincoln responded by saying that there was "so much assumption of facts, and so much of menace as to consequences" that he would not submit to Shields to give a fuller answer to the letter. Lincoln regarded the letter as insulting. The exchange created an impasse. The way out of the impasse was a duel.

When Molly first heard that Jim Shields had gone to Simeon Francis to demand the identity of Aunt 'Becca, she laughed aloud. What did he propose to do? Fight a duel over a joke? Have someone killed, maybe himself, on account of some political lampoon? How like his over-elaborate set of manners! The real joke was demanding that people who were bartering eggs and butter for a pair of shoes pay their taxes in gold. By soliciting a duel, Shields would only make himself more of a laughingstock.

Then she heard that Shields had gone chasing up to Tremont with a second to thrust a letter of challenge into Lincoln's hands. At that she felt a pang of alarm. The broguish Shields was serious!

Would they duel? Was Lincoln safe? Had she brought this about?

From Simeon Francis, Molly heard that a minuet of dueling niceties was taking place in Tremont. Shields's first letter demanded retraction of personal abuse. Lincoln refused the letter. Shields wrote a second one. Lincoln disdained to negotiate about the second note until Shields had withdrawn his first.

Molly thought: "How like men! They'd rather fight than be sensible." Still she wanted assurance that Lincoln was safe. And no one could give her that assurance.

Lincoln returned hurriedly from Tazewell County, arriving in Springfield after dark. He stopped at Bill Butler's house, refreshed himself and wrote a note to Molly that he'd been composing in his head all the way from Tremont. Then he spurred his mount up Quality Hill. When he arrived outside the Edwards house, candles were burning in the dining room and kitchen. He tied the horse to a tree. Staying in the shadows, he circled the stable and hurried across the stable yard. He climbed to the back porch on tiptoe and, peeking through the porch window, saw the Irish girl washing dishes while the stable boy dried them. Lincoln knocked quietly at the door. He went back to the window and saw the pair stop their work, surprised at the knock. Lincoln knocked again. When he heard footsteps approaching, he retreated into shadows. After a moment the door opened. The stable boy peeked outside.

"Evening," Lincoln said, still standing in the shadows. The stable boy came onto the porch. Lincoln moved into the light.

"Mr. Lincoln."

"Please give this note to Miss Molly." Lincoln offered an envelope.

The stable boy looked at him. "Everyone's talking about your dueling Mr. Shields," he said.

"Are they? I hadn't heard."

"If the sheriff catches you, he'll throw you in jail."

"Then he better not catch me."

The stable boy regarded Lincoln with admiration. "My money's on you."

"Could you take this note to Miss Molly?"

"Maybe she wants to take it from you herself."

"The Edwardses don't need to know I'm here," Lincoln said. "Nobody else either. You know what I mean?"

The young man smiled conspiratorially. "You think you're the only feller who goes calling on the sly? Mum's the word." He disappeared into the house.

Lincoln waited in the shadows for what seemed forever, fearing every moment that Ninian would burst onto the porch, and the secrecy of his courtship would end. Finally the door opened. Molly stepped out. Lincoln softly spoke her name. "It's you!" she whispered, coming to him. They embraced, kissed. "They said I was wanted in the kitchen, then told me to come out here."

Lincoln led her off the porch into the darkness of the stable yard. He explained that Shields was bent on dueling to save his reputation and that he could not blame him. He had been a fool to call him a liar in print. "I must've been influenced by bad company."

"You two aren't honestly going to duel, are you?" Molly asked.

Lincoln chuckled at Molly's concern. "He's the one who'll get hurt." He kissed her forehead.

"We're fighting with broadswords. I got familiar with them in the Black Hawk War. I've got the reach on Shields by half a foot. He challenged me, so I choose the weapons and make up the rules. I won't get hurt."

"You don't think it won't hurt you to kill—"

"Nobody's going to get killed."

"—or maim Jim Shields? We were all foolish to insult him."

Maybe cooler heads would prevail, Lincoln said, and they wouldn't even fight. Dueling would not polish their reputations. It didn't help that all Springfield was gossiping about it. He'd been warned about arrest at the Butler house. Since dueling was illegal in Illinois, punishable by a year in the penitentiary, he might be arrested. To avoid that he was leaving early the next morning for Jacksonville. A friend there had broadswords. He would meet Shields later in the week on an island in the Mississippi. It was Missouri territory and dueling was legal there.

"Please don't do this," Molly requested. "I've been worried out of my mind. Can't you just a-pologize? After all, it was meant in fun."

"Shields won't be happy," Lincoln assured her, "until he gets hurt."

Molly's mouth was open to protest. But she knew that each gender had its ailments. Women suffered from "female trouble." Men were similarly susceptible to "male trouble," to various kinds of fighting, the most ritualized of which was dueling. Women could not understand it. Molly knew she mustn't argue with Lincoln about this. She leaned against him. He held her to him.

Finally she said, "I best go in before Elizabeth finds us out here." She looked at him for a long moment, as if she might never see him again, and hurried inside.

The next day Molly went to the offices of the *Sangamo Journal* and appealed to Simeon Francis. "Is there no way to stop this insanity?" she asked. Francis shook his head.

"But this is ridiculous!" Molly exclaimed. "Somebody's not actually going to get killed over those silly articles, are they? Can't someone stop it?" She felt frantic. Was Francis going to allow someone to die? She asked, "What if I claimed authorship of those articles?"

"Lincoln would be humiliated."

"Isn't that better than someone's getting hurt?"

"Shields knows Lincoln wrote it. Lincoln won't apologize until Shields withdraws his first letter."

"Oh, you men! Don't you see how crazy it is?"

"Lincoln won't be the one to get hurt," Francis assured her.

"Why should anyone get hurt? Lincoln doesn't want to kill Shields! Or anyone! You know how he gets. The saddest man in the world. That's how he'll be if— We can't let this happen!"

Francis explained that Lincoln had chosen to his advantage in selecting cavalry broadswords. It was true that Shields had taught sword fighting in Canada before coming to Illinois, but broadswords were large and heavy. A youth wielding an axe had muscled Lincoln's shoulders and arms. Moreover, Lincoln had specified that each duelist must fight within a confined space; crossing out of it would mean forfeiting the duel. "Lincoln would like to settle this amicably," Francis assured her, "but if he's pushed to it, he can split Shields from the crown of his head to the tip of his tailbone. And serve him up as cutlets." Molly wished they were dueling with feather dusters.

During the next days Molly waited impatiently for news. She paced the floor. At night she hardly slept. Alone in her room, she prayed for Lincoln's safe passage through this trial. And for her own. Now that she and Lincoln were friends again, now that something akin to a courtship was blossoming between them, she blamed herself for flirting with him in a way that encouraged him to ridicule Jim Shields and push his vaulting vanity to a challenge. Obviously, calling him a liar in print was going too far.

Over in Jacksonville, Lincoln was accustoming himself to wielding a broadsword, hacking away at scarecrows. He found himself more easily winded than he expected. An afternoon of broadsword practice made his shoulders ache. True, he had swung axes for days on end as an eighteen-year-old, but that was fifteen years ago. These days he sat in offices and supposedly used his head. It was more difficult than he'd expected to stay inside the enclosure he had mandated. He had set up logs to approximate that enclosure and had tripped over them several times. If he tripped in the duel, it would be Shields who split open the head he had been using, though not very intelligently.

If he were truly using his head, Lincoln thought as he left Jacksonville for Missouri, he would go to Shields and acknowledge that one of his failings was to go too far in political ridicule: everyone knew that he had behaved badly in "skinning" poor Jesse Thomas. He would admit this fault and tender an apology. But he couldn't do that; honor was at stake. Yet what could be more honorable than to be man enough to admit a mistake? But Shields wanted blood. Only severed limbs—and possibly his or Lincoln's death—could avenge his honor. True, the sight of Shields with his Irish anger in full flame made Lincoln want to squish him as he might a June bug. That was why he had been bullheadedly legalistic when Shields first sought redress. He could not mention that Molly and Julia were a party to the joke; no gentleman would contemplate such a thing. The pressure to duel had taken on a momentum of its own. His and Shields's seconds were itching for the fight, strutting around like generals to Napoleon, organizing the duel with an excess of politesse. So he and Shields would go at each other with broadswords.

CHAPTER

18

After hearing the disturbing news that Lincoln and Shields intended to duel, John Hardin rode hurriedly to Springfield from the circuit court in Carrollton. When he called at the Edwards home, Molly told him: "Yes, it's true. Ridiculous, isn't it?" Ninian and Elizabeth were both away; Molly was staying with the children. As they were drinking coffee, despairing of male honor rituals and exchanging family news, Molly moved beside her cousin. In a whisper she said, "I have something to tell you. In confidence. Can you promise to keep my secret, Cousin John?"

He studied her for a moment. At last he nodded gravely.

"You'll never breathe a word of what I'm going to tell you to Ninian or Elizabeth or anyone else?"

"My, my!" he said. "All right, I promise."

"A year and a half ago," she began, "when we had Christmas with you in Jacksonville. You remember?"

He nodded again.

"Mr. Lincoln asked for my hand and I agreed to marry him."

"But you broke it off."

"No," Molly whispered. "He did." She lowered her eyes so that Cousin John could not see what it cost her to admit this. He did not allow his face or his manner to betray his surprise. "Ninian took him to the woodshed and catalogued his deficiencies. So he thought it best for me—" She shrugged.

Hardin asked, "Does the duel have something to do with you?"

"I'm seeing him again," Molly acknowledged. "Secretly. That's what you must never tell." Cousin John's expression showed its surprise. "We meet at the home of friends," Molly hastened to assure him. "We are never unchaperoned. Never. Sometimes girlfriends of mine are with us." Her cousin looked doubtful. "He has always acted honorably toward me. Always."

"And his intentions are . . . ?"

"We aren't there yet." Hardin set his mouth in disapproval. "You must understand how difficult it is for him, knowing how much Ninian and Elizabeth disapprove."

Hardin took his coffee cup and brought it slowly to his lips. He drank thoughtfully. When he lowered the cup, Molly refreshed his coffee. At last he asked, "Are you the reason for this duel?"

"Yes," Molly admitted. "I'm the cause of it." She explained how the Lost Township letters came to be. How they provided a means for her and Lincoln and another young lady, whom she did not name, to joke and flirt and become partners in a conspiracy of harmless political fun-making.

"Lincoln called Shields a liar," Hardin said. "That's not harmless."

"Lincoln didn't call him that," Molly insisted. "Aunt 'Becca did." She explained that she and her friend were responsible for the third letter and the poem; she did not know who had written the first letter. "Now that fool Shields is pretending to be so deeply offended by a little joshing that he wants to shed blood."

332

"Shields is something of a fool," Hardin agreed. "That's all the more reason to be careful. But if a man called me a liar in print, I'd certainly go after him."

"And get one of you killed?" Molly was now so agitated that she began to walk about the parlor. "You'd do that?"

"I wouldn't duel him. I'd thrash him."

"Shields can't thrash Mr. Lincoln. He hardly stands taller than I do."

Hardin watched the agitated young woman pace about the room. "You must understand, Molly, young men come here out of nowhere. Some are honorable; some are scoundrels. If a man is honorable, as I believe Shields is, fool though he may be, his most prized possession is his reputation. He can't allow himself to be called a liar."

"It was all in fun."

"Fun for you, not for him." Molly began to cry in frustration. Hardin watched her. Finally he said, "You're in love with Lincoln." She did not answer, wiping the tears off her cheeks. "And have been for all these months."

"I don't know what I'll do if he's hurt." Her tears began to flow faster. Hardin watched her, knowing he could offer no comfort. Suddenly she implored, "You must never tell them that I'm seeing him!" Hardin nodded. She stood for a moment, weeping. Finally she said, "Please excuse me," and hurried from the room.

An hour after dawn the sky was clear, the air still, cool and humid. Mist lay over the river. Two skiffs pushed out into the current. Boatmen rowed them across to Missouri, where the flood plain of the two great rivers, the Mississippi and the Missouri, lay flat and wooded and ready to receive men who chose to avenge their honor in combat. The boatmen rowed toward the island where they knew a third skiff would be resting. When they saw it, they pulled toward it, jumped from their skiffs and beached them on the shore. Lincoln and his second, Bill Butler, stepped out of one, neither speaking. Lincoln, sad-faced, stared at his feet, consciously ignoring the hearty adversary clamoring from the adjacent skiff. As he came ashore with Colonel Whiteside, Shields loudly proclaimed, "We have a good day for this business. It's rotten when there's wind or rain. A pity to fight for one's honor, but I'll be glad to have mine restored."

The men moved onto a meadow where four others, official friends of the adversaries, had come at dawn to prepare the dueling ground. Each adversary had chosen a doctor as a friend: for Lincoln, Elias Merryman; for Shields, Tom Hope. Along with Lincoln's friend Springfield lawyer Albert Bledsoe and Shields's friend Bill Ewing, Speaker of the House in the Legislature, the doctors had erected a plank ten feet long in the black earth. It was set on edge. The duelists would fight across it. They had marked back lines parallel to the plank at a distance of the length of a broadsword plus three feet. If either duelist crossed over his back line, he would forfeit the contest.

By eight o'clock the mist had lifted. Sunlight shone on the dueling ground. A light breeze stirred the autumn leaves. The adversaries stood on either side of the plank, both stripped to the waist. Shields limbered his body, swinging his arms. Lincoln did knee bends and rolled his shoulders. The seconds stepped forward to present the broadswords. Shields examined the pair of swords and chose the one he preferred. He tested its heft, went to his side of the plank and began to swing his sword. Lincoln took the remaining sword, stepped to his side of the plank, lifted the sword over his head and brought it down with the force that had turned scarecrows into sticks.

The adversaries were now ready for battle. But neither they nor their seconds and friends felt any rush to commence.

"Ho there! Ho there!" came a cry from off the river. A skiff approached.

"Shall we finish this business?" Shields asked.

But no one, not even he, was in a hurry. The men stood watching the oarsman row the skiff toward shore. It contained John Hardin. "Ho there," he shouted. "I want to parley."

The seconds and friends would not proceed with the duel until Hardin had been heard. Lincoln and Shields left the dueling ground and huddled separately with their companions. Whiteside and Merryman went to talk with Hardin. Lincoln watched them consult. Finally Merryman came to him.

"Hardin wants to settle this business amicably," Merryman reported. "He proposes that the matter be referred to four mediators. Shields says, 'Let's get on with it,' but there are eight gentlemen here. He's willing to let them mediate. I said I had to consult with you."

"Does either one of us really want to slash at the other with a broadsword?" Lincoln asked. "And get punctured in the process? Let's settle it now." He looked over at the men clustered around Hardin. "I've already written a note to Shields, saying that I would acknowledge writing the second letter signed 'Rebecca,' but only that one, if he would withdraw his insulting letter."

"Will you apologize?" Merryman asked.

"I'll say that the article was written for political effect. That it was never my intention to injure the personal or private character of Shields or his standing as a gentleman." After a moment Lincoln added, "Or my standing as a gentleman. Along with jumping out the Legislature window, this was about the damnedest fool thing I've ever done." Merryman looked up from noting down Lincoln's stipulations. He started back to the conclave of friends.

Molly received a note from Eliza Francis, inviting her to tea. She hurried through the back lanes, knowing this invitation must bring news of Lincoln. Perhaps she would see him. When Eliza opened the door, there was a smile on her face. "Good news," she said. "Come in." Molly entered the parlor, hoping to see Lincoln. He was not there. She went to the window. Might she see him coming along the road? Behind a screen of leaves she beheld a man's legs, limping beside a cane. Lincoln? Injured? She was about to rush out the door when the man came into view. Not Lincoln. She laughed with relief. "Is there news of our friend?" she asked.

"Come into the kitchen with me," Eliza invited. "I have scones in the oven."

Molly followed her into the kitchen. "Is there news of the duel?" she demanded. "Please tell me!" But Eliza only opened the oven door and tested the scones with a broom straw. A knock sounded at the front door. Molly felt her heart jump into her throat. Fear paralyzed her legs.

"Would you get the door?" Eliza asked.

Molly reasserted her control over her legs. She entered the living room and found Lincoln standing before her. She flew into his arms. They kissed and held one another. "Are you whole?" Molly asked him. "I've been praying for you night and day."

When Eliza entered the parlor with a tray of tea and scones, Lincoln said with a grin, ""I may still be a little pale, my dear ladies, but you are not beholding a ghost who came here across the River Styx. This is a chastened and wiser, very living man."

"You do look a trifle thinner, Mr. Lincoln," Molly teased, "though I hardly knew you had it in you to grow thinner. How are you chastened?"

"By my gracious adversary." Molly guffawed at this designation. "Shields has made me see the evils of my ways. I've written unsigned ridicule since I was a boy. But I have done with that forever."

"We are very glad to see you, Mr. Lincoln, safe and sound," said Eliza. "And now if you'll excuse me, I've got duties in the kitchen."

As soon as she had gone, Molly hopped onto a hassock and opened her arms for a repeat greeting of her tall and somewhat thinner friend. They kissed and held each other for a very long time. When Lincoln relaxed his grip, Molly only clasped him tighter. He renewed his grasp and held her against him. After a lengthy embrace, the sounds of Eliza moving around the kitchen brought them back to the everyday world. Molly gave Lincoln a we-best-stop-for-now kiss, jumped off the hassock and led him to a sofa. "Was it awful?" she asked. She prepared his tea for him. "I'm sure you were magnificent with Jim Shields cowering before you."

Lincoln put his arm about his friend—she stopped pouring tea—and drew her close. "The truth is I was the one cowering."

"That I do not believe!"

"I was shaking like a lap dog eliminating a peach pit."

"Mr. Lincoln!" Molly giggled, happy to see him relaxed enough to let his earthiness peep out. "I don't believe a word of it."

He stretched back on the sofa, his arm still holding her close, and felt that pleasant warmth and confidence in his surroundings that gave birth to exaggeration. "I looked across that plank at what I'd always considered a pipsqueak. Leprechaun Shields! And yet it was like I was the pipsqueak, a scrawny little David, and he was Goliath of Gath, enormous on the plains of Abraham."

"Little Jim Shields? Nonsense!"

"He looked twice as big as Lorenzo Dow Thompson, the giant who threw me when we wrassled for a campground in the Black Hawk War. We were stripped to our waists and, believe me, the muscles on Jim Shields's chest and arms rippled like a wheat field in a strong breeze. I looked down at my scarecrow's chest and it was stippled with goose flesh. I looked like a plucked chicken. Felt like one, too."

Molly laughed. "We must have the *Sangamo Journal* publish this account of the proceedings."

"Shields's broadsword looked eight feet long. And mine hardly a foot. He held his as if it was weightless, and my arms were aching holding mine. My nervous sweat was stinking up the air. All I wanted was to run behind a bush and toss up the breakfast I hadn't had and go hide. Then across the water, like an angel voice singing out, I

338

heard, 'Don't kill each other yet! Hold on! I'm coming!' It was Hardin."

"My, my! How had he heard about that business?"

"He insisted on mediating. Would not be put off about it. And I had the magnanimity, if I do say so, to put up my tiny sword when I saw that Shields was willing to put down his very large one. And that was the Great Mississippi River Battle of the Titans."

They sat side by side, her head against his shoulder, for a long time, sipping tea, nibbling at scones, enjoying the warmth of their bodies where they touched, and watched a breeze tug orange and red leaves off the dogwoods outside the window. Lincoln thought about how pleasant it was to have this woman beside him, to bask in her admiration, and to laugh at her teasing. After a time he told her, "When I was walking back to my skiff, my shirt and coat back on, Hardin sidled up to me. He said, 'I have a cousin in Springfield who would never have forgiven me if you went back there with a hole cut in you by a broadsword."

"Hmm," said Molly. "I wonder who that cousin might be. . . ."

"Yes, I wonder. Hardin has so many in this town." As they sat there, Lincoln thought there was a letter he must write. Must write it today.

Finally Molly asked, "Did I bring this trouble on you?"

"I expect you did. That's what I get for flirting with you."

"I'm a dangerous woman."

"I believe you are."

Lincoln returned to the office he shared with Stephen Logan and began a letter to Joshua Speed.

He noted that, although he had survived a brush with dueling, the fever for it still gripped the town. Shields, who seemed to have learned nothing from the trip to Missouri, had challenged Bill Butler to a contest—at sunrise, with rifles at one hundred yards—but Whiteside, still Shields's second, had nixed the combat.

Lincoln closed his letter in this way:

"But I began this letter not for what I have been writing, but to say something on that subject which you know to be of such infinite solicitude to me. The immense sufferings you endured from the first days of September till the middle of February you never tried to conceal from me, and I well understood."

Speed had become engaged to Fanny Henning in September and married her in February. Lincoln continued:

"You have now been the husband of a lovely woman nearly eight months. That you are happier now than the day you married her, I well know, for without, you could not be living. But I have your word for it, too, and the returning elasticity of spirits which is manifested in your letters. But I want to ask you a close question: 'Are you in *feeling* as well as *judgment* glad you are married as you are?' From anybody but me this would be an impudent question not to be tolerated, but I know you will pardon it in me. Please answer it quickly, as I am impatient to know."

Lincoln received an answer from Speed by return mail. The Kentuckian assured his friend that he was wondrously glad in both feeling and judgment that he had married. He speculated that only one circumstance could have provoked such an inquiry, and he urged Lincoln to take the plunge.

The letter roused Lincoln both to exultation and panic, and he girded himself for the discussion that had been on his mind for months.

When he next went to the Francis home, Molly served him apple cider, fresh from the press, and told him about her efforts to begin teaching four-year-old Julia her first lessons. As she did, Eliza came from the kitchen, making sufficient noise to warn them of her entry, and announced she was going across the road to borrow eggs.

When she had gone, Molly turned to Lincoln, a devilish light in her eye, and observed, "Mr. Lincoln, we are alone together in this house." Her eyes shone with an intensity that sent a flush of nervousness and excitement through him.

He swallowed hard. "I know." He kissed her firmly, lengthily.

"If I'm not mistaken," Molly said, "it will take Eliza quite a spell to get those eggs."

Lincoln kissed her once again, mightily, and realized that his hands were beginning to move of their own free will. "Miss Molly," he said, "you ought not to be alone in a house with me without a chaperone." Molly cocked her head and smiled, flirting, inviting his attentions in a manner that took his breath away. "I'm thinking of your reputation."

"Reputation be damned!" Lincoln laughed nervously. Molly grinned. "I can think of no one I'd rather be alone with in a house."

Lincoln moved away from her on the sofa. Molly looked at him invitingly and smiled. Lincoln tucked his hands under his thighs. "I'm sitting on my hands to keep them out of trouble."

"What kind of trouble might that be?" Molly inquired. She materialized beside him and settled herself on his lap.

"I've just escaped a scrape with death, and I don't want Ninian Edwards coming after me with a rifle."

"Really? And you're one of the Titans of the Mississippi?"

"Oh, Puss!" he said. He freed his hands from beneath his legs, wrapped his arms about her and pulled her to him. They kissed. He laid his head on her shoulder, his forehead against her neck. "I think about you all the time."

She kissed his hair, held his head close to her.

"I've been asking myself over and over, Can you ever forgive me for what I did to you?"

"I never held it against you."

He pulled her close, sought her lips again. "I humiliated you. Disgraced myself. Trampled your reputation and my own honor."

"I'm a package a man wants to think carefully about before taking it home."

"I got so sick afterwards." Molly nodded. "I hoped you might come to me."

"I wanted to. Elizabeth and Ninian forbade it. I kept hoping you might call."

"I didn't have the strength to get myself back up to the Edwards house. Or the courage. I was afraid to let you see me. The way I looked you'd've— I'd've scared you so much your lovely brown hair would have turned white."

Molly laughed and pulled Lincoln's face to her to kiss it. "Oh, Abraham! What a couple of years it's been. Elizabeth was after me every minute to write you that letter. When I did write it, she disapproved of what I said. I was all wrong, she maintained, to extend you the privilege of renewing your suit."

"When I got that letter, the hypo overwhelmed me. I could scarcely function."

"When I heard nothing from you," said Molly, "I felt the same way. But, of course, I had to pretend to be the gay belle in society."

For a time they said nothing, holding one another.

Finally Lincoln asked, "If we could go back two years to where we were, would you do it?" Molly murmured companionably, snuggling against him, but did not answer. "If I asked you to marry me, what would you say?"

"Mr. Lincoln! That is no way—"

"You would say, 'I don't see you down on your knee.' " Lincoln laughed and gave her a squeeze. "Wouldn't you, Puss? You said that once before and it brought me two years of pain."

"You are not a romantic person!"

"You are a difficult woman!"

"I'm sitting on your lap, trading kisses with you, in a house without a chaperone, and you wonder what I'd say if you proposed to me!"

"You'd ask, 'Did you lose your confidence two years ago?' And I'd admit that I did. You'd ask, 'Have you got it back?' And I'd say, 'Yes, I have. I want you to be my wife. I've still got some debts, but I can provide for you now. Not the way Edwards provides for Elizabeth—' "

"I don't want that, Abraham."

"I can provide a good life. I've left the Legislature to concentrate on the law. I'm partnered with the best lawyer in the state. What would you say?"

"I'd say, 'If we do this, we don't tell anyone till the day it happens.' "

"When do we do it?"

"I've waited two years," said Molly. "I don't need to wait any longer."

"I'll get a ring."

"Not a word to anyone."

"No one!" Lincoln held her close and kissed her. "I wonder if you could get off me for a moment," he said.

"Am I too heavy?" Abashed, Molly jumped off his lap and stood before him.

Lincoln slid from the sofa and bowed before her on one knee.

"You are mocking me!" she said, playfully striking his shoulder.

"Woman, I'm committing my life to you." They looked at one another. "Miss Molly, will you do me the honor of marrying me?"

Molly leaned down to kiss him.

On the morning of November 4, just a month after writing Joshua Speed, Lincoln burst in on breakfast at the home of Parson Dresser. The parson stood, wiping coffee from his lips, as Lincoln announced, "I want to get hitched tonight." Dresser looked surprised. He knew Lincoln, though not as a churchgoer, and was unaware of his paying court to any young woman of his congregation. "That is," Lincoln elaborated, "Mary Todd and I mean to get hitched."

The parson grinned. "Does she know about this?" he asked.

"She does," Lincoln assured him, "but I'm pretty sure Mr. and Mrs. Edwards do not. We've been courting in secret."

"And fighting duels. Was that a feature of the courtship?"

"Father, don't ask him that!" said the parson's wife. She rose and gave Lincoln a hug.

"I reckon it was," acknowledged Lincoln. "Since I didn't get killed, we decided to tie the knot."

Parson Dresser congratulated Lincoln and inquired where the ceremony was to be performed.

Lincoln asked if the parsonage was available. Dresser knew the Edwardses would object, but it was not their wedding. He agreed to perform the ceremony in the parsonage.

Lincoln hurried through town to the room where Jim Matheny was lodging, found him still in bed and asked him to serve as his best man. Shortly afterwards he met Ninian Edwards on the street. "Edwards," Lincoln said, "you should know that Molly and I are getting hitched tonight."

Because an aristocrat never gets ruffled, Ninian greeted this news with equanimity. But surprise showed in his eyes. As soon as Lincoln was gone, he hurried to his horse and galloped up the hill with the news.

By this time Molly had informed Elizabeth of the couple's plans. "In the parsonage?" cried Elizabeth. "In the parsonage?" Her cries reverberated in the room like crows cawing in a tree. "I won't hear of it. Remember, Mary, you are a Todd!"

Ninian arrived, out of breath although the horse had done the running. "What's this about Molly's getting married tonight?" he asked his wife when he found her. "And to Lincoln? Lincoln?"

"It's true," his wife told him.

Ninian frowned deeply with confusion. "But they haven't even seen each other in eighteen months!"

"Now I know where Molly's been running off to in the afternoons," said Elizabeth. "And I thought she just wanted to get out of the house."

Ninian and Elizabeth sought the privacy of their bedroom in order to discuss this development. "Can we allow this to happen?" she asked.

Ninian pointed out that since both Molly and Lincoln were of age, they could do what they wanted. The town's better people might commiserate with the Edwardses about the match, but he doubted that they would support family interference. "People tend to wish for the best with a young couple." Elizabeth nodded, knowing, if they interfered, that the town would wonder for whom they were saving Molly. She was almost twenty-four, moving toward spinsterhood. Ninian spoke the thought that had occurred to him, riding up the hill. "She's been with us three and a half years. Do we want her here indefinitely?"

"They've been having secret rendezvous," Elizabeth confided, "Molly and Lincoln." She stared at her hands when she said the words, for she was too embarrassed to look her husband in the eye. Hesitantly he asked if the rendezvous were chaperoned. "So she claims," Elizabeth said, but they both knew that Molly would not, could not, ever admit to unchaperoned meetings with a man. Suddenly both were silent, sharing the same thought, a thought they almost dared not clothe in words. "If something 'regrettable' happened. . ." Again Elizabeth gazed at her hands, feeling that already she had said too much.

Fearfully they looked at one another. Ninian embraced his wife. Softly into her ear he whispered, "Something 'regrettable' would be a lot worse than this marriage. Think of having to live that down." Elizabeth nodded, her head against his chest. Pulling away, she wiped tears from her eyes. "We will have to accept this turn of events," he told her. He handed her a handkerchief.

She blew her nose, drew herself erect and said, quite firmly, "The family must be seen to support her."

"Here you are!" a smiling Molly said, as they opened the door to leave the bedroom. "Lincoln and I are getting married tonight at the parsonage," she told Ninian. "We hope you'll come."

"Indeed, we'll come," said Elizabeth. "But the wedding must be in this house." Her tone brooked no argument. "You are a Todd," Elizabeth reminded her sister. "The wedding will be in this house."

Ninian agreed. "What would people think if—"

"You could have given us some advance notice," complained Elizabeth.

Molly smiled to herself. They all understood why things were being done this way.

It was a Friday. Lincoln was not appearing in court that day. He found the ample Colonel George Washington Spottswood at the Globe Tavern and verified his reservation for a room he could rent for several months. As it turned out, Fanny and Will Wallace had only recently moved their young family from the Globe. Lincoln and Molly would start their marriage in the same room where her sister and the sweet doctor had launched theirs.

Up on the hill Elizabeth and Ninian prevailed. The wedding would be at the Edwards home. Perhaps that was best, Molly thought. No need to create bad feeling with her relations and gossip in the town by insisting on the parsonage. Lincoln had not set foot in the house in almost two years, and after tonight, for all she cared, he need never set foot in it again. The cook could bake a cake and brew some coffee; that would be preferable to the beer and gingerbread from Dickey's Bakery that they had thought of for the parsonage.

Lincoln picked up the wedding ring he had had engraved for Molly with the words "Love Is Eternal." She hurried to the Jaynes and the Rodneys to notify Julia and Anna that they would be needed as bridesmaids. "It's happening at last!" said Julia. "I'm so pleased for you!"

Molly ran to the home of Dr. John Todd and told her cousin Elizabeth, "I'm going to be married tonight to Mr. Lincoln, and I want you to stand up with me." When the girl complained she had nothing to wear, Molly got her to wash and iron her best white dress.

Molly hurried to the new home of her sister Fanny Wallace. "I'm a limb of Satan," she exclaimed exultantly. "I've been seeing Mr. Lincoln secretly for months, and we're getting married tonight at Elizabeth's. Please come!" Fanny tried to hide her astonishment. Secret courtship! Heavens! After a moment she realized the news was exciting. "I knew you'd marry a Springfield man," she said.

On such a momentous day Lincoln took refuge in his office. A note from Molly informed him that the wedding was to be at the Edwards home. That news set him to thinking, to pacing. He reread Speed's letter of reassurance and went off to tell the parson of the change in plans.

He dressed for the ceremony at the home of Bill Butler. Sarah Rickard approved his appearance, and Elizabeth Butler tied his tie while her children kept asking, "Where you goin' all dressed up?"

Lincoln and Matheny took a carriage up the hill, both of them thinking that weddings were something for women. Men tolerated them and participated to acknowledge that they were tamed.

In a room off the parlor, Molly was smoothing her embroidered white muslin dress before a mirror, Elizabeth fussing at its hem, Ninian standing behind her, and the three bridesmaids whispering nervously across the room, when she heard Lincoln arrive. Her heart beat faster as she heard him greet Will Wallace and Parson Dresser, and she smiled to herself in the mirror for she had never been surer of anything in her life. A knock sounded at the door. Fanny peeked in. "Everything's ready," she said quietly. She smiled at Molly. "How lovely you look!" Molly smiled back. Elizabeth rose and stepped back beside Ninian, releasing Molly from the Edwards guardianship. "Mr. Lincoln's in his place and the guests are waiting." Molly's sisters left the room.

Molly heard the piano begin to play the march she had chosen. The bridesmaids lined up. "Here we go!" whispered one of them, and they started out the door. Molly took Ninian's arm, and they moved through the thirty guests that had been assembled at such short notice.

Lincoln stood, tall and grave, at the fireplace. He smiled at her as she drew near. Molly and Lincoln exchanged their vows, repeating them as the parson read them out, but for those few minutes, it was for Molly as if she and Lincoln were alone together in the room. He slipped the ring on her finger. Parson Dresser pronounced them man and wife, and they kissed before God and their guests.

They greeted their friends and shared with them coffee and cake still warm from the baking. Shortly afterwards Molly and Lincoln got into the carriage that awaited them. They drove to the Globe Tavern to begin their life together. And to face whatever it was that destiny had in mind for them.

AFTERWORD

In April 1843, five and a half months after the Lincoln wedding, James Conkling drove a buggy to Bloomington, Illinois, to participate in the proceedings of the circuit court. Getting there was difficult. He encountered "miserable roads, deep sloughs, execrable bridges, swollen streams, drenching rain, high winds." "I have arrived here yesterday afternoon," he wrote his wife, Mercy Ann, "after quite a tedious journey."

In Bloomington, he noted, he "found Lincoln desperately homesick and turning his head frequently toward the south."

*   *

HISTORICAL NOTES

It would be nice to say that this novel is based on fact and largely, of course, it is. Abraham Lincoln is probably the most studied person in American history, and the potential source material for a work like this one encompasses hundreds of volumes.

But in this case it is closer to the truth to say that the story is not so much based on fact as it involves a variety of interpretations of recollections of Lincoln and Mary Todd, most of them collected after—often well after—Lincoln's assassination in 1865. That means a quarter century had passed between the time the events took place and the time the recollections were given. The passage of time fogs memories. They are colored by personal reactions to the people involved. History itself can have a distorting effect. An informant could hardly give a recollection of Lincoln after 1865, for example, without his Civil War struggles, his emancipation of the slaves, and his assassination influencing that recollection.

Moreover, for some of the principal events of this story there are no facts. For example, were Lincoln and Mary Todd actually engaged to be married in late December 1840? We assume that sometime in the autumn or early winter of that year the couple had reached an understanding about marrying. But there seems to have been no engagement party. If there was an engagement, many of their friends seem not to have known of it. When Mary wrote her friend Mercy Ann Levering sometime in December, she talked about her social life but did not mention an engagement. As a result, someone writing about the Lincoln-Mary Todd courtship has to interpret what happened.

Novels are built of scenes. Where possible, I've based scenes on fact: for example, the scene where Lincoln and his friends toss the shoemaker into the horse trough and invite his wife to beat him. This incident's factuality seems indisputable because we know the names of the men who helped Lincoln do this. I believe that it is placed here at about the time it would have actually occurred, in mid-1839. Another example is Stephen Douglas's attack on Simeon Francis. Several sources make it clear that the attack actually took place. Molly Todd's witnessing it is the author's invention.

There are scenes based on what may very well be fact. Lincoln's descending through the trapdoor in the courtroom ceiling to defend his friend Ned Baker is one of these. William Herndon claims to have seen this occur (see *Herndon's Life of Lincoln*, p. 158). But one has learned to treat Herndon skeptically. (Paul Angle, a Lincoln scholar who annotated Herndon's text, offering corrections, notes, p. 315, that "when Herndon states a fact as of his own knowledge, it may be relied upon as true." This lends credence to the trapdoor story.) Once again, Molly's witnessing the event is invention.

Other scenes were built on factual reports. It's generally—though not universally—agreed, for example, that Eliza Francis invited Lincoln and Mary Todd to a party in order to effect their reconciliation. I've invented what was said at the party.

Still other scenes are total inventions. Lincoln's proposing to Molly while they collect firewood at the Hardins is an example. The interview

354

between Lincoln and Ninian Edwards and the breakup scene are others.

While writing the chapters, I carefully foot-noted the text. Obviously, this is not the kind of book that requires footnotes.

The notes address these topics. Perhaps the most important of these are:

Who was Mary Todd?

My own view is that Mary Todd—Molly Todd, as I have chosen to call her—has been very ill-used by history. We know that as a young woman she was vivacious, witty and sharp-tongued. If she was not a beauty, she was certainly pretty and animated. Probably what later generations would call "cute." Certainly she had a sense of where she'd come from: if you were a Todd from Kentucky, you did not forget it. Some may have seen her as proud; Herndon certainly did. But her pride—if that's what it was—did not keep her from reaching out to Lincoln once she had perceived his unusual qualities. "She loved show and power," her older sister Elizabeth Edwards told Herndon (see p. 166), "and was the most ambitious woman I ever knew." (Elizabeth, who had married wealth and position and into the Illinois aristocracy of the day, would almost certainly have considered ambition a contemptible quality.) Precisely what Mary was ambitious for is not clear. Not for wealth nor for social position. If she had been ambitious for those, she would not have chosen Lincoln. Perhaps she was ambitious for validation and for some recognition of Lincoln's and her own political skills. Her girlish boasts that she intended to marry a President of the United States, which very much bothered Elizabeth (see Herndon, p. 166-167), seem simply to have been expressions of her vivacity and wit. They were remembered mainly in light of her having actually married a future one.

Molly had a lively intelligence, and in her time was probably as well educated as any woman in the United States. Interested in politics, she was no doubt keenly aware of the intellectual and professional limitations under which women of her day were forced to exist. If Molly were alive today, one could imagine her as a lawyer in her own right, as a political operative or the head of an NGO. It was her misfortune to be caged in the social strictures of the nineteenth century. It's my hunch that her outbursts of temper that became more pronounced later on stemmed in part from the high degree of frustration a confining domestic life imposed upon her.

One cannot help wondering why "the Todd girls" left the established society of Lexington, Kentucky, for the small prairie town of Springfield, Illinois? Elizabeth, the oldest sister, settled there because she had made an advantageous marriage into the first family of Illinois, one that enjoyed wealth, position and social prestige. But why did Frances and Molly follow her? One reason, it seems clear, was to escape Miss Betsey, the stepmother Molly so disliked. Illinois seems to have been settled first from the south, and many of the first settlers were men from Kentucky. Perhaps many of the most interesting men of Kentucky, men of good family like Lincoln's friend Joshua Speed, had followed opportunity to Illinois. And so perhaps the Todd girls followed them. One wonders, too, if the fact that slavery was illegal in Illinois also held attractions. In a slavery economy, women of good family, released from household drudgery by slave labor, could spend their married lives producing children for their husbands. This is what Molly's mother seems to have done. She produced seven children in twelve and a half years and died, probably of childbed fevers, at the age of thirty-one. Molly's father, Robert Todd, set out almost immediately to find a new wife and set her to providing him children. One wonders if women felt less pressure to have such large families in Illinois—the Todd girls had fewer children than their mother—and if that possibility attracted them to the prairie town.

If Molly Todd has been ill-used by history, why is this the case? I believe there are two main reasons. The first is that Mary Todd Lincoln did not— for very understandable and very human reasons—weather the challenges of her later life in admirable fashion. Those challenges included the untimely deaths of three sons, criticism and animosity directed toward her as First Lady, due in part to her own actions, and the assassination of her husband, all of which led to a descent into near insanity in her last years. Moreover, she had a sharp tongue and it made her enemies.

The circumstances of her later years made it impossible for Mary Todd Lincoln to be perceived as the storybook wife of a storybook husband. Lincoln's achievements as President, the example he set as a self-made man who had risen from ignoble beginnings, and the assassination seen as a martyrdom made it difficult, if not impossible, for his widow to find a place for herself in the myth that was fast created about him. When she failed to do this, Mary became a kind of witch figure at whose feet could be laid the blame for problems that a more charitable view would have laid elsewhere. At a time before the development of psychiatry, the deep-seated psychological problems of her later years were regarded without understanding or sympathy.

The second factor is that William Herndon, Lincoln's law partner and an influential biographer, contributed to—if he did not create—the witch-figure image. "There is no doubt that Herndon and Mary Lincoln cordially detested each other," writes David Donald in his biography of Herndon (p. 348). Herndon can be admiring of her, saying, for instance, on page 237: "In his [Lincoln's] struggles, both in the law and for political advancement, his wife shared his sacrifices. She was a plucky little woman, and in fact endowed with a more restless ambition than he. She was gifted with a rare insight into the motives that actuate mankind, and there is no doubt that much of Lincoln's success was in a measure attributable to her acuteness and the stimulus of her influence."

While this, it seems to me, is undoubtedly true, Herndon has already poisoned his reader against Molly. He has made a kind of harridan of her. On page 181 he writes: "To me it has always seemed plain that Mr. Lincoln married Mary Todd to save his honor, and in doing that he sacrificed his domestic peace. He searched himself subjectively, introspectively, thoroughly; he knew that he did not love her, but he had promised to marry her!" He goes on to say, page 182: "Until that fatal New Year's day in 1841"—the day on which it's assumed that Lincoln broke his engagement to Molly—"she may have loved him, but his action on that occasion forfeited her affection. He had crushed her proud, womanly spirit. She felt degraded in the eyes of the world. Love fled at the approach of revenge. . . . Whether Mrs. Lincoln really was moved by the spirit of revenge or not she acted along the lines of human conduct. She led her husband a wild and merry dance."

Herndon's is such a harsh judgment that it is difficult to credit it. Alas! It is largely based on the false premise that on New Year's Day, 1841, Lincoln jilted Molly Todd at the altar. But this never happened. Nonetheless, Herndon reported—or, more accurately, concocted a report about—a supposed wedding, pages 169, 170. Trying to figure out what had actually occurred on that fatal first of January, Herndon concluded—and wrote as fact—that a wedding between Lincoln and Molly Todd had been scheduled for that day. "Careful preparations for the happy occasion were made at the Edwards mansion," Herndon wrote. "The house underwent the customary renovation; the furniture was properly arranged, the rooms neatly decorated, the supper prepared, and the guests invited. . . . The bride, bedecked in veil and silken gown, and nervously toying with the flowers in her hair, sat in the adjoining room. Nothing was lacking but the groom." Eventually, he wrote, "it became apparent that Lincoln, the principal in this little drama, had purposefully failed to appear!"

All of this is poppycock, nonsense, Herndon's animosity getting the better of him. There was no wedding scheduled. Lincoln did not stand up Molly Todd at the altar. But Herndon's seemingly authoritative report that this had happened—and that Lincoln had reason to fear marrying Molly Todd—all contributed to the perception of her as a witch figure. Moreover, for decades it sent historians and biographers much more careful than Herndon down false paths. For example, Carl Sandburg (*The Prairie Years*, one-volume version,

p. 260) and Albert Beveridge (vol. 2, p. 16) do not question Herndon's account; Benjamin Thomas, writing somewhat later in 1952, concluded, "Herndon's explanation does not fit the facts" (p. 86).

Having carefully combed the sources, Douglas Wilson comes to conclusions very different from those of most modern historians. He posits that, when he returned from heavy campaigning in southern Illinois, Lincoln realized that he did not love Molly Todd; that "the fatal first" does not allude to the breakup of the engagement, but rather to Speed's sale of his interest in the James C. Bell & Co. store to Charles Hurst. Wilson believes that Lincoln broke off the engagement because he had, along with Speed, fallen in love with Molly's beauteous cousin Matilda Edwards, although he never pursued an attachment to Matilda. Wilson accepts Herndon's basic notion that Lincoln married Molly Todd because it was what honor required of him. (See Wilson, *Honor's Voice*, Chapters 7 and 8.)

Admittedly some sources provide a basis for Wilson's conclusions. But my own sense of character leads me to doubt them. It may be a bit sentimental to suppose that the Lincoln-Molly Todd pairing was wholly a love match, but I find it difficult to believe that so canny an operator as Lincoln would have, after an almost two-year hiatus from Springfield aristocracy, tied himself forever to a woman for whom he felt no affection. In my view that assumption does not make us admire an honor-bound Lincoln, but diminishes him. This is taking the Honest Abe myth to ludicrous lengths.

My view is that Herndon's portrayal of Molly Todd as a woman any sensible man would want to escape marrying or would marry only to regain his honor dishonors the kind of helpmeet Molly actually was. Herndon makes Molly out to be one of the crosses Lincoln had to bear. In fact, she was closer to being, as he later writes, at least partly responsible for Lincoln's success. To repeat what was earlier quoted from Herndon: Molly "was gifted with a rare insight into the motives that actuate mankind, and there is no doubt that much of Lincoln's success was in a measure attributable to her acuteness and the stimulus of her influence."

A letter, found in the Lincoln Library, from fellow lawyer James Conkling gives us a firsthand picture of Lincoln only a few months after his marriage. The letter is dated April 18, 1843. Conkling has traveled by buggy to attend the circuit court at Bloomington. He writes his wife: "Jumped fences and waded mudholes—fine sport and about 8 o'clock reached Bloomington. Found Lincoln desperately homesick and turning his head frequently toward the south." This report does not accord with the notion that Lincoln married only at the call of his honor or that he traveled the circuit to get away from home. I quote this letter in the Afterword.

In this work we take Molly only as far as her wedding day. That problems plagued her after this time there can be no doubt. But up until November 4, 1842, we see a young woman of spirit and wit patiently biding her time over some eighteen difficult months when she had no contact with the man she hoped to marry. She did not denigrate or belittle him. If she was difficult later on, at this time she kept her own counsel and waited for events to turn things around for her as eventually they did.

Knowledgeable people will contend that I've whitewashed her character. I disagree. I'm merely trying to play fair with her up to November 4, 1842.

For some very sad reading about the Lincoln marriage, see Michael Burlingame, *The Inner World of Abraham Lincoln*, Chapter 9, page 237. The chapter comprises fifty-seven pages of text (exclusive of footnotes, of which there are 425).

For a more compassionate view, written from a woman's experience, see Doris Kearns Goodwin, *Team of Rivals*. Goodwin notes that Molly Todd's background and training ill-prepared her for the domestic life Lincoln offered.

For perceptive peeks at the Lincolns' domestic life early in the marriage, see Donald, *Lincoln*, pages 94-96, 107-109.

Perhaps the fairest way to close these notes about Molly Todd is to quote the final section of the chapter titled "Courtship and Marriage" from Benjamin Thomas's *Abraham Lincoln: A Biography* (1952, pp. 90, 91):

"The years of marriage that followed offer contrasts as striking as those between the bride and groom, who were opposites in almost every way. She was short and inclined to corpulence, he was tall and lean. He was slow-moving, easygoing, she precipitate and volatile. He had the humblest of backgrounds, hers was aristocratic. He was a man of simple tastes, she liked fine clothes and jewelry. His personality and mind were the sort that grow continuously, hers remained essentially in a set mold. Both had ambitions, but her determination was so much more intense than his that it would be like a relentless prod, impelling him onward whenever he might be disposed to lag.

"She willingly made sacrifices. Their first home was the Globe Tavern, a modest place, where they lived simply. Here their first child, Robert Todd Lincoln, was born on August 1, 1843. About five months later they paid fifteen hundred dollars for a plain frame residence of a story and a half, a few blocks southeast of the business district, where they lived until they went to Washington. Lincoln curried his own horse, milked his own cow, cut and carried firewood. Three more babies came: Edward Baker, William Wallace, and Thomas, whom they called Tad. Eddy died when he was four; Tad had a cleft palate and lisped, handicaps that endeared him all the more to his father.

"Lincoln was not an easy man to live with. His careless ways and dowdy dress, and his interludes of abstraction and dejection must have annoyed his wife. But Mary learned to overlook his shortcomings. Their letters, written when they were apart, reveal sincere affection. They went to parties together and they entertained. Together they met defeats and rejoiced in victories.

"Lincoln was indulgent as a father and left the upbringing of the children largely to 'Mother' who was forbearing and overstrict by turns. Her whole nature took on a sort of instability as time went on. Devoted, even possessive toward her husband, she was eager to make him happy. But small matters upset her and brought on fits of temper. Servants found her difficult to please; she quarreled with tradesmen and neighbors. She suffered violent headaches, known now to have been warnings of mental illness, and these sometimes made her utterly unreasonable. Lincoln bore it all as best he could, taking her tongue-lashings, yielding to her whims whenever possible, offering excuses to the neighbors, trying to make allowances for the affectionate wife and mother he knew she was at heart. When her upbraidings became unbearable he would not talk back or censure her, but simply slip off quietly to his office.

"Gossips have overstressed these unpleasant aspects of their life together; they were not always present by any means. For the most part Lincoln and Mary were happy with each other. Yet there was the other side, nor can it be ignored. It was unquestionably a factor in shaping Lincoln's character. For over the slow fires of misery that he learned to keep banked and under heavy pressure deep within him, his innate qualities of patience, tolerance, forbearance, and forgiveness were tempered and refined."

Why "Molly" Todd?

We know Lincoln called Mary Todd "Molly." In a letter to Speed during the period of the breakup, he refers to her in this way. Probably others did, too.

This novel represents an effort to portray the "Molly-ness" of this woman. As I see it, calling her "Mary" invites the reader to view her through the lens of the shrew myth created about her. Calling her "Molly" invites the reader to view her with new eyes. Storytelling requires specificity. Molly Todd was more specifically the woman I was seeking to portray than was the misleading, shopworn Mary Todd.

Mary Todd Lincoln and William Herndon

In his 1948 biography of William Herndon, *Lincoln's Herndon*, David Donald (also a biographer of Lincoln, *Lincoln*, 1995) allows the reader to piece together the difficult relationship between Molly Todd and William Herndon, born within two weeks of one another in December 1818. They met at a dance in 1837 when they were both eighteen and Molly was a belle visiting from Lexington. When Herndon compared her graceful dancing to the "ease of a serpent," he set the relationship on a negative footing forever. (I have used that encounter, setting it two years later than it evidently occurred.)

Donald reports that Herndon, who had bunked with Lincoln, Speed and Hurst in the room above Speed's store prior to his marriage, "strongly opposed this marriage [that of Lincoln to Molly] into the wealth and aristocracy of Springfield." Molly disliked her husband's choice of a partner and never invited him into the Lincoln home for a meal, despite an active legal partnership that the men shared over sixteen years. Moreover, Molly snubbed Herndon when he made his visit to the White House in 1862. (See Donald, *Herndon*, pp. 188, 189.)

Gathering material on Lincoln after his assassination, Herndon asked Molly for biographical information. They met secretly in September 1866, when she came to Springfield to visit her husband's tomb. She provided the requested information, shaving five years off her age, and the meeting between two people who did not like each other seems to have gone well. (Donald, *Herndon*, pp. 190, 191.)

Later that year Herndon gave a lecture about Lincoln's life in New Salem, the fruit of a research trip. The trip had turned up reports of Lincoln's engagement to Ann Rutledge, a story that appealed to the deeply romantic Herndon. From the perspective of the twenty-first century it's difficult to understand why this information was regarded at the time as shocking. Sensing a whiff of scandal, however, Herndon kept it confidential for a time, then decided to make it public out of a fear that a writer colleague who had looked through his papers might scoop him on it.

Herndon seems to have been motivated by a desire to portray Lincoln not as a martyred demigod, as he was being increasingly presented, but in the fullness of his personality. Moreover, Herndon feared that a pamphlet Lincoln had written in New Salem questioning religion would come to light and be used to damage his reputation. That Lincoln should have had a serious romance in his twenties surprises no one today, but Herndon's revelation of his engagement to Ann Rutledge, her death and Lincoln's bout with near insanity, much of this Herndon embroidery, created a storm of controversy. Unquestionably his timing was bad; the country was still coming to terms with Lincoln's assassination. Even worse was Herndon's inference that Lincoln had never loved another woman; this suggested that he had not loved his wife, the mother of his children.

Herndon's revelations and exaggerations were widely regarded as a slur on Mrs. Lincoln. They brought a visit from Lincoln's son Robert Todd Lincoln. He asked Herndon that "nothing may be published by you which after *careful consideration* will seem apt to cause pain to my father's family." By this time Mary Lincoln had lost a husband and two sons and was living in seclusion; her solid mental foundation was slipping away. "I hope you will consider this matter carefully," the young Lincoln continued, "for once done there is no undoing." (See Donald, *Lincoln's Herndon*, Chapter 15 on Ann Rutledge, pp. 218-241.) In 1872 Ward Hill Lamon's biography of Lincoln appeared, ghostwritten by a Democrat using biographical material, much of it raw and undigested, some of it speculation, gathered by Herndon. (Lincoln's supposed jilting of Molly Todd was one of the speculations.) The book failed to find an audience. Wanting to profit from it, the ghost writer involved Herndon in a controversy about Lincoln's religion. Herndon composed yet another lecture, this one about Lincoln's religion, in which he quoted Mrs. Lincoln as saying that her husband was not "a technical Christian." Donald writes, "That pitiful widow," (by this time a third son, Thomas, known as Tad, had died) "about to be committed to a mental sanatorium, was prevailed upon to denounce Herndon and to repudiate the interview in which she had declared that Lincoln 'was not a technical Christian.'" That repudiation, he continues, "was a signal for Herndon to loose all his long stored-up hatred for Mary Lincoln. For once he had caught this most vulnerable and most detested of his enemies in a factual error, and he produced a public letter to show Mrs. Lincoln up as an irresponsible liar." (Donald, *Herndon*, p. 280.)

If Herndon had seemed to triumph over Molly at this point, his real revenge came with the publication of his *Life of Lincoln* in 1889, seven years after her death.

A word about Abraham Lincoln

Abraham Lincoln is by no means the only self-made man in American history. His time was full of them, and in this work there are two other noteworthy examples, Stephen A. Douglas and James Shields. Even so, one admires the journey on which Lincoln set himself: out of a poor-white, scratching-the-soil, eking-out-a-living boyhood into a quest for what he called "distinction."

The law and politics were both means of pursuing that quest. At least to pursue the law, a man needed a rudimentary education. Lincoln was able to acquire the needed education mainly through his own reading. He did not have the advantages that Stephen A. Douglas, for example, enjoyed of schooling in upper New York State at Brandon Academy and Canandaigua Academy, but had to provide for himself whatever education he was able to achieve. He is said to have first visited Molly Todd with a Euclidean geometry text in his possession (see Ishbel Ross, *The President's Wife: Mary Todd Lincoln*, p. 30). The humility of that action must have made a significant impression on Molly Todd. It revealed Lincoln's respect for her education and her intellect and demonstrated his own teachableness.

One has the sense that Douglas was totally consumed by politics and the art of political maneuver. Lincoln's interest in poetry, storytelling and the art of the written word offers evidence of Lincoln's broader horizons. Lincoln was a conscious literary practitioner. He tried his hand at poetry and honed his literary skills until he was able to write speeches of true nobility. Even today, schoolchildren still memorize the Gettysburg Address.

P. M. Zall's *Abe Lincoln Laughing: Humorous Anecdotes from Original Stories By and About Abraham Lincoln* traces the origins of stories similar to the ones Lincoln told. Since some of these origins are far anterior to Lincoln's own time, one wonders if as a youth Lincoln read jestbooks, as some were called, and began at an early age to practice telling them, learning how to shape them to apply to changing circumstances. It seems clear that mastering the art of storytelling was a conscious part of Lincoln's education. Certainly storytelling skills opened opportunities for him. They may have been largely responsible for his first election to the Illinois Legislature.

If the pairing with Molly Todd in some ways seems curious due to the fact that they were such contrasts to one another, in other ways they seem extremely well matched. If perhaps most men do not wish to be paired with a woman smarter or better educated than they, the Lincoln who sought more education was well matched with a woman as well-educated as any in the country at that time. Each had his area of savvy. If Lincoln had the common touch, Molly could give him access to strata of society where he badly needed a guide. Her conviction that he possessed nobility of character made it possible for her to do this. They also seem well paired in terms of ambition. Herndon wrote (p. 304) "His ambition was a little engine that knew no rest." As Lincoln's law partner for many years, Herndon was certainly well placed to know about this. The couple's similar interest in politics also bonded them.

In addition, it's my hunch that neither Molly nor Lincoln really had a wide selection of possible mates to choose from. Although many young men had come west to find opportunity so that in Springfield there were vastly more single men than single women, still Molly was, in fact, confined to men belonging to the Coterie. Molly's biographers do not offer evidence of a young woman of wit and vivacity who was overwhelmed with marriage proposals. Her sharp tongue doubtless had something to do with this. Her education and background may have made her seem intimidating. Although they were well matched in many ways, Douglas seems not to have asked for her hand. Edwin (Bat) Webb seems to have been the only serious alternative to Lincoln. His age and his children disqualified him.

As for Lincoln, his ambition and pursuit of distinction led him to reach for a connection with a Coterie-level woman. This is not to suggest that Lincoln married Molly Todd to gain social access; I don't think that's the case. But the fact that she offered this must have enhanced her attraction. There's no question that Lincoln "married up." Despite whatever attraction he felt for her, Sarah Rickard could not have pushed Lincoln to the heights that Molly did. Had he married Sarah, it's likely that he would have remained an increasingly prosperous Springfield lawyer, paterfamilias to a large and happy family, a man who would never have attained the kind of distinction that makes him important to us.

Perhaps it's appropriate to note here that this work acquaints us with three other rather amazing men. Stephen Douglas's meteoric rise continued. He became a Congressman in 1843, a Senator in 1846. At a time when Lincoln remained largely unknown, Douglas became a national politician and a leader of the Democratic Party, running for the Presidency in 1860 as a candidate of the Northern Democrats. He died, probably of typhoid fever, in June 1861, just at the beginning of the Civil War.

If known at all to Americans these days, James Shields may be known as the Illinois politician who challenged Lincoln to a duel that never

371

occurred. Since he's the butt of the jokes in the "Lost Townships" letters, he may seem a buffoon. In fact, he was a serious and skilled politician and a talented attorney. Lincoln badly overstepped the line in calling Shields "a liar" in print. If Shields's challenging him to a duel seems an extravagant reaction, that act points up the care men took at the time to protect their reputations. (The "Lost Township" letters and "the skinning of Thomas" made Lincoln cut back on political ridicule. He never again wrote unsigned pieces lampooning opponents.) Shields served as a general in the Mexican War and later in the Civil War. He was appointed Governor of Oregon in 1848 and had the unusual distinction of serving as a United States Senator from three states, Illinois, Minnesota and Missouri.

John J. Hardin was a third amazing man. (He probably did not accompany Molly on her 1839 trip from Lexington to Springfield, but she would certainly have been chaperoned by some male relative.) Hardin served as a Congressman and was expected to have a bright political future in Illinois until he was killed leading troops in the Mexican War.

How did Lincoln and Molly Todd become engaged?

Researchers really know very little about how, when or where Molly Todd and Abraham Lincoln became engaged. Molly's letter to Mercy Ann Levering, dated merely December 1840, can be provisionally dated around the 15th due to its reference to the excursion to Jacksonville "next week." (For the letter, see Turner, *Mary Todd Lincoln: Her Life and Letters*, pp. 19-22.) William Baringer's chronology, *Lincoln Day By Day*, shows that Lincoln was in Springfield continuously during the first three weeks of the month on business at the Legislature. Lincoln took care of legal business in Springfield on December 22. He may have been gone from December 23 to December 28, and the excursion to Jacksonville must have occurred during the Legislature's Christmas recess. The Legislature was back in business on December 29; Lincoln introduced a bill on that day. (See Baringer, pp. 148-150.)

In her December letter Molly tells Merce Levering that "Mr. Webb" is "our principal lion." What to make of this? The most obvious conclusion is that Molly and Lincoln were not yet engaged at the time the letter was written. My reading of Molly is that she is careful not to disclose matters that she does not want known. For example, in the July letter she mentions to Merce "between ourselves" that she has received unexpected letters, which historians have concluded may have been from Lincoln. But she is careful not to reveal their author. Molly knows that local gossip is also flowing back and forth between Merce and local attorney James Conkling, whom she later married. If Lincoln had proposed and he and Molly were still keeping that news to themselves, would Molly have deliberately thrown Merce off the track? My hunch is that she would not have done this. Therefore, I conclude that Lincoln must have proposed to Molly sometime between mid-December and the beginning of the next year.

Did they actually become engaged? Perhaps not. Few people seem to have known about this engagement. So was it an "understanding," but not yet an engagement? Some couples want to taste and test the idea before speaking the news.

To become an engagement, did an understanding need the approval of Ninian and Elizabeth Edwards? Possibly. Might they have heard about the understanding, but refused their blessing and so kept the news from becoming widespread? Possibly.

Does it seem likely that Lincoln needed some encouragement to offer a proposal? The evidence suggests he did. So I have Molly suggesting that Webb might ask for her hand. Would a man actually say, "You're not going to marry him? You're going to marry me"? This is how my father-in-law proposed to my wife's mother when they were dancing together in Washington, D.C., and discussing her fiancé in far-off California. That marriage lasted over fifty years.

Others posit that Lincoln and Molly Todd became engaged—or at least came to an understanding about marrying—much earlier than this. Douglas Wilson, for example, suggests that in the autumn Lincoln became engaged to a "creature of excitement" (Mary). But after campaigning hard in southern Illinois, he returned to Springfield to realize that his infatuation was over. Moreover, according to Wilson, he fell in love with and wanted to marry Matilda Edwards, to whom Joshua Speed had already proposed or was about to. In Wilson's view, "All of this made a shambles of Lincoln's emotional life and caused his slide into the deep depression of mid-January." (See Wilson, *Honor's Voice*, pp. 228-231.) This analysis requires rethinking the meaning of "the fatal first of January" and reappraising the timeline of events in the last months of 1840.

In regard to Matilda Edwards, David Donald suggests (*Lincoln*, p. 612) that "Mary Todd was looking for a face-saving reason for Lincoln's actions." If Matilda actually played a role—though without any awareness of doing so on her part—we have to rethink how mature Lincoln's affection for Molly actually was. Perhaps we should. Matilda seems to have refused proposals of marriage not only from Speed, but also from Stephen A. Douglas, whom she refused for having bad morals (Wilson, "Fatal First"). Can Lincoln have been so bowled over by Matilda's quietness and beauty that he broke off his engagement to Molly? (Burlingame also accepts that Lincoln "fell desperately in love with [Matilda], and proposed to her, but she rejected him." p. 315.)

In considering Wilson's analysis it strikes me as unlikely that, if Lincoln had recently broken an engagement to her, Molly would go off on an excursion to Jacksonville with him and Matilda, the new object of his infatuation, or that she would never have spread gossip about him after he had spurned her.

At several places in his *Life of Lincoln,* Herndon tells us that Lincoln often remarked, "It's a good thing I'm not a woman because I can never say no." This suggests yet another possibility about the engagement, namely that the subject was broached by Molly and so persistently urged on Lincoln that he finally agreed. On reflection he changed his mind. Then two years later something of the same sort happened again, and this time Lincoln went through with the marriage. This possibility gives a certain plausibility to Wilson's reading of Lincoln's deciding that honor required him to marry Molly.

Plausible? Perhaps. Likely? I think not. It's possible to believe that if Molly urged the marriage and Lincoln couldn't find the nerve to go through with it, Molly would have felt ashamed of her urging and did not hold Lincoln's timidity against him. But given Molly's wit and the sharpness of her tongue, it strikes me as unlikely that in this case she would control her tongue throughout 1841 and 1842.

Lincoln's life story is one of a man setting his sights on things he seemed unlikely to achieve, of his reaching without stint for things that seemed beyond his grasp. He relentlessly pursued Senate seats, abandoning his law practice for six months in 1858 to campaign and debate Douglas, this at a time when he had a family of growing boys. (Although he won the popular vote, he lost the seat to Douglas because the Legislature elected Senators.) Did Lincoln relentlessly pursue what he wanted only in the realm of politics? No. Molly obviously encouraged his interest in her, but it strains credibility to suppose that the pursuit was all on her side.

Did Ninian and Elizabeth Edwards oppose Lincoln's marrying Elizabeth's sister?

As is the case with virtually every aspect of this courtship, the facts are few, leaving much to interpretation. Opinion on almost every point is divided.

When Herndon interviewed the Edwardses, more than a quarter century after the courtship, and also after the martyred President's assassination, notes from the Ninian interview stated, "Edwards admits that he wanted Speed to marry Miss Edwards and Lincoln Miss Todd: He gave me policy reasons for it. . . ." In her interview Elizabeth stated, "I told Mary my impression that they were not suited, or, as some persons who believe matches are made in heaven would say, not intended for each other." (See Herndon, p. 167.) For Herndon, Elizabeth Edwards also so misremembered aspects of that relationship as to baffle researchers and historians for decades. The question arises: Could a misremembrance of such proportion result from anything other than hostility to Lincoln?

What do other biographers of Lincoln or Mary Todd have to say?

Carl Sandburg (*The Prairie Years*, one-volume version, p. 70): "Ninian W. Edwards and his wife had argued [Mary] was throwing herself away; it wasn't a match; she and Lincoln came from different classes in society."

Albert J. Beveridge (*Abraham Lincoln*, 1809-1858, Vol. 2 Years of Discipline, p. 14): "But the Todd and Edwards families scorned and detested the Hanks and Lincoln family; and Mary, especially," [quoting Herndon] "held the Hanks tribe in contempt and the Lincoln family generally—the old folks in particular, a feeling which she never overcame."

Paul Simon (*Lincoln's Preparation For Greatness*, pp. 236, 237): "The engagement was frowned upon by the Ninian Edwards family with whom Mary was staying. Perhaps the aristocratic Ninian W. Edwards told Mary and Lincoln that the match was not a good one. . . ."

"A son of the Edwards later said, 'My mother and my father at that time didn't want Mary to marry Mr. Lincoln. . . . When my mother saw that things were becoming serious between Lincoln and Mary, she treated him rather coldly. . . . During 1841 and 1842 my mother did what she could to break up the match.' "

And most damning of all: "Perhaps part of the difficulty was due to the strange character of Ninian W. Edwards, an unpopular man with his legislative colleagues, and a man embittered by the Whigs in Sangamon County who had slated Lincoln for re-election to the House while unceremoniously dropping Edwards. It would be in line with the somewhat warped Edwards' personality to harbor a grudge."

Oscar and Lilian Handlin (*Abraham Lincoln and The Union*, p. 53): "Elizabeth and Ninian Edwards, aware of familial responsibilities, sternly told Mary that the match was unsuitable and would certainly lead to unhappiness. Lincoln's future was dubious, the marriage was beneath the family. The man was a useful political ally—not potential kin."

Stephen B. Oates (*With Malice Toward None: The Life of Abraham Lincoln*, p. 55): "At this point [engagement] Ninian and Elizabeth Edwards stepped in and tried to break up the romance. . . . As a consequence, said the imperious Edwardses, [Lincoln] was no longer welcome in their home. All of which upset Mary. . . .

"Lincoln was devastated. The hostility of the Todd and Edwards families—especially Elizabeth—caused incalculable pain in one so insecure about himself and so resentful of his own family that he hadn't visited his father in over nine years. One of Lincoln's greatest sorrows—from his view—was that he'd worked himself to the bone for recognition and success and yet had carried a social albatross about his neck: the lack of family respectability. No wonder he never discussed his background in Springfield high society. What could he say in the presence of Elizabeth and Ninian Edwards? That his father was all but illiterate? That the origins of his real mother were obscure?

"As winter came on, Lincoln sank into a profound depression about the way Mary's people had rejected him."

Douglas Wilson ("Abraham Lincoln and 'That Fatal First of January,' " *Civil War History*, Vol. 38, 1992, pp. 101-130) quotes Herndon's interview with Ninian. "Edwards admits that he wanted Speed to marry Miss Edwards and Lincoln Miss Todd: He gave me policy reasons for it—the substance of which I have given in another place." (p. 107) Wilson's theory is that Lincoln broke off the engagement after falling in love with Matilda Edwards. It is set forth in his work *Honor's Voice*. As a result, Wilson takes little notice of possible interference by Ninian and Elizabeth.

Ruth Painter Randall (*Mary Lincoln: Biography of a Marriage*, p. 47): "Albert S. Edwards, son of Mr. and Mrs. Ninian Edwards, years later said that the cause of the break in the engagement was the opposition and disapproval of his parents. They had nothing against Lincoln except his poverty and lack of prospects, but they thought he could not support Mary in a manner which they felt to be essential. . . .

"There is indirect evidence that Mrs. John Todd Stuart gave the same account, saying that Mary herself told her that the Edwardses forced the breaking of the engagement by their opposition.

"Ninian W. Edwards 'was naturally and constitutionally an aristocrat,' wrote one of his colleagues in the state legislature, 'and he hated democracy . . . as the devil is said to hate holy water.' "

Jean Baker (*Mary Todd Lincoln*, p. 89): "At home Mary Todd heard other reasons that made her hesitate before marrying Abraham Lincoln. Her sister Elizabeth, who bore the name of her mother, took seriously her surrogate parenthood and challenged any courting by the rustic, socially primitive Lincoln. 'I warned Mary that she and Mr. Lincoln were not suitable. Mr. Edwards and myself believed they were different in nature, and education and raising.' " (Baker's presumably quoting a Herndon interview in these last two sentences.)

Baker writes that Mary's flirtations during a socially busy last week of the year provoked Lincoln's jealousy and caused the rupture of the engagement, a view that strikes me as unlikely in a man as mature as Lincoln and in one with so much riding on a marriage that would notably affect his social and professional position in Springfield.

Ishbel Ross (*The President's Wife: Mary Todd Lincoln*, p. 40): "Both young men [Lincoln and Speed] were anxious to marry, but at this point they wavered, lacking confidence in their own capacity to make good husbands. Lincoln was doubly troubled because of the social gap between Mary and him and the outspoken criticism of her relatives."

She continues (p. 41): "Conkling felt sure that Mary had jilted [Lincoln]. Speed thought that it was the other way around, but all believed that the attitude of the Edwards family figured strongly in the broken engagement."

And she adds: "Mrs. John Todd Stuart attributed the broken engagement directly to Mr. and Mrs. Edwards."

Justin and Linda Leavitt Turner (*Mary Todd Lincoln: Her Life and Letters* p. 24) endorse Ruth Randall's conclusions, writing: "She offered two factors as probably combining to precipitate the breakup and the eighteen-month estrangement that followed: Lincoln's extreme sensitivity, coupled with the adamant opposition of Mary Todd's family, particularly Ninian and Elizabeth Edwards."

How did the breakup occur?

Most of what we know about the circumstances of the breakup of the engagement come from Joshua Speed's report to William Herndon (see Herndon's *Life of Lincoln*, pp. 168, 169) given a quarter century after the events took place.

Most modern historians and biographers agree that the engagement—or the "embrigglement" as one of them calls it—was broken on January 1, 1841, the date that Lincoln later referred to, in a letter to Joshua Speed, as "the fatal first of January." And they agree that it was Lincoln who broke it off. Some believe that Lincoln lost confidence in himself, in his ability to provide for Molly in a manner that would insure her happiness. As David Donald puts it (*Lincoln*, p. 87), "His nerve snapped." In a letter to Speed dated July 4, 1842, Lincoln wrote, "I must gain confidence in my own ability to keep my resolves when they are made" (Herndon, p. 177). Others—Ruth Randall, for instance—see the breakup largely as a result of the opposition of Ninian and Elizabeth Edwards as it affected a proud, sensitive and socially disadvantaged man.

As mentioned above, Douglas Wilson takes an entirely different view.

Herndon's famous gaffe, reporting a wedding that never took place, for some years bedeviled people trying to sort out these matters.

Did Lincoln lose his nerve?

Donald says Lincoln panicked, lost his nerve. Donald emphasizes economic considerations (*Lincoln*, p. 86). Lincoln "now had an income of more than $1000 a year from his legal practice, plus his salary as a state legislator, but neither source was certain. His law partnership [with John Todd Stuart] was about to be dissolved. . . . Lincoln was not even assured of his income from the state legislature. With the collapse of the internal improvements system and the resulting bankruptcy of the state, he and his associates had come under increasingly bitter, and sometimes personal attack. His political popularity was declining. . . . He had resolved not to stand for reelection when his present term in the legislature expired. Thus in 1840 he was a man without reliable income, who had no savings and owned no house but probably still owed something on his 'National Debt' [a debt owed in New Salem]. . . . He knew that he could not give Mary the life of wealth and luxury to which she was accustomed."

Donald also seeks deeper uncertainties. He continues: "These anxieties covered his deeper uncertainties about marriage. Like Speed . . . he was probably still sexually inexperienced."

If Donald is right that Lincoln lost his nerve, his coming face-to-face with a reach for his destiny (marrying Molly Todd) and then losing his nerve about actually grasping that destiny must have been a blow to his sense of himself. He seemed to be on the way to becoming something almost inconceivable to himself, given the Indiana farm boy he had once been. But he didn't think he could bring it off. He feared that instead of giving Molly happiness (which is what every woman hoped to get from marriage), he could only bring her uncertain prospects, diminished status, unhappiness. And he wasn't willing to do that.

Lincoln's going to pieces after breaking off the engagement must have been, in an ironic way, very flattering to Molly. So how can we possibly believe Wilson's theory that Lincoln went to pieces when he escaped a bad match and was free to pursue the woman (Matilda) whom Wilson says he loved? Moreover, he seems to have marshaled no pursuit.

Jean Baker's theory about the breakup

Jean Baker (*Mary Todd Lincoln*, p. 90ff) believes both Molly and Lincoln were at fault in the breakup. She has Lincoln, who had promised to escort Molly to a dance, turning up so late that she had left without him. To punish him when he turned up, she flirted with "the faithful Edwin Webb." "Furious at her dalliance," writes Baker, "Abraham appeared 'grim and determined' (according to Mary's sister) at the Edwards home," and had to wait until New Year's callers left the home. "The resulting quarrel over Edwin Webb . . . ended their courtship."

This theory suggests that Lincoln and Molly were reacting like present-day teenagers. Perhaps that's valid. After all, men and women inhabited very different spheres at that time. But it suggests an immaturity, particularly in Lincoln, that belies our understanding of him.

Baker continues (p. 94): "In view of the personalities of the principals, the romance would never have revived unless both had shared in its destruction. A unilateral wound to such sensitive psyches would have been beyond healing." She sees the "Lost Townships" letters as being a way for Lincoln and Molly to approach the subject of matrimony through the characters of Shields and Aunt 'Becca, who have married by the final letter.

Baker seems to have derived this scenario from the reminiscences of Emilie Todd Helm, Molly's half-sister, whose daughter Katherine wrote the book *Mary, Wife of Lincoln*. She proposes the broken date idea, but has Molly flirting with Stephen A. Douglas, with whom Molly's name had been linked. (See Randall, *Mary Todd Lincoln: Biography of a Marriage*, p. 44.)

In *Mary Todd Lincoln: Her Life and Letters* Justin G. Turner and Linda Leavitt Turner make this comment about Katherine Helm's account (p. 23): "Katherine Helm, in her biography of her aunt, contended that Lincoln, suddenly 'panic-stricken' at the prospect of providing for this pampered creature (Mary), used her flirtation with Stephen Douglas as an excuse to end the relationship." Thus, in their view, this immature jealousy was only a cover for more serious concerns. That certainly seems a more plausible reading of the situation.

The breakup according to Benjamin P. Thomas

Thomas in *Abraham Lincoln: A Biography* takes a position stressing health conditions. He writes (p. 86): "Lincoln had a moody temperament. At times his melancholy became so acute as to be an actual mental ailment known as hypochondria. . . . The symptoms and causes [which Thomas lists] fit Lincoln's case exactly, for he had been working hard and long, and he was worried about his true feelings respecting Miss Todd. Wretchedly despondent and uncertain of himself, he explained his condition to her, and she, realizing that his perplexity and dejection were beyond his control, released him from the engagement, but at the same time hoped he would renew the courtship when he had recovered."

He continues: "This is the only explanation consistent with the documentary evidence and with Mary's personality. Had Lincoln failed to appear for a wedding the proud and high-spirited Mary would never have forgiven him."

The breakup according to Stephen B. Oates

In *With Malice Toward None* Oates takes a position similar to that of Ruth Randall, especially in blaming the Edwardses' interference. He writes (p. 55): "At this point Ninian and Elizabeth Edwards stepped in and tried to break up the romance. For Mary to see Lincoln was one thing. But to marry him was quite another. And the Lexington Todds emphatically agreed." [I have not stumbled on this family factor elsewhere.] "After all, Mary came from a proud and educated family. By contrast, Lincoln was from 'nowhere' and his future was 'nebulous.' As a consequence, said the imperious Edwardses, he was no longer welcome at their home."

Oates continues, "In despair, [Lincoln] remarked that one *d* was enough to spell God. But it took two *d's* to spell Todd."

Oates does not try to set the scene of the breakup. He merely states (p. 56): "Lincoln apparently told Mary that he could neither support a wife nor make her happy and asked her to release him, which she gracefully did. She was not bitter about it and sympathized with his anguish, but still she was hurt."

Doris Kearns Goodwin's thoughts about the breakup

In *Team of Rivals* Goodwin notes that "the inner lives of men and women living long ago are never easy to recover," especially when, as in this case, virtually no correspondence survives. She posits that "the very qualities that had first attracted the couple to each other may have become sources of conflict." She suggests that "Mary may have precipitated the break," but "more likely, Lincoln's misgivings prompted a retreat." She notes recent scholarship about Matilda Edwards, but supposes that Lincoln's fascination with Matilda, which she assumes existed, was "merely a distraction surrounding his impending marriage to Mary."

How did the reconciliation move to marriage?

Of course, we can only speculate. But why not?

My hunch is that the first secret meetings at the Francis house were not easy to arrange. One imagines Lincoln being slow to move to the social initiative—although Emilie Todd Helm, Molly's half sister, did report Lincoln's paying a call on

Molly, Euclid geometry book in hand, the day after he met her. (Ishbel Ross, p. 30, is the source for Euclid; she appears to be following Emilie Todd Helm.) For her part, Molly may have been fearful that appearing too eager to rekindle the romance might queer it. So I speculate that Eliza Francis helped the couple to meet, possibly with the assistance of her husband, a great friend of Lincoln's.

In addition, the meetings were probably not all that frequent at the beginning. According to Baringer's *Lincoln Day By Day*, Lincoln spent most of the summer in Springfield with the exception of about ten days on circuit from June 6 to June 15.

It's my hunch that the "Lost Townships" letters provided a time of high flirtation for Molly and Lincoln. Molly's biographer Jean Baker goes so far as to suggest that they represented a way for Lincoln and Molly to discuss marriage inside a context that seemed political (pp. 95, 96). "In terms of personal politics," she writes, "the Rebecca letters provided a comic theater where, with laughter, Abraham Lincoln and Mary Todd ended their estrangement."

According to Baringer, Lincoln learned that the Whig candidate for governor had been defeated on August 12. This may have provoked the anti-Democratic ridicule of the first Rebecca letter, published in the *Sangamo Journal* on August 19. Some scholars believe that Lincoln wrote the letter; others disagree. The second letter, which I think Lincoln and Molly must have discussed before its creation, appeared in the *Journal* on September 2, two weeks after the first. Shields must have appealed almost immediately to Simeon Francis to know the identity of the writer. The third and fourth letters—the third being Julia

Jayne's satiric letter and the fourth Molly's poem—appeared in the *Journal* on September 9, the following week. Lincoln received Shields's first note in Tremont where the Tazewell Circuit Court was in session on September 17. Lincoln drew up dueling instructions on September 20. On September 22 the duel was called off. Lincoln was busy with court work the following week, and dueling fever ran high in Springfield with the possibility of a Shields-William Butler duel and another between Shields's and Lincoln's seconds, Whiteside and Merryman. Calm returned by October 4.

It's my assumption that sometime between September 22, when the duel with Shields was called off, and October 4 Lincoln decided to ask Molly to marry him. It strikes me as doubtful that, having already broken a first engagement, Lincoln would officially propose to Molly until he was certain he intended to marry her. All he needed to overcome any doubts was Joshua Speed's assurance that he was glad he'd married "in *feeling* as well as *judgment.*" Lincoln wrote Speed on October 5 asking for this assurance. Within a month Lincoln and Molly Todd were married. Is it reasonable to think that Speed, Lincoln's best friend, would have urged him to marry if he had known that Lincoln was marrying only to heed "honor's voice"?

Why did they marry?

Lincoln was within three months of his thirty-fourth birthday. He had established himself as a lawyer and was in partnership with a talented attorney. He was undoubtedly ready to settle down. He seems to have been living at the Butler home, apparently a kind of boarding house, for over a year. It's likely that he was ready to have a wife and a home of his own. He liked Molly; she understood and admired him and was prepared to make allowances for his deficiencies. In many ways they were very well matched. The match was socially advantageous to him. This is why lots of men get married; some people call it love.

As for Molly, it's clear she loved and admired him. She was within about six weeks of her twenty-fourth birthday, well along for a woman of her time to marry in Illinois. She was undoubtedly anxious to get out of her sister's home; she had lived with the Edwardses for about three and a half years. She wanted a home of her own.

If Ninian and Elizabeth had broken up the engagement, were they in a position to foil this new plan of marriage? Probably not. Molly and Lincoln seem to have sprung the news on them when it was all but a *fait accompli*. Both were of age. By the time the Edwardses learned of the plan, Parson Dresser had already agreed to marry the couple that evening in the parsonage. Perhaps Ninian and Elizabeth did not even try to stop it. Would Ninian have wanted his sharp-tongued sister-in-law, by now in danger of spinsterhood, lodging at his home indefinitely? He knew that an attempt to thwart the plan would unleash unending tirades from Molly. Moreover, another Edwards child was on the way. According to the website "Early Settlers of Sangamon County," Elizabeth Edwards bore a third child, Elizabeth, on January 7, 1843. The Edwards home may have been getting too crowded to easily house Molly. But it was important for the Edwardses' reputation in Springfield that the ceremony take place at their home.

Did Lincoln love his wife? Did Mary Todd Lincoln love her husband?

These are appropriate questions. Why? Because a number of Lincoln scholars have concluded that Lincoln did not love his wife. In fact, they argue, he bore her as a cross. (See Douglas Wilson.) And because others contend that Molly intentionally made her husband's life a hell. (See Herndon.)

But, for me, the questions are impossible to answer.

Why impossible? Well, what exactly do they mean? Do they mean, Did the Lincolns love one another in a kind of idealized way? If so, the answer has to be that real men and real women do not love in ideal ways. Real people love because the beloved charms, intrigues or enchants them, makes them laugh, makes them feel good about themselves, makes life without the beloved seem lonely, empty, unsatisfying, maybe even impossible. They love in spite of the fact that the beloved may exasperate, frustrate or embarrass them. They love despite the beloved's deficiencies and annoying quirks of character. People who love one another share experiences that bind them together; they form a bond of loyalty and treat each other with respect.

The Lincolns seem to have done all this.

Did the Lincolns love each other "romantically" at the time of their marriage, when this book ends? Yes. They had just overcome the challenge of the duel. They had been courting secretly and successfully, against the wishes of her family, and had decided to get married whatever anyone thought. This is highly romantic stuff.

Handling the challenge to duel was a real test. Lincoln could have thought, This woman is nothing but trouble, and revealed both the secret courtship and Molly as one of the letter writers. Not without some loss of face, it's true. But dueling was no child's game. Duelers did get killed or maimed. Instead Lincoln kept faith with Molly. Although she must have been deeply worried, she held her tongue. Molly's success in this courtship required her for two years to do just that: hold her tongue.

Once the marriage was well established, unquestionably there were challenges. My hunch is that neither of these people was easy to live with. Molly's sins are well established. But Lincoln could get abstracted and forgetful of family niceties, and he was an untalented father, loving his sons but unwilling to discipline them. At times there must have been high degrees of frustration in the Lincoln household. Both were ambitious for him to achieve high office, and it kept eluding them. It kept going to lesser men. Then, when it came, what a pile of woes to handle!

There must also have been frustrations from the fact that they came from such different backgrounds. People from the same background often share the same values. Or if they don't, at least they know how those values were instilled. Lincoln and Molly must have had different values about many things, stemming from their different backgrounds—how to handle servants, to cite a trivial example.

My hunch is that their experiences of loss may have brought them closer. Lincoln lost his mother and sister as a young person. Molly lost her mother and was shunted away from her father's second family. Losing children may have drawn them together; Molly was inconsolable for a long period after their second son, Eddy, died seven years into the marriage.

It's not easy to define what love is in a relationship that becomes a marriage. But as I see the matter, it's hard to exclude it from the Lincolns' relationship.

Could Lincoln have ascended to greatness without first surmounting the challenges of the courtship?

Is the courtship story just an interesting romantic tale? Or is it also about a crucial aspect of Lincoln's self-development?

The courtship story serves as a way of watching Lincoln grow into an expanded sense of himself. The young Lincoln kept reaching beyond his background for experiences, for opportunities—in New Salem, in the Black Hawk War, in Springfield and in courting Molly Todd. This last was a reach for which he did not have the background, the education or the finesse. But Molly recognized in him a nobility of character that was enough for her.

Ninian Edwards did not see that nobility of character. (Never saw it, in fact. He did not support Lincoln's reach for the Presidency—speaking of reaches—but instead supported Douglas.) When Ninian called Lincoln for overreaching, Lincoln seems to have buckled. He lost confidence in himself (and possibly in Molly) and broke off the engagement. He went into a tailspin of depression so serious friends thought he might commit suicide.

What caused the crisis was that he accepted Ninian's measure of him and its consequences. In the following twenty-two months he rejected that measure and figured out who he was. He left the law partnership with John Todd Stuart. Stuart was often in Washington, serving as a Congressman and thus not useful as a mentor. He associated himself with Stephen A. Logan, then generally regarded as probably the best practicing attorney in Illinois. He did not stand again for the legislature, deciding to be more serious about the law. He shunned social life.

He began to define himself more seriously. What gave reality to that self-definition? The fact that Molly Todd affirmed it. In the eighteen months when they did not see one another, Molly seems not to have denigrated Lincoln. She invited him to renew his suit. She kept her own counsel while playing the role of Springfield's brightest "ornament." When they began to see each other again in secret, both had grown. Molly supported Lincoln's new self-definition, flirted him into a disastrous mistake, saw him through the imbroglio and married him.

If he'd married Ann Rutledge or Sarah Rickard, he might have been happier. But we never would have heard of him.

Sarah Rickard and Joshua Speed

It seems pretty clear that Lincoln had a friendship with—and an attraction for—Sarah Rickard, the teenaged sister of Elizabeth Butler, wife of William Butler. Lincoln took his meals with the Butlers and the various relatives who came to their table. It seems unlikely that Lincoln had what one might term a "romance" with Sarah. But it seems highly likely that he asked her to be his wife. Sarah reported to Herndon many years later that Lincoln had proposed to her. (See Wilson, *Herndon's Informants*, under Sarah Rickard.)

It also seems clear that a relationship existed between Sarah and Joshua Speed. (The notion that Speed had a fickle heart seems to have been no exaggeration.) Wilson writes in "Fatal First" (p. 128), "In sending copies of Lincoln's letters, Speed told Herndon: 'I have eraced (sic) a name which I do not wish published. If I have failed to do it any where, strike it out when you come to it—That is the word Sarah.'"

After Speed returned to Kentucky and became engaged, Lincoln wrote him, "One thing I can tell you which I know you will be glad to hear: and that is, that I have seen Sarah, and scrutinized her feelings as well as I could, and am fully convinced, she is far happier now, than she has been for the last fifteen months past."

It's possible that Speed wished Sarah's name to be excised out of deference to his wife. He had been married for twenty plus years when he sent Lincoln's letters to Herndon. Or perhaps he wanted them excised as a courtesy to Sarah. But the emphasis he gives the matter suggests that he wished aspects of the relationship hidden.

It's a curious fact that Lincoln and Speed both seemed terrified of marriage—in contrast to young Billy Herndon, who was happy to embrace it. A number of scholars and biographers have remarked on this reluctance. The fact that marriage was regarded as a contract, forever in force, may have had something to do with this reluctance. However, Baringer's *Day By Day* shows that Lincoln handled a number of divorce cases. I wonder if the reluctance had something to do with the fact that, on Lincoln's part, he had had so little contact with women while, on Speed's part, he had

had so much. Speed seems to have been en-amored of both Sarah Rickard and Matilda Ed-wards at about the same time. Perhaps his fa-mously fickle heart made him believe he could never be happy committed to one woman.

Letters, Stories, Campaign Songs

The excerpts from Molly's letters to Mercy Ann Levering quoted in Chapters 7, 8 and 11 are from actual letters Molly wrote. See Turner, *Mary Todd Lincoln: Her Life And Letters*.

The excerpt of Lincoln's letter to Joshua Speed quoted in Chapter 12 is available in numerous sources. See *Collected Works*.

The "Lost Township" Letters are given in their extraordinary entirety in Herndon. See also *Collected Works*.

Lincoln's stories have been adapted from the compilation by P. M. Zall called *Abe Lincoln Laughing: Humorous Anecdotes from Original Stories by and About Abraham Lincoln* and from Benjamin Thomas's essay "Lincoln's Humor" in his collection titled *"Lincoln's Humor" and Other Essays*.

Lyrics from the 1840 campaign songs are quoted from Arthur Schlesinger's *The Age of Jackson* and from Freeman Cleaves's *Old Tippecanoe: William Henry Harrison and His Times*.

BIBLIOGRAPHY

Baker, Jean. *Mary Todd Lincoln: A Biography.* New York, W. W. Norton & Company, 1987.

Baringer, William E. *Lincoln Day By Day: A Chronology 1809-1865,* Vol. 1: 1809-1848. Washington, Lincoln Sesquicentennial Commission, 1960.

Barringer, Floyd S. *Tour Of Historical Springfield.* apparently privately published 1971.

Beveridge, Albert J. *Abraham Lincoln 1809-1858,* Vol. 2 "Years of Discipline." Boston, Houghton Mifflin, 1928.

Boritt, G. S. *Lincoln and the Economics of the American Dream.* Memphis, Memphis State University Press, 1978.

Burlingame, Michael. *The Inner World of Abraham Lincoln.* Urbana and Chicago, University of Illinois Press, 1994.

Cleaves, Freeman. *Old Tippecanoe: William Henry Harrison and His Times.* New York, Charles Scribner's Sons, 1939.

Clemens, Samuel (Mark Twain). *Life on the Mississippi.*

Condon, William H. *The Life of Major General James Shields: Hero of Three Wars and Senator from Three States*. Chicago, Press of the Blakely Printing Co., 1900.

Delbanco, Andrew, ed. *The Portable Abraham Lincoln*. New York, Viking, 1992.

Dictionary of American Biography: Baker, Edwards, Hardin, Shields.

Donald, David Herbert. *Lincoln*. New York, Simon and Schuster, 1995.

Donald, David. *Lincoln's Herndon*. New York, Alfred A. Knopf, 1948.

Duff, John J. *A. Lincoln: Prairie Lawyer*. New York, Rinehart & Co., 1960.

Gavin, Rev. Jeff G. *Past Sites of Springfield: A Historic Guide to the Downtown Area*. Manuscript in Old State House Library 1983.

Goodwin, Doris Kearns. *Team of Rivals*. New York, Simon and Schuster, 2005.

Green, James A. *William Henry Harrison: His Life and Times*. Richmond, Garrett and Massie, Incorporated, 1941.

Handlin, Oscar and Lilian. *Abraham Lincoln and the Union*. Boston, Little, Brown & Co., 1980.

Herndon, William H. and Weik, Jesse W. *Life of Lincoln*. New York, Da Capo Press, 1983, an "unabridged republication" of the 1942 edition edited and annotated by Paul M. Angle.

Hickey, James T. "The Lincolns' Globe Tavern: A Study in Tracing the History of a Nineteenth-Century Building," *Journal of the Illinois State Historical Society at Springfield.*

Hill, Frederick Trevor. *Lincoln the Lawyer.* New York, Century & Co., 1906.

Johannsen, Robert W. *Stephen A. Douglas.* London, Oxford University Press, 1973.

Lincoln, Abraham. *Collected Works*, Vol. 1, Roy P. Basler, ed. Rutgers University Press, New Brunswick, N.J., 1953.

Oates, Stephen B. *With Malice Toward None: The Life of Abraham Lincoln.* New York, Harper & Row, 1977.

Peterson, Norma Lois. *The Presidencies of William Henry Harrison and John Tyler.* Lawrence, University of Kansas, 1989.

Pratt, Harry E. *Lincoln 1809-1839: Being the Day-to-Day Activities of Abraham Lincoln from February 12, 1809 to December 31, 1839.* Springfield, Il., The Abraham Lincoln Association.

Randall, Ruth Painter. *I Mary: A Biography of the Girl Who Married Abraham Lincoln.* Boston, Little, Brown & Company, 1959.

————. *Mary Lincoln: Biography of a Marriage.* Boston, Little, Brown & Company, 1953.

————. *The Courtship of Mr. Lincoln.* Boston, Little, Brown & Company, 1957.

Remini, Robert V. *Andrew Jackson and the Bank War*. New York, W W Norton & Company, 1967.

—————. *The Life of Andrew Jackson*. New York, Harper & Row, 1988.

Ross, Ishbel. *The President's Wife: Mary Todd Lincoln*. New York, G. P. Putnam's Sons, 1973.

Sandburg, Carl and Angle, Paul. *Abraham Lincoln: The Prairie Years*. Abridged edition. New York, Harcourt, Brace & World, Inc.

Schlesinger, Arthur M., Jr. *The Age of Jackson*. Boston, Little, Brown & Co., 1945.

Simon, Paul. *Lincoln's Preparation for Greatness*. Norman, University of Oklahoma Press, 1965.

Suppiger, Joseph E. *The Intimate Lincoln*. London and Lanhan, N.Y., University Press of America, 1985.

Thomas, Benjamin P. *Abraham Lincoln: A Biography*. New York, Alfred A. Knopf, 1952.

—————. *"Lincoln's Humor" and Other Essays*. Urbana and Chicago, University of Illinois Press, 2002.

Turner, Justin G. and Turner, Linda Levitt, eds. *Mary Todd Lincoln: Her Life and Letters*. New York, Alfred A. Knopf, 1972.

Wilson, Douglas L. *Honor's Voice: The Transformation of Abraham Lincoln*. New York Alfred A. Knopf, 1998.

———. "Abraham Lincoln and 'That Fatal First of January,' " *Civil War History*, Vol. 38, 1992, pp. 101–130.

Wilson, Douglas L. and Davis, Rodney O. *Herndon's Informants*. Urbana and Chicago, University of Illinois, 1998.

Zall, P. M. *Abe Lincoln Laughing: Humorous Anecdotes from Original Stories by and About Abraham Lincoln*. Berkeley, University of California Press, 1982.